THE WINTER ROAD

I push both the spearhead and the end of the arrow that's in my shoulder back through me a bit. A freezing spike of pain. My senses lighten to wisps, I fall away from the ground, my chest fit to burst, my blood warming my belly and the dirt under me. Why am I angry that it's all over? The sun keeps climbing, the pebbles rattle and hum as the song of the earth runs through me – beating hooves, distant cries, roots of trees stretching and drinking. I hum to quieten the pain. It's my part in the song but I was always part of the song, I just haven't been listening. The birch trees shush me. Snowy peaks crack like thunder in the distance. The sky is blue like his eyes, fathomless.

"I'm coming," I says. He knows I'm coming. I just have to hold out my hand.

By Adrian Selby

Snakewood
The Winter Road

THE WINTER ROAD

ADRIAN SELBY

www.orbitbooks.net

ORBIT

First published in Great Britain in 2018 by Orbit

1 3 5 7 9 10 8 6 4 2

A CIP catalogue record for this book is
available from the British Library.

ISBN 978-0-356-50837-5

Typeset in Apollo MT Std by Palimpsest Book Production Ltd,
Falkirk, Stirlingshire
Printed and bound in Great Britain by Clays Ltd, Elcograf S.p.A.

Papers used by Orbit are from well-managed forests
and other responsible sources.

Orbit
An imprint of
Little, Brown Book Group
Carmelite House
50 Victoria Embankment
London EC4Y 0DZ

An Hachette UK Company
www.hachette.co.uk

www.orbitbooks.net

To Martha, Will and Molly.
I love you beyond all measure.

THE CIRCLE

CRUTTER-VURI

GOSPEAKS

EECHERSEN CLAN

ELDER HILL

R. CRITH

HILLFAST

TAPPER'S WAY

FALDON RIDGE

THE SEDGEWAY

THE

R. BRAEG

ABLITCH

THE CASSIES

SEKKERSON CLAN

THE SHIELD

CARLESSEN CLAN

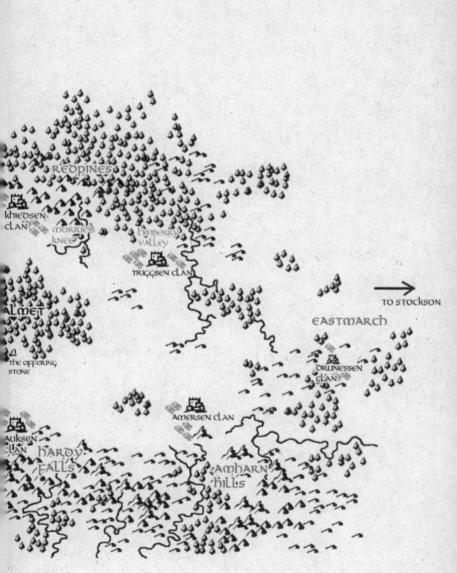

REDPINES

KHIEDSEN
CLAN

MORRIE'S
KNEE

LIMBERRY
VALLEY

TRIGGSEN CLAN

ALMEIT

TO STOCKSON

EASTMARCH

THE OFFERING
STONE

DRUNESSEN
CLAN

AMERSEN CLAN

AUKSEN
CLAN

HARDY
FALLS

AMHARN
HILLS

Part One

Chapter 1

You will fail, Teyr Amondsen.

My eyes open. The truth wakes me.

You will fail.

I had slept against a tree to keep the weight off my arm, off my face. My tongue runs over the abscesses in my mouth, the many holes there. My left eye is swollen shut, my cheek broken again, three days ago, falling from a narrow trail after a deer I'd stuck with my only spear.

I close my eyes and listen, desperate to confirm my solitude. A river, quick and throaty over rocks and stones. A grebe's whinnying screech.

I take off one of the boots I'd stolen, see again the face of the man who'd worn them as I strangled him. I feel my toes, my soles, assess the damage. Numb, blisters weeping. My toes are swelling like my fingers, burning like my face. I need a fire, cicely root, fireweed. I have to be grateful my nose was broken clean. A smashed-up nose is a death sentence in the hinterlands. If you can't sniff for plant you're a bag of fresh walking meat. You need plant to heal, plant to kill.

If I keep on after this river I can maybe steal a knife, some plant and warmer clothes. These are Carlessen clan lands, the coast is beyond them. I'm going to live there, get Aude's screaming out of my head, the horns of the whiteboys, the whisperings of the Oskoro who would not, despite a thousand fuck offs and thrown stones in the black forests and blue frozen mountains, let be their debt to me.

The grebe screeches again. Eggs!

I pull on the boot with my right arm, my left strapped against me and healing, itself broken again in my fall.

I pick up my spade and the small sack that I'd put Mosa's shirt in, the spade something of a walking stick to help me along the mossy banks and wretched tracks. Snow was making a last stand among the roots of birch trees, a few weeks yet from thawing out. A few handfuls ease my gums.

The sky is violet and pink ahead of the sun, the woods and banks blue black, snow and earth. I stumble towards the river, a chance to wash my wounds once I've found some nests and broken a few branches for a fire.

The grebes screech at me as I crack their eggs and drink the yolks. I find five in all and they ease my hunger. If a grebe gets close enough I'll eat well. The sun edges over the hills to the east and I am glad to see better, through my one good eye. The river is strong up here, my ears will miss much.

I drop the deerskins I use for a cloak and unbutton my shirt. I didn't have to kill the man I stole that from. I loosen the threads to the discreet pockets that are sewn shut and take a pinch of snuff from one. It's good plant, good for sniffing out what I need. Feels like I've jammed two shards of ice into my nose and I gasp like I'm drowning, cry a bit and then press another pinch to my tongue, pulling the thread on the pocket tight after. Now the scents and smells of the world are as clear to me as my seeing it. For a short while I can sniff plant like a wolf smells prey.

I forget my pains. Now I'm back in woodland I have to find some cicely. The sharp aniseed smell leads me to it, as I'd hoped. I dig some up, chopping around the roots with the spade to protect them. Around me a leaden, tarry smell of birch trees, moss warming on stones, but also wild onion, birch belets. Food for another day or so.

I wash the cicely roots and I'm packing my mouth with them when I hear bells and the throaty grunts of reindeer. Herders. The river had obscured the sounds, and on the bank I have no cover to hide myself in. I cuss and fight to keep some control of myself. No good comes of people out here.

The reindeer come out through the trees and towards the river. Four men, walking. Nokes — by which I mean their skin is clear and free of the colours that mark out soldiers who use the gifts of plant heavily, the strong and dangerous fightbrews. Three have spears, whips for the deer, one bowman. There's a dog led by one of them, gets a nose of me and starts barking to be let free. Man holding him's smoking a pipe, and a golden beard thick and long as a scarf can't hide a smirk as he measures me up. The herd start fanning out on the bank. Forty feet. Thirty feet.

"Hail!" I shout, spitting out my cicely roots to do it. My broken cheek and swelling make it hard for me to form the greeting. I try to stand a bit more upright, to not look like I need the spade to support my weight.

"Hail. Ir vuttu nask mae?" Carlessen lingo. I don't know it.

I shake my head, speaking Abra lingo. "Auksen clan. Have you got woollens to spare? I'm frostbitten." I hold up my good hand, my fingertips silver grey.

He speaks to the others. There's some laughter. I recognise a word amid their own tongue, they're talking about my colour, for I was a soldier once, my skin coloured to an iron rust and grey veins from years of fightbrews. One of them isn't so sure, knowing I must know how to fight, but I reckon the rest of me isn't exactly putting them off thoughts of some games. Colour alone isn't going to settle it. Shit. I reach inside my shirt for some of the small white amony flowers I'd picked in the passes above us to the north.

"No no no. Drop." He gestures for me to drop the spade and the amony. He lets a little of the dog's lead go as well. The bowman unshoulders his bow.

At least the stakes are clear, and I feel calmer for it. He has to be fucked if he thinks I'm going to do a word he says, let alone think his dog could hurt me.

He has nothing that can hurt me, only kill me.

"No, no, no," I says, mimicking him before swallowing a mouthful of the amony and lifting the spade up from the ground to get a grip closer to its middle. I edge back to the river, feeling best I can for some solid flat earth among the pebbles and reeds.

He smiles and nods to the bowman, like this is the way he was hoping it would go, but that isn't true. The bowman looses an arrow. Fool could've stepped forward twenty feet and made sure of me but I throw myself forward. Not quick enough, the amony hadn't got going. Arrow hits my left shoulder. It stops me a moment, the shock of it. He's readying another arrow, so I scream and run at the reindeer that strayed near me, the one with the bell, the one they all follow. It startles and leaps away, heading downstream, the herd give chase.

Time and again I made ready to die these last nine months. I'm ready now, and glad to take some rapists with me. I run forward while they're distracted by how much harder their day is now going to be chasing down the herd. The one with the pipe swears and lets his dog go at me while one of the spears fumbles in his pockets for a whistle to call the herd, running off after them.

Dogs are predictable. It runs up, makes ready to leap and I catch it hard with the spade. It falls, howling, and I get the edge of the spade deep into its neck. I look at the three men left before me.

"Reindeer! You'll lose them, you sad fuckers!" They'll understand "reindeer" at least.

The pipe smoker draws a sword, just as my amony beats its drum. I don't know how much I took but it hits me like a horse just then. I shudder, lose control of myself, my piss running down my legs as my teeth start grinding. I gasp for air, the sun peeling open my eyes, rays bleaching my bones. My new strength is giddying, the amony fills me with fire.

He moves in and swings. He's not very good at this. The flat of my spade sends his thrust past me and I flip it to a reverse grip and drive it hard into his head, opening his mouth both sides back to his ears. I kick him out of my way and run at the bowman behind him. He looses an arrow, and it shears the skin from my skull as it flies past, almost pulling my good eyeball out with it, the blood blinding me instantly. He doesn't know how to fight close, but I'm blind in both eyes now and I'm relying on the sense the amony gives me, half my training done blind all my life for moments like this. I kick him in the gut, drop the spade and put my fist into his head, my hearing, smell exquisite in detail. He falls and I get down on his chest and my good hand seeks his face, shoving it into the earth to stop its writhing, drive my one good thumb through an eye far as it'll go. A shout behind me, I twist to jump clear but the spear goes through me. Out my front it comes, clean out of my guts. I hold the shaft at my belly and spin about, ripping the spear out of his hands, his grip no doubt weakened a moment with the flush of his success. I hear him backing away, jabbering in his lingo "Ildesmur! Ildesmur!" I know this name well enough, he speaks of the ghostly mothers of vengeance, the tale of the War Crows. I scream, a high, foul scritching that sends him running into the trees.

My blood rolls down my belly into my leggings. There's too much of it. Killed by a bunch of fucking nokes. No more than I deserve. I fall to my knees as I realise, fully, that it's over. The river sounds close, an arm's length away maybe. I fall forward, put my arm out, but it gives and I push both the spearhead and the end of the arrow that's in my shoulder back through me a bit. A freezing spike of pain. My senses lighten to wisps, I fall away from the ground, my chest fit to burst, my blood warming my belly and the dirt under me. Why am I angry that it's all over? The sun keeps climbing, the pebbles rattle and hum as the song of the earth runs through me − beating hooves, distant cries, roots of trees stretching and drinking. I hum to quieten the pain. It's my part in the song but I was always part of the song, I just haven't been listening. The birch trees shush me. Snowy peaks crack like thunder in the distance. The sky is blue like his eyes, fathomless.

'I'm coming,' I says. He knows I'm coming. I just have to hold out my hand.

Chapter 2

A Year Before

"You will fail, Teyr Amondsen."

"I will not. I cannot."

I was standing before the chief of Citadel Hillfast, Chief Othbutter. We was in his chamber of justice. He has a simple wooden chair up on a modest dais he believes gives his people the right impression of his priorities. His gut and the jewels braided into his beard speak otherwise. The jug of wine, red as his fat spud of a nose, also speaks otherwise.

Stood next to him his high cleark, Tobber, a beech-coloured broom brought to life, long narrow face and smooth bald head. Tobber has told me I will fail. He stood as a master of an academy would stand before his class, for he had an audience, mostly the merchants that make up my competition along with representatives of Othbutter's favoured clans. A king and courtiers in all but name, crowding the room so it was hot and thick with the smoke of pipes and whispers.

"I think she's far more prepared than you think, Tob," said Othbutter. "She takes my captain, an escort of my best men, she has employed an excellent drudha to mix her plant and your most capable cleark, she takes my brother here as well, to do my justice. Our clans in the Circle need our support from the bandits that terrorise them. Master Amondsen presents us with an interesting solution." Othbutter had a table to his left, on which stood his jug and a plate, from which he picked and folded two big slices of beef into his mouth.

"She has not the trust of any of the clans who live in the Circle," said the high cleark to the room. Othbutter's brother Crogan muttered a "Hear, hear."

"One of Khiedsen's sons, Samma Khiese, now terrorises the Sedgeway and the Gospeaks and claims himself lord of the Circle and all its clans, including her clan, the one she abandoned. Steel, not tribute or errant daughters, is what they require."

Chief Othbutter looked at me, expecting me to continue the rebuttal, defend my honour.

"We will clear out whatever bandits we find," I said. "I've done it all my life as a soldier. But this expedition isn't just signing some contracts and trading plant, it's about spending profit, my profit, towards strengthening our rule of law. It's about reconnecting the Circle to all of us, so that my clan and all the clans there have good reason to bury those enmities that lead them now to blood. The routes through to Elder Hill, before even we reach the Sedgeway and the Circle beyond, are difficult if not impossible half the year for want of work to drain land or build cord roads and rip raps and keep them. I aim to forge a proper road beyond Elder Hill, right across the Circle as far as Stockson and the busy markets your fathers will no doubt have fondly remembered to you. Citadel Hillfast might then rekindle the good relations with Citadel Forontir that we once enjoyed."

Tob paused for effect as my words were met with murmurings of disbelief. "Yes, Amondsen, I hear that you will build forts from your own chests of gold, drive out bandits, keep hundreds of miles of road maintained from here to Stockson and yet charge nothing for it. You would do what our chief it seems cannot, with but a handful of men and a few wagons. Maybe somebody here not already hired by you or sleeping with you would offer a wager as to your success?"

Before a silence could burnish his point I spoke. "The chief has many more responsibilities than I, problems up north with the Larchlands and Kreigh Moors biggest among them. I'll set an example to all the merchants." I cursed myself the moment I spoke these words, for they did me no favours with those assembled, for all that I spoke true. "The merchants of Hillfast have responsibilities other than filling our purses and lining our cloaks with fur and silk. These forts, this road that my people are building, will further my own prosperity, you can bet on that, but they will help the people of the Circle, grow the common purse through taxes and in so doing raise us all up."

A peal of laughter then that Tobber allowed before saying, "I look forward to seeing all our beggars and slaves bedecked in the silk and ermine that will fall behind your bountiful wagons!" This made the nokes laugh harder and even Othbutter smiled, though in looking on me his eyes pleaded innocence.

"A man as travelled as yourself, Cleark Tobber," I continued, the irony of that sending further ripples of laughter through the crowd, "would have seen Farlsgrad's Post Houses for himself and seen what service they do for the people, easily triple the distance walked or ridden in a day." Fuck him, he'd get seasick crossing a stream and he knew it. "And tell me, Tobber, what else should I do with my coin if not empower Hillfast in its trade? Do you know any good whores I should go piss it all on?"

That got a lot more laughs, and it infuriated that sad old prick for we all knew enough what his pleasure was with girls. I could never weave words as well as others though, that's as good as it got from me. I'm more used to giving orders than winning people over.

I looked behind me to Aude. He smiled and winked. He was still worried there might be some move to stop this dream of mine at the final hour, but the chief had signed and sealed commendations and proposals for the clan chiefs, giving my caravan his authority.

Then Tobber started up again. "Did you know, Chief Othbutter, that she means to take this caravan to the Almet, the dark forest at the heart of the Circle? She means to get the monsters living there, the Oskoro, to swear fealty to your staff. Is that right, Amondsen? But will you recognise them amid the other trees? Will you get within a mile of them before their spores put you to sleep and they feast on your flesh?"

"It's pig shit, Chief. All my years there we never had anything bad from these people. Tributes have always been paid to them and they've saved lives in return, my own for one. Until we forge a friendship, the Almet won't be the common ground it used to be, a neutral place where we can meet the clans, a place of peace and not blood, made so by the Oskoro and respected by all who live in those lands."

"Well well, Amondsen, if you could harness their drudhaic power, I'm sure our troubles in the Circle would soon be over. I won't fault her for trying, Tobber," said Othbutter.

The Oskoro would not be used, but they would be in my debt from the gift I had for them, though what that could mean for us was as hard to fathom as they were.

"Cleark Tobber," said Othbutter, "you have spoken well in favour of your chief's interests, as always. However, I will

12

not leave these merchants to fend for themselves in the Circle when they are doing much to fill our coffers, not least by giving your clearks an ease of passage. We are done, masters. Amondsen, I wish your path swift and dry." He stood to signal the gathering was ended. The high cleark bowed and walked past me without a nod or a word. We locked arms for a farewell, me and the chief, and I took Aude's arm and led him out of the chamber into the main avenue that runs parallel to the dockside the far side of Othbutter's court.

"That might have gone better," I said. "They think it's a ruse, a way of getting one over on them and nothing more."

"You upset the merchants gathered there to be sure, but there's none there that don't already despise your success. Too proud to be part of it and all."

"I saw pity for an amusing child."

"Who, except Chalky Knossen, who's coming with you, has even a slip of your ambition? You show them their sorry limits." He leaned in to kiss my head as we walked.

"Aye, perhaps. Can we walk back to the house? Might be the last bit of time we get to ourselves for a while."

We wound our way up through the carts and children, plant-addicted droopers and hawkers of the streets of Hillfast, edging the slums and the merchant's store sheds. Those guarding them I knew well enough to ask after, teasing word of their masters out of habit, for I would not be back in Hillfast for a year. Then it was up through the steep cobbled lanes of the farmers' huts onto the Crackmore path, a hill that led up to our house amid the cliffs.

"How are you?" he said once we'd crested the hill and turned to look back over Hillfast, as we always did on this climb. I guessed he was meaning how I was since we'd argued the previous day. Knowing we might meet resistance on the road, I had tried a day brew, a dayer as we called it, something

13

a bit less than the fightbrews I took to enhance my skills as a mercenary all those years ago. I lost control of the dayer, it being the first time since then I was putting my body back through it. My cleark Thornsen had taken our son Mosa out for the day while I tried it, but it didn't go so well for Aude, who had stayed with me, and I had hurt him during the rise, when my body was fighting with the hard, violent thrill the dayer caused.

"I'm excited to be getting going at last. I've gone over our tactics with Othbutter's captain, Eirin, Thad as well, but I have a duty for you too, and Mosa won't be back for a while." I give him a wink but he didn't return it and it stung.

He was a slender, beautiful man, ropes of black hair swept to one side which I kept wanting to tuck behind his ear framing the sharp ridge of his cheek. Today the cheek was bruised.

"Well, some instruction on getting our son to eat fish would be welcome. He tried bilt too, rabbit and reindeer. It didn't go well, seems he can only eat their meat fresh," he said.

"I'm sure he'll take to bilt with no other choice." I took his hand in mine for the rest of the walk and let the breeze and the gulls fill our silence as we approached our house because I didn't know how better to fill it.

Near the gate was our two wagons and the packhorses. We'd got some boys from the shed up to help us. Thad, my drudha, was there too, overseeing the plant we were looking to trade or gift.

"Teyr! Did you get Othbutter's scribble on our scrolls?" he asked.

"I did. We ride out tomorrow."

"Purses for our mercs?"

"Yes, those and all. Sanger, Yalle and her crew, all paid retainers." He nodded and turned back to the chests that he'd packed the jars and bottles of prepped plant in.

"I'm going to cook us all some eggs and pitties," said Aude. He put his hands on my shoulders then.

"I'm sorry, bluebell," I said, wanting to reach out and touch his cheek but not daring to try.

"No, Teyr, you told me how it would be, that you might lose yourself. I didn't think . . . well, I don't know."

"I would say there's no excuse, but it took hold of me, I couldn't stone it. I . . ."

He kissed me, the gentle crackle of his whiskers compressed to the softness of his lips. He always closed his eyes. I mostly closed mine, except that day, and when I saw his eyes open, I felt the hint of a smile in his mouth that cradled all else we felt.

"We've a lot to do if we're going to prove that dusty cinch Tobber wrong." With that remark he gated off what we could not speak of to protect what his kiss reaffirmed. I watched as he walked away against the sun, his familiar off-kilter stride, shoulder slightly higher on the right, back straight up as a plank of wood, all from a twist in his left foot from his being born that would never right.

I had a well of confidence when I first courted him. My asking around after him got back to Tarrigsen, who he worked for. Tarry was a merchant, had been like a father to me when I'd returned from soldiering with a fortune for savage work done for the armies of Jua and Marola. Aude had started with Tarrigsen a while after I served an apprenticeship there. Wine and fucking had lost their appeal quite quickly after I'd landed in Hillfast. I was a curiosity, a bet even, a barren woman with the strength of two men cold — by cold I mean without a brew — but

15

a little too old, so I began to hear. I had thought, for all the years I was taking purses, that I just needed enough to pay out and sit on my arse getting soaked on good wine, stilling out on kannab and eating fine beef twice a day. And while I was doing that I knew I was only trying to chase out what was gnawing at my guts, that I couldn't settle with the idea that all I did with my life was kill people for coin and then drink myself to death. So I had begun to use my knowledge of the world and give it the weight of my coin. I became a merchant and was developing a "concern", as the other merchants would say, and they might have meant both senses of the word in saying it. Tarrigsen the merchant had also travelled far and wide, and when, one day, he took a seat at my side in the Mash Fist tavern down on the south quay he explained to me exactly what I was feeling, finding the heart of my thoughts so quickly I almost choked on my rum.

"There's the look of a seaman, Teyr, staring at a horizon while sat in a tavern. You in't the first soldier to nurse her cup and wonder if she could go about the world killing and getting rich and be happy coming back home. But you also in't the first to realise, now all the killing's done, that a life smithing at the same forge for twenty year or keeping tally of an old ass's coin don't make a man poor in his spit and spirit."

"Well said, Master Tarrigsen. And you mentioning the work of a cleark is a bit of what brings you in your finery here among the deckhands, carters and soaks, I imagine."

He laughed, clacked my cup with his and drained it, putting it down heavy on the table to get old Geary to hear it and splash us out a couple more from a bottle kept put away for me.

"He's my best cleark is Aude, and you in't the only

16

merchant's got his scent in their nose. Much as I love you, I won't be fucked with by any merchant of Hillfast, whether she paid the colour or not."

"Well, it's not really his letters or his tallying I've discovered an interest in, Tarry."

He raised an eyebrow. "Good, well, along with the merchants I'm having to slap away, there's also one or two women that have an eye for him as you do. I recall now I sent him over to get your scribble on the Shares. Had his boy with him I believe, Mosa."

It had been a week before. Aude had earnest, gentle blue eyes that I very much liked looking at and he sang rhymes to the boy on his shoulders amid our pleasantries. Mosa was playing with the piece of amber his father had on a necklace. I must have apologised for my appearance, for I'd spent the morning shifting sacks in my shed, and he'd said to that only that I looked fine.

"You know his keep, Mosa's mother, she . . ."

"Yes Tarry, Thornsen told me a bit about it, you know how the clearks go, tight like a virgin's cinch with each other."

"Ahh Thornsen, an excellent cleark, you're lucky to have him, but yes, they spill more of our secrets than they do their own ale when they finish their day, I'll bet," he said. "But her dying giving birth to the lad is well known. It snuffed the drink out of him rightly. Caring for a dut'll do that when there's nobody else, I guess."

"I need a reason to see him. Can you give me one?"

He laughed again at that. "How many men have you led into war, how many killed, and you're after me cooking up some story so you can give him that look you women give us." And he made to flick his hair about and look at me sort of side on.

"Ha! Any women you didn't have to pay for ever look at you like that, Tarry? I bet these others after him got proper long hair though, not a head like this, no axe blades giving their lips an extra curl either."

"There's few got your brains and your means. We both know there's a bit of chatter about you around the quays, more than a few merchants got their cocks in a twist because they won't be half the trader you'll be, and the gangers can't put up any muscle worth a shit to take a slice of what you'll make, you having paid the colour. You want to go courting Aude to keep you warm at night, I'll be happy for both of you. Poach him as cleark and you won't find a ship'll take your interest or your cargo from Hillfast to Northspur, not while I'm breathing."

"I'll never do that to you, Tarry. There's my word."

"And I'll take it. Now don't wear him out."

I've harpooned whales, been holed up in blizzards in the Sathanti Peaks surrounded but unseen by a hundred enemies. I've been a castellan, I helped the great Khasgal found his own throne, wedding the most inspirational and powerful woman I'd ever met, the only other woman he loved. You would think then that I wouldn't be short of things to talk about when I called on Aude to go riding for an afternoon. Tarrigsen had Mosa, saying he was going to get him helping make us all some supper. Tarry loved this man and his boy, that was clear.

On that ride I learned Aude was naturally quiet. We must have done a couple of leagues before I managed to speak, saying I was a bit surprised he would agree to a ride with someone Tarrigsen was having to keep a backeye out for when it come to trade. And he rode on for a few moments, smiling to himself and just said, "But you're beautiful." I wasn't expecting that of course, I know I'm not a painting, not after my life, and he'd have seen me blush if it wasn't for the colouring over my face from the years of the skin rubs and how the fightbrews had changed it. Nazz'd wet himself, and Ruifsen, if they could have seen me shy like a young lass, having known what I was like on campaign with them when I was a few years younger.

Aude took a keen interest in plant, more than anyone I knew that wasn't a soldier, and we'd stop when we saw this or that, and it filled up most of what we talked of. There was a run of chestnut trees flowering, and we climbed a couple to get us a few handfuls of their teardrop leaves and some hunks of bark. He said he knew a good infusion for coughs and breathing troubles that I used to get a lot of when taking the brews, and that Mosa would get from time to time. He didn't make a fuss either like some men had when I, having been a soldier and also a deckhand, flew up a tree faster than he did. Even asked me to lend him a hand up. I liked that he had no idea how to work up to a kiss, and it quieted him enough when I took the initiative that I realised I might have been the first he'd kissed since his keep, Mosa's mother, had died.

Of Mosa he couldn't speak enough, two summers old and a handful by all accounts, having found his feet and now pulling on anything left near the edge of tables, including a bottle of ink, which, even with cleaning, left him looking like he'd soldiered and paid the colour down in Jua. They sat me next to Mosa that night after our ride out. I tried eating my stew and helping Mosa with his, but not without getting the odd spoonful in the face from his bursts of excitement or frustration. I sang a few songs I knew and pulled some faces, which got the boy laughing, and it felt nice, filled my heart up.

19

Before the end of summer Aude had moved with Mosa up to my house, which pleased my kitchen girls and everyone else besides, it seems. By winter the boy called me Ma. I looked up at Aude the moment Mosa said it, for it made me tearful. He said, "That's right, she's Ma to you and her crew, I think. Isn't that right, Ma?"

He was smiling too, and much moved, I think, and he give Mosa a kiss. That was the happiest I've been.

Chapter 3

Now

Her eyes are closed.

My eyes are closed. I'm warm, heavy and safe.

She must not move until the red drum beats.

A thump, a single unignorable knock. And it's mine, I feel it. Either my finger twitches or I try to twitch it. And between these two moments and the flutters of sinew and muscle that follow I know I am held, swaddled. A fingernail of cold air irritates the back of my throat.

When she wakes, she must choose.

Not swaddled. Buried.

Reach up and leave us, or stay and begin her service.

My lungs pull and nothing happens. I spasm; warm wet earth binds me, holds shut my eyes. I pull again. A gurgle, something slithering into my throat from my nose, earth filling in behind it. I try to cough and force this fluid, this jelly, out of a channel — no, a pipe jammed solid in the side of my mouth. I'm shaking, convulsing in this bed, I drive my arms up, fingers wriggling, shoulders, chest; head straining to be upright. The weight on my arms falls away;

they're freed, and with the realisation that I am close to the surface I pull up my knees and kick myself by inches out of my grave, twisting onto my side to retch up and out this reed in my mouth and the thick cold slime that floods from my nose. I clutch my throat, maddened and terrified of the great weight pressing against my chest still. Then I realise what was missing by its return: my heart beating, now a demented pounding that has remembered its duty. I sneeze and cough up more of the slime, wheezing, breathing too fast, shallow gulps crackling, and I'm coughing out this green fluid streaked black with blood. Before I can open my eyes I'm gone again, my galloping heart an agony.

Fucking Oskoro.

The air's more blue, I shiver and start awake. I try to open my eyes. My left eye, less swollen now, sees along my arm, sees vomit and whatever mix it was the Oskoro put inside me to stop me breathing. My right eye won't open, I can't move it, the one that the edge of the arrow caught. I reach up and there's a press on it, a thick hard skin of wax spread over my face, a mask. It feels like I've got sand in my head, my nose full of the wax's smell, honey and sour milk.

The wind has picked up, licking about two big rocks at each of my shoulders. The river is yards away. I want its cold to kill me.

"Your debt's paid. Fuck off." My throat and mouth are dry and raw, the words fall out of me like wood shavings.

The wind's saying I'm naked. The river's ready to give me my wish. Grebes and woodpeckers call undisturbed, so I'm alone.

I could lie here, cover the earth back over me like bed furs, curl up like a girl again, wake in the dark as my ma leaned in through our curtain. She'd say to me, my ma, "Up

then, your pitties ain't marching themselves to the pan."
Candle in her hand, red wool hat, a gift from Sukie Auksen,
who loved her before my da won her with his songs and his
hips. Thruun, my little brother, was cutched into me, thumb
loose in his mouth and sleeping like the dead, for even stone
will stir from time to time.

Give us a hand up then, Ma, if I'm to go on living.

The rock at my right takes her place and I pull myself
up. I blink her candle away and squat to piss. I feel a
poultice crack as I do, on my back, and look down at
where the spear had come through me. I can feel something
like a thread of yarn moving between the mash over the
holes in my back and belly and I know it was Oskoro
drudhanry, for they had plants with roots that could find
a grip in the ropes of gut and the muscle and bones and
blood of bodies, knit themselves into a feast of veins and
drink their due.

It takes me a moment more of feeling around the wounds
to realise I'm using my left arm. I move it carefully, for the
arrow wound's been done above my left bab too and it
wouldn't do to break the mash up early. I say early but I've
got no idea how long I've been buried.

I hobble forward into the river, unsteady as the stabbing
pins of waking muscles scritch with each step.

This is a river running clear, pebbles and boulders its
bed, blurred by its force. It makes me gasp and cuss as I go
in. I plunge under and the current strips me raw. If I open
my mouth and fall back I can end it. I won't get up. My
bones would settle into the ground and my blood would
find his blood, for we died far from our bloodlands and
would be free. Their gates are locked.

My heart is beating too hard though, which is its own
answer. The river runs through me, a heavy embracing

rushing force inside and out of me, calling me to act, to follow its example.

I leave the river as the sun sets, clean, but I won't survive the night without clothes or a fire. As I look down at the shallow pit the Oskoro put me in to heal, I see a ribbon of leather I had not noticed, running between it and a mound of earth a few feet away. I kneel at this mound, the ribbon disappearing into it. I dig aside the dirt and pull at the leather. A sack is buried, with a bow and quiver of arrows. It had all likely belonged to the herders.

A thick tunic, leggings and boots are in the sack, a noke's fieldbelt, cheese and a flask. There are furs in the pit and a good knife, as well as the sack holding Mosa's shirt and the spade I had with me before. I dry myself off a bit with the furs and put the clothes on.

I will go to live on the coast, follow this river.

So I hide from the farmers, sniffers and herders, survive in the weeks since my death, using the skills my ma taught me. The river gets fatter and slower. Aoig, what the Old Kingdoms call the sun, melts the snow and brings the world to life proper. I could feel it before, on a brew, what we called the song of the earth, when the brew makes every sense stand out like an agony, and the world wants to tell you too much and you can lose yourself and die in it if you haven't been trained. But when I cracked open the wax over my face and rubbed away the poultice I could now see the song with my right eye, though I'm hard pressed to describe it.

Judging by my reflection, a pale streak is all that's left of that herder's arrow, there's the knot of scar at the side of my eye, a lattice of bark and skin, and my eyeball is now all dark like gravy, rolling about the socket like it's bathed in sand, like it's an eye that don't belong there.

This sight invades my other senses. If I shut my left eye, the pattern of what I see is different: I see the land's living, I taste it, a sight beyond any fightbrew, a sight that disturbs my dreams with vapours of a knowledge perhaps only the Oskoro understand. All these weeks since I opened that eye I have tried to travel in the twilight, as no amount of beech leaves or poppy seeds eases the headaches and sickness that two different eyes cause. This is the sight of an eagle and we were not made to live with it.

Standing stones are carved at the borders between the lands of Carlessen's Families, their grazing rights and sniffing rights and farmland. The land evens out, valleys running ahead to vales and plains. I have not been here before. I follow still the course of the river, a vein of life, food and water, both foraged and stolen. There are many more guards and watchers at theits than I had reckoned with coming out of the mountains. The warlord's arm is lengthening. So I keep my distance from the river as I follow it, sleep in trees. But the peace I manage to take from the solitude is robbed from me when I'm woken only days out of the valleys the Nakvi-Russ river runs along. Horns, horns of the whiteboys, their screaming, maddening howl, like animals being slaughtered. Like people being slaughtered. These sounds blow through the birch and pine about me, blow past me from the west, at the river. The horns pull tears from my old eye. I hold my head and think about breathing, to only breathe, to stone the fear. The horns are death.

I string the bow and leap down to the ground from the bough I rested in. I take some snuff to clear and fill my chest for running. Birds take flight, darting out of the edge of woods near a theit; nine, ten huts, pens of pigs, chickens and plant fields. Those that live there are running about gathering their children, men and women taking up spears and passing between them a small bag, some plant to give them a lift. I see the beard hoop of the family's leader, weavings in his keep's hair, and it's those two who stand just ahead of five men. The horns are sounding from the trees to the north of their theit. I glimpse, from this higher vantage point, figures moving between tree trunks, their horns echoing over the dell this Family have their home in.

They make them wait. It's what they do. The horns fill the rising morning, scratching at the nerves, shrill screams that trigger the theit's own babies and children.

One of the men standing behind their chief starts shouting, looses an arrow in defiance. The horns stop. A man staggers out of the treeline, crying out for their surrender. He has stumps where his hands were, blackened strips of cloth over them. He holds them up in front of him like he can't get used to them. The chief tries to shout over him. Two of the men behind the chief then run forward to help what must be one of their kin. I almost cry out, it's so obvious to me. They make forty yards to their man when I see the shivers in the air from the flight of arrows, cutting them both down. The maimed man falls to his knees at their side howling, leaning to one who must be a brother. Two more, a man and a woman, come from different huts, each with a bow and spear to make up the five again that stand with the chief. Then a horseman nudges his mount out from the trees. He wears leathers, field-belt, but his face, head and hands are chalked white.

"Line up the boys, Orgrif! Swear fealty to Samma Khiese! Feed our army with four of your kin and a quarter of your plant and the rest of you live!" Two flaming arrows are loosed, each thirty yards short of the nearest hut, but the intent is clear. The whiteboy knows the chief's name. Could be a Seikkerson or an Auksen lad, accent suggesting one of those clans. Fucking traitor.

Orgrif looks to his keep then, and the knot of kin behind him. They speak, and he turns back to the whiteboy and throws down his spear and bow. The others follow.

I'm relieved. Nobody else needs to die if Orgrif isn't stupid, and I can move on, keep ahead of them.

As his keep runs forward to the man on his knees, Orgrif whistles for the others in his theit to come out. Riders trot forward from the trees, nine in a line. Four dismount as they get to where Orgrif and the others are standing. There's shouting and cussing from his people as the boys, four in all, are presented to the whiteboys. It worries me for they don't know what the whiteboys will do if they are crossed.

Hard to hear then what is said, as I'm still over the river. The lead rider, and he carried himself as a leader, walks up to the boys. One spits at him as he leans close, catches him good in the face. I grip my bow and tears spring from my eyes. I'm not ready to watch a torturing. The boy's mother shouts something. The lead rider puts the boy on the ground with one hard punch. Orgrif makes to move, but a man behind him steps to him and puts a hand on his shoulder.

The leader puts the boot into the boy, kicks his face a few times, then reaches down to grab him by his tunic and pull him towards his crew. I want to throw up, sick with fear for the boy, who can't be more than Mosa's age.

The other whiteboys ready themselves, all liplicking for some violence as I put an arrow against the bow and draw. I have to stifle a thrill then as I line up the shot; it's this changed eye, so easy to judge distance, so clear the sense of the air moving between the arrowhead and the leader's back. I've never been more sure of a shot. I hold my breath and let the arrow go, a thrilling certainty to its arc over the river as it hits the leader's back and makes him stagger forward. As it hits him I move behind the tree I dropped out of.

Shouts start up. I draw another arrow, nock it and step out of the trees again, hungry to feel that assurance, for it quelled my fear. The arrow hits one of the mounted riders in his neck as he stares down at his leader and he falls dead from his horse. I'm spotted now so I step further out from the tree, to goad them now they're leaderless. One of them looses an arrow. It will land behind me, missing my shoulder by a foot or so. I still hold my breath as it flashes past me and I raise my bow again, everyone now looking over the river at me. I loose two more arrows as the whiteboys mount up and head for me. One hits a whiteboy as he drives his horse into the river, the other just misses its mark but catches the horse behind it in the neck, the rider thrown to the bank. The family see what's happening, and a cry goes up from a couple of them despite Orgrif's protest, and they run for the fallen rider.

I run into the trees, take some amony and pray to a magist it isn't too much to kill me.

The slope rises steeply amid the trees. I climb up some banks and wait, listening.

"It gets worse for you, you don't come out now!" says one of them.

"Grenned's chops are smacking for meat, ain't they," says another.

He's shushed. Three of them give away their positions clear as day, though there's more than that about. They speak because they're nervous, because they haven't been trained not to. These aren't whiteboys then, or Khiese now thinks some chalk paste's enough. I still count three to listen for. I pick up a stone and throw it twenty or so yards, its knock against a trunk echoing. A shuffling and whispering about fifteen yards down the slope from me gives away another two.

I lean out, loose an arrow that hits one of them and lean back in. The boy next to him shrieks and I hear him make a move away from the one I just dropped.

There's whispering, but the amony's strong enough that I'm able to hear one calling for them to retreat. "She's paid," he whispers. "Brewed," says another. Good. I hear from the soft footfall that they're approaching my position. Some of their sightlines, if they're with bows, will be stopped by the trees about us. There's a thrill then I don't, can't dwell on, the same as when I rushed those herders. Moments from now it might be nothing matters. As I move out from the tree again, bow raised, I take all doubt and choice away. I'm free.

As the first arrow punches into the chest of one of the whiteboys and begins drowning him in his own blood I've drawn the bow again, easy as yawning, and I kill a second one of them, high in the middle of his chest.

Two more of them cry out and run at me with spears, ignoring the boy that called for their retreat. I run towards them, only the knife, and I do it because I have only the knife, because nobody does that against spears. I judge the better of the two from his stance and go for him. I'm quick enough, though I have no brew in me but what amony gives.

He couldn't have had more than twenty or so summers this one, seems paralysed before me, thrusting the spear at me like I'm to be shooed away. I parry it and step inside, quicker and stronger than him. Stab him twice as he tries to fend me off, take the spear before either he or it hit the ground and keep moving. I have lost the place of those others around me and expect an arrow to hit me before I get my back to a trunk, facing the other of these two. He's no older, quivering, blowing too hard as he readies himself. He slaps his spear into the bind, I roll it and push the point of mine

29

through his eye. No movement to my sides. I close my eyes. One left. I hear him then, he's running, north through the trees, denying me a shot at him. Trouble's coming back double. The people of this theit are dead if they don't flee.

I walk out of the trees and wave to the settlers so they know I'm not one of those who attacked them. The horses the whiteboys rode towards me I approach quiet and make my whispers. I could use a horse. They seem easy enough and are happy to be led with my awful singing back through the river and up to the huts.

A woman comes over; man behind her must have been her keep.

"I don't know the Carlessen lingo. Abra or Common?" I ask as I tie the horses to a garden fence. I see Orgrif has gone to join his keep with the wounded man and his dead kin.

"You kilt them?" says the woman before me. She's got grey straw for hair, whitening at the roots, and a pale leathery face in which I can see, I think, trust and concern. Her man was aiming to be relaxed with both hands on his spear like it was a staff, but he looks jumpy as a rabbit now I'm close.

"I did. One got away. More trouble's coming."

"Thucksen's boy that was, the one leading them out of the trees. His family are five mile northwest and never worth the leather on a lash. You know this Khiese?"

Words lock in my throat; I can only nod. "There'll be more of them, and you'll all pay. I have to speak to Orgrif."

"I'm Braidie," she says, "come on." She hooks her thin hard old arm in mine and leads me through the plant garden and up a path towards where the others are gathered, mothers holding their boys and girls close, while the one that was punched is hugging his ma while she puts a paste on him where the skin's split, shushing him all the while. His eye's all puffed and red.

She looks up at me as I come near.

"I owe you his life, his honour," she says.

I shake my head. "He strengthened his rope with that one spit." Which is a saying to mean he did his family and his line proud.

She cocks her head towards Orgrif, who looks up from the wounded man outside the camp. "He give us all up for nine boys with some chalk on their heads."

"That in't the only way to see it, Grumma," says one of the spearmen who was stood with Orgrif a short while ago. "That spit's going to bring this Khiese on all of us, and that brewed-up bitch there just sealed it," he says, looking over at me.

"Pity you didn't stand up to them, Annik, but then you can barely stand up to your sister when she's knocking your lazy backside around your plant runs," says Braidie.

Orgrif comes over then. He nods at me, but they all have questions.

"How's Murin?" asks Grumma.

"Mell's seeing to him," he says before turning to me. "You, you've got colour, you have any plant'll help him? He's in a bad way."

"I'll see if I can help," I says.

Mell, Orgrif's keep, is kneeling over this Murin, rubbing something into his gums when I get there, poppy most likely, for I saw a run of it as I brought the horses up. Murin's on his back now, shivering and mumbling. His stumps wasn't done with a sharp enough edge or belted and bandaged soon enough. She'd washed them with vinegar from what I could smell, but it was obvious he'd lost too much blood.

"Not much I can do, Mell," I say. I wasn't wasting birch or bistort on a dead man.

"He's got a baby not a season old, and a boy too," she

31

says, and she wipes her eyes with one hand while smoothing his head with another.

"Where's his keep?"

"Ydka? Sniffing, she'll be a league or two south."

I put a hand on her shoulder. "I'm sorry."

"What's your name?"

"Teyr. Teyr Amondsen. What Family are you?"

"We're Kelssens, of the Carlessen clan. Amondsen, your Family is part of the Auksen clan? You look beat up, sorry for saying. Was it these whiteboys we've been hearing about?"

"Yes." I had to pen my thoughts in. I take a breath. "You're not safe now this has happened." That Annik put the thought in me that my shooting the whiteboy might well have been the wrong thing to do, for all that the boy who spat at him would have been kicked to death.

Murin stops shivering and is still. He had been looking up at the sky and not at us the whole time.

"He must have seen the magist Halfussen calling for him," I say.

Mell leans over Murin's body to that of the one he fell down to weep over, who must have been his brother, shot by the whiteboys. She takes their hands and puts them in each other's.

"They'll go into our tapestry together now," she says. She turns to me, and if my eyes are full it's because there's two I love that I hope have found the same path, and it's them that's brought me to my own knees next to Mell.

She puts her arms about me, and I can smell the flowers fresh braided into her hair. Her neck is hot, her cheek wet and I'm overwhelmed, for all this time since Khiese left me to die I've not held or been held by another. I pull away quickly because I can't go back there.

"Sorry." I stand up and wipe my face and recover myself.

Mell stands too. She's good to look on, thirty years or so. There's a way some have, a posture and a sympathy in the eyes for sorrow that disarms and welcomes, and she has it. It becomes apparent as we walk back to the theit and the gathering turns to us both, even Orgrif turns. It reminds me why I left my own family, for the strength of women never opens the way to their getting any power or recognition short of the subtle strings that the mothers of chiefs can pull.

"They're coming back, Mell, more of them too. You need to tell your kin to leave here."

She says nothing.

"They're saying Orgrif give up your sons too easily."

"I won't bring him dishonour by speaking against him." She could be my ma.

The whole theit's out now, ranged about Orgrif, fifty odd, including the children. She speaks to them.

"There was nothing we could do for Murin. Someone needs to go and find Ydka and her dut. This is Teyr, she's Auksen clan." As she says it she's looking about the family until she sees the boy, seven years or so, who must have been Murin's son. Mell goes over to him and kneels down to hug him. She's leaving the gathering to Orgrif of course.

"I'll fetch Ydka," says a man standing by. "Can I take one o' those horses?"

"Yes, I would like to keep one of them to move on, if you'd show me that kindness, but the rest are yours."

"You come down from the Auksen lands then?" asks Orgrif.

"I did." He wasn't getting my life story, and it was true to a point.

"I heard something of this Khiese, this warlord, a few weeks back when I was down at the dock. Is he all over the Circle? Has he taken Hillfast?"

33

"If he has I haven't heard it. You'd do well to gather what you can carry and move south. The Carlessens need to know what's coming."

"I don't think we will, Teyr. These are our bloodlands." As Orgrif says this I look about and see Annik among those calling out their approval to this.

"They'll be your bloodlands when you return, if Carlessen is honourable. Or you'll all die when next the horns sound."

"These whiteboys in't for much if an old and paid-out drooper like you got their measure," says a woman from behind Annik. She's heavy-looking, Annik's sister no doubt, a clay pipe in the corner of her mouth, though I can see it isn't lit. The heat of those about me is somehow as clear to my eye as a smell is to my nose.

"Must have missed seein' the shots she made from over the river then, Femke, best I ever saw," says Braidie.

"If all of you could shoot well it wouldn't be enough for what's coming." I look back at the horses tied there. Walk away. They couldn't stop me if I did. Maybe my being here is giving them the grit to stay and I curse the thought.

"You seem to know a bit about what's coming," says Orgrif. "Will you help us set?"

Fuck.

I look about at this Family. I bet Steid Carlessen barely knows they exist except when his collectors come calling. They're on their own, something Khiese's relied on when bringing the Circle clans together against Othbutter.

I wish for a purse I can hide behind, some orders that deny me a choice. I look at Murin's son and the other younger duts about. I look at the mothers. They don't have the look that speaks of a confidence I'll take their side. Probably think that, being a woman having ruined her body with brews, what could I know about the bond of love for a child? Fuck

34

them. Here's why I'll do it. It's because I get to kill more whiteboys, and Auksen and Seikkerson clan traitors at that. Because I can't, even after all I suffered at Khiese's hands, bring myself to leave these people to die, and dying myself's something I've been neighbours with for longer than I can remember.

"I'll stay, for what it's worth. I'll die with you rather than see you all butchered alone. These whiteboys, they start with burning your plant, killing your animals. They will try not to kill you for a while. The horns will go on for days. There's nothing we can do until they get too close and make a mistake. It's likely they'll leave you without food if there's enough of them to come in at you and do all that quickly. But they'll leave then; they'll just watch you, and retreat if you go out after them, pick you off as you do it. Then when you've lost hope and you're starving, then they'll come in at you. You want to stay here? I doubt any of us'll live. I know all about your honour; I hope it keeps you warm when you're surrounded by your dead."

I don't do myself a favour with them in saying that; they're all shouting at me, bit of spit sent my way too. They haven't the sense to see I could kill every last one of them on my own, and I paid out (meaning I had stopped paying the price of taking fightbrews) years ago.

"Enough!" shouts Orgrif. "We have our dead to bury. This woman is an Amondsen, a Family of the Auksen clan. Good blood. They've done us no wrong and she stands with us against what's to come. She's right to warn us, but I'm calling arms. We need mixes made; bring your plant and belts to Mell and help her make them up. Annik, Kirvotte, Grigg, bring your spades." He turns to me then. "Stay at our hearth tonight, our guest."

I inventory the horses' saddles and lead them into a shelter with the theit's three other horses. They are good enough stock; they'd make these people some good coin in any other run of luck. I find a sword, which is welcome, for these people rely on a smith in the theit that Braidie said the whiteboys come from. I would learn we had no more than four swords between us, though many more spears and some hatchets.

Their best fletcher was being buried so I ask Braidie to get others I can teach it to. Whole Family don't have more than fifty or so arrows with their sniffers out.

I help best I can with the milk churning once I've set some of the younger ones off to find us some good wood, and it's a way to burn off the rest of the amony I took. I have a chance at some unguarded sleep and I don't want to waste it trying to stone my thoughts back from the dark.

Mell wakes me late in the evening. Theirs is a larger hut and she sits around the firepit with Orgrif and three young men who are dressed ready for the watch I proposed. They're nokes but the best archers they have.

"Goodnight, Teyr? I hope you slept," says Mell. She's ladling some broth in a pot over the fire.

"These boys are on watch with you," says Orgrif. "Maege, Erlif and Kirvotte. Teyr is your chief tonight. You do as she says."

"Can you see out of that eye?" says Erlif. He's got a cockiness about him, making the most of being a boy, I think, for he isn't more than thirteen or fourteen years and Maege nudges him to shush him. He's likely to be tricky and we don't need that tonight.

"I can't too well without this paste I use in it. Can you help me?" I say. Before he has time to say anything I've got the leather pouch from my sack and I take out a small stick.

The plant in the stick needs to be melted before it's applied, as it's sealed in a guira gum mix to keep it fresh. I hand it to him. "You need to warm it till the end starts to run, then you'll need to run it over my eye. Think you can do it, Erlif? Do you have a steady hand?"

"Steadier than this pair," he says, knocking Kirvotte's knee. He takes the stick but I grab his wrist as he does. He's surprised at my strength. "You have to be steady, Erlif, or you'll blind me." His smile's gone and he just nods. He leans over the pit, heats up the stick and then turns back to me. Mell's behind him, smiling; she knows I'm exaggerating the danger, though it doesn't much surprise me that Orgrif's still not twigged.

"I'm going to hold my eyelids back, Erlif. Go easy, like you're running your finger over a girl's lips."

"Like he's ever done that before," says Maege.

"Shut your hole."

He's up close now, heel of his hand on my cheek, tongue poking out with concentration as he brings the stick to my eye. I'm glad of the help for the eye'll get a better soak than I can manage on my own. When I woke from that pit the Oskoro put me in and found these sticks that smelled just like them, something like burned kannab and honey, I knew they must have been for the bark and whatever other wounds they'd healed. They must use this oil on their own bodies.

I blink back the warm oil off the stick and it eases the eye a bit.

"Good work, Erlif." He smiles. We've built some trust. It's how I was taught.

"Maege's cricky for you, he told me," says Erlif.

"No, I'm not!"

"He is, keeps talking about how he wants a squeeze of Blackeye's babs."

37

The boy's head bows, I can almost feel his face flush. Orgrif laughs loudly and Mell squeezes her mouth tight against the same.

"If you three are running the watch with me then we do it as soldiers. Reason you've got to help each other like Erlif's done and Maege's going to do is because you can't prep for a war alone. You have to get past thinking with your cinch or your cock. Am I clear? Can you be soldiers?"

They nod, though Kirvotte's smirked at my mention of both. Orgrif raises his eyebrows.

"Maege, you can do my spear wound and my arrow wound. There's bark in them, needs washing with more of the oil comes from warming that stick." I daren't tell them it's Oskoro drudhanry. No saying what they'll then think, like it's infectious or something. I pull my tunic off over my head, just a woollen shirt underneath. I turn my back on the boys and lift it.

"Maege, it can be hotter for these wounds." The bark'll drink up that oil. I hear a murmur as he does the bark. They can see the mess I'm in, the scars, the lumps and the knots from all the beatings and brews.

"Good work, Maege," I say as I turn back to face him. "I'll do the front myself."

He half smiles and shuffles back to sit with the others on a bench near the firepit.

"Seen holes like that on pigs I stuck," says Orgrif, "not ever on someone still living."

"In't many drudhas up to healing this sort of damage. But while you boys have had a go at rubbing my eye and my back, I'm sorry to say it's my turn to prep you for our watch. You heard of the luta leaf?" None in the tent have.

"Let's have our broth. And Mell, do you have a stick they can bite on?"

That takes the wind out of their sails, and they look at

each other nervously now. Once we're done with the broth I take four luta leaves from a strip of alka-guira that keeps them moist, for they're thin enough to see through, like the film from a slice of onion, and a fuck lot less pleasant to put in your eyes.

"Who's first? Kirvotte? Want to show the other two how it's done?"

"What do I have to do?"

"You're going to lift up each eyelid, I'm going to slip a leaf under them, onto your eye, then you're going to take that stick and bite down on it while you keep your eyes closed for a count of twenty."

He looks over at Orgrif, who has a smile appearing on his face.

"What are you laughing at, Chief?" he says.

"You're braver than me."

"Ready?" I says.

"Go on," says Erlif. "This should be funny."

Kirvotte shakes his head, leans in towards me and lifts up his left eyelid. I press the leaf on it.

"Quick, the other one, keep that eye shut!"

He lifts the other lid and on goes another leaf. I push the stick in his mouth just as he starts blowing and punching the ground. I put my thumbs on his eyes and with my hands keep his head still till the pain retreats.

He opens his eyes and instinctively grabs my arm. "On my rope it's killing me!"

He looks then at the other two.

"Fuck a goat, your eyes are all different, they've gone a bit like hers," says Erlif.

"The leaf's melted, its juice has soaked into his eye. You need to get outside, Kirvotte, it's bright enough in here you might do them some damage."

He can't stand up and leave quick enough.

"Who's next?" I says.

They needed a few slaps during the first watch. Luta changes how you see the world in more ways than the obvious. Next night was more work-like; we was in trees about the perimeter of the camp but so's we could see each other. Luta made it easy to spot even small gestures to say what might be wrong, and I taught them some signs to help tell what they were seeing while we waited. Fear give them some discipline for sure.

My days was helping Braidie, Mell and the others with plant, and also caulking their boat for an escape, stashing a bit of food and coin in it to take off downriver, though there'd be no more room than for eight or so in it.

Third night out the horns start their screeching and soon enough the camp's out. Turns out some of the women are better archers than the men, and it takes some cussing and argument to ensure they get the mixes they need to do good work during an attack.

I tell my boys in the trees to drop their brews. They are mild enough they won't make mince out of their brains, but should at least give them a clean rise. A short while later and Kirvotte's signing that there's two below him. I sign him to keep his place and keep signing back what he's seeing.

I thought the luta might have an effect on the eye that the Oskoro changed when they healed it, but I discover it is already more potent than anything the luta can give. I see the two whiteboys passing through the trees, past Kirvotte and blowing their horns as they then come near Maege. I'd given the boys sporebags. I'd seen them used over in Farlsgrad, belet and plant heads harvested when they were heavy with spores and cut and dried inside eggshells that were gummed whole again.

Of course, it makes no difference what instructions I'd given Annik and the others at the theit; they show themselves, shouting back at the woods and giving away their numbers and arms and readiness. Idiots.

I watch the boys and they watch me as the night wears on. Then, there's movement enough it's easy for all of us to pick up on. Below Kirvotte I can see twelve whiteboys, their heads almost glowing against the more drab greens and olives that the luta turns the world into.

He's signing their presence and numbers to me. Then they pause among the trees at the edge of the treeline and I see one sparking up a torch, which gets passed around for each of them to put to arrows. They move out of the treeline to prepare their shots. I sign for Kirvotte to throw his eggs at them. His timing is good; they're raising their bows to shoot, and the eggs, hitting the grass, make barely a noise. One of the whiteboys coughs and lets an arrow go, but he loses the full draw and it flies flat and hits the grass harmlessly some way from the first of the huts. A horn then goes up in the camp as they've seen the fire arrows lit. Maege then signs, and I see below his tree a number of whiteboys come running through. Whatever routine they'd worked was now blown off course by seeing the bowmen coughing and choking and scrambling for their masks. I sign for Maege to hold his own attack. The whiteboys run out into the clearing around the theit, waving spears and swords and shouting as they head for the fences and the runs of plant this Family would be hard pressed to lose. Annik and about five of the other men move out to face them, and about them Femke and two of the other women start loosing arrows. The whiteboys read the range well and are quick on whatever brew they've had.

The whiteboys run in to hurl a couple of spears. Annik then gives a shout and, clearly heartened by the sight of those on their knees choking and useless, thinks this is it. I feel straight away it's wrong, it's too obvious. I'm on the verge of whistling them to stay back at the huts when I hear below me a twig snap. I was caught up too much in what is before me, but now I refocus, there are forty-odd whiteboys snaking their way through the trees. This is a complete fucking slaughter, and I'm dead if I make a move. I look over at my boys still in the trees and give them commands and a sign to hold.

Sure enough, the forty below me start running across the clearing aiming to kill off what they knew would be most of the able fighting men and women of the theit. I give them about twenty yards and sign for my boys to drop out of the trees and start shooting at the whiteboys who lured out Annik and his men.

On the ground now, I step out from the treeline and drop an egg into the pouch of a sling that Mell had given me. The whiteboys have not seen properly what happened to the archers, and with their shouting I manage to get at least three eggs away, two hitting shoulders to give them cause to stop where the eggs broke. They shout then for masks as the spores get in them. My bow's out and I start bringing them down, one by one. I'm spotted of course but with the engagement ahead of them they're caught in two minds. One of them barks orders – it's in their own tongue, I don't get – it, and about ten of them turn and run back at me. Two have shields out and move to the front. I turn and run for the huts, bringing them in range of Femke and the other archers. The luta helps me pick out the divots and roots and stones that could, in this darkness, trip me. A couple of them fall and so prove their own sight mix isn't up to much, and it gives me some small hope that their drudha won't have prepped them much for the poison we made up.

The women start shooting arrows past me, one at least a bit too close, but I drop a shoulder as I see it thread a wave in the air a moment before it's gone and has hit one of those chasing me.

In the clearing, despite our efforts, there's twenty or more whiteboys running at Annik's handful. I can only hope Kirvotte and the others did as they was told and was running back through the trees on the far side of the settlement to make the numbers up among the huts. The screaming starts as axes and spears find their marks. I leap a fence into an empty pen, throw my bow and remaining arrows over towards a nearby hut, and turn and wait for them to come at me. I'm breathing too hard, but the sword feels good, the doubt's gone and I'm squaring up to these traitors when Braidie shouts at me, starts screaming my name. The first of the whiteboys leaps clean over the fence, wild delight in his eyes, drool hanging in strings off his chin. His brew's been badly measured and he's gritching out, pure and ravenous for murder. I manage to get the lean on his spear and stick him in the gut. My mistake is not pushing through to finish him because two more are up on the fence and coming at me. As I knock his spear to the ground he comes forward again bare-handed. I'm meeting another spear with my sword so he's on me in a moment. I've got a knife out, turn side on to slide the second spear past me as it comes in, and I kick out. As the first man gets his hands on my throat I bring the knife up through his jaw. The two with spears reposition as they're blocked by their kin from a straight thrust, so I pull him back with me using the knife in his head, his rotten breath and hot fingers still squeezing my throat. I can't breathe, and this fucker isn't dying, he's grinning.

There's a shout to my right, sounds like my boys, and they're shooting at the others who have come after me. Someone lands from the fence behind me and I'm a heartbeat from pulling the knife out of this whiteboy's head and thrusting it behind me when Femke the archer runs past me with axe and a shield, the woman's howling like a wolf in the Frenzy. My head begins to pound. It feels like I'm retreating from my body under his fierce grip and I find myself backed up against the opposite fence in this pen. I've got no choice, moments from another death, so I go for a pouch on my belt, my last eggshell full of spores. He's opened his jaw with hoarse, watery laughter, forcing it down the knife's blade, so I crush the egg in his mouth and pull out the knife. The spores explode around us. He's got the worst of it and the paralysis is almost instant. I fall to my knees, coughing and retching as much from being strangled as with the spores that are finding their way through the alka-soaked rags I'm wearing for a mask. My skin's itching and my eyes, even with the luta, are swelling.

"Teyr!" It's Braidie shouting at me, somewhere behind me. I reach for the fence and feel my way up and over it towards her.

"Braidie, help me, I'm blinded. River moss with an arnica, bistort or labror tincture!"

I'm moving towards the sound of her running, the hand that takes mine is cold and wet.

"I have some river moss in our hut, but I've got Ydka and our children and there's a bowman over the river, I can't get these duts to the boat." She'd read the end of this settlement as soon and as clearly as I had. "Those duts'll only live if you go with them, you can't die here." My eyes feel like they're frying now. Braidie fusses about in the bag of plant she's carrying. For a moment my black eye trembles, I have

44

this strange thought that it is responding to something I smell a moment later. Braidie opens my eyelids, one eye at a time, I can hear her chewing and she spits onto my eyeballs whatever mix it is I smell, the scent of labror in there a welcome hint I might see again shortly. I hear footsteps running up behind her, a child out of breath.

"Na Braidie!" says a boy. "Someone's shooting at us down by the boat. I can't find Crettie, Na, I can't find her!"

"Shush now, where's Brek?"

"He was trying to get on the boat, Mell's gone down there, they turned over Da's cart and they're behind it. Ydka can't do nothing because she's carrying her dut."

The juice from Braidie's spit is like cold milk on my eyes, the spores are running out with the tears. I take the moss she's kept in alka and squeeze the fluids from the mixture into my mouth, an astringent for my throat, which is sore from the spores.

"Here," she says, and she gives me her quiver and bow, taking up a hatchet for herself.

"Take Teyr to the boat. She'll help you all better than any of us."

I begin to speak but she sharply cuts me off.

"Protect our rope and honour, Teyr Amondsen, take these children away that they might come back one day." She puts a hand to my cheek a moment, then we turn as two white-boys come running at us. I shove the boy back so he falls over, and I use the quiver to knock the first spear past me. The other of them has an axe, which I'm grateful for as it means he'll need to get closer to me. Braidie pushes past me, flushed with some sort of brew. I can feel it, the heat of it, the violence of it I can almost read with my eye.

"Leave!" she bellows.

Her axe bites at least one of them. The boy with me is

45

up off his arse and running down the slope towards the river and the cart that's near their boat, so I have to leave her, and I know she's going to die.

"Teyr!" It's Maege, he's running across the gardens, "Teyr, help us. Orgrif's holed up with a few in his house, they're setting fire to it."

He's covered in blood, his quiver's empty and he's shivering and gasping for air. I have to calm him.

"I'm sorry, Maege, I can't. I've sworn to protect the Family's children, I have to make sure they get on the boat now if they're to live. Can you help me with the archer over the river that's stopping us getting to the boat?" He looks over and on the luta sees what's happening well enough.

"I see him. There's just the one of them. Teyr, Erlif and Kirvotte, they . . ."

"I know, I know, Maege, and I'm sorry. And we're out of spores, so each moment now we have to make clear in our heads, no grief and no pain or they'll have died for nothing. Take Braidie's quiver. When you see me wave start putting arrows over him, keep him behind that birch trunk until I can get us going." I take a few arrows from the quiver and hand them to him.

He looks down at the arrows in his hands, but I can feel the resolve building, I can see it in the tightening of his lips and around his eyes as the frown softens. "But we . . . Right, right I'll do it."

"Mell's down there, I'm hoping I can save her too. Orgrif would want nothing else." I put my hands on his shoulders, bring his face close to mine. "You honour this Family, your tapestry. Breathe slow and hold it for the shot; you'll pass out if you keep blowing like that." I give him a wink, like I'm teaching an old goat how to kick.

He smiles. "I will."

I follow the boy on through a run of veg. Mell stands as we approach though crouched still against the upturned cart. Brek is there, along with Ydka, Murin's boy and some other children.

"Maege's going to cover us from that archer. When I give the signal, you need to run down to the boat. Brek, I want you to untie it while Ydka and Mell get on it."

"No, Teyr, it's you who must go. I can't leave this theit, my Family, Orgrif either. You're their best chance of living, not me."

"Mell . . ."

"No!" she shouts. I follow her eyes towards Maege, who's turned away from us and is shooting five whiteboys charging at him. I then see what she's seen, the thatch of her long-house roof crash in, Orgrif running out to the whiteboys waiting for him.

I look around me and the children are staring back at their people dying. Mell draws a sword, too finely worked and shining to my sore, luta-filled eyes to have ever been used. She looks back.

"Go! You swore to help this theit, you'll save them, save the Kelssen rope." She doesn't wait but runs on. Moments later she cries out, I can see the trail of the arrow's flight as a momentary flicker. She's hit in the thigh and falls over. Maege is overwhelmed. I turn to the children. One of the girls is screaming at what she's seeing.

"Children!" I shout. "You run for the boat."

"We'll be shot," says Brek.

"You won't. Ydka, I need you to help me lead these duts."

I look at Murin's boy and a girl next to him, the next two oldest. "Take their hands and follow Ydka."

"Come on!" she says. Her baby's crying in the wrap that's tied against her chest as she runs out.

I take an arrow and nock it. They're running down to the boat, the older ones holding the hands of the littler ones, dragging them along as they bawl. I empty myself of breath. Maege and Mell are being hacked to death somewhere behind me as the archer steps out from behind the tree to find a target to draw on.

I let the arrow fly, but he's already spotted them all running for the boat and looses an arrow at them. My arrow punches through his face and throws him back. I'm running before he hits the ground.

"Teyr!" It's the boy that brought me down from Braidie's. I look down the bank and Ydka and the children have frozen. The arrow's hit Brek in the shoulder and he's crying out.

"Ydka, get them on the fucking boat! You, Murin's boy, start untying it!" I turn to the boy who's been hit; he's panting, staring down in disbelief at the arrow shaft sticking out of him.

"Stay with me, Brek. I'm sorry, lad, but this is going to hurt."

I drag him up and over my shoulder. He thrashes about in pain as I follow the children down the bank to the river. The children splash through the shallows and onto the boat. Murin's boy unwinds the rope and with my spare hand I grab the younger children by their hoods and tunics and throw them into the boat. They know well enough to crowd the far end as I heave Brek onto the boat, and he hits it with a yelp before I'm pushing us out into the river.

"One of you take the rudder. Ydka, take the paddle if you can, keep us in the main current."

One of the girls, clutching a sack, pushes past me. "I'll do it, it's my da's boat."

I kneel down beside Brek. I'm only going to save his life if I stone all else to silence. The noise vanishes and I'm

48

opening the boy's mouth and dropping in some cicely followed by a rub of some poppy wax on his gums and tongue.

His breathing settles in moments, so I pull the arrow out with as quick and sharp a tug as I can manage. He winces and cries out but it is already a softened pain. I sniff the wound and the blood that's dribbling from it. Larkspur from the smell, a simple enough poison. If it was henbane he'd be dead now. I have powdered arnica; I press it into the wound and put a strip of gummed bark over it to seal it.

I can't look back as I take the rudder from the dut, but I have to watch instead their stricken faces, either hidden in the shirts of their kin or else staring at their huts, the fires reflected in their eyes.

The river bends and the trees take the massacre from us. I need to give them something else to put their minds on.

"Is Brek the oldest child here?" I ask. Ydka's boy nods. He's cutched into his ma.

"How old is he?"

"Eleven years."

"What's your name? And can you tell me who's in the boat with us?"

"I'm Jorno. This is my ma." Ydka watches me as she paddles, can see that I'm trying to calm them by getting them to talk.

Brek's fingers are tracing along the cork I've put in his shoulder. He'll need a touch more poppy come the morning. He had a strong dose. He won't be speaking much till daylight.

"There's Aggie, she's three years," says Jorno. She is sucking her thumb, eyes fighting to stay awake in the arms of her brother, who has a cloak must have been his ma's over them both.

"That's her brother, he's six. His name's Litten." He's

49

watching me, big for his age, plaited yellow hair and streaks of tears in the dirt of his face and chin trembling, trying to keep himself together.

"I'm Dottke," says the girl next to Brek, who's wearing a grown-up's boots with a tunic too small and short in the arms and a cap that again must have been her ma's for she keeps having to push it back from falling over her eyes. Her hands are bloodied and the sack she's holding for dear life must have been given for this escape. I lean back to give her room because she wants to help with the steering.

"What's your name and where are you taking us?" she says.

"Her name's Teyr, but Maege and Kirvotte was calling her Blackeye," says Jorno, "and she killed twenty of those white-faces, I saw her shooting them and fighting them on her own."

"Why is your eye black?" says Dottke.

"The Oskoro put it in there," I says, hoping to close off the questioning. "My name's Teyr, I'm just trying to keep you alive. We have to find somewhere for you to go that will take care of you all."

"Can they see us through your eye? The Oskoro?" asks Jorno.

"Don't be stupid," says Dottke.

"Fuck off, Dott," he says.

"Don't swear!" hisses Ydka, who gives Jorno a cuff.

"Hey hey, easy now. Don't fight. You all got enough worries, haven't you?" I says.

They don't say anything to this, though Ydka pulls Jorno closer and kisses the head of her dut, who's whimpering and wriggling against her chest.

"They're all dead in't they, Blackeye?" says Dottke.

We hear the horns in the distance and they all look sorrowful and are quiet a while.

"I'm sorry."

I could say more to these duts about their bravery, Mell, Braidie, Orgrif and my boys. They killed a lot of whiteboys. There will be some awful torture ahead of any still alive in that theit. I keep my mouth shut instead and steer us on.

Chapter 4

Then

I was surprised to see old Tarrigsen waiting when me and Aude got back from Othbutter's court. He hadn't been up here since the van was assembling but he's stood in our main room trying to grab Mosa as he ran about him. We'd left Mosa with my cleark Ammie that morning, and it smelled like she was preparing pitties in the kitchen. Aude embraced him before leaving us to it.

"Hello, Tarry. It's lovely to see you up here."

"I don't come enough, I know, I love it up here, cleaner air. Plays havoc with my chest though, that climb. But I had to be here today though, eh? I understand it's tomorrow the van moves out. You're the gossip of the guildhall tonight, I'm sure. A mad old woman blowing her fortune and making Othbutter look bad is what I'll guess they'd be saying."

I went over to hug him, and I could hear his wheezing as I did.

"It's Uncle Tarry, Ma," said Mosa, stopping next to me. "Are you stopping for pitties, Unc?"

"No, lad, you've all got to be off before light tomorrow,

I expect. You'll need to bed down early. Go see what your da's doing in the kitchen, I'll bet he could use the help."

Mosa wrapped his arms around me and looked up at me before he ran out.

"Look, one of my front teeth has gone. Can you see the new one?"

"Let's have a look." I took his head in my hands, smoothing his fine blond hair away from his cheeks and turning him towards the candle over the fireplace.

"Smile then." He grinned, teeth like chips of frozen milk, two small gaps, top and bottom at the front, which he pushed his tongue against.

"I gave the tooth to Da," he said.

"Run along then, tell Da I want some extra cheese with my pitties, but no extra teeth."

He left us stood before the hearth, a welcome heat seeping through my coat from the fire.

"A fine lad and not fond of swords as far as I can see," said Tarrigsen.

"No, he's starting his letters once we're back from this. I'll need a clever young man to take our work forward."

"Aaaah Teyr, careful. I can tell you that children are slippier than an oiled eel when it comes to your directing their lives." He coughed then, a nasty hacking he needed a cloth for.

"Are you all right? Your chest sounds worse today."

"I'm fine, it's age and you get used to it. There's no pipe-weed or infusions that will make me young again. Come, walk me out."

"I've only just got here. Are you sure you can't stay?"

"I can't. I made myself useful, double-checked the inventory with Thad and wore myself out chasing Mosa around."

We'd walked a short way from the house when he stopped us, out of earshot of those inside.

"You have the seed?" he asked.

"I do. Keep the other one in case something happens. I don't think we'll have trouble getting to the Almet forest, but I'd hate to lose both seeds for the want of caution."

"I'll keep the other one safe, Teyr. I hope the Oskoro come when they learn you have a seed for the Flower of Fates." The Oskoro had always lived in the Almet, the forest at the heart of the Circle, shunned over time as they experimented more and more radically with plant on and in their bodies. The Flower of Fates, rarest and most potent of all plants, had a place at the heart of their lives and their beliefs.

"I hope they come too. I made a promise to their brethren in Khasgal a long time ago, and I mean to keep it."

"Teyr, there is no chance for peace in the Circle without the Oskoro. You know this. They are its heart, its living heart not its folklore, and they will do much to unite the people of the Circle, as they once did. But they can't while spears and arrows are all that greet them. Put that seed in the Offering Stone, make sure they see you do it, and you'll have a strong ally. The drudha the seed will inhabit will become a potent force in all the citadels, if we can recover our old friendships."

"I know."

"The clan leaders would not Walk together anywhere else but the Almet if you're wishing to align them again with Othbutter. I don't envy you that challenge, or managing his brother's shitty diplomacy; Crogan's more stupid than a dog on the droop. But plant speaks to all, as the saying goes. Oskoro plant will bring them to heel."

"The Oskoro haven't treated with anybody I've ever heard from."

"Has anyone yet asked the right questions? Shown them good intent? Peace?"

He did not expect an answer but embraced me again, so awfully weak compared to that of feeling crushed in his arms in years gone by. Then he took my hands in his. They were cold and they trembled a little and I became worried for him.

"I'm proud of you, Teyr. Bringing the Circle back its peace, bringing trade. I would say I wished I had thought of it myself, but I'm twenty years too old."

"Twenty years wiser maybe."

"No, Teyr. It isn't wisdom, hiding out here on the coast and leaving all those old clans to fall back to tribal ways, where once all Hillfast's prosperity was shared. You're doing what I wish I'd done, put a mirror up to the rest of us here, all those in the guildhall gossiping about that mad cratch blowing her fortune while they swindle Othbutter for tithes that might go to fixing up the broken trails they complain to him about. I have good standing here in Hillfast, but what difference have I made, how changed is the world for the fortune I've amassed from it? You're better than all of us, Teyr, to drive this road through the hinterlands of the Circle, to bring wealth and plant to those good clans Othbutter has ignored – we've all ignored – for the safer, more profitable trade up the coast. He rules a divided land and you will be the one to heal it.

"I can perhaps do you some good by keeping an eye on Cleark Thornsen while you're away, not that he'll need it, you have the best high cleark in the northern Sar. But I'll look out for your interests wherever we share a port, my girl."

He put his jumpcrick bones to his big pipe then, lighting bacca in a heavy-looking bowl of plain black wood that looked more like stone.

"Pack enough of Thad's Golden Brown mix and you might just float back and save your breath entirely," I said.

He smiled as he filled the air between us with a delicious silky orange-smelling smoke.

"He's a fine drudha. Go on, I'll take a pound of it if you leave it with Thornsen. You can't want his whole stock of Brown with you or what'll there be to come back for?"

It wasn't the foulest of winters, and our heading off the next day was done with us knowing that we was on the cusp of spring, the first buds on branches, and cranes sighted down south of the Gassies marshes, meaning that Lake Cutter would be full of them in a few weeks.

Apart from the mercenaries and soldiers we had to protect the van, there was Othbutter's brother Crogan; overweight, looked like he hadn't travelled further than the guildhall in his life, though he at least had the good sense to listen to whichever tailor and cobbler served him, for his boots looked strong and his wool cloak fur-lined and plain grey. He had a seal, coin and parchments that give him the power to cut a deal if we had to with whoever might stand in our way.

There was also merchants, clearks and the families of a number of Othbutter's soldiers who was heading to Ablitch Fort under our protection, and would go their own way once we hit my first outpost.

I needed experience in the Circle but it was hard to come by. I'd hired an old mercenary, Sanger, the only other in our party to have been there before besides me. He had a younger man, Jem, with him. Tarrigsen had recommended both for their cool heads and fast hands. Sanger was older than me, a white stubble around his bald head, but he lifted our kegs easily for how ordinary he seemed, and that seeming ordinary was a priceless quality.

I picked Yalle and her crew, Steyning and Bela, on Cleark

Thornsen's recommendation. They was in their prime, expensive, gave off an easy arrogance, all flushed green with the top-ups of Steyning's brew, skin rubs giving their skin that waxy hard shine. They'd been on a few campaigns out east in Lagrad and was a lot more field-ready than Othbutter's guard. Steyning was a drudha, I expected she would give us an edge in the wild. Both Yalle and Steyning were lean, both cropped their hair to a thick stubble like Sanger, but blonde as cream, striking against their colour. Bela was bigger, more a pit fighter than a trail runner in stature, a thick long black ponytail I envied, twice the heft of Yalle and a mischief about her and her talk the other soldiers soon warmed to.

Eirin Bredssen was Othbutter's own captain. Her letnants were Skallern and Jinsy, each with twelve men. I'd seen her about Hillfast, ignoring the duts that shouted "Clubber" after her, for her one hand was badly deformed from childhood and she'd had a lump of steel made as a glove for it, a fist that felt no pain. She was as big as Bela, but stern with her crew, fastidious about duty and their good order. I learned that she was the first Bredssen to rise to anything and therefore fanatically loyal to Hillfast and Othbutter. And while the thought of some well-drilled but wet soldiers of Othbutter's didn't burnish my confidence, I knew at least she'd keep them in line and hold true.

Rounding out the van was a couple of merchants: Chalky Knossen, who put in coin and hoped to find new partners in Stockson, bringing his family with him; Theik Blackmore was a bit different, and bought into sharing my risk on the outpost at Faldon Ridge, paying for many of its soldiers and craftsmen. He was going to stay at Faldon Ridge to help establish it. My outpost castellans was already in place. I'd chosen a Cassican called Omar for Faldon Ridge and an ex-Farlsgrad soldier called Fitblood for Tapper's Way, a lovely big old barrel of a man who Mosa couldn't wait to meet again. Omar and Fitblood's crews had worked towards each other to make the route up to the edge of the Circle quick and sound. I was aiming to run an outpost myself near my own clan lands and move on when I thought best, through the Eastmarch and beyond to Stockson in Forontir. I had other outposts north up the coast and south. One day I hoped to see all these outposts joined by good roads and trails so all the clans across Hillfast could more easily trade with each other.

We had a good fast run through the frozen vales inland from the coast to Tapper's Way on the river Braeg. Faldon Ridge was the main outpost and my first to go up. This one was newest, only half built, but it was already catching good trade on the Braeg as it ran north to the Warrens and south to Ablitch and the Gassies. There was a half-built stone wall around a few sheds, barracks for the crews busy cutting and laying stones and working wood. There was already runs for the animals of course. Surrounding the outpost was easily a hundred or so tents of those who saw the chance of some coin and work, along with some resting up with their wagons. From duts to tinkers to hands looking for work, they all sat about their fires or was fixing up their wagons or cooking. I was glad to see that the stones and wood for the outpost was all guarded and fenced off. We was all eyed carefully as we moved our van through. Nobody was in a mood to risk a bit of filching off our wagons with Eirin's crew leading their horses alongside them, her having them keep their cloaks and armour clean, Othbutter's green and gold standing out.

Stood in the middle of it all, hands on his hips, was Fitblood. He was the size of a tree, a big firm belly probably the only difference between the man now and the man who made quartermaster of the Farlsgrad First Guard eight years before. Eight years since he paid out and ran the tallies and scrolls for them well enough I paid him double to do it for me not two years ago when I first begun planning this venture. I waited for Crogan to dismount along with Eirin, Yalle and old Sanger.

"Master Amondsen. Good day!" he bellowed, before raising a hand to stop me from saying something back, turning instead to four riders who had trotted up behind him.

"Bruissen! On your return from the bridge I want to know that the lime and alum has arrived. I also want to know if he needs any more men, I've got eight scratching around somewhere wanting five pennies a day plus rations. Now, my apologies, Master Amondsen," and Bruissen knew not to wait to be dismissed so rode out with his men, "where is your handsome Mosa and your good man Aude?"

I got off my horse and hugged him.

"Who's this lot with you?" he said. So I did the introductions.

"You built this, Amondsen? Chief not covering coin?" said Chalky.

"We did, though Othbutter give us this bit of land. We're also building a bridge over the Braeg."

Chalky looked over at Crogan then, who might have been thinking about the opportunity for tithes lost because his brother likely didn't understand what I was up to.

"It seems we did give her this land. I expect our chief or Tobber agreed a cut on what you'll take from the bridge?" said Crogan.

"I'm not charging anything for people to use that bridge."

"You've lost your senses," said Yalle, who'd trotted up behind me as Aude clasped arms with Fitblood and the huge man took up Mosa, holding him high in the air.

"Have I?"

"Bargemen'll be pissed off, and there's a few wooden bridges northeast a bit who'll lose out."

"Not my concern. I won't charge. There's a straight trail east we're making good with cords – by which I mean cord roads – that meets my bridge first. And those others? They aren't maintained like they should be. Any van with a load worth anything is forced to ask the bargemen to make crossings, and now they won't have to. Fuck the bargemen. Thieving bastards been robbing us merchants blind for years, right, Chalky?"

"That is true. Your bridge will save coin and time on the crossing, if it can cope with the floodwater."

"Of course it can cope, Master Knossen," said Fitblood, who held Mosa against his vast chest. "It is a construction for which I have the best design, with farlswood roots and stone arches. The mason is from Elder Hill, the finest in the region."

"Your coin to throw away, I reckon," said Yalle, "but I would be charging a toll."

"If she was the sort of master to charge a toll for it, I doubt she'd have persuaded me to leave Farlsgrad, good lady. If you haven't seen the Farlsgrad roads they call the Wheel, you might not understand what Master Amondsen is looking to achieve. You'll all have her to thank in years to come as these good roads and outposts bring this country together as they have in Farlsgrad."

"Yalle's right, however, isn't she?" says Crogan. "All this is hardly profitable. Can't really understand why you're doing it when you got it easy back at Hillfast."

"I'll make enough from charging the vans and others that come through if they want to make use of our service. I told you why back at Hillfast, didn't I? It's about me doing some good, not just getting rich."

"Yes, still doesn't make sense given you don't owe any of

these people fealty, but there we are. I hope Faldon Ridge is a bit further along than this outpost in its building. The Elder Hill chief, Fierksen, is down to meet us there and I doubt it's to congratulate you, Amondsen."

"How long are we staying for, Master?" said Sanger, the old mercenary, reading the need to interrupt how this was going.

"Tonight only. There's no real place to shelter all of us here at the moment, but we could all use some good hot food and a keg or two to wash it down."

"I'll see to it, Master," said Othbutter. "The stables at least are finished, as are some of the barracks we can put the families in, if they don't mind squashing up. There are two messengers of Chief Othbutter's staying, besides your van, paying only their food as instructed. Now, Mosa, I see a lot of other children in your van, and I'll need the help of all of you to find a box of honeyed apples I've lost!" Mosa yelped and tore himself from Fitblood, running down the line of wagons and horses to shout at the children. Fitblood led us through the farlswood gates, waxed to a shining red that almost glowed in the small part of the wall that was complete.

"These are beautiful," said Aude, nodding to the gates. They was something I insisted on. I did a lot of trade over the Sar for them and I loved the wood, thought it would make a good impression on those who come by the outposts. We led our horses to the stables ahead of the rest of the van, finding stalls next to each other. He ducked under the wood panel into my pen while I was undoing the clasp and slid his hands about my waist, standing behind me. I could feel him harden, and his hand slid up from my waist to my breast, fingers rounding its curve, lifting my nipple.

"There's a boy four stalls down," I whispered far too loudly. It didn't stop me from reaching back to grab his backside and press him against me. I wanted to feel it, I wanted to tease him too, though I felt a flush of lust that threatened to blot out the world. The heat of my horse and the smell of mud and sweat almost pushed me over the edge.

I turned into his arms, glancing down before meeting his eyes. "I think we ought to check on the horses later, after the feast, ensure they're comfortable in here. You agree?"

"I do, bluebell." His fringe fell forward, tickling my nose as we kissed. I tucked it behind his ear.

"I wasn't talking to you." I bumped my hips against his cock. He held me with one arm and traced the back of my head with a finger, running circles over the stubble and tufts that I braided, calming us both down. I could see he was deep in thought as he looked at me.

"Teyr, while I knew you had to be away all these months making this happen, as stupid as it sounds I still didn't expect, well, all this. All those plans have become real and they're around us. I was watching the others, Chalky, Crogan, Yalle, when we arrived at the gate. A look passed between them. One could have read contempt in it, but I doubt it was that. I think it was a bit of admiration. You know I had my own doubts these last couple of years. But you've won us all over and I'm more proud of you than you could ever know. You've changed this bit of world already."

"You have a silver tongue, I'll give you that. There's a lot to do here, and if they was exchanging looks, then I think they're keeping their doubts about my sensibilities tucked away a bit. Faldon Ridge outpost is built already, I can't wait for you to see it. I need them to see it too; I can't have them losing respect for me and what I'm doing here." I held him close for a bit then, needing his reassurance, enjoying the quiet after the stable boy shuffled off. Soon enough I felt him rear up against me again.

"You don't give up, do you? Get your tack off your horse, and we need to find Mosa before he's sick on Fitblood's apples. I can't imagine we'll be back in here before having at least one roasted pig each, if I know Fitblood, but you're going nowhere else tonight before we sleep."

There was a feast. Spits was set up in the main hall, and though the roof wasn't completed it was a dry night. Of course it wasn't built for such numbers and we all helped the servants and men garrisoned here to cook the meat and keep mugs filled. Many took their food outside.

The children had all fallen in love with Fitblood and followed him about, waiting for him to spin around and roar as he went through the hall, full of jokes, arms full of platters. I entered the hall and took a seat next to Thad, who had himself just lit a pipe and joined our mercenaries, who was all sat together, Yalle and her crew, old Sanger and Jem.

"Our leader!" said Bela, one of Yalle's crew and a few ales in. "Aude is your keep, isn't he?"

"He is," said Yalle quickly, "and you should remember it when your hands start wandering, Bel."

"If they wander tonight, they'll wander over to Jem, in't that right, lovely?" She was sat next to Jem and she leaned against the pretty young man, pushing her babs out a touch. "But say, Teyr, 'sides your coin, which you're splashing around on all this, what does Aude . . ."

"See in me? I ask myself that, so you don't have to." I forced a laugh out with her and tapped her mug with mine. Then I leaned over to Yalle and put my lips to her ears: "We're out before dawn tomorrow, the days are short as it is. She needs to be ready. She also needs to address me as Master Amondsen or Master, while I'm the purse."

"She will be ready, you shouldn't doubt me on that."

"I've a livener if there's any problem with Bela," said Thad quietly, "caffin and shiel. One snort and you're a league out of your bed and flying south for winter before you've got your boots on. Trust me."

"Thank you, Thad, but we've got a mix for our girl," said Steyning, who Thad hadn't thought was much more than a cooker, which is to say, an amateur, when they first went over preparations for the van.

"You're not paying colour lately, Master Amondsen?" said Yalle.

"No, I'm paying you and Sanger."

Sanger smiled.

"I admire your confidence," said Yalle. "I heard you were once useful with a blade and bow. But time rusts us all."

"It does, sadly."

She'd made her point, though Bela smirking nearly earned her the edge of my plate in her face. I had gone back on the dayers, the day brews that give a lift but are not close to the speed of thought or body of a proper fightbrew. Still, my veins was swollen and jet-black again. I had to explain it to Mosa, who thought I was becoming sick. I hoped I wouldn't need to go back on the fightbrews ever again, they wasn't something I wanted Mosa or Aude to see me on. I turned to Sanger, who'd been quietly watching us and was watching everything else, I'm sure. He had some bark in his neck and some slivers in large cuts on his arms. They'd been worked in well by whatever drudha had done them, and it was the first time I'd seen the old man out of his chainmail, just a loose shirt on with an open neck. Like the other mercenaries he still wore his belt. I used to wear mine everywhere too. I missed it often, even all these years since I last wore one; kept going to adjust it or move the pouches around my legs when I was sitting down. It was your life on campaign, lose it and die.

"Sanger, everything good? Anything you, Jem or the horses need before we move on to Elder Hill?"

He shook his head. I looked over at Jem, who was glancing at Yalle. Easy to understand why, she was fine to look on. She had noticed his attention, a thoughtfulness on her then that I realised was her deciding what she might do about it. Jem said about as much as Sanger those last few days out of Hillfast. Pair of them had done the north coast runs, but Sanger had been further afield, past the Circle and east towards Lagrad, fighting at the borders there, though he hadn't come across Yalle, who'd taken purses that way too. Jem was a good kid, I couldn't see him as a mercenary at all. He could do tricks for the children which had a few of Eirin's boys smirking and making some comments, for he could have been thought sullen when he was around us, doing whatever Sanger was bidding, almost like his slave.

"How's Jem?" I asked. "Can't read him. Don't seem as worn with this life as he might, if he's not as wet as you're saying."

"He's quiet," Sanger said. "He looks up to you. He puts his purses aside once his plant's paid, aiming to get a share on a boat. He not spoken to you about it?"

"No."

"It's why I have him. He's got a good heart but he is ruthless about a purse, no distractions, morally flexible once he's signed. He finds a way to keep the man in him away from the killer. Like there was two of him in the one head."

"Perfect mercenary then."

"Ay, maybe. Say, Master, you're sure about the brews? Circle clans barely trust each other, and coming out of winter they'll be flinty, especially with this bandit preying on them."

"We come from the chief. We keep south Circle then we've only got two clans to think about and whatever bandits and crews are out there. They won't have drudhas."

He leaned in then to whisper. "They know the land, they got numbers. You should be assuming that. Your van's organised, or I wouldn't have taken the purse, but get yourself on the brews again and I'll feel a lot better about the Second Lady of Khasgal's run making it." That was a title I hadn't heard in a good while, one I didn't deserve.

He sat back, and I doubt the others heard it, Yalle asking Jem about his purses and Bela watching Jem too, a pair of leopards flattering a sheep.

Mosa ran up then, throwing his arms around me from behind. "Save me from Fitblood, Ma! He's chasing us!" His fingers was sticky with honey. I turned and saw his lips was glazed with it too.

"Well now, the one place Fitblood isn't going to get you is in your bed. I need to get you to the barracks without him seeing, don't I." I turned to face him, saw Fitblood approaching and gestured with heavy eyelids that I needed to get Mosa off to sleep. I took him up in my arms and walked him through the benches. Aude was watching us from his table and we winked at each other before I passed through the great doors and into the main run.

"Are we going tomorrow?" said Mosa.

"Yes, bluebell. It will still be dark, and the moon you see there, it'll be on that side of the sky when we head off. "

"I want to stay."

"And I want you to meet my family; my brother and uncle and all the Family children." He put his cheek on my shoulder and yawned. The excitement was dying in the cold.

"Have you made friends with the other children?"

"Mmm." He was settling.

"And what did you play tonight? Was Fitblood a wolf?"

"He was, it was the Frenzy and he was king of the wolf pack. Will we be out when the Frenzy happens again?"

"No, son, it's once a year the wolves eat the amony and go wild. We will be in Forontir by autumn, when it flowers. And when did you last see a wolf anyway?"

"I haven't. What are they like?"

"Just really big fierce dogs, and they get much bigger during the Frenzy, taller than you."

"Da said you used to drink fightbrews, and you got bigger and stronger than any man and could lift trees out of the ground with your hands."

I laughed. "They do make you stronger. Thad makes them for the soldiers who protect us. They have amony in them as well. His brew is famous, ended up in the Roan Province's principal recipe book, *The Eyes of Trahsar*. He made a fair old bag of coin for that."

"Can I drink one so I can get strong? Will it change my skin so it's like yours too?"

"It would change your skin after a while, but no, bluebell, they make you feel very bad, and you're sick for a long time after you drink one. If I took one I'd worry that I'd scare you. I wouldn't be anything like your ma, I might not even recognise you it would change me so much."

"Why do you drink them, then?"

"Because if you don't you won't win a fight with someone who has drunk one. If I ever do drink one it would only be so I could protect you. Now, I think this is your mat. Me and your da will be coming to bed soon."

We'd found our way to the small barracks the families had been given for their children. I nodded to a couple of the women who must have been wives or sisters of the soldiers heading to Ablitch Fort, Othbutter wanting more of a garrison there. They'd keep an eye on him.

"What's it like in the Circle, Ma? Lour said there's tree monsters and the clans there eat anyone they find sneaking on their land." Lour was one of his friends back at Hillfast.

I put furs over him and sat next to him on the mat. He turned towards me and curled up his legs to lean into me. He had hot hands, damp from running about the outpost. "Has Lour ever been there? Of course he hasn't, the daft boy. The Circle is beautiful. I used to camp out in the Highmoor with my own ma when I was a girl. The grasses run for miles, the sky so big and blue it makes you dizzy and sometimes you see buffalo herds, not in their thousands, but in their hundreds of thousands. And I grew up in the Amondsen Family, which was part of the Auksen clan, on the south edge of the Circle. That is where my rope is bound to the earth and always will be." It moved me to say it, for I'd not think about my clan's lands for months at a time, then a memory of them would stop me still, right into my belly.

"Why did you leave?"

"A story like that makes me think you're asking because you're just wanting to stay awake when it's late. If I didn't leave, how could I have met you and your da?"

He said nothing to that, grinning because I'd guessed his game.

The next day we said farewell to those staying at Tapper's or going down to Ablitch Fort. The van now would be the one looking to cross the Circle. Eirin marched her crew out ahead of the van each morning and waited for us at a site they'd prepared for us to camp at in the evening. We expected no real trouble this close to Hillfast and on the main highway to Elder Hill and my outpost at Faldon Ridge, but she made sure there was always a camp and a fire going when the van rolled in. There was a few days of Yalle asking Eirin how the march went, or it was Bela or Steyning making remarks about Eirin doing foot and sword drills after supper and not before, a constant nipping at her, questioning her, so I had to have a word with Yalle before Eirin did something stupid. All very well, I said to her, asking whether I was going to pay the colour again, but if she couldn't work with Eirin it didn't matter what I did. She shut up for a bit after that, and in a couple of weeks we was at Faldon Ridge. Ground was softening as we went but the Gassies, the vast marshes that come with the thaw, hadn't yet fully sprung to life with their plagues of mosquies. We picked up the River Crith, which fed the Gassies from the Crutter-Vuri hills far to the north of us, and we arrived at Faldon Ridge and my outpost late at night, pushing on the few hours rather than stop short, principally because of the heavy rain that had been battering us all day.

Here was the outpost as I knew I'd find it, good stone walls around it, ditch dug, walls manned and torches lit. Around the main farlswood gates the stables and runs on the same layout as the other outposts being built.

This uniformity, this sense of the familiar, was something I always craved on campaign. I wanted a messenger or crewman working for me to ride from one outpost to another and know where to go for whatever he needed to do.

Besides the camp of those who lived off or was travelling through Faldon I wasn't expecting to see so many men and women with Clan Eeghersen's sign on their shields and on banners, their red and black chequers. The Eeghersens was a clan from the northwest side of the circle, known for their salt trade. The rest of them was all hid in cloaks and hoods. These must have been Fierksens, the Family that ran Elder Hill, who owed fealty to Grithie Eeghersen. It was like a warband camped around my outpost, and I had to wonder why they thought to bring so many for such a short trip.

They saw the Othbutter green and gold of our own banners and surcoats so didn't much stir as we rolled in towards the gates, keeping to whatever shelter and warmth they could.

Omar had come out and was waiting to greet us.

He'd been a mason much in demand after paying out the colour, and had already proven his quality with the bridges south to Ablitch and east to the Sedgeway. Almost the opposite of Fitblood, he was slight as a sapling, even in his furs, had a walking stick from a fall from rigging years before and he was pressing down with little effect a mighty bushel of black hair that surrendered to no one, not even the downpour.

"Master Amondsen, a great pleasure. As you'll see, the outpost is much changed, and the markets here have crept from their positions on the Crith to buzz around us more closely, earning us thirty silver a month so far. It will be a challenge to find you all somewhere to sleep tonight, for Chief Fierksen from Elder Hill is here, anticipating Crogan's arrival. Do not worry, we are quite prepared for a feast, though only a few of you will be able to sit in the longhouse."

"Thank you, Omar," I said.

"Lord Crogan," said Omar as he walked behind me. He spoke Common, though he had taken time to learn Abra and some other lingos besides.

"Do we feast tonight?"

"No, my lord, it's late with nothing prepared. Tomorrow it must be."

"I'm sure your crew will appreciate the rest, eh Amondsen?"

"They will."

"I'll be in the longhouse, a chance at least for a few cups with Shean." Shean was Chief Fierksen's first name.

He walked past us and left us stood there.

"I'll have Tarret find spots where he can for your wagons;

our guards will look out for them and give Captain Eirin's crew a chance at some rest. Now, the cord roads north . . ." he began.

"Omar, I've just ridden most of the day, you can report tomorrow."

"Ah, my apologies, Master Amondsen, let us at least share a jug and a pipe tonight after we've settled your van in. It's been a hard few weeks here and your counsel would greatly help."

Even while finding spots for our wagons and horses I caught snaps of chatter about the Circle and the troubles there. I won't lie, it was making me a bit sour, for going after a bandit wasn't easy work and I'd not done it in many years. Three days of rain had taken everyone else's good humour as well, and as we made our way to the gates into the outpost I saw Eirin had her soldiers form a line outside it so she could give them orders. Yalle, Bela and Steyning, a bit of uisge or ale in them, I guessed, was passing down the line behind Eirin and taking the piss. I saw Jinsy, one of Eirin's captains, start shouting at Bela. Steyning stepped forward and threw a punch, catching Jinsy but not putting him down, then Eirin turned and dropped Steyning, her club fist putting the drudha on her backside. Sanger moved in at the same time as Yalle and he was between Eirin and Yalle.

"What the fucking hell is going on here!" I shouted as I moved in. "Sanger, this is my shit, you should go with Jem and find you some shelter and food." Sanger nodded and moved off into the outpost, whistling for Jem.

"Eirin, Crewman Jinsy stepped over the line."

"He knows it, Master. I'm more concerned by the discipline, or lack of it, in Yalle's crew."

Yalle was about to speak but I cut her off. "Yalle, the point of hiring your crew was because of your experience.

I assumed you had some. Start giving a fuck. Keep your crew in line."

"Amondsen, when a brew goes down, when we're working, you'll know you won't have hired better. When we're walking, we expect some ribbing can be enjoyed with other men without them crying about it."

"Your opinion's noted. And next time it's Master Amondsen."

I told the others around us to move away, leaving me with Eirin and Yalle. I was grateful for the wind and a heavier burst of rain for scattering everyone to the buildings about.

"You don't need me telling you how shit like this poisons orders. Jinsy and Bela might be stuck together on rec, and if they aren't tight, if they lose focus a moment, it could kill us all. I'm in command, not Crogan." I softened it a touch then; I still couldn't believe I was needing to do this, so wanted to end this lashing on a better note. "Might be the easy going so far is giving minds a chance to wander. Let's make sure we're on a proper van drill once we're out on the Sedgeway. It's Eirin's decision on how she keeps a crew in the lands where we're welcomed. It's my decision how that goes in the wild."

They said nothing. I clasped their arms each in turn. Neither was that happy of course, not helped that we were all fucking soaked.

Omar come up again as they walked off, a big torch hissing with the rain.

"You said there was a cup had my name on it?" I asked.

"I have some kannab tea and a fire lit in the office."

"Sounds like urgent business to me."

He led us to the shed at the left of the gate, through which was the office of the clearks and Omar's quarters. With our cloaks leaving dark water trails on the stone floor he pushed chairs up to the hearth and poured out some water from the copper kettle into our bowls, adding powdered kannab and a spoon of cloudberry jam from a jar under the windowsill. I was glad the cold and wet masked the trembling in my fingers.

"Imbala, Omar, this is most welcome." I took a large swig of the tea, desperate to get some kannab inside me. I was feeling spiky. The dayers had got me on edge, and stoning them was something I was having to relearn.

"Imbala." This was his word for love. He took a sip of his drink and picked up some rags that had been drying on the hearth to press against his thick coils of hair. Little colour remained in his veins of the brews, or the skin rubs, his black skin now just faded in places, as though covered in patches of dust.

"I cannot say how happy I am with your work here. It's fucking beautiful."

"Aaah, thank you, Master Amondsen. My admiration for the people of Hillfast grows each day. You do not look to see others want if you have anything to spare yourself, for you know how vulnerable everyone is to the land, wolves and snow. The Eeghersens had been coming since we built our bridge to cross the Crith, Seikkersons too, and the Eeghersen salt was good trade, their furs as well."

"I saw we have a coal shed. But why did you say 'had been coming'?"

"Something to talk about with Crogan, for the shed's empty, no Seikkerson vans have been this way in a while. Those soldiers out there are the first we've seen of any Eeghersen clan in all that time. They would run in a cart of salt a month, but no more. Then, five months ago as winter set in, some riders came over from the Seikkersons, said they'd be the last through because of this Khiedsen man murdering anyone and everyone that wouldn't recognise him as lord of the Circle. They were on their way west but didn't say where. I wish I had asked more of them, but this outpost demands every breath."

"I'm glad you told me, Omar. We'll have to parley with this Khiese and see what negotiations can be had."

"Khiese's why Fierksen's here. There's trouble, Master. You're not a moment too soon."

The following day I went about the outpost with Omar, meeting all those who we employed, from the clearks to the guards, the smith, carpenters and farmers. I remembered most from my last visit and took time to ask after them and their families. It was something Khasgal taught me the value of and the reason he could annex Khasgal's Landing at all and make it a power in the Western Sar, for he took pains to remember all those who would not otherwise merit a lord's attention and so they was fierce loyal to him.

With Fierksen here I bid Omar put a feast together to see us off onto the Sedgeway and ensure he had the welcome he might expect from Crogan visiting, for the Fierksens was strong allies with the Othbutters.

As with our short stay at Tapper's Way, many of the crews joining for the feast was out in barracks or on wagons with their plates and cups, and the rest of us in the main hall. We was in our cups and pipes on the high table: me, Omar, Crogan, Fierksen and their advisers.

Omar raised his cup. "A toast to welcome our neighbours at Elder Hill and my two masters, Master Amondsen and Crogan Othbutter."

All of us raised our cups except Fierksen, who simply drained his cup and banged it for a boy to come fill it again.

"Chief, we are welcomed by Castellan Omar, you eat at Master Amondsen's table. You should remember your manners," said Crogan.

Fierksen's long wild beard glistened with grease as he chewed and slurped his way through his thoughts.

"This we're eating, paid for with the trade gained from us, my family. Paid for through land given at my borders by you, Crogan. Seems you put these merchants of Hillfast over your sworn families."

"Chief, this outpost demands much from those Families near and about; we do good trade with you in turn," said Omar.

"There's vans would use my own barges and our bridge at Ruggy's Gap and now our host has built bridges south of us and don't charge for their upkeep. It's taking food out of our mouths, Crogan – my family are upset – yet this woman's ambition is the least of our troubles."

"Maybe we feast first and retire so that I might hear your grievance in our pipes, my friend."

"You might hear my grievance now, Crogan, for if this gathering is what you're giving us in answer to Crutter and Grithie Eeghersen's plea for help – some pig, ale and thirty-odd soldiers protecting some rich merchants – then I should want to know whether you have any idea what is going on out here."

"We've had nothing from Crutter, no message."

"Pigshit, Crogan, this was near a month ago. You should have had messengers."

"We've had nothing. Tell me, what news? We understand there is a bandit that roves about the Circle raiding, but we've not learned this from Crutter, just the vans that have come through."

"So if these soldiers are here to rid us of him, why do I see families and merchants all set for a good long trip?"

"It's not our principal reason for coming out here, Chief," I began.

"No, it isn't, woman. Seems you can lead Othbutter's own guard and his brother to whatever profitable purpose suits you, for I see Captain Eirin down there at a table, but it don't seem to be to stop us Eeghersens being raided to the north."

Thad put his hand on mine at that point, for he must have seen me tense.

"Shean," said Crogan, "my brother sends us to build relations we have wrongly neglected in the Circle. I am here to do justice, I bring trade and gifts. I am here also to listen to grievances such as this. Chief Othbutter is listening, Fierksen, he is sorry he did not listen sooner. I have to ask, however, why you feel there ought to be more soldiers here. You've brought many yourself."

"These whiteboys as they're being called, they seem to be everywhere, that's why. Four families sworn to Eeghersen, all have had boys taken, food and plant, on pain of death. I've got Family chiefs telling me these gangs turn up like the dead come back, all bone-white and half mad. This Khiedsen boy, calls himself Khiese, he's talking about uniting the Circle against you, Crogan. Grithie got a posse together and run them off Meilerssen's theit not three weeks ago. Nobody's heard from the Meilerssens since then, and I sent a runner up there and he come back saying place looks abandoned. Hopefully they in't all dead, and he saw no sign of it, but my lands near the Sedgeway as they are, and the bridges, might be something this Khiese is looking at. Might even be looking at this outpost of yours, woman."

"I'll have a man go back to Hillfast and secure some soldiers to come out to Elder Hill," said Crogan.

"Aye, good. Weiden Crutter will also help us. They at least have sent someone here to tell us that they'll see us right," said Fierksen.

Crogan looked pissed off at this but said nothing. Might

be he was wondering, like I was, what the Crutters was up to for they long coveted the staff of the ruling clan.

"Any other families having problems, Chief?" I said.

"I suppose you'll find out. You heading north to see Grithie then, Crogan?"

"Seikkersons are first," I said. "We go there then to the Almet, to the heart of the Circle. We will parley with the Oskoro. I will make sure we return to see Grithie on our way back through."

"You'll what? Didn't you just hear me talking about us being raided by the Khiedsens and you what? You think you'll wish up an army of baby-snatching tree fuckers to solve my problems?"

"This expedition is about nothing other than us uniting all the clans of the Circle. But we only do this through the Almet, to walk there once again, and that's why we need the Oskoro," I said.

"I'm speaking with Crogan. I want the thoughts of a woman who long ago betrayed her own rope for coin I'll let you know." I give Crogan a look then, expecting something from him, but he tightened his lips, a sign I should leave this to him. I stood up, Thad standing with me, not sure whether I was about to drop Fierksen on his back.

"Chief Fierksen, you are in my house, on my land whether or not I got a cock or cinch. Your horses will be led from our stables at dawn, and you'd better be up early enough to sit your fat arse on one or you're walking home."

I left the table and walked out of the longhouse. I was shaking a bit. Thad caught up with me and we saw Chalky and Aude standing by the outpost gates, which was open, talking to the guards there while sharing some pipes.

"Here she is!" said Chalky.

Chalky was the Hillfast merchant who was coming with

me all the way through the Circle. He had brought his whole family, wife Edma, his son, an albino like him, and his two young girls, who was a bit older than Mosa. Chalky was a weaselly, canny junior partner in a larger merchant interest, but he was looking to settle in Stockson, as I was for a while, and get a slice of the plant trade that was coming up from Ahmstad and Donag. He was hoping they'd make him a full partner, not least because he was taking note of all he'd seen so far of my plans. Fine by me, he'd be my man by the time we hit Stockson.

"Hope you're all talking about something other than that fucking bandit," I said.

They give each other a look.

"Right, what have you heard?" I held out my pipe for Thad to pack it.

"Heard off a man bringing his family through from an Eeghersen theit," said Chalky. "He's camped outside with Fierksen's lot. Seems this Khiese is bloodthirsty, gutting and stringing up those coming through the Circle, which weren't many anyway as, if you'll pardon me, the clans there in't exactly friendly. Spoke of a strange howling, not wolves, more like screaming, and almost every night he heard it echoing over the hills and woods. Apparently it's them as makes this noise."

"And I killed twenty men single-handed on a dayer," I said, "before scaling a fort's walls and ending a siege by bedding the castellan so vigorously he fell asleep so I could take the keys to the fort's secret gates. Lots of stories seem to gain weight and colour as they go from mouth to mouth."

"That's a fair point," said Chalky, who paused a moment to wonder at how unusual and specific my answer seemed to be, "but if there's something to all this, if it's not just that we got to negotiate with the clans there, which you said was going to be straightforward, will we turn back?"

"Clans have dealt with bandits, I saw my own da do it more than once. We're going to show them all there's another way. If we fail then fine, we'll come back."

They seemed settled enough with this and shortly Chalky's boy Calut joined us as he'd started his pipe a few months previous and was looking for a sly pinch of kannab himself while his ma Edma wasn't in sight.

"You looking after your ma, Cal?" said Chalky.

"Course. Ma asked if Thad or that other drudha got something for her hands. Skin's cracking again and she says she can't stop scratching."

"Go on, tell her I'll come by with something later," said Thad, who was slurring a bit as he handed back my pipe. I pulled on the pipe and savoured a sweet smoke that pleased my nose while my throat and then my head went numb. I was already worrying less about preparations for the next day.

"Aude and me have been talking, and I've got to say, Amondsen, well done. These outposts you built are run thrannie by that Omar and Fitblood. Must've took a lot of coin for that and these trails have been laid."

"You have had a guess at how much as well, I reckon. Remember Thiek has paid in for this outpost. He'll have an interest in it."

"I haven't told them what it's cost, my love," said Aude.

Chalky laughed at this and held up his hand. "Course I've wondered. You done well, old girl. Makes Othbutter look bad though don't it? Less he lays claim to this somehow. Crogan's no better, looking for a bit of glory, I expect."

"He's going to be as much use as a severed cock out in the hinterland." I took another pull on the pipe. It was turning my head to jam and butterflies.

"When were you last back there with your family?" said

Thad. Aude had asked me the same the previous night as I cutched him and Mosa.

"It was about eight years ago, just after we come back off campaign. You stopped with Nazz but I couldn't face him, not without I might have killed him for how he trapped us and left us for dead. I went back to see Ma and Da instead, but both had gone into our bloodlands. Just my brother Thruun was left, polishing the family chain and strutting about the settlement. He made a speech saying how grand our da was, never mind our ma. Couldn't find it in himself to give her a mention, even after she's buried."

"That's the way there as it is anywhere when you're a woman," said Thad. "Unless you're a drudha or you're paying the colour, it's just fucking and farming. And Teyr Amondsen wasn't for farming."

That got us all laughing.

"How will your brother feel when we refer to you as Master Amondsen? You were meant to give up the name as a girl, if I recall custom in the Circle correctly, take Aude's," said Chalky. He held a hand up then quick. "I'm not meaning anything by that, mind you, don't think I am."

"Course not," says Aude, "she's done more than me in my life, why should it be my name against it?" They all nodded at this, Thad putting his hand on Aude's shoulder, moved a bit by that, I think.

"He won't like it, my brother. It'll feed a view that I think I'm better than them for not giving up the name once he'd been born. Maybe it'll inspire the girls there to see what a girl can do, that we deserve our own names to be part of the weave. That said, these babs are the only clue they'll have I'm a woman with my skin all rust-red and my head shaved and looking like this." By "weave" I meant the Family tapestry, the litany of the rope, names of fathers and sons

80

only, names of future sons and all, to make it seem inevitable, make it seem like your family must prevail.

"I have to say I agree with Sanger about you paying the colour again," said Thad. "It's been many years, and those are wild lands, no law but what Families decide, and living's hard, they think with their guts and blades."

"I don't . . . I know, I didn't want Mosa or Aude to see me going through stoning fightbrews."

"You're a veteran. They know that."

"I want to wait until we've got a better sense of the lands."

Thad shook his head. "Taking my number-four cold could kill you, no matter you were on it for years."

He was right. Fightbrews was volatile, you didn't know how much juice was in each one, how potent the amony or caffin was. One bad batch could lose a war, whether it be too weak or too strong. Never mind that it could simply kill you if it wasn't mixed right.

"You know your plant, Thad, it's always an even brew when you're cooking."

He nodded and huddled into his furs. "Glad spring's here. I'll take rain over snow all day long."

Still, for all what I said, when I looked over at the firepit at a couple of boys spooning fat on a pig they'd spitted and hung, I thought back to me and my brother Thruun doing the same as duts. I'd spoon on the fat from a small bucket for the feasts my da would hold if old Auksen come to our settlement with his retinue, usually to do justice and agree tithes for Hillfast. Thruun would sit with me at the pig and cut away at the crispy shining stripes of brown and blackened skin. With a nod he'd toss the odd strip up for me to catch in my mouth, my hands being busy with the ladle and bucket. I'd hold the nob of fat and meat in my teeth while I blew over it, then I'd bite down and it would flake apart into delicious splinters. Seems like all these laws and customs for men and against women don't get noticed when we're all duts. I wish it could be like that again.

"How's the blisters, Aude? And how's Mosa coping," said Thad. "There's some fair walking to be done yet to her family's longhouse in Amondell."

"Mosa is coping with this travelling better than I am, he's enjoying it. I'm a boy of streets and docks, not all these miles of grasses, trees and fucking awful wind. How do you not go mad with it howling over the heights and on the plains?"

"How do you not go mad with all the shouting and the stink of fish and whales and shit in the streets?" I said.

"That's the smell of adventure, the smell of the sea."

"It's the smell of shit is what it is." I kissed him.

"Put him down, Teyr," said Chalky.

"Let's have a toast and finish these," said Aude. "I'm dreading the start tomorrow already." They raised their cups to me. "To you, Teyr Amondsen."

My cup was empty, but my line was inevitable. "To me."

The van rolled out the next morning. I said farewell to Thiek Blackmore, who was going to stay and help Omar with the outpost, and I did rounds with Eirin and Yalle, inventory with Thad and Chalky. Eirin's crew was front and back, an easy pace led by the horses in the dark before dawn. As I'd promised them, we did a full van drill and it went well, giving us some confidence in things being ordered, expectations of each other, soldier and noke, being clear. We slept a bit better too for believing we had a good watch going at nights and good scouting and flagging in the days. The mountains of the Crutter-Vuri lit up pink with the first sun, but around us was all shining frost and black rutted earth of the tracks we had to follow east to the Crith. We pushed it some on the first day on the hard ground to the river. These was lowlands, willows stood sentinel over frozen pools and bone-coloured sedge. Mosa and Chalky's girls mimicked the throaty gargling of the brown-hooded tarmigans, which was their attempt to aid a few of Jinsy's bowmen, thinking the tarmigans would come at us to see off a threat. Too early for eggs but I took my shortbow and shot one that flew out of the grass. Skallern's swords give a cheer and howled at Jinsy's bowmen, two of whom missed before a third one found another bird.

It put us in good spirits and singing was soon taken up, though here I knew that Aude would find few equals, his high clear voice earning whistles from men and women alike as he sang verses from *The Doom of Hedler*, when the ill-fated love Hedler holds for the magist Halfussen turns her mad with grief as he returns, heartbroken, to the sky out of duty to Sillindar's call.

Some heavy sleet made it tough going for us through to the Breke, the main bridge over the Crith if you're leaving or going to Elder Hill or Faldon. We took it over my own bridge as we was hoping for more news from a well-travelled trail. Must have been over a hundred years old now, the work of the mason Beddesen, or Stoneheart as he was called by many both here and back at Hillfast, where he had built the chief's hall and the guildhall. Fierksen had five men posted at the bridge, tucked away in their hut keeping dry. I asked their letnant about the comings and goings and there was fuck all from the Sedgeway, just barges and boats on the river and few enough of them.

After a night at the bridge we moved on east into the Sedgeway. The next week or so would be hard going as the land rose. To the south, hills, now mottled black and white as the snows receded, climbed to the peaks against which we'd find the main Seikkerson settlement, the first we'd have to secure the trust and support of if this road through the Circle was to succeed. North rose the mountains proper of the Crutter-Vuri, and the first clan to the north was the Eeghersens. The Sedgeway was a sort of channel into the plains of the Circle as the hills curved away east on both sides around wide plains and forests. Around the Circle was the rest of its clans, each sharing some part of the plains. In the middle, in the heart of the Circle, was the Almet, and the Oskoro within it. It was generations ago that all the clan leaders last undertook what we called "Walks" in the Almet forest; families making keeps with each other, blood ties to ensure peace, justice to be decided. None now went near the heart of the Circle by all accounts, the plains around the Almet went unclaimed and unwalked. Our route would take us into the Seikkerson lands southwest of it, but I was nervous and keen to go there and see the Oskoro, give them the gift I saved them all these years.

With five carts and more horses heavy loaded we had to keep to the main trails over the lower hills that was the Seikkersons' borders. Eirin had sent a few outriders ahead to get a view of how the trails was looking and whether we'd get any problems keeping the carts moving. We had planks and rope for the heavy mud of the thaws and for fording streams. Two of the outriders we'd sent ahead had waited for us to catch up and with them was three men looking much the worse for the weather. One seemed unable to stand and was scratching his head and looking about him as though he'd mislaid a mug of beer in a tavern. The other two had the downward look, I thought, of men fearing for their lives.

"They were screaming and running when we rode up,

thinking we meant to kill them," said one of our riders. Crogan walked forward with me and Eirin.

"I'm Crogan Othbutter, brother to the chief. You are safe here." He looked them up and down. They was muddied, one nursed an arm, none had packs or cloaks. The only one that seemed to pay attention to Crogan and the rest of us held what must have been a flask. He had a knife, the only weapon between any of them I could see.

"Afin! Afin! This is a van, a proper van, not whiteboys." He had tears in his eyes and he clutched the good arm of his friend. He looked at the carts desperately. "You must have something you can spare us from these wagons? Water we found yesterday, but Crosh, him on his knees there, he took badly to some mushrooms he found that we swore were bracky-tops, but they don't mek you sick if you cut the stem."

"Thad, Steyning!" I shouted back. "Need something to empty a man's belly and fast."

"I'm Afin," said the other man, and as he spoke I could see a wild tiredness in his eyes, grass in bloodied clumps of hair and swellings where cuts had infected. From his breath at ten paces I knew him to have some infection in his mouth as well. "We come from Aeller's Hill. This van is a welcome sight to us all."

Yalle walked up. "What's stopping us?" She took a look at the three sorry men. "This? You're serious, Master? We're going to run into a lot more than these so soon after winter. Too fucking work-shy and soaked or addled on shiel."

"Afin, I'm Lord Crogan, Chief Othbutter's brother. How did you come to be like this?" Crogan had half an eye on Yalle as he said it. She shook her head. Afin was distracted, looking about at us all.

"Your lordship, have you come to settle on clan matters?

We've been put out by men who have said they're from the elder Seikkerson and they rode us off the land. But they was the whiteboys of Khiese. I am Lanny Gildersen, second in line to the Gildersen house." This was the first man who spoke to us.

"No, Lanny," said Afin. "I told you: Elder Seikkerson dun't know anything of them, he wouldn't stand with anyone against your family."

"Respectfully, Master," said Yalle, "if we're intent on giving away supplies to liars and beggars, I'll have Bela throw them some bilt and we move on."

"No." This was Thad, who had walked between us to the men. "We are here to build bridges and make good relations between Hillfast and all the clans through the Circle."

"Seikkerson is with Khiese," said Afin, "you didn't see the seal." They was arguing with each other, ignoring us.

"This is true?" said Crogan, trying to intervene with as much dignity as their ignorance allowed him. "Seikkerson has abandoned your family for some bandit? It makes no sense. Gildersen and Seikkerson have had peace for generations, as close an alliance as can be expected among those competing for clan rights. Your family have been allies, have you not?" Yalle then interrupted him, though she was talking to me.

"Steyning will not be wasting plant on beggars yet to prove they are who they say."

Thad glared at me as he started mixing a drink for Crosh, who was now groaning. Crogan said nothing but also gave me a stare by way of reply to her.

"We'll waste our plant then, Yalle. You are correct to question this as it strictly falls outside your purse's terms. These are Hillfast people. We are Hillfast people and we will help them."

Thad went about his work with a practised economy. He saw a chance to exercise his healing art and we watched as he went about it, though Yalle excused herself and led Steyning away by the arm, who had shortly arrived. Crosh seemed a lot more at ease after his drink, until it hit his belly and sent him running for the nearest trees while we helped Afin with his pain.

Lanny Gildersen was who he said he was, give word of his Family and clan that satisfied us, and he spoke some more after a drink. "Seikkerson was demanding far more in tithes and tribute than he had previously and upset all his affiliated Families. Us Gildersens being proud enough refused him. I can see how Afin could think what followed was him, but I can't believe it. A few days after our messenger returned from sending our refusal a number of horsemen came and forced our men out of our main settlement. They killed everyone who resisted. The horses and the horsemen were daubed in chalk perhaps, or white masks – it wasn't clear for they arrived at night and dropped sporebags all about, addling us and giving us visions."

They remembered little more and was keen to be on their way once Crosh was upright and they was given a bag of water, some bread and lard. I told them they'd need to keep west until they reached Faldon Ridge outpost and to ask for Omar.

As we prepared them, Aude and Mosa come up to me.

"Are they good now, Ma?" said Mosa.

"Yes Mo, they have no home so we'll give them some food and send them to our outpost over the Crith bridge."

He was pleased with this. "They don't look well. Who hurt them?"

"I don't know."

"She's been kind, your mother," said Lanny. "She seen

there's plenty here to help her people with and she's shared it." He smiled at Mosa and Aude.

"I'm sorry you've been expelled from your homeland," said Aude. Lanny looked down and nodded.

"We should go, Lanny," said Afin. "We're grateful to you, Othbutter, and to you, Amondsen." He put his arm around Lanny and called to Crosh, who could only hobble. The three of them was talking as they helped each other along.

I leaned into Aude, enjoying the way he'd stretch his neck a fraction to fit my head under his jaw, and I kissed the amber stone of his necklace. About us the van prepared to get moving.

"Are you missing that morning drenching under the falls?" I said. "I can smell your sweat."

We had a small fall, near the house, that he'd stand under every day, coming back red and shivering as though he'd been slapped all over.

"I am missing it. There hasn't been time for more than a wash from a barrel since we left." I knew from the flat way he said it, not rising to the tease, that his mind wasn't on the answer.

"What's the matter?"

"Sorry, bluebell, it's just those three. If one is a Gildersen heir of sorts, well, if all three of them are from that clan, why aren't they asking us to go there and defend them, help them take back their land? Where's the fight? I know, I know, I'm no fighter, but they tell us they've been run off their land by a bandit, these whiteboys, and they then just walk away? Even a whipped dog whines."

I wish I'd paid full heed. We moved on, the outriders having told us of a good spot for the horses near a large stream we'd be able to ford with the long cords we'd brought for getting the carts through heavier ground and over runs like this. We built a fire up while Eirin organised watches, and after potatoes and some cured cod Chalky had provided we settled down. Mosa lay between Aude and me. I was out cold when the horn blew.

We all woke with the shock of it. I jumped up, Aude put his hand to my leg to steady me and Mosa instinctively hugged into his da. I heard arrows, the huff of bowstrings and shouting from around us in the camp. There was grunting and gasping to my right. One of our soldiers must have been on watch on a dayer but was now staring at an arrow sticking out of his chest. He started pulling it out, tugging at it with a look of disbelief on his face.

We'd put the carts around us in a rough circle. There was figures swarming over them, cutting at the ropes that held down the boxes. One of Eirin's crew was trying to get up from his knees, using his shield to hold off a man in a thick surcoat who was stabbing at him with a spear.

Aude tapped my hip. I looked back and it was my sword and scabbard. He held the latter while I drew it. "Keep him underneath you," I hissed.

"Eirin!" I called. I could hear her yelling for her captains, Jinsy and Skallern. A man landed from a nearby cart, came at me.

"Ma!" screamed Mosa. The man thrust his knife. I barely escaped it with the instinct of years of training, the knife cutting up the sleeve of my fur, dragging over my skin. My movement gave me the momentum to push his arm across him, seeking the line crossways to his. I put the sword in his side before kicking him to the floor. My blade was coated with paste from the scabbard so he'd die quick. I glanced once more at Mosa as I lit up. He was staring at me wide-eyed. Aude had his arms around our boy, breathing hard, trying to control himself. For now he didn't matter. I looked around me. Dark figures was everywhere. Eight of them had set about soldiers barely awake, beating or strangling them. Boxes was hitting the ground as the carts were being stripped. Yalle shouted, I heard Thad's hiss, he must have been fighting but I couldn't see either of them. No time for a dayer, my belt was in a sack at my feet. Fucking stupid. I dashed for the nearest cart. One of the two men on it dropped down and ran at me, a shortsword but no armour or strength. I forced him into a clumsy parry, he had no training. I ran him through and jumped at the other one, who had dropped the sack he was holding to better run from me. Old Sanger appeared next to me, scared the fucking life out of me and distracted me enough the thief managed to run into the grasses. "Master, I . . ." A scream, then another. An arrow hit the cart next to us. I squinted to see the dim shape of the archer, reaching for another arrow.

"Bow, twenty yards straight beyond the cart," I whispered, pointing him out. Sanger nodded, looked past me to my right, Jem was there, shield ready and licking his fingers with his other hand, must have taken a dayer mix from his belt. He then ran for the bowman. I heard Jinsy and Skallern shouting at their crew, then a scream from my right; one of our bowman had been hit in the thigh with an arrow. Behind me Aude shouted for Thad to help the wounded man. Sanger nudged me to get me to move and ran to where a soldier was rolling on the ground with one of the attackers. As we closed on them, one of their crew appeared from the side of one of Crogan's wagons. He had a nailed lump of wood raised waiting for a clear hit. A spear punched through him. It was Skallern. I looked about us, three men was running away with sacks or bags they'd looted. Seven or eight more was crowding two of Eirin's. I pushed Sanger to follow me and I ran at them. One saw the new threat and come at us, his stupidity getting the better of him. Sanger was quicker than me and he stepped in front of me, smartly disarming and killing what was another poorly armed and ragged-looking man. They wasn't trained, they wasn't proper bandits. My arm was numbing where I'd been scratched.

"Thad, I'm cut!" He'd dressed the bowman's arrow wound, I could smell the elm and bellwort ointment on him when he got to me. Seeing movement on one of the other supply carts, Thad threw a powderball from a bag on his belt, the dust exploding in the faces of the men trying to loosen the ropes and pull down boxes. They screamed, clawing at their eyes and throats.

I followed him. He killed them off as they was spluttering and retching.

"Oh fuck. This is Afin from the road," he said. "So much for our charity."

Neither of the bandits wore armour, one knife between them and the man with Afin barefoot. Thad took a bottle from a loop on his belt, turned to me and poured a measure of chestnut vinegar along the length of my cut. Fucking agony. He saw I had no belt so opened his mouth for me to mimic him and put a thumb of caffin butter on my tongue. He ran off to tend to those lying around the camp, the soldiers that had been attacked, some killed, others wounded.

More cries went up as we organised ourselves under Eirin and Yalle. I could see more clearly now. There must have been forty or fifty that had ambushed us, but they had little to defend themselves against our training as we fought back.

"Amondsen!" It was Chalky. I ran over the embers of the fire to where he was kneeling over Cride, our carpenter. It looked as though he'd fallen from a cart, might have been smoking a pipe up late with the lads on watch but he was dead now.

"Poor bastard. Where's your family?"

"Safe, Skallern and two of his are moving them to Aude and Mosa."

I went after anyone I didn't recognise, though I caught only two while many more fled for their lives. As I expected, and hoped, Eirin called her men back to the camp to form guard at the wagons. They obeyed despite their dayers giving them shivers, and they was gnashing their teeth and shouting and cursing with bloodlust.

Torches was lit and we called lines. Seven dead: our carpenter, the two guards Eirin had put up, two of our labourers and two of Jinsy's men. Jem and Sanger come back covered in blood and carrying a sack each.

On the tally we lost oil, a week or so's rations, a few pounds of bacca, salt, flasks of honey and two packs of plant that was going to make gifts. Worth a few gold at least.

Crogan was first of course, starting on Eirin the moment the count's done, and Thad and Steyning reported on the state of those wounded. A lot of the line was blowing with what the fighting and fear took out of them. Mosa's looking at me, first time he's seen me kill and I'm sorry for it. Might be the first time he's seen anything like this, and Aude's holding him and smoothing his hair as he shudders with nerves. Chalky's daughters was crying, his keep holding them close to her. Eirin's crew was gathering about their fallen and they went through their embraces, rituals and hollering for each other and for the dead, all of it trying to stone the fires of their brew. I think I should blow Mosa a kiss, show him I'm still me, but I can smell the blood on me, and the caffin mix has sharpened the stink and sorrow of everything so loud, clear and strong in my nose and on my tongue I want to scream. I heard crying far off, voices arguing on the wind. Somewhere somebody shouts as though in victory. Perhaps it's his first food in days.

"Anything to say, Master Amondsen?" shouted Crogan.
"I expected better."

Eirin was at the front of her line, her head bowed a moment.
I glanced at Yalle and her crew, but they was checking over
their belts.

"What will you do now, Captain," I said to Eirin, "when
we set up camp tomorrow night?"

"Four guards, caffin mix, two shifts."

"Should have brought a dog," said Chalky, but he kept his
eyes on the ground as he realised he was speaking to soldiers
still all noisy for blood. However, he was right, to a point.

"I've looked over your men, Eirin, the dead guards. No
sign of struggle I could see, looking at the grass about them.
On their pipes, I'll bet. You seem clear and commanding at
running them and drilling them and they seem to follow
you about waggy and bright, but close your eyes and they
dissolve into rookies." This was Sanger, the voice of experience. He had a smooth and deep way of speaking that carried,
demanded to be listened to.

She nodded, and I knew then she needed no more humil-
iation, though her crew needed to hear what Sanger said.

"Captain Eirin did all she could do in running the drills
and moving the van camp to camp," I said. "Not a lot more
she can be found wanting for if they don't obey her orders.
It's a short while before dawn, I think. Eirin and me need
some help digging a pit for the dead before we move out.
Who'll help?"

A few of those in the lines looked about each other. Yalle's
crew wasn't offering, which was a pity.

"I'll do it," said Aude. He'd let Chalky's keep take Mosa
to her children so he could come and stand with me, and it
would have been shameful for Eirin had Skallern not then
spoken and said they'd bury their dead and ours besides,

without help, for it was their failure. It was right and I accepted it because it was about them saving some honour. I said no more on it and put my arm in Aude's.

"Sorry Mosa had to see me like this. Sorry you have to see it. I'm struggling to stone it – control it, I mean. I'm going to dig a while and that might help me come down off this butter of Thad's."

"You kept us alive, Teyr. I . . ."

"Go on, you thought it would have been safer, that we'd have been better prepared if I'd been paying the colour again."

I felt him nod. "I just . . . When you're on the brews you get . . . You change."

"I know. I go out of my mind for a time." I withdrew my arm, for he hadn't drawn me in or towards him as he would usually do. It was that subtle fear of me, the force that was filling me, and it always made me sick to see it in him.

"Who'll speak for them?" Aude meant the families of the dead, someone who would wind them into their rope, adding them to the line of fathers past.

"Eirin must," I said. "She'll keep something of theirs, to be returned home and put in their bloodlands. I didn't think you had an affinity for such customs?"

"I don't. The dead fill the earth everywhere. Is there a square yard of it that remains yet a virgin to blood? But I understand these men may have believed they must return somehow to their bloodlands. These are the rites we should respect if this expedition is to succeed."

Aude knew I too did not care for the rites, but then as a woman such rituals concerned only with the need for sons to continue the line was a weakness of our families and clans that was mocked by many in all the lands I'd travelled in except Farlsgrad. I loved those of my family I knew, but my heart was cold to our customs.

"Ma!" Mosa shouted. He ran over to us from Chalky's family and stopped just short of us, even though I had my arm out.

"How many did you kill, Ma? I saw you kill three."

"I'm sorry, bluebell, but I did kill them, they was taking our food and they was killing us. I had to protect you. They was hungry and you can get hungry enough you'll risk your life to eat. I wish I didn't have to kill them."

"Was it the men we saw yesterday?"

"Yes. We give them food but they might have been planning to steal from us."

"Have you had a fightbrew, then? Can you lift Da up in the air?"

"She can, Mo, she's much stronger than me." He smiled, and I mistook it for an invitation.

"I can lift him up without a fightbrew." I put my hands under Aude's arms, bent my knees a bit. He flinched. With a gasp I straightened up, lifting him off the ground. He tapped my arms.

Mosa clapped. "What's the matter, Da? Ma, spin him around."

I looked up at him. "Shall I?"

He shook his head. "Put me down, love."

I lowered him quickly. "You've put on weight," I said and reached up to put my arms around him. He put his hands on my forearms as I did it, pushed my hands together and kissed my fingertips. It was a gentle refusal.

"You're shaking, Ma. What's the matter?"

"I'm fine, it's the brew, but it should wear off."

"Let me get us a flask of potskas, a snifter will do us good and I brought a little flask of it," said Aude, who went over to his horse.

It hasn't always been easy for us. "The colour stains inside and out," as the saying goes.

95

"You look like you're ready to jump up and down, Ma. Your eyes are funny too, like candles are in them. What can you see?"

"The butter that Thad gives me helps me see much clearer in the dark, and I can hear things far away and smell things far away too. I can smell grissom, there must be some nearby, but I can also hear Skallern peeing behind that tree over there."

Mosa cackled with delight. Then, looking at the trees around us, frowned.

"How do you know it's Skallern?"

It took a few days for the van to recover to some sort of normal routine. We was all quiet and agitated, tempers short. We slowed too as we got into the hillier ground of the Seikkerson clan. Ironback and Beiddsen was the Seikkerson-sworn families I recalled in this region, though their respective boundaries was a mystery to me. Both families was known to us Fasties merchants through Elder Hill and west. They mined iron, the Beiddsens more coal. Chalky called them blackies, like most of us merchants did, both for their trade and for the Ironbacks particularly dying their leathers black with vitriol, which was also a good trade for them and a better trade for us. There was heavy mists as the land rose to the hills, and we took the well-known passes to the main run into Seikkerson land among the snowy barren heights and lush valleys, the beauty of which could surprise you around almost every turn of the trail, and where the Families spent their time with their reindeer most of the year apart from summer.

Over the week that followed we went slow with the wagons, ground was shitty with the thaw. We saw a few more people that looked to be starving or else ill with the winter in these hills. I ignored all pleas to discourage these people from coming near us, for we needed to know what lay ahead. There was a da and two boys about ten or twelve summers the pair. Crogan wasn't keen on giving them any of our supplies, the piece of shit, and it was Aude who put some berries we'd gathered into the man's hands with a few copper pieces, though he'd have to have got near the river before he could find anyone could make much use of them.

As we pushed into Ironback land we was approached by four riders, all in the Family's long black shawls. Heavy dark cloud muffled the morning, and likely would the whole day. Crogan stepped out front so I had to quickly ride up from the wagons near the middle of the van. He could easily make this much harder than it needed to be.

"I'm Crogan Othbutter, brother to the chief. We come for trade and a greet with the clan, while I come to hear your news and if required, dispense the chief's justice." He'd caught some sort of cold, a head full of snot, a finger of which he snorted onto the ground next to my horse.

"I'm Teyr Amondsen, a merchant. We have plant: amony, alka, shiel, as well as tanned leathers, gifts should you require them. I would talk with your chief as well, for it is not only trade we seek."

They looked to be on Kreigh drafts, heavy and easy horses. One raised his hand to the others and pulled back his hood. He had fine blond hair, plaited, his beard short, both thinned and streaked darker in places with the effects of fightbrews.

The boy I'd known had grown to be handsome, even through the colour; a languid confidence, a haughtiness in the expression. His men relaxed at his gesture. He took his time looking over us, men and horses stamping in the cold. Eirin and Jinsy walked their horses behind us, the green and white chequered shields and cloaks leaving no doubt they was Hillfast guards.

"Jeife Seikkerson, another brother to a chief. Would rather talk Abra than Common." He nodded at Crogan and smiled before looking me over. Bela whistled from somewhere behind me. Jeife kept his eyes on mine and continued in Abra, the language of my childhood.

"Amondsen. A ghost tells me you built the outpost at Faldon Ridge, a bridge and roads too."

"A ghost?"

"No one goes west now, Khiese commands it. But ghosts roam as they will." He wore a pleased-with-himself smile.

"You're in Ironback colours. Seikkersons wear grey, the owl," I said.

"I'm still Seikkerson, but I run the Ironback family now. Khiese asked me to kill Gredden and I'm not one to refuse him."

"You killed one of your sworn chiefs?" asked Crogan. We was all stunned at this. It was hard to know what to say.

"Do you swear allegiance to Hillfast or this Khiese?" said Crogan.

Jeife turned in his saddle to look at the men behind him. Their hoods were still up, hard to see any more than beards, the odd braid. He was signing to them, hard to see it, just his hand moving against his back. Eirin whistled at this. I turned to see that Yalle, Sanger and Eirin's crews was in the saddle themselves and fanned out across the trail around the wagons. One of Seikkerson's crew nodded to him. He turned, took in the changed positions of our soldiers and shrugged.

"Hillfast."

"I'm surprised it needed consultation, Jeife," said Crogan.

I dismounted and whispered into his ear. Thankfully he repeated what I'd said. "I would be honoured if you'd lead us to your brother at Crimore. I come with gifts from our chief. With the loyalty and good work of Masters Amondsen and Knossen, we mean to strengthen Hillfast, running a road through the Circle to Stockson."

One of Seikkerson's riders coughed, an obvious gesture of derision or disagreement. As I was close to him I squeezed Crogan's shoulder before he could rise to the insult. I needed to find out about Khiese and I now had the opportunity to spend some time with Seikkerson.

"Lead us on, Jeife Seikkerson; if you wish I can tell you more of my outposts and plans for my road."

"And I expect you'll wish to hear more of Khiese." He turned his horse about before I could answer and led us along heathland, the briars and grasses bent east against the years of prevailing westerlies.

Crimore was the main Seikkerson settlement, a stone longhouse with a stone tower at one end of it on a natural motte with two palisade-walled baileys stretching down the side of a valley. Ours was the only way in, a river cutting through and past us from a waterfall and cliffs at the far end of the valley. Our track was heavy going with mud from what must have been recent flooding. We all got filthy getting the planks down and the wagons over them.

Here we saw the lie of Jeife Seikkerson, for the banners flying along the stone walls was not those of the owl. The Khiedsen banner was a high ash tree, red on brown. These was black flags, the red ash upside down. As we got closer a murmur went through the van. The outer bailey's fence of stakes was decorated with naked bodies – blackened skin, distorted and torn, savaged by birds. Some was mostly bones, patchworks of flesh and sinew all that remained.

A few soldiers come out, while more sentries was at platforms against the fort walls, no doubt on a seeing mix. Men and women took up bows among the smaller longhouses, huts and animal runs.

Jeife shouted out in their local Abra whatever was needed to reassure them and they stood down.

Aude was walking alongside me and our horse, the pair of us exhausted and muddied from helping with the wagons. Mosa rode, rocking in the saddle and no doubt himself tired after running with Chalky's girls around the van. He hadn't, thankfully, noticed what was on the fort's walls.

"You've been here before," said Aude.

"I have. They don't hang bodies out like this, not for anything. Or they didn't. Jeife's da was chief when I was last here as a girl, same blond hair, but had paid colour hard. He had the shakes far worse than me, a pipe of kannab might as well have been stitched to his mouth. I don't think he could even have fed himself without it. Last I saw Jeife he was chasing me about, a girl of thirteen years I was, visiting with old Auksen and my da, who was trying to teach me plant and hunting. I say trying because I knew more than he did, out with my ma for years sniffing and snaring game while he was trying to make something of my brother in the dealings with Seikkerson here and the Amersens and Carlessens down south. So one year he brought me along. I think he was aiming to see what my brother would do for the clan while we was away.

"Back then I had beautiful hair, before the colour, and Jeife kept asking for a strand of it, and though at the time I thought boys was stupid, Jeife was the first I ever thought about kissing." I give him a dig with my elbow. He shook his head, smiling.

"He couldn't tally your ledgers like I can."

"No, you always make it right."

"I thought Cleark Thornsen did your counting, Ma, not Da."

"Well, he doesn't tally all of them, Mo," I said. Mo yawned and his eyes drooped.

"I have to see Jeife's brother, who'll be the chief. Thende was always the cleverer. I hope he can help me understand this."

"Those banners bother you and all, don't they?" said Aude. "You've not taken your eyes off them." He'd caught me looking up at the fort as we talked.

"Not near as bad as the poor Seikkersons on those walls. It makes me sick to see it. The banner's a Khiedsen banner, disrespected in the way it's been altered, but to fly it over a clan's home settlement, well, why aren't this Khiese's men here, occupying the fort? How far does his influence extend?"

He said nothing. He'd followed my line of thought.

"I'll need to speak to Crogan. We'll push on to Auksen lands, I want to know what's happened to my family."

"Of course."

I hid it from him, but seeing banners where they shouldn't be, thinking of my family's own colours deposed, burned me up inside, and it was upsetting me because I wasn't expecting to feel like that about a place I hadn't been for eight years. With Ma and Da gone there was nothing, or so I thought. But there's a knot, must be in all of us, mustn't it, a protectiveness when we think of the fields, faces and songs that rise in our memories on our thinking of home. I know I said what I said about my ancestors, that rope of elder, da and son, but nobody wants their name to just vanish from the world.

We come to the outer bailey. Jeife dismounted and give the reins to one of the men – must have been a guard, though he had no colour.

I stood with Crogan, Eirin and Chalky. Chalky nudged me and pointed up to the tower. There was a bowman up there and alongside him another, a figure bone-white as though caked in chalk, skin and head; bare-chested, eyes painted black. He dwarfed the bowman. As Jeife began speaking he left the lookout, descending out of sight inside.

"You shall feast with my brother, he is aware of your coming."

"That would be your ghost, I guess," I said, pointing to the tower where the man stood.

"Who, the sentry? No, I sent a rider here before we rode up to your van. Bring the wagons inside. I will find our quarter, he will arrange where your retinue will sleep. Master Amondsen, I would be honoured if you would sing your Family creed after we have eaten. You sang it so beautifully as a girl." He held out an arm for me to take. Patronising shit. I took his arm and we strode ahead of the others along the wide track sloping up through Crimore to the fort. It was an insult to Crogan of course and I was fine with it.

"Your keep, the skinny one?"

"Aude, yes."

"Looks tame. Did it take long?"

"Do you think he should have bigger muscles? Some colour?"

"Can't be much to get your juices going when his woollens come off."

"I can see why your brother's the chief, Jeife. If you had any wit you'd be able to answer those questions on your own, as well as understand that they're too stupid to get my hackles up."

"That your boy, with him?"

"What do you think?"

He shrugged. "I didn't hear of a fightbrew didn't take a woman's womb."

"He calls me Ma, it's good enough for me."

I kept looking for a sign of the man painted white, but there was nothing. The van had brought most of the

Seikkerson family out of their huts, the workshops and off the runs. The children was quiet.

We was nearing the inner bailey and the chief's longhouse itself. The arched doors split open, grand enough but diminished against the memory I had of them as a girl. Thende would be out to greet us.

"You're flying a banner I don't recognise. It insults the Khiedsens."

"It is Khiese's banner. He is lord of these lands, though once was exiled from his own. My clever brother Thende did not lose many of our family before he realised Khiese's might. Khiese is a man of his word. Always. Obey him and all is well. Cross him and he is savage, without mercy." He gestured to where we had seen the dead on the outer fence.

"This is Citadel Hillfast, Jeife. The Circle is still part of the lands of the citadel."

"No, Teyr, it isn't."

Thende walked out of the longhouse and down the steps cut into the motte. His colours were pale, a faint yellowy green. He must have paid out many years ago, no doubt when he was made chief. He was taller than Jeife, towering over his guards as though they was children, though rangier than an infantryman, a strong runner. He wore the long, intricately carved gold beard ring of the Seikkerson chief but was almost bald.

"Lord Crogan Othbutter of Hillfast. Masters Amondsen and Knossen. My hall is yours."

The others had caught up to me and Jeife as we waited for Thende.

"Elder Seikkerson," said Crogan, "may Haluim keep us safe. We bring gifts, among them a new recipe for your book that our chief wishes to share with all the clans."

They clasped arms. Crogan would have also said "we bring

justice", but he was clever enough to leave that out, though all about would be aware it was unsaid. Now, in front of a gathering, wasn't a time for questioning fealty. That would come later.

I lingered a moment as Thende gestured for us all to join him inside the longhouse. Looking back down the hill, I saw how beautiful this valley was, the faint hiss of the waterfall to our right behind the chatter and churning songs, snow on the high ridges and now only in patches as this fertile land come to life again. The settlement's children should have been happier than they were. Mosa was up on Aude's shoulders as they too looked across the valley and the cold clear river to the hills beyond. At home he'd drag me out at this time of year to harvest moss, shiel and any other plant we could find, always hoping for that rare pea-sized budding flower of the blueheart. I told him he'd get a silver piece for each one, all of which he kept in a small bag in a secret hole in the floor of our bedroom. But these children seemed listless in their doorways or on the skirts of their mas. I'd seen it before many times, always after a slaughter or some other horror.

I waved down to Aude before turning to enter the longhouse. Little had changed, barracks to the right, the chief's feasting hall ahead and the forges and workshops to the left. Still no sign of the painted man.

Inside the feasting hall a second firepit was being prepared for the evening, the main pit giving off a welcome warmth. On the far side of the hall an open archway led through to Thende's just, where he would sit over disputes, and beyond that was his own room.

"See that Lord Crogan's retinue and I aren't disturbed," Thende told a guard. Jeife was stood with Crogan, Chalky and me.

"Jeife, could you see Lord Crogan's soldiers and the mercenaries have spots to lie tonight."

I give Jeife enough of a hint of a grin to sting him, and the guard closed the door to Thende's room. I was glad to see he still slept on straw, though in a wooden frame well worked with carvings of hunting and beautiful depictions of the plant we made so much use of in these parts. There was an equally ornate desk set sideways on to a huge hearth and fire, though on it was folded robes and woollens that must have been washed for him. Shutters was open high on the walls, but they did nothing to lift a weak and sorry light.

"Your father, your entire rope, must wish you severed for flying whatever that banner is over Crimore," said Crogan, the moment the door had shut.

Thende looked hesitant, nodded, struggling with Crogan's openly hostile way of speaking.

"Khiese came, brought with him forty-two boys, all of them were twelve to twenty summers at most, six from each of our Families. He had twice as many as we could have mustered, painted white, well armed. Looked like the dead risen and put a fright among my people"

"Whiteboys, there was one at the top of this tower as we walked into Crimore," I said.

"No, there couldn't have been."

"What happened?" said Chalky before I could press him on it.

"Well, Khiese stood at the gates, out of bowshot. One of his painted men, huge man, not of these parts, shouted out that if we didn't allow him to make his case for ruling over the Circle he would slaughter us all. We stayed quiet. The first instinct, the first thought any of us had I'm sure, was defiance, for the insult would be hard to wear on the High

Family of a clan. But Khiese's flag flies above us and so you have an answer.

"I said I would hear Khiese. Taking boys of my clan, from our Families about, with no word reaching me was a shock to me. I needed to understand him better, whether he was a mouthpiece for some other power. He spoke softly, standing where you four are stood now, not even the size of Teyr, though he had a rich green web – as the veins are sometimes called – and a dark yellow colour such as you would see on wildmen. Hard to see at first what men or women would fear in him. He told me he had the Khiedsens, Triggsens and salt-trading Eeghersens swearing fealty to him. I laughed at him, Triggsens and Eeghersens being big proud clans. He was calm, understood in a strange way why I might have laughed, told me what I was thinking, reminded me the Khiedsens were the most feared clan north of the Circle. He is a Khiedsen, or was. Took the name Khiese instead of Khiedsen to dishonour them. Said he was chief of the Khiedsens and all those clans and now, he said to me, yours." Thende looked at me at this point.

"I was about to tell him what a problem that would be for both of us when he told me himself. My Families had already sworn him fealty, they would not raise a sword for me. I would not get our tithe, nor men and women to manage our borders and farmlands, and here of course he meant plant rights. He told me we were under siege if I did not fly his banner. He told me Jeife was ready to take my place if I wished to die with honour."

"That is a serious dishonour upon him. It would get Jeife killed among the Amondsens," I said.

"Why aren't you dead? What do your people think of you?" said Crogan.

"They're alive to think it. The dead you see on the walls were those that went against him."

106

"Every one of you alive has betrayed the clan. They've betrayed Hillfast."

"What would you do, Crogan?" he said. "You might call him a savage when you look at our walls, but that is merely the price of defiance. Better soldiers, better equipped than the handful I've got here, no way of getting a bird to Hillfast and, besides, what would be the use when we see nothing of the Othbutters, no justice, no arms. Would you have me burn this whole Family for pride? For a flag?"

"Yes, Crogan, what would you do?" I added. Fuck him. Not the wit to see Thende was neutered, nor yet that a struggle would have taken place if Khiese had been alone in this room with Thende. Crogan stepped to me, his face inches from mine, his jowls and neck quivering as he spoke.

"What could you know, Amondsen, of honour, multiplying your coin while playing at mother? You took purses wherever they were fattest, left your family before you could even begin to repay them for raising you." He turned back to Thende. "I wouldn't have believed him, Thende. I would have had him killed. I would have killed him myself." Thende saw me ball my fist and put out a hand to stay me from doing something stupid.

"I drew my sword, for I saw he had none," he said. "I thrust, he spun on one leg, back bent and palmed the blade away. He moved in and winded me, his elbow, his fist in my face. I was on my knees and I'd lost two teeth in a breath. Before I could flinch he had his thumbs on my eyes. 'I understand,' he said. 'You had no choice, me alone, unarmed.' So he stood back, looked at me like he was my da all disappointed in me, said, 'You can try again, once more, first move, but I'll kill you if you don't kill me, and I hope you'd put your clan over your own honour, as hard as that must be.'" Thende was silent for a moment. The confidence he

107

had put out when he greeted us at the gates was gone. He was broken, I could see it now, shoulders curved in, drooping at the neck like he had an anvil on a necklace.

"What shall we do now then, Crogan?" I asked. It was that or beat him to the ground. He knew fuck all about why I'd left home. Besides that, we really had a problem. Khiese's hold on the Circle was worse than we could have thought.

Thende looked at me then.

"Khiese said the Auksen clan are falling into line, all their families. He could be lying."

"We'll go after him," said Crogan. "It seems he's ambushed a great many Families unready or unable to cope with his crew of whiteboys. We've brought our own crew, Hillfast's best. You'll give us his whereabouts."

"You should have taken more interest in the Circle these last few years, and this might not have happened, Khiese might not have gained so much ground," said Thende. "Your collectors used to come for your tithes and return with our tidings, our requests for justice, which went always unanswered. Little wonder vans like yours need so many soldiers when Hillfast guards are a distant memory on the Sedgeway. I'll give you his whereabouts. He's gone east, I expect, for that side of the Circle is still free and the way east still open."

Crogan was bubbling up like a lid on a boiling pan, so I applied the finish.

"You wouldn't even be here now if it wasn't for my own coin and my interest in bringing the Circle into the new world."

"Fuck you, you bald bitch," spat Crogan. "Your insolence will find its way to my brother. He'll tax you until your arse squeaks if he doesn't tear you open as a traitor. Thende, we'll have a speech prepared for the feast. You will renew your fealty to Hillfast. Your people will see some pride restored."

Thende's smile was belied by his eyes. Crogan turned and left, slamming the door behind him.

"I'll head down to the van and do the night checks with Eirin," said Chalky.

The wood's whistling and cracking filled the silence now we was alone. A tear slid from Thende's eye. I was close enough to reach out. He let me press it away with my thumb.

"We'll see Khiese and we'll deal with him. We've got a good crew, good drudhas."

"You'll need to apologise to Crogan later. I appreciate your words, Teyr, but I don't swear fealty to Othbutter and Hillfast. Crogan's not as stupid as you think he is, Teyr. He knows I must refuse him tonight and so damn myself before my people, who have seen you all arrive as a sign that they might be free of this Khiese, that you're here to rescue us."

"Crogan's not Circle, he's not made here like you or me. Amondsens and Auksens have parley and arrangements with Crimore for generations. Our ropes are woven."

"You haven't been here since you were a girl, remember?"

"I'm here now. Here for all the clans."

"So is Khiese."

"He brings extortion and cruelty, not trade and wealth. The clans can prosper, winters need not be so full of chance, so full of hunger and fear."

Thende thought on this a moment before walking over to a shelf and taking down a glass jug, a heavy and beautifully blown piece with a square of embroidered linen over the top. Wiping the inside of a couple of cups with the linen, he poured us a measure of uisge.

"A good life," he said. And so saying he broke my heart. We toasted it. I looked up at him again and saw in his trembling lips he was set. He couldn't live without honour, and Crogan coming here, my coming here, forced his compromise, his shame, to its crisis. I put my arms around him, held him to let him know I knew, let him know I wasn't going to talk him out of it. Politics might be more tactical in other lands, but in the Circle you are measured only in honour. If you're dishonoured, you have nothing. I never had much time for that way of things, but it was thick enough in my blood to understand his position, and I was sorry. I spoke in Abra then, our own lingo.

"Jeife used to follow me around when I visited with my da, make a prick of himself. He even showed it to me once, sorry little thing. But I know you used to . . . what was that word we used? You used to be cricky for me?" I felt him smile above my head, for I came up no further than his chest.

"Jeife used to tease me over and over," he said. "I made you a posey but couldn't give it to you, the last time you came. Your da kept a fierce eye on us both, I'm sure, and I had some hope that my own da would see a match for us and not that nose-picking crier of old Auksen's."

I leaned my head back to look up at him. "You'd have been a fool to make me a keep, Thende Seikkerson."

I leaned against him again. I wanted the last person he said a word to to be good to him.

"You didn't marry the nose-picker then?"

"I didn't," he said. "I have no heir, neither does Jeife, but he'll need one."

"You've been a better elder than Jeife, I'm sure of it."

"We're about to find out. Look, Teyr, Samma Khiese bested me easily without even a sword; he doesn't look much but don't be fooled. He's dangerous because he's got them believing, utterly, that he's going to command the Circle and he'll rise against Hillfast. All those years a bandit, he's hard and he knows these lands, knows as well the hard life we've all got now we don't walk the Almet and settle our issues

110

there. A man like that, who can speak to hardship and turn these clans and their sworn families to his purpose through his reason as much as his cruelty, knows no bounds to ambition, and he was mighty full of himself and confident when I saw him. It might well be strong-founded, such confidence, but it means he won't rest with these clans that he's taken. He's still young. The capital, Hillfast, is next, then the whole citadel, for who, north and west, could stop him?"

I could have stayed talking with him longer, anything to delay what was going to be a turn for the worse for all hereabout with Jeife succeeding him. I wish I'd known him better, but that would have meant staying home, duts and sewing and cleaning for some pig-shit heir to a herd.

"Can you fetch it, the green bottle, size of Jeife's self-respect, wrapped in a rag on the right side of that box in the corner? I'll leave a note making clear this was my own action, not yours. Send the guard in when you leave, so she sees me alive and well."

He stood as I returned with it, just a tongue-full of liquid in it, stoppered with wax. He looked down at me and his air had changed, calm, getting his head in order.

"A long life, Teyr Amondsen, it was good to meet you again. Your ma would be proud."

"So would yours, Chief Seikkerson."

I hugged him again and left quickly, to better help him with the resolve he had mustered.

"He's asked to be left alone while he prepares for the feast, but wanted to speak to you," I said to his guard. I glanced at Thende as she walked into the room. He smiled to himself, and it shone, the fear and doubt dissolved.

I found Eirin, Thad, Yalle and old Sanger, gathered them up outside the longhouse near the rear wall.

"Thende's killed himself, with poison. He wasn't going to

swear fealty to Hillfast. Jeife is going to be the elder and I don't trust him as far as I could spit him." I had to explain what happened with Crogan earlier. "Make sure Skallern and Jinsy have extra guards on dayers at the wagons, make sure Chalky's family, Aude, Mosa and all those we need to protect are near you in the hall."

"Jeife won't make a move against us – it'll be a bloodbath, even with the prospect of Crogan as hostage," said Sanger.

"I only agree with that if we're also ready. But looking too ready will make him think we're behind it," said Yalle.

"I don't see it, Yalle, we have nothing to gain by killing Thende, not in his own house," I said.

"Crogan comes over as a bit stupid, could be they view his disgust at the Khiedsen banner as an unbearable insult," said Sanger.

"I still don't see it, not as guests."

"I'll have my men make sure the horses are fed and ready if needed. I'll put Skallern on arranging his crew around the hall," said Eirin. "You're going to tell Crogan, Master Amondsen? Or shall I? He needs to know."

"He does," said Sanger.

"I'll find him," I said.

Couldn't help be a bit worried for Aude and Mosa, but we had time before the alarm would be raised. I got some more of the caffin butter off Thad and hid a knife in a pocket I had made inside the shift I put on for the night. I put our packs ready, told Aude what he needed to know about these precautions.

Crogan was put in a nearby hut that belonged to the smith; the man's wife and his boy moved to a neighbour.

Crogan was with his cleark and Chalky. He'd found the smith's chair and had his feet out and his legwraps, socks and boots drying at the fire.

"There you are, Amondsen. We've talked over what to do if Thende pledges fealty with this Khiese."

"And."

"And I'd like you to hear it. You're not stupid, you may have something to add. Plainly, if Thende swears for Khiese we must take him hostage. I saw Eirin readying her men just now and told her that it was important she be ready to command her soldiers to kill all who oppose us when I confront Thende about his disloyalty. You ought to command your mercenaries to be ready also, we'll have need of them."

"Except Thende's dead."

"What?"

"He took the honourable way out, as you'd encouraged him to do."

I did a good job in not adding to that.

"I've heard no horn or cries to that end from the fort."

"He was giving me time to leave and to talk to the guard so there would be no question it was suicide and not some plot of ours to avenge his lack of fealty to your brother. They won't discover him until he doesn't answer the door to his room. We won't have long."

"I see you chose not to come straight to me with your knowledge of this."

"No, Crogan, I went straight to Eirin and Yalle and ensured that our horses and our van was readied and additional guards was brewed up and watching them, as well as ensured that Skallern will set his crew throughout the feasting tables to give us an edge if Jeife, who'll assume the beard ring and sword of the elder, chooses to blame us or indeed tries to take you hostage. Jeife is very much for Khiese."

Crogan stood and looked around him, presumably for his sword. "Right, well, good plan, Amondsen."

"He's not going to swear for you, Crogan, what will you do?" said Chalky.

"We need a parley with Khiese himself, I won't give Jeife the respect if he's just one of his bitches."

"We don't have the crew to stop Khiese from just taking you a hostage for Hillfast," I said.

"Tell us what you would do then, Amondsen."

Good question. I wasn't rightly sure, but it wasn't facing Khiese direct, not from what Thende said. In truth too I was sour because it was going to be a lot harder to speak to the people of the Circle, to pursue my road. Othbutter would need to send more soldiers, an overwhelming force to end it quick, and there was no way he could muster that number quickly enough.

"We need to know more, Crogan. He's a bit more than a bandit, that much we now know. I need to know if my family and the Auksen clan are his or not, because if not, we might have a place from which we can find enough strength to beat him, a place we might defend, to make it hard for him. We've got plant and soldiers enough to defend a fort like this if we can find just fifty or so who know how to loose an arrow. I know these lands better than he does, even all these years later. We can make him pay for every yard he attempts."

"If your family's already Khiese's, we're dead," said Chalky.

"But we now know more, we learn more of his numbers, how his chain of command works, his letnants, scouts, plant, anything. Othbutter is going to need this knowledge if he's to send anyone in with a chance. We could head south out of the Hanging Falls where us Amondsens have our main settle and be out of the Circle and in Carlessen lands in days, even if it means spoiling the van for the sake of haste."

"I'll speak to Eirin about this idea of yours, Amondsen," said Crogan. "For now we go to the feast. If Jeife assumes the hoop and sword, he might reveal something of Khiese's plans and number. I know what's needed here – humility. I think I can manage that."

I glanced a moment at the others in the room and made my way out.

I was walking with Aude and Mosa from the stables where we were due to shelter for the night when I heard the shouting.

"Put Mosa up on your back," I whispered to Aude as five of the sentries come running up the hill from the walls on the outer bailey. Ahead of us walked Crogan and Eirin and his cleark, and Jeife come out of the longhouse's main doors with two men, stopping when he saw us.

"What's the matter!" called Crogan.

"Elder Thende, my brother, he's dead," said Jeife. "Crogan, Amondsen, you need to follow me."

"Lord Crogan to you, Jeife."

"You are in my house, Crogan. Crimore is mine and my brother has been killed, not hours after you arrive here and had audience with him. This matter will be investigated and," he paused, "your help is appreciated."

I squeezed Aude's shoulder and pinched Mosa's cheek before walking up the slope with Crogan to where Jeife stood.

"There is no hoop or sword of the Crimore elder about you, Jeife," said Crogan. "You may wish your people to see your declaration done properly, not shouted out without their support."

I could have fucking killed him.

"Take us inside Jeife," I said. "Tell us what happened. I left your brother in good spirits, it seemed, an hour or so ago. Indeed, he asked me to bid his guard go into him after I left. Have you not spoken to the guard?"

He hadn't, a curse at the edge of his mouth, eyes on me sharp like cut glass. He tilted his head a fraction in the direction of one of his guards.

"Jalley, get Heikke to Thende's room." He strode back inside, expecting us to follow. I had to trust that Eirin, Sanger and Yalle had us covered everywhere but in Thende's quarters.

Once in the room, I saw that Thende's body was in the corner with a blanket over it. I couldn't hide my upset at seeing that gentle man dead on the ground. My tears flowed free.

"You look upset, Amondsen."

"We shared a drink barely an hour ago. He was a good man."

The chairs we'd sat in had been turned round. Jeife sat down but did not bid either of us take the other chair. Heikke came in with three other guards escorting her.

"Step forward, Heikke. I'd like a full report in front of these two. You apparently saw my brother last, is this true?"

"Yes, my lord, he called me in after she left. He asked about—"

"I don't give a shit. How long were you in here before you left?"

"Long enough for a slug of his uisge, my lord, and a seat there at the fire with him."

"And when you left him?"

"He wished me well, my family well, was stood right before that chair you're sat in."

It was silent a moment. Thende had made sure no blame could be cast on us, it seemed. I enjoyed watching Jeife try to act thoughtful, maybe thinking it was him using this silence to get us a bit uncomfortable with it. Good on Crogan, he didn't say a word either.

"I'm sorry about your trade mission, Amondsen," said Jeife. "Such good intentions laid low by the Othbutter clan's lack of interest in your homeland. We are united under Khiese as we have never been before, the Circle clans. Maybe Khiese will be interested in trading our riches for silks we don't need or plant we don't need. I doubt it. Maybe your caravan is the beginning of a suitable tribute to him."

I smiled. He wore a muster belt, used for ceremonies normally, three pouches, three bottles, usually empty, but I could smell radish, a telltale sign of the Galerin mushroom, freshly made in the pouch to be this strong. He had his rider's shortsword in its scabbard, and as I made it appear I was seeking my words, I saw his fingers twitching, a dayer was working its way in.

"Are you expecting trouble, Jeife? You seem ready to kick off."

"I was concerned we had an assassin in our midst, Amondsen. Nobody ever died of taking precautions."

"We won't be turning over our caravan to you, Jeife. I'm just sorry your clan won't benefit from our gifts, particularly if you insist on not swearing fealty to the Othbutters."

"Do you think, here in Crimore, there is actually a choice?"

Crogan glanced behind him, he was nervous. He looked to me. I heard the guards behind me making subtle movements, the whispers of hilts being loosened in scabbards.

"Vans like this take precautions, Jeife," I said. "Especially where we see good banners replaced with bad. I reckon we should all walk out of here, call everyone in for the feast to tell them of the death of their elder and to toast you. What you say then to your people is up to you, but we won't stay where we're not welcome. I look forward to some fine words for your brother."

My heart had quickened, these words setting a course for

life or death. I unclasped my hands from behind my back and smoothed the sides of my dress and apron, my fingers that bit closer to my knife. My hands trembled anyway, more so now on Thad's caffin butter, and Jeife was wise enough to look me over and see I too was rising. It was all I could do not to grind my teeth. I wouldn't have stood a chance against four, three perhaps, but they all had reach on me with their side-swords. I was lucky that one adjusted his feet slightly, allowing me to place where he was behind me. He was slightly too close. My advantage. Through the doors we could hear the main feasting hall filling up, shouting and laughter, a flute in the hands of a dut from the sounds of it, but with the chamber of justice between Thende's quarters and the hall, we'd have little chance of being heard.

"I don't need you to tell me I should speak well of my brother. I loved him. You shall lead us through to the feasting hall and stand with us as I welcome the people of Crimore and Hillfast to eat and drink at our benches. I shall still want a song, Teyr, to begin our eating with."

He nodded to those behind us, and the guards stepped forward, holding our shoulders to steer us ahead of them towards the hall. I considered a move but I couldn't be sure what Jeife was thinking. Crogan and I was both pushed forward, and as we walked through the doors into the chamber of justice I heard them draw their swords behind us. The doors to the feasting hall were shut, a shout would not raise the alarm quickly enough to save us. Jeife would kill us the moment we entered the hall. The merest blink of Mosa's peril in my mind was enough.

I was pushed with a left hand, meaning no soldier out on my left side, so I knew where the guard would be stood behind me. I drew my knife, spun round and jumped forward. His arm come up but I was under it and I punched the knife into his side and smacked down hard on his sword hand, knocking it to the floor. I kicked him backwards and went for the blade. The guard next to him reacted, turning and thrusting her sword at me. I twisted, parrying with my knife, but I wasn't quick enough, the edge of the sword slicing into my left arm as it went by me. I stepped back instinctively and she kicked the sword away. Jeife had moved to Crogan, his own side-sword's point in Crogan's back. The guard on the ground was groaning, his hand over the wound under his arm, blood dribbling through his fingers.

"Drop the knife, Amondsen. Shout anything, Crogan dies."

"Jeife, help me?" The poison was shutting the guard down. He spluttered and fell still.

"She's killed Liggsen, Jeife, she's fucking killed him," hissed one of the other guards. She pushed past Crogan to come at me. Jeife thrust his sword out to check her path.

"Yes, she has, Eirsen. Hold your piss. Amondsen, drop the knife."

I felt blood run down the edge of my hand and finger. I had to hope I was still immune to Hillfast poisons or that the blade was clean.

"You don't want to hurt Crogan. It will make things very difficult for you. It may not be what Khiese wants." I dropped the knife.

"Thank you, Amondsen. Now, shall we try entering the hall again? Get in front, alongside this fat cunt."

I stepped to Crogan, who was sweating now, breathing hard. Jeife stood the other side of Crogan and knocked on the door with the pommel of his sword. It opened, a blast of heat from the pits, the light of the torches and smoke in the air drowning my senses, the sharp sour stink of a sweaty crowd, the crackling and tang of meat and fat. Frantically I looked for Aude and Mosa among the faces. Hand on his

119

back, Jeife nudged Crogan forward. Cups started banging as we was noticed. "Jeife! Jeife! Jeife!" "Where's Thende?" "Start us off, Jeife! Blessing of Haluim!"

Jeife held a hand up to hush the hall, and the shushes echoed along the benches and tables. I saw a few of Skallern's men now, Eirin was to my left, twelve feet away. She saw the blood running down my arm and the drawn swords of the guards and signed immediately to the others, unseen by Jeife himself, who then spoke.

"Once we might have seen the visit of Crogan Othbutter as a great favour, coming as he does with promise of trade, the support of the citadel and his family. But when were the Othbutters last here? Only their tax collectors bother us, and that regularly enough. But here is the brother of the great chief himself. He came to tell Elder Thende, my own brother, that he must swear fealty to the Othbutters after we have all sworn fealty to our new lord, Samma Khiese."

The room was silent now. If there was any lingering hope about us of some sort of escape from Khiese it was gone. A couple of the nearest Seikkersons now noticed I was bleeding, the drip of blood visible to them as it hit the stone floor at my feet. Some others noticed Jeife's sword was drawn and held point down behind Crogan. Crogan looked about him for his men. Some of those present at the benches began to move, uncrossing legs or reaching for hidden daggers. I still couldn't find Mosa or Aude.

"But I have awful news, caused by Othbutter's visit. Elder Thende is dead, poisoned in his own room."

Gasps and murmurs. A couple cried, "No!"

"It seems Othbutter's demand to renew his fealty, when his commitment to Khiese already cost this clan and this family so much, cemented my poor brother's struggle with his honour. He came reluctantly to understand the wisdom

120

of Samma Khiese, as you know. I, your new elder, have no such difficulty understanding who our master is."

It was quick, the thrust. He angled the blade up and drove it through Crogan in a swift and fluid movement. The point of the sword forced out the wool of his tunic at the front. Crogan gasped aloud, arms rigid in shock, as though he'd been plunged into an icy pool. Jeife's other hand held his shoulder to keep him still while he drew out the sword. He pulled Crogan to the floor at his side, Crogan still alive enough to try to sit himself up on quivering arms. Crogan looked over at me, but as he leaned on one arm to reach for me with the other it gave way and he slumped to the floor, dead.

Jeife turned to me, I was grabbed by the two guards behind me, one squeezing my cut, which made me cry out.

"Ma!" shouted Mosa, near the back at the main front doors. I saw him then, just about, Aude too. Jem was with them and drawing knives.

"Captain Eirin, your men are unarmed," said Jeife. "It would be awful if any attempt to harm me or my people should lead to Amondsen's death, so I hope they won't try to leave."

He looked at one of the men on a nearby bench, who nodded and gestured to three more, who took up their swords from the floor beneath their table and moved to the main doors.

"Now, Amondsen, you know the value of your caravan and you know the value of your life and the lives of all those who have brought it to us at Crimore. Your crew may choose to fight, or you can tell them not to. At least that way you get to live and take Crogan's head back to his brother."

I clenched my teeth with the pain in my arm, looked at Aude holding Mosa, Aude's face aghast, awaiting the killing blow. For my part I saw only Othbutter's fury should I go back to him with his brother's head. I saw the requisition of my forts for his use, a compensation I would again be forced to be grateful for against his own threat of my keep's life, my boy's life. Still my thoughts revolved, my eyes filling up, a well of anger and helplessness, looking for a proposal, a way through. The soldiers sensed it, gripped me tighter, causing a further spasm of pain. I was kicked in the backs of my knees, dropping me.

"You see a mercenary's true colours now, my friends. She's thinking of how much gold, how much profit she will not now make. She is struggling to decide which to choose, gold or family. This is the girl who disrespected her own family, kept the name of her rope, rightfully her brother's, left them and the Auksens who had raised her and fed her. We're grateful to you, Amondsen, the people of Crimore will live well off the supplies, the plant. We should perhaps also consider acquiring your recipes. Where are your drudhas?"

He looked out at the crowd. In those moments I felt a stillness wash through me, though I cannot tell you why, and I realised both he and I had underestimated us a moment before the arrow hit him. The caffin butter, Thad's dayer, I struggled to stone it, get it under control. All my feelings and senses overwhelmed me as much as they raised me towards the highest sense of my self. But it meant I was too focused on looking for my own solution, the best action I could take, and I ignored the possible outcomes an experienced and well-paid handful of mercenaries could add, all because the brew narrowed the world to my body's sense of it and I'd lost the ability to push that back out onto the world, to join and not merely receive its song.

The arrow come from above, one of the shutters in the roof above this end of the hall. It hit Jeife in his right shoulder, precise, forcing him to drop his sword. I looked up, another shutter was above me, saw Yalle and Sanger. An arrow was loosed straight down into the head of one of the guards behind me. A third arrow then, from one of the bigger shutters open over the firepits, through the neck of another guard stood just behind Jeife.

As Jeife cried out and the men and women in the hall panicked, Thad stood up.

"Silence!" In his hands were two thin waxed cotton bags full of coldfire stones. I could faintly smell them with the dayer, an alluring sharp tang at the back of my mouth. He walked to the firepit and held them over it. The hall fell silent but for Jeife whimpering along with the children, whose parents were shushing them.

"If these bags are dropped into those firepits and the shutters above us are closed, those of us without salve or treated mask will choke and vomit themselves to death. I would hate to kill good people, for none of you have made this terrible mistake."

I turned to face the guard who'd been ready to kill me. He dropped his sword.

"Mercy," he said. No fucking chance. I threw myself at him, swung a right, which he put his arm up to deflect too late. I caught him clean in the side of the head and put him down.

"Teyr!" shouted Eirin, who ran over and pulled me off him. I'd got a few punches in before I was hauled up easily by her. She put her face up close to mine. "Stone it, Amondsen. Breathe." I pushed her back, my hands up to show I'd heard her. The guard flinched when I caught his eye. He had no colour, easy to forget how the nokes can fear us.

"Someone get this arrow out," hissed Jeife, looking at me. He'd fallen to his knees in pain. The main doors opened, and Jinsy and the others walked in with the sentries that had been left out on duty in the settlement.

"Thad will," I said, "and I hope he takes his fucking time about it. Eirin, get some of your boys to get Crogan out of here, tell Steyning to clean him up."

I took Jeife by his wounded shoulder and pulled him up.

"Ma! No!" shouted Mosa from the back as Jeife cried out.

It caught me for a moment, like someone had played the right note on a horn but the rest of the players was inside my head filling it with a vicious noise. It give me pause to look out at all these farmers and labourers, sniffers and crafters. Some had risen from their seats, ready to die fighting with their bare hands.

"I'm not Samma Khiese. Crogan was not Samma Khiese. We both respect the Seikkerson rope. We will not hang you or your sons and daughters from the walls like Khiese. You are free and will come to no harm if you do not resist our leaving. You may well swear Jeife Seikkerson in as chief of these lands. We respect that as well. I cannot make you swear fealty to anyone else. But consider the wisdom of your choice. If I find the Auksen clan are yet free then we may be able to resist this Khiese and you can once again be the masters of Crimore Vale."

I found I had nothing else to say. Jeife would win them back because he had a clever tongue. Othbutter's failings in all but his collection of tax would have been felt in all their purses and harvests over the years. What did he benefit them? I could offer nothing while Khiese was free and dangerous. Some murmuring began and I had lost their attention. Thad moved in to take the arrow out of Jeife and stitch up the hole.

Eirin ordered everyone out of the hall along with the people of Crimore. Jeife grunted but did his best not to show the pain of having an arrow cut out. Thad worked quickly with plant and gut to stitch and poultice the wound it left.

"What poison is in me?" asked Jeife.

"None," said Thad. "We hoped not to have to kill anyone if it came to this, but . . ."

He helped Jeife up.

"We're leaving," I said. "You won't get in our way."

"A fine speech, Teyr, but the Auksens belong to Khiese."

"I'm sorry to hear it."

"Caravan like yours, too big to hide, too small to make a difference. You're heading to your death, all of you."

He gestured to the one guard who remained with him to follow him through to the just.

"My fucking arm hurts," I said after he'd left.

"His was the worse wound," said Thad.

"How did you know mine wasn't poisoned?" I knew the answer though, I just wanted it confirmed.

"I watched you, no sign of any poison from my seeing you walk in until now. Took a moment to notice the stain and the blood, there's a bit of smoke in here from those pigs."

He cut and tore my sleeve and prepared another needle and gut.

"We'll take some cuts of pig for the trip out of the valley, make sure everyone's had something fresh and there might be some scraps to salt." I was saying that with a few cusses and some moaning as he did a fine job.

"Cut's clean, a bit of something on the blade from what I can smell, but if anything the rust would be more deadly." After he'd finished and packed everything up he took up one of the carving knives and cut a big pile of slices of meat onto a serving tray. He left me to my thoughts as he did it, stopping only to wipe his hands and get his pipe going.

"You can carry those bags of coldfire stones," he said when he was done. "We need to talk with Eirin and the others when we find somewhere to stop, Teyr."

"I know. I need to think a bit."

Outside, all of us was watched by the settlement. I saw Jinsy and Skallern's crew going door to door and taking arrows from the men and women about us, for they all could use a bow as with all clans about the Circle, being always at each other's throats as I said before. Thad passed the meat about our crew.

I went over to where the horses was tied and found Aude and Mosa. Mosa still looked upset and come over to hug me.

"I've got the saddle and bags," said Aude, but he didn't stop what he was doing so he was struggling with what had happened.

"I thought you were going to die, Ma." Mosa started sobbing into my dress. I ran my fingers through his hair, the heat from his scalp warming my fingertips. I was feeling sleepy, the dayer wearing off and my nerves getting worse, my fingers trembling again. I felt low and a bit ratty. I was grateful for Thad's mix in the poultice for it felt cool and numb, some part of that the night air on my bare arm too.

"I was scared too, Mo. But we've got good soldiers here. They thought there might be trouble and they sneaked up onto the roof of the longhouse ready to help without being seen."

"Your arm's hurt; will it get better?" He pointed but wouldn't go near it. "Are you still bleeding, Ma?"

"Aude?" I said.

"Let's talk when we get going," he said.

"No, Mo, it's not bleeding, it's drying up now. I'll need to wash it all off soon. Thad has put plant on it and it'll be healed up in no time."

"What happened?"

"Well, before I come into the hall where you were sat with your da, I tried to attack one of them with a knife I

126

had hidden, but she had a sword and she cut my arm. I did it because I thought they was going to kill me."

His bottom lip tucked up and his eyes filled and he touched my arm as gently as he could.

"I know where Da keeps his potsa. You and Da always end up laughing and singing when you drink that. Da will get it, won't you?"

"It's a good idea," I said, "but I'll have some later, bluebell. We need to get moving, as we aren't welcome here no more."

There was hollering along the line as the carts was put on the horses and Steyning and Yalle put Crogan's body onto one of them, dusted and bound. It would be wrong to put him over a horse in front of these people.

Eirin led us out of Crimore. Jeife watched us from the longhouse doors and his people gazed at us silently as we made our way back to the river and started along the track out of the valley. The younger children waved, one or two had their hands smacked as they did it, but whether this was born out of hostility to us or even respect or sorrow for what happened to Crogan it was hard to say.

I trotted up and down the line myself to speak to everyone and see that they was good and answer any questions they had, for many of them wasn't in the hall to see what had happened. When I reached Thad and Eirin near the front, they confirmed Crogan's cleark's count of plant and gifts was intact. We took nothing but arrows from Crimore in our own defence, but we would leave them no gifts until their own banner was raised again.

"How long do we go tonight?" said Thad.

"Couple of hours should get us out of the mud by the river and up onto harder ground in the hills. At the head of the valley you remember we saw a spot might be worth a camp if we wasn't so close to Crimore? Feels like a good place to go now and work out our next step," said Eirin. I went to say something but she held a hand up.

"Sorry, Master Amondsen, but this needs a proper talk with all of us settled and thinking right."

She was right. I could see even by her lantern she looked worn out, her dayer was taking its toll, but also maybe Crogan's death had shaken her. It was obvious, thinking back on it as we followed the hill trails, that she was feeling personally guilty for Crogan's death. I had to make sure Yalle wasn't going to push her on it, so found her in the line and we had a few words, but she wasn't interested in badmouthing Eirin, if only because she was paying the dayer too.

The clearing we had found was likely a spot for those moving herds or else a place to rest for vans that come through going east or west.

Crimore would be somewhere below us, but the hills was heavily wooded, obscuring it. Skallern put a few soldiers about, and Sanger and Jem went back down the trail to watch for any riders coming out of Crimore. I was hoping they might spot the whiteboy I'd seen, for he had never appeared afterwards.

Aude put Mosa in Chalky's wagon with his family for some warmth as the wind had teeth up here, roaring through the trees. I was wrapped in my woollens on the cart that had our things on it among supplies for trading. He patted and spoke to our mares and our packhorse, Thunder, who was called that on account of the time Mosa was stood behind her when she lifted her tail and splattered him with dung. I watched him as he spoke to them. Aude was good with the horses, they loved him and always made for him the moment he was in sight. He come over then and jumped up into the cart with me, undid the clasp on his cloak and put it about our shoulders. We was silent for a bit, arms around each other. He fidgeted like he wanted to say something. I listened to him catch his breath and then try to control his breathing. He was trying not to cry.

"Sorry, bluebell," Aude said. "I didn't want Mosa to see me get in a mess. I wasn't ready to . . . Well, Jeife killed Crogan as quick as clicking your fingers, and I saw you were hurt and for a moment I thought I was going to have to — and Mosa was going to have to — watch you die. And . . ." His eyes filled up. "And I froze, my love. He would have done it and I didn't shout, I did fuck all." He wiped his eyes, angry with himself.

"Ho now, Aude." I put my arm across his waist and turned into him to cutch him.

"You told me all those stories from when you paid the colour, the things you did, and I saw that and wanted to be sick. Not much use to you, am I? You were calm as a cow with swords at your back."

"It's the life I had, bluebell. Stoning and paying the colour, it changes you." And I hated that we both was thinking of what I skirted around in what I was saying. I tried to edge my words towards it. "You learn to go cold, keep thinking. Course I was fretful, but it was my worrying for you and Mosa, forcing all this on you. We're alive. We've learned something and we won't get caught like that again."

We was alive. Made it another night, that was what me, Nazz and Ruifsen would have said back in our army days.

"I expect you'll be needed by Eirin and Yalle soon, decide what's to be done with Crogan and this van."

I tipped my head to the side so I could rest it against his. "What would you do now?" I said.

"I'm just sorry this isn't going as you'd hoped. This Khiese seems like a serious threat. That clan down below us is

129

beaten, in spit and spirit. And your clan too may be the same."

"They won't be. I can't see it. I know that he pitted the Seikkersons' families against Thende, but there was always bad blood with the Ironbacks in particular. There's little vigour in the twist of their ropes. Auksen's loved by all the Families sworn to his. Doubt they'll let him down."

"The woman I made my keep I love for many reasons, and your reason, your cleverness, is chief among them. So you must think, *What if he's got to my people?*"

"And you, Aude, have lime jam on your tongue, sweet and sharp. Course I'm worried about it a bit. Maybe I don't know how the family are, but we had good recipes and Auksen was a hard fucker last I saw him, like his da. I have to think that if Khiese walked our sons up to his walls he'd not give up his clan. Thende was a good man, but goodness is wanted in the Old Kingdoms with their laws in writing and their standing militia able to protect it. Out here in the Circle it can be weak."

"You're not ready to give up on it all just now then?"

"No." I said it too quickly, too hard, like a slap. As I was walking up the hill out of Crimore I knew we was nearly halfway across the Circle, and I was only a week or two from my own family.

He reached behind him and felt about in a sack, pulling out of it a flask of potskas. I took a good slug, savoured its fiery aniseed. I kissed him on his cheek then, as he was taking his own swig. I hated that he had some doubt about me, and I hated, as I looked about me, that I was wanting to bawl for how it had all gone. I didn't want him to see me upset, but that's one thing. I could not let any of the van see me upset. So I kissed him, though a tear on my cheek touched his and he felt it.

130

"You mustn't cry now if Eirin comes over. Spadeface, Chalky's little girls call her." I smiled at that.

"No, that's not right. She's been at the gruet sure," which is a Fasties way of saying she was big all over, "but she's fine to look on. And what about Yalle? What about me?"

"They aren't going to tell me what they call you, are they. Yalle, well, she has that small sharp nose and drawn-in cheeks and she's tall and slim so she's the Pickaxe."

"I think she'd be fine with that. Spadeface and the Pickaxe. I just wish they got on more."

"It's down to you. It always is. We're with you, Mosa and I. A 'stroll in the big country' is vanner's humour, a way of saying it isn't easy. You need to see if anyone else has the heart for a stroll now, with Crogan dead. It'll take a good crew if you want to keep us safe."

I looked behind us, as we was facing outward from the camp, which our wagons was arranged around in a half-circle. They was in their pipes, and Thad was playing his flute, a sailor song, "Crackerdock", that had them tapping along with their hands and reminded me of days spent drinking and smoking with Thad, Nazz and Ruifsen down in the Roan Province, before greed tore it all apart. Thad was doing a fine job keeping their spirits up, something he always managed on a campaign or a van.

I kissed Aude and jumped down off the wagon to join Thad and the others. As they saw me approach, Thad finished the verse with a flourish so's they'd stop singing.

"I didn't mean for you all to stop."

"Come and sit with us," said Thad. "We know we've all got to talk, and I don't think we'll get much sleep before we head out of here tonight."

"And the question is which way," said Eirin.

"We should toast Crogan before anything else," I said,

surprised that Eirin hadn't already decided. I raised Aude's flask of potskas and passed it to those that didn't have one themselves and we all said a line or two about him, Eirin recalling him falling off the edge of the dock once while pissing and her having to fish him out, Skallern's keep slapping him in front of the crown prince of Farlsgrad for saying she was pregnant when she wasn't. I said something about the Othbutters' support for merchants but I was fooling no one and began to wish I'd not offered the toast, though it was right.

Yalle and Steyning was there, along with Sanger. The rest of the crew was either guarding or in their pipes about the wagons, spreading us out as a precaution against sporebags.

"I want to toast you all too, that saved my life and maybe all our lives down there. To debts that cannot be paid!" And they responded.

"I haven't ever been one for a speech," I started.

"Pig shit," said Thad, scratching out his pipe bowl, and this got a laugh.

"Well, when I'm forced to. Now I'm forced to. We had come to build relations with the clans of the Circle. We haven't done it because of this Khiese. But I believe he hasn't got to the Auksens or further east so I want to go on. First we have to make our way to the Almet, to the heart of the Circle. It's even more important we push hard to get there. I don't know what help we'll get, but the gift I have for them they won't be able to ignore. Their help could make all the difference. With or without them, we then make for the Auksen settle. Unless Khiese's got a standing army he won't have the crew to cover all that land, nor maintain it from those Families that might want to fight back at him. So if we go on I need all of you, because with all of you we got enough to make him think about hitting us. Sorry to say it would mean leaving Crogan here, because the two it would take to cart him back to Hillfast are two we could do with."

"And if he has got to them?" This was Sanger. "Then you can't deliver my purse."

"Agreed," said Steyning, "and the terms were clear, two-thirds of the final amount to be paid if we couldn't reach Stockson. Are you saying you'll pay up once we know if Khiese runs your clan? Because that's what's happened; I don't think Jeife was lying about that."

"Yes."

"First sign of trouble, eh, Steyning?" said Skallern, who was a veteran of Hillfast's militia, mostly up in the Moors.

"Master Amondsen understands us," said Yalle.

"I'm sure there's a purse for avenging Crogan's death," said Eirin, but she hadn't thought this through before saying it.

"That would mean killing Jeife for one, then going after Khiese. How much silver do you have in your packs, Captain?" said Steyning.

She shook her head. They never dealt with mercenaries much of course. "I'm for seeing the Auksens," she said. "Crogan can be buried tonight, in this clearing. We were meant to bring the Chief's justice and support to the Circle; turning back to Hillfast means we'd fail him."

"We're all agreed?" I said quickly. I was thrilled we would move on with so little disagreement. The Auksens and my own family was my main hope of turning about the ambitions of this Khiese. Few of us here would have any fear of his crew with a fort and more to fight alongside us in familiar lands.

"We are, Master Amondsen," said Sanger, who rose and stretched. "Let's find us some wood." He whistled for Jem. I looked over to where I heard movement on the back of one of the supply wagons, where Bela seemed all wrapped around Jem, who did his best to right his leggings under the thick oilskin they was sharing.

I stood and walked over to Aude. He jumped down off the wagon and stood before me.

"Do you need me for anything?" He smiled. I'll never get past the joy of seeing him smile at me.

"We're burying Crogan here and pushing on to the Almet, then down to Auksen lands and my clan."

"Right."

I could see he was nervous and I could understand that.

I heard a horse approach at a canter, it was one of Eirin's that we'd posted as a lookout on the track back along the hill nearer Crimore.

"Captain Eirin about, Master Amondsen?"

"She's in the camp."

"Can you hear it, Master? Perhaps not, if you're only on dayers. It's horns," said the rider.

We walked away from the campfires down the track a bit, and I could hear it, just, with any falling off of the wind to quieten the pines. It was a screeching of sorts, high on the air.

"Too far for Crimore. That over east near the Shield forest, do you think, Woodsen?" I said.

"Yes, Master, feels like it." The rest of us gathered to listen. Only those of us on Thad's dayer could hear the horns; Steyning's wasn't refined enough. It put her nose out of joint a bit but there we are.

"What shall we do, Master?" said Eirin.

"We give Crogan Othbutter up to his tapestry, to Halfussen. Then we head for the Almet, prepped and ready for whoever is blowing those horns."

"They sound like people screaming for their lives," said Bela.

"They're meant to," said Sanger.

"Do they have soldiers, the Oskoro?" said Eirin.

"I don't know."

"Do we get a few of their drudhas in return?" said Thad.

"I don't know that either. But if Khiese gets anywhere near us in the next few days, I feel better about being in the Almet than anywhere else bar my bloodlands."

"I'm glad it gives you some comfort, Master Amondsen," said Eirin. "Hope you can share that with my crew, because they're shitting it."

Chapter 5

Now

The swollen river makes us faster as we head away from the burned-out Kelssen theit, home of these children and Ydka, mother to two of them. It has been raining hard, and they have long since gone through crying about what's happened.

"Pot's filling up quick, Blackeye."

The girl Dottke is smiling now despite the cold rain hammering down as though it hates us. The one pot that had been stashed in the boat with the pack of food, clothes and plant is filling up nicely with water and should replenish our flasks.

Brek is asleep next to me. The arrow-shot boy woke in the night and a finger of opia eased him off again. Ydka's baby starts whining, barely an hour after she last give him her bab. She jerks awake, her hands moving around under the cloak she's wrapped in, helping it onto her nipple. She pulls a face before looking over at me.

"Think he was born with teeth, this one."

"Does he have a name, Ydka?"

"Not until he's a year. My ma was clear on that rightly

from the moment she heard I was with him. Same with me as it was with Jorno."

"A Fasties woman then." Which meant, among other things, the da wouldn't have really had a say, not least because these was hard lands and nobody wanted, in Hillfast winters, to be stitching names into the weave only to unpick them before spring.

"I'm sorry for your family," I says, "for Murin and all the Kelssens." She looks about us, only Dottke awake, but she has lain back down and curled up into Litten and Aggie.

"Thank you, Amondsen." She'd been crying in the night. This miserable and bitter dawn, a mist fogging up the lands beyond the banks of the river, give us a solitude and quiet that is needed. It hides us too, though the sounds of the horns faded in the dark hours before dawn. I don't think we are being followed.

"Whose lands will we be in now?" I ask, looking to put her mind onto something useful.

"Jannissens. There's a river dock we'll come to shortly. Nakvi-Russ joins the Nakvi-Anssi and the docks are just past their joining."

She looks ahead at the river. We're not talking about how we go from here; what I will do, what I won't do, what will happen to these children. I have given no promises, no word, and that is as it is meant. I don't want this. From the moment Ydka's keep come out of the trees, freshly mutilated by the whiteboys, I hadn't wanted this.

I'm tired. I lift the hood back away from my head to let the cold rain soak me and keep me awake.

"I didn't want to say something the last few days you been with us, but you been beaten haven't you? Was it the whiteboys did it?"

"Yes," I says.

"You paid colour though, you must've seen a few of them off too. Were you working for Othbutter then?"

"No, I . . . I used to be a merchant, in the port of Hillfast. We was attacked when I was coming back to my homeland."

"You got away with your life. You must owe Sillindar." This is a saying meaning that it is thanks to the magists that I am still alive. I have fuck all to thank a magist for, this much is true. I have even less reason to tell her my troubles.

"I do owe Sillindar, among others."

"How come you're not headed back to Hillfast then? You lose the shirt off your back, as the saying goes? Is there a way you can help us now?"

"There's nothing for me at Hillfast. I expect there's debts, mind, I don't rightly know." I look about me at the sleeping children. Ydka's dut wriggles about again, he's fed and he's awake. She lifts him up a bit from her babs and arranges a hood over both of them to protect him from the rain.

I think about Mosa and I need to look away from her, though my face is now so soaked she might not notice my tears. My face still hurts, cheek and eyes still puffy to the touch. Swelling has gone down a bit in my mouth. Seems like the spear I took and this change in my eye and the scar next to it hurt less in every way than what Khiese did to me. The woollens and boots the Oskoro left me from the herders are at least helping with my feet and the cold. I don't know what they'd have used the bodies for.

"Where will you go?" says Ydka.

"To the port, then south to Jua or over the Sar somewhere. I got my letters so maybe a cleark, enough to feed me and to put the citadels behind me."

"First time I seen a bit of light in your eyes, you saying that, Amondsen. I see you mean it."

She says it with a smile but I feel there's a bit of sadness too and she never meant for me to feel guilty about wanting to leave them, but she is alone with the last of her family, last of all the Kelssens, in this small boat.

A couple of the duts are whispering and it's the littlest girl, Aggie, who pokes her head out of the blanket.

"I'm hungry. Where's Ma, is she coming?"

"Ssshh, Aggie, she's not." This was her brother, Litten. He's looking at me and I do my best with a frown to persuade him to hold telling her for now and he says no more than that.

"There's a few bits in the sack there," says Ydka. She points under the stern sheet I'm sat on while I work the scull. I drag the sack over to Ydka, and the movement of Aggie and Litten wakes the other children.

"Breakfast," says Ydka. I watch them as they take the broken bread. They can hardly look at me as they nibble away. They're staring at the sides of the boat or out onto the river, and the previous night will be at the front of their thoughts. She's young, Ydka, young to have a dut and Jorno, who must have been nine or so years old.

"You had Jorno young, must have," I says.

She's chewing on some bread herself, and it seems to diminish her age further, cowed by the rain alongside the children, letting it moisten what is in her fingers.

"I was fourteen years. My da promised me to Murin as Orgrif hadn't the women enough to give him any choice and you know how it is with the blood. It helped my own ma wasn't from these parts either." She means by this the mixing of clans that is seen to strengthen blood. She's got hair a bit darker than the children in the boat, darker than Jorno's too, like wet sand to their dry. I look at Jorno as she's talking but he doesn't seem to be listening. "More important for the match was a stretch of some three

139

acres that was around here, Gabb's Pen, where I was sniffing a few days ago as you know. It was known to be good land for hazel and with that come the belets and of course the henbane if you're lucky. Orgrif felt Murin was worth it."

"He was very lucky, I think." She's a fine beauty too and I feel she'd lift a bit to hear it. Her smile and the joy for her duts as she gives them comfort are startling, like a fierce sun flashing through cloud, beautiful enough I feel my own cheeks flush a bit.

"So this is your own family's land we're passing through?" I says.

"Not my family no more and not for years. I weave the Kelssen rope now."

This is more true now than it was yesterday morning. It's possible I might have been sold off like she had, and thousands like her, but for the Amondsens being a bigger family.

Of course Jorno was listening though. He leans against Ydka and hides his face.

"I want Ma!" shouts Aggie. "I want to go home."

"And me," says Dottke.

"You can't go back, bluebell," I says. "And there isn't an easy way to say this. Those men with the painted faces, they . . . well, they burned your theit. All your homes are gone, and your mas and das are gone and all, I'm sorry to say."

"They kilt them all is what she's saying," says Brek, who's not opened his eyes but is clearly listening.

Litten gets upset now, and he starts crying and he's only got Aggie to hold on to, who sees her brother upset and so she cries too and it hurts me the way Aggie cutches into him. Me and Ydka have to let them cry, and she hums for them a bit, reaching over to hug them in her spare arm.

"I need more of that rub, Blackeye," says Brek, meaning the opia.

"You don't. I'll look at your wound when we get to the docks, for now you'll have to hold till we reach it."

"It's hurting bad."

I lean over him. "You sound like a drooper. You need your wits in this world, now more than ever with this lot to care for, don't you think?"

It pleases me to see him firm up, not liking the comparison. There's two ways people go when they get their first good taste of opia. They either shrink, like their bodies want to settle around it, and after years of seeing droopers, that shrinking's done long before they're robbing and killing for it. Or, like Brek, you tell them they don't need it and they see it right, see the weakness looking to rob them, and they knock it back as much out of fear as of hate.

Late morning and voices – shouting, singing, whistling – are carrying through the last of the mist on the river. The rain's cleared and there's a bit of blue peppering the sky. The Russ and the Ansi join and I need Ydka's help to oar us to a small rotted-looking pier in the current. It's a small dock, no more than ten piers for barges, though a few more are tied to posts around.

I haven't slept and I need to badly. I step out of the boat and tie it. There's a couple of stone houses but the rest is tents, paddocks for the horses or dog teams doing the hauls or sleds up through the riverways, and so a lot of yapping and howling, in part from the men about.

We might as well have been a boatful of honey-glazed boar meat to all those that watch us through their pipe smoke. We are noticed by all who are stood about taking the air, or distracted from their haggling over the wares here:

piles of raw and filthy furs, kegs of whale oil from the coast, linens, cottons and fish. The smell of stews and frying oils catches the attention of the children most and they look about for the source of the smoke drifting to us through the vanners, bargemen and scratchers at their business.

The moment we're off the boat a man walks up, the only one about with a weapon in hand, a spear. He's wearing a leather jerkin but it's old and worn enough it should be torn up and used for polishing.

"Four bits, that spot there you're tethered to. Pouch of bacca might cover it." He's got one tooth and black gums, no taller than me with his back straight. He knows he isn't comparing as well as he's used to, for though he's been at the gruet he's a noke, and colour is colour.

"Spare us, sir," I says. "We're out of the Kelssens. There's trouble, we escaped with our lives. We only want to ask a bit of food and some furs and we're gone again."

I've taken my fieldbelt off of course, I don't want to use it up yet to bargain for something to eat, but we have a purse with us that Mell had stashed in the boat. The children are standing behind me. I need to see to Brek's shoulder but showing some colour to these men is a bit more important in giving them pause. The guard sees Ydka then, who's been kneeling with the duts to straighten out their tunics and whisper them some rules to follow. As she straightens up his eyes widen some, seeing her beauty, but before he can speak there's another appears behind him. His beard hoop's carved, Carlessen rings engraved on it, the five Families of the Carlessen clan linked together. He's older, grey beard stained with bacca spit and a tunic stained worse than a beer cloth.

"Nothing for trade in the boat that I can see. These your slaves, soldier?"

He's speaking King's Common, likely then from the Carlessen port.

"Are you the quartermaster?" I ask.

"Not me. Name?"

Like he was having that. "I'm Seikkerson, these are Kelssens and they aren't slaves. You got whiteboys, Samma Khiese, a day or so away. You have to tell your quarter. They killed everyone but these here."

He frowns, like I'd gaffed.

"She's talking about that bandit up in the Circle, Dakka," says the guard. "You not listened to those coming in off the Ansi last few weeks?"

"Been laid up with my chest, in't I. You must have a belt on you, Seikkerson, you paid colour, and you old wheezers always have to pack it, even after paying out."

"You think I should just give you my plant?" It's too confrontational, and I instantly regret it, but who the fuck thinks plant's there for the taking off an old merc like me, surely not a man his age.

"You won't help me then?" He's given me a way back in, saving a bit of honour for us both.

"Might have something can be threaded into your bacca, but I'd need to see. I lost a lot when I was attacked." The state of my face should be plain to see.

"Much appreciated, Seikkerson." He looks over those with me, eyes also lingering a bit on Ydka.

"What happened?"

"Whiteboys, this bandit's soldiers that he has covered in chalk and paint, they come in and burned the Kelssen theit to the ground. Boy there's got an arrow wound. I just about managed to get away, the chief asking me to take the children to safety. They've killed everyone else." I say this last bit quieter, enough noise about us to mask it with Ydka now talking to the duts, and they didn't need to hear it said again.

"Nowt's happened like this round here for many years. I can hardly believe it," says Dakka.

Another man shouts over at us then − dressed well, a clean tunic and beard, and he's fat with fine living, boots shining with wax and a rich green cloak with a bronze clasp that is finely worked.

"Hope you're not bargaining on those children without me getting a chance to bid, Dakka," he calls.

He comes over, leaving what must be a couple more guards behind him.

"What's he offered? I have a drudha can cure a dozen ailments. You'll get a better deal from me because I can sell them for more if they're in better shape. Wait, they're not chained?"

"They're not slaves either," I says.

There are a fair few questions queued up in the corners of his mouth but a few looks are exchanged between him and the other two and he straightens up to leave.

"My mistake. I'm Gressop, of the Bethessens, Clan Carlessen of course."

"I'm a Seikkerson, my name's . . . Well, I'm called Blackeye by these duts."

"Yes, been looking at that, looks in a bad way," says Dakka.

"Like the rest of her," says the guard. Dakka finds this funny.

"You're in trouble?" says Gressop.

"We all are. I need to see the quarter, but first I need to see if someone has enough kindness to spare these children some food and furs."

He is about to ask about our trouble when Dakka interrupts. "I'll tell you shortly, Gress. Look, Seikkerson, we get hundreds of beggars through here with their stories of bandits and other shit. Good luck getting a man here to give food away for nothing in return. Pay your bits to my man Eddler here and you'll have this fine pier till tomorrow at dawn."

He leads Gressop away. I get the pouch and pay the bits and so Eddler leaves as well.

"How much did Mell put in there?" says Ydka, of the pouch.

"Another ten bits and a silver, been clipped as well, though we might get away with it."

"Let's get the duts some stew and a bit of that fish and be going," she says.

"How? That won't get us far down the river and then we're all out."

"Your belt?"

"No. No, not yet."

She gives me a dirty look. "Let me have the pouch. I'll get them something and bring you and Brek back a bite. Might be I can get a bit more pity with this dut." With that they walk off.

Brek's struggling with the pain as I clean and cover the bark with cotton.

"It's itching bad," he says.

"It will while the bark knits in. Isn't much of a wound, but bark's the best for drawing out the poison. It's thirsty is bark."

"What are we going to do?" he asks.

"Get enough food to make the run to the Carlessens' port." I say no more because that's as far as the plan goes, as far as I go. They need an almshouse and some work if they aren't going to die.

I hear a scream then despite all the other noise of the market, a child, and there's too few of them here for it not to be one of mine.

I start walking towards the smell of the food, the direction Ydka took them. Dottke runs up, tells me Jorno got into some sort of trouble and now Ydka's in trouble. Sure enough, a few men are surrounding her, must be dock guards. One's holding Jorno, who's trying to kick out, while Aggie and Litten are holding on to Ydka's dress. She sees me, she's upset and desperate.

"A boy snatched the pouch as I was paying for some bowls of stew off this one. I can't pay."

"Where did he go?"

"Oi, you with her, can you pay for the stew she just give these duts?"

"Beggars get beaten," says one of the other two. One of them's paid colour, faded like me though, been off the brews a while longer by the looks of him. Him and his mate have clubs in hand, though the one who's holding Jorno against him hasn't used it on him.

"You saw what happened then, she had coin. Did you see who run off with it?" I look about us, but there's a crowd here, we're near a couple of pavilions that are set up for clearks and auctions and such. A boy could have ducked round any number of corners here.

"Well, it might be we can spare your slaves that bit of gone-off turnip and piss you call a stew, eh, Ces?"

A look that has some sort of meaning passes between them, and it don't feel right.

"I'm going to let this little one go, you should tell him how much a club hurts."

"Jorno, stand with your ma. We're grateful for this," I says.

"You got plant you can trade for more," says Ydka to me.

"She has?" This was Ces, the old man who's standing over his pot and a pile of dirty bowls. "You got a bit of white seed?"

I shake my head. "Is it for your throat or can't you shit?"

That brings a laugh from the dock guards and a smirk from Ydka.

"Throat of course." Cow shit. He was saving face. He rubs the front of his throat under a short filthy beard to make better his lie.

"I can put a finger of mallow root in some hot water. Should help your throat."

He looks grateful, and it seems only the two of us here know its main use is for his guts.

"Fetch it and there's another bowl or two of this fine stew for these duts."

He dips two of the dirty bowls back into the pot, gives one to Ydka and one to Litten.

I'm surprised a moment that he'd do this before getting his mallow, surprised at the two dock guards standing here with us as someone behind me hits the mud, and a roar goes up from five or six men drinking outside the tent of a brewer. The man fallen over is too soaked to get back to his feet easily and another, smaller man, quite young to look at, is in a rage, kicking him in the gut while being cheered on. The man on the ground is drunk enough to be laughing, and in a flash he grabs the other's leg mid-swing and pushes him back off balance, knocking over a few plates and mugs. The brewer's shouting out now for help, so why are the dock guards standing here?

When I look back from the scrap they've walked off towards the pens.

The old man selling his stew catches my eye, looking about him before whispering, "Boat."

Fuckers was keeping an eye on me.

I splash through the muddy tracks, past the two men fighting and the growing ring of herders, sniffers and vanners looking for a moment's circus.

At the pier I see Brek sat up and he's crying.

"I was shouting for you!" he says. It's clear before he says it that we've been robbed. There's no sack under the stern sheet, my sword's gone and my own sack, with Mosa's shirt in it. I feel sick, my belly's flipped upside down inside me. I can't have lost it, not after this winter and all these months, all I've been through.

"Where did they go? Hey, Brek, it's fine, come here." There isn't any gain in squeezing him now for whoever did this. There's a connection here, given the old cook couldn't have said anything while the guards was standing with us, keeping us there.

I sit next to Brek, who tries to adjust himself to better let me sit next to him without the boat rocking too much. I put my arm about him, gentle at his shoulder. He's having a proper cry now, heaving and emptying all the last day out of him, I think. It'll hit them all once the hunger's eased back a bit.

His crying ends with the usual shudders and snotty sleeve. He leans behind him then fetches out my sack, which would have been lying beneath him when the robber come.

"Oh Brek," I says. I kiss him.

"I was propping myself up with it to have a look about. When he come I just moved a bit so's he couldn't see it."

I take the sack, small, grey leather, covered in my sweat and blood with no care or wax given to it since I found it forty yards from a dead man's cart before midwinter in the high hills of Hardy. The worn leather drawstring is tied tight. The weight is right, barely more than the sack itself.

"What's in it?" he asks.

"Something precious." I loop it across my body.

"I'm sorry, Blackeye, I was scared and I didn't want to be."

148

"Don't be. I'll fetch Ydka and the duts back here and go looking for our things."

He tells me what the man looked like, tells me who was stood near when it happened. His description isn't going to be much use, a plaited blond beard and a brown hooded cloak, though this man did have a few teeth missing.

Ydka and the others I send back to the boat to see out the afternoon while I make up the mallow root decoction for the cook.

"Tell me about the quarter here," I ask him.

He's boiled up some water and I strip the guira and mallow and press them out into a bowl he's prepared.

"Leb Carlessen, face like a bald ferret, can't be much over twenty, dresses fine enough and I reckon has been put here to keep him out of the port's taverns and to learn how to do something useful instead. About as straight as a horseshoe is the trouble. He quickly got used by a couple of brothers who cut their rope a few years back down southeast near Hope lands. I reckon Forontir would pay a bit to see their heads. Now he's got them as his clearks."

"Names?"

"Westal and Gressop. Westal's paid colour. You know, I saw him playing with the woman Leb keeps around, out when I was foraging a week or so back. Kept my head down or he might have cut it off. Could be something you could wedge between them."

"Leb's got that longhouse just off the two big piers I saw coming in?" I ask.

"He has."

He confirms there's only one way in or out of the long-house. He's as grateful for the brew as I am for that bit about Westal.

I walk through the few other stalls that are set up and

past some fires been made by those who are stopping over for the night. There's a lot of eyes on me, woman who paid colour, and I'm sure my black eye don't help. It's rubbing bad and I need some oil on it. I'm desperately tired and hungry now, but I want to go walk around this longhouse of Leb Carlessen's before I head back to the boat to get some rest. I don't know how I'm going to feed the duts next.

I walk a route around the staging post and Leb's longhouse, a habit from my soldiering, looking for runs in and out of the place. Sure as the old cook said, just the one door. As I return along the piers I can see Gressop at our boat, Leb's man, the would-be slaver from earlier. He's alone, standing with Ydka slightly apart from the children in the boat, and turns when he sees the children and Ydka look at me approaching.

"Aaah, Seikkerson."

"What's going on, Ydka?"

"He wants to help us." There are tears in her eyes as she cradles the baby.

"I do. I heard of your misfortune from two of Carlessen's guards."

"I'm sure you did."

I see a shade of tightness in his jaw, his lips. He doesn't realise how much I can see, thinks perhaps my eye is worse than normal, or even blind, not far better.

"I can help Ydka and she can help all of you."

"Ydka, what the fuck is going on?"

"Don't, Amondsen."

"Amondsen?" he says.

"Oh Teyr, sorry, I'm sorry." I hold a hand up to shush her.

"I said my name was Seikkerson. It's not, I'm Amondsen rope. I was being cautious."

"Of course, I understand." He swallows as he says it, as if the name caught him by surprise, as if it means something to him.

"So what do you mean by saying that Ydka can help all of us?"

"Ydka is beautiful, like Sillindar made a woman out of honey if I may say so, and, even better, she's milking for that dut. I know a merchant with a number of main ten cargo interests – sorry, I'm saying that he's very rich – and he will need a wet nurse come the summer."

"A slave, then."

"There are slaves and there are slaves, as you must know if you've paid the colour. You'll have seen slaves broken in mines and you'll have seen slaves living well. I have been plain about this with Ydka."

"Who's going to see Litten, Aggie, Dottke and Brek right then, with that food and coin?"

"Well, her older boy, Jorno, he's not—"

"No."

"Amondsen . . ." says Ydka, a tremor in her voice telling me she has talked about Jorno finding his own way – with me, she must think.

I look past her. Jorno is wrapped in a cloak and sat next to Brek. They're all laughing at something Aggie must have said, as she's cross and Litten has to hold her from rocking the boat too much. The sound of them at play rings a heavy and cold bell, and for a moment I'm hearing the harbour bell from the apple trees of my old garden. He's hiding, I'm counting to ten.

"You're abandoning your son as well as all these duts of your Family? You'd sever your rope?"

"Don't talk to me about rope, Amondsen. You give your Family nothing. You said as much to Mell the other night

151

and I heard you clear enough. This is about feeding my dut and keeping the Kelssen rope, all that's left of it. You stopped to help the theit and you didn't have to, so you made it your work to care for them now."

"Like fuck I did," I hiss.

"Five silver coins and food for the journey should see you south," says Gressop over us. "If Jorno finds an alms-house to take him in the port then I'm sure some form of correspondence would be allowed. My friend will not open his doors to a family, and what then would Ydka and the rest of you do if you insisted on her refusing me? This sacrifice she makes now will help all these children until you can find something better for them. But, sorry, I forget that you have so many more important things to do, you would leave them."

A moment where I see my fist hammer into his face passes.

"We'll find some food, Ydka. I can hunt, I can sniff."

She glances back to Jorno before looking again at me.

"Look at you, Amondsen. Look at us. Scrabbling around for hazelnuts and belets? No proper woollens or boots for the next few weeks? Is it better or worse for my boys, now my Murin's gone and our theit's gone? We're not going hungry and right now we choose either nothing or five silver and food for all these."

I turn to Gressop, whose concern is smeared thin across his face. "Gressop, if your family name was in need of even an ounce of honour you'd be supporting these Kelssens, you oily piece of shit. You're all one clan. I'm going to speak to Leb."

"That's a good idea. We should do that."

That wasn't the answer I thought he'd give. Something smells bad about all of this.

"They your men, Gressop?" says Ydka.

Gressop and I turn to look behind us. I see a couple of

men leading horses through the main run, but their backs are to us and they're soon obscured by others loading and unloading barges.

"No idea," says Gressop.

"They was looking our way, like they knew you."

"Not seen them before, and dock guards wouldn't be leading horses through the main run," he says.

He was right about them not being guards. The horses are thick with mud and saddlebags and the men's cloaks just as dirty. They'd just come in and looked road heavy, as we used to say back on campaign.

"We should speak to Leb, Amondsen," says Gressop. "Sooner we can work this out the better. It'll rain shortly."

I shiver, a reflex that's my body's way of slapping me awake. I barely heard him, and he's waiting for me to answer, seeing sleep crowding at my eyes. I want to argue with him about charity, but I have no idea if the Bethessens and Kelssens are close or not. His family's honour does not move him, at least as much as I can see. I look up and see the black clouds building from the west. There's nowhere for the children to shelter except we'd have to beg people for a corner of their pavilion or covered wagon.

"Amondsen, he's waiting," says Ydka. And Gressop's now behind me, waiting for me on the edge of the main run.

"We need to talk later, Ydka. A slave is a slave."

She doesn't answer. If anything I'm hardening her in favour of Gressop's offer of slavery, not the opposite.

"I'll be back later, Brek. Dottke, can you look after him?"

"Yes, Captain Blackeye." She's pleased with herself for saying it and I'm warmed by it.

Gressop leads me to the longhouse. Two men who paid colour are standing at the door to it, both been at the gruet and must be from further south, darker hair, shaved faces. They do their best to look at me like I'm dirt. Then the one speaks, and it's Common.

"Belt." I don't like it, any of it. I managed to get a lick of amony while Gressop walked in front of me moments ago, so if there's trouble I might only have the advantage in the next half an hour or less.

It's small enough inside, even humble. A fine but plain high-backed chair is at the far end of the room. Must be Leb sitting on the chair, from the old cook's description. Lad has lost most of his hair already, just a band around the sides he keeps razored and a sad little moustache in need of a good dinner. The more interesting face by far is on the man to his left, standing in leathers, belt and blade. He's scarred worse than me, an expression that's calm, that weary expectant look in the eyes that a long day won't end quietly. No spears about the room, that's something in my favour. He must be Westal.

Leb stands, adds a few inches to his height. He puts on a frown to make himself appear more serious.

"Gressop?" he says.

"This is Teyr Amondsen, Quarterman. She's arrived this morning from the Kelssen theit upriver. Burned to the ground, she tells us. She, along with a delightful young mother and some orphans, are all that survived."

Leb looks to Westal and back at Gressop. Westal subtly shifts his feet, maybe doesn't know he's doing it, his back straightens. It feels like me or my name is getting this reaction. I'm glad of the amony, it's taken me away out of the exhaustion I was feeling, though I'll likely drop where I'm standing when it wears off. For now the world is as sharp as needles to my eyes and ears.

"Well, we have a friend down at port looking for a fine

young wet nurse, so I offered a fair sum to this girl and Amondsen here that would more than help her see the children safe somewhere. Food enough to get them there too. She thought, however, that I should just give her and these Kelssens alms for the honour of it."

Westal looks me over carefully. He's not amused like Leb is. He'll be the most trouble.

"Teyr Amondsen," says Leb. "There's a name to rattle the old scabbard, eh?"

"You heard it before?" I says.

"Well . . ."

But he's said enough, for he can't know me. I had an agreement with Tarrigsen in Hillfast about leaving trade with this clan to him, for a price, so I'd not dealt directly with any at Port Carl. I'm about to make a move on them when Sillindar chooses to smile on me. A woman walks through from a doorway behind Leb's chair. I see a desk and scrolls, but I don't see ink on her fingers, which are as white as the babs she's got only half covered by a dress of more use down in sunny Jua than here. Her glance at Westal the moment before she reaches Leb's side is enough to seal it.

"Fladdie, can you leave us for a while. I'll send Hekkl for you later."

"Yes, Quarterman." There's little formality in her speaking.

"Best not send Westal, eh Leb," I says, "it'll take him a few minutes longer to fetch her, from what I've heard."

There's a delightful moment as Leb turns to look at Westal, Fladdie's mouth drops open and Westal looks over at both of them.

This moment's all I need.

I run at Westal, Gressop yells but I'm at him. The world narrows itself into only balls, eyes and throat. He's good enough close in, sadly. He leans as my fist comes in. I catch his neck and it's enough to give me another moment to kick his knee back. But he's as calm as me, our learning done in alleys and battlefields, so he shifts balance to the other knee. He won't have time for his sword and wastes none trying to free it. Leb shouts for the men out front. I have to press Westal again because right now he's the only one has a weapon. He grabs my leg as I kick again and I use it as an anchor to launch a kick to his head with my other foot. I don't land well enough from that however. The other two have come in and I hear steel drawing from scabbards. Westal has staggered backwards, stunned for a moment, but in righting myself I can take no more advantage of it. Still I have to rush him, give him or the men with swords behind me no time. He sets himself and throws a punch as I come in, uppercut. My guts are ready and I'm too close for it to go near my head. His punch rattles my ribs and I gasp but manage to jab a knuckle in his eye, pull his head up with his beard and punch his throat. Footsteps behind me. I push Westal to my side so I can fall forward to my belly, winded, fighting for my breath. A grunt accompanies the thrust of the sword, inches above where I fell. I turn my head to see him ready for another thrust, but I'm on the ground, he has to close. As he stands over my legs, thinking the winding I've got's done me, I shift my weight so I can kick his balls. As he goes down I yell out, desperate and hoping someone outside might hear and interrupt them. I go for the man's sword, get close into him, risk a stabbing as he hits his knees. His sword's up but the kick's emptied him. I grab and twist his wrist, a disarm. Just as the sword leaves his helpless fingers and drops into mine I feel something hit the side of my head, a fragment of nausea and everything's gone.

* * *

156

Flickering torchlight squirms its way into my eyes. Left eye won't open, swollen and as solid as an iron slingshot. My black eye needs almost no light to see. Some time has passed. I keep still: two I can make out in front of me. I'm sitting on a chair in Leb's longhouse still, my arms tied behind my back and legs bound to it.

"She's still alive, thank Sillindar. You're a fucking idiot, Westal. Kill her and I'll make sure it's you stood in front of Othbutter." This was Gressop.

"Suck me, Gress, think I give a shit?" The words are whispered – dry, forced out. Good. Tells me my punch still hurt him, tells me not long has passed. "I'm bored. Bored of us yessing and noing that lamb of a boy. When we going to make some real coin?"

"Easy to forget the frostbite and starving, hiding from the militia and posses trying to string us up by our gizzies. Yet you're always forgetting."

Westal spits. I hear some talking at the door then.

"Who's there, Hekkl?" says Gressop.

A new voice from the doorway, letting in the sounds and smells of evening fires.

"I've scrolls for Leb. I'm to see they're given to one of you as he's not here."

"On the table in the back room there. You have a seal?"

"Scrolls are waxed. For Leb only."

A woman. The voice has given me pause. Why do I think I know it? I open my eye a sliver and see colours flashing with her movement as she nears and passes me to the room at the back of the longhouse. I've worked out that these colours come with the smells, like the eye can see what I smell. She's wearing a fieldbelt, and she's taken something, it's on her breath.

"Who's that?" she says.

"None of your fucking business," says Westal.

"Excuse me, I didn't hear you?"

I smile.

"He said fuck off," says Gressop.

"I don't think we will," she says.

"What?"

She draws her sword, the slick sound giving away that it's pasted. Someone opens the door and comes in.

"Where's Leb?" they say, but muffled, must be masked. A man, another voice that dances about my memory.

Westal's drawn his sword. "You're not taking her, if that's your plan."

"Sporebag says we are," says the man.

"You won't make it out of Carlessen land alive."

"Amondsen, I'm cutting you free," says the woman. She's near now. I hear the leather of her belt and armour cracking, smell the dayer on her breath. Then I feel a sack go over my head. Westal, seeing what this means, moves towards us, but Gressop screams and I know the sporebag's been thrown, a splash of blues and purples is all my eye sees. The woman's got me by the arm and I'm being stood up, my legs trembling, knees in pain. Gressop and Westal start choking, there's a brief smack of swords and then repeated stabbing.

"Take this," she says. I feel the hilt of a sword against my fingers.

"I can hardly fucking see," I says, but I take it. "Where's the guard, Hekkl?"

"Leyden's told him Leb's wanted here. That man he just killed was right: we won't make it out of Carlessen land if we leave this lot alive."

"For me?"

"Master Amondsen, I'm one of your vanners working Ablitch – everyone calls me Cherry. I put the bag on your

158

head because anyone finds out it's you, it'll be a death sentence for Cleark Thornsen as well as you if he's found to be hiding your whereabouts."

"Cherry? Oh Sillindar, is that you, Jairu? I haven't seen you in near a year."

"Yes, yes, it's me. Leyden told me it was you, on the boat earlier. Your whole guild had orders from Thornsen to keep a lookout for you on our runs, stop at every stagepost and riverdock and theit to ask after you. Here, hold your head still." I hear her at her belt, then she takes the hood off and presses something wet and cool over my eyes, river moss in it, burdock. It's tingling, and I feel the water and blood leak out.

"Good mix," I says.

"One of Thad's."

I see him the moment she says his name, singing on a ship, filling his pipe with bacca, holding me as we leave Marola, betrayed by our own.

"Master Amondsen, I know yer got questions, as many as we have for you," says Leyden, "but first we have to do this Leb Carlessen."

"Why?"

"There's a bounty on you. Othbutter."

"What?"

"Othbutter's got you down for killing his brother. Got sent his hoop and sword from the Seikkersons. How did you not know?"

My mind's spinning. There's no time to catch up. They've been reckless, they haven't thought it through, too young. I'm moved, how they just acted as they did from the moment they saw me, but killing Leb was making trouble for these two and Thornsen, who's given them the order to find me.

"Right," I says, "we can't go over this now. You've been

seen, word'll spread if you kill Leb. He's the only one with any clout in Hillfast and these two was running him. I was told they was gangers got their claws in. Might be we did him a favour in killing them. Cherry, tie my hands back up, sword on me, when he comes in say you found me killing them. Say you'll take his seal and me downriver to his uncle. I bet Thornsen didn't give you the Amondsen seal, did he?"

Leyden smiles. "Nope, gave us Carlessen's." I send a wish up to Sillindar for Thornsen's savvy.

Cherry'd just got my hands tied when Leb walks in. Hekkl's with him and he straight away levels his spear at us all.

"Get out!" shouts Hekkl.

"Wait," says Cherry. "We're Carlessen vanners. Stopped this one trying to leave as we were putting our scrolls in. She says she got loose and killed these two."

"She did?" He puts up a hand to relax Hekkl. "Check she's tied, Hekkl. You two, back up against the door." They do as they're told.

He's rougher than he needs to be of course. He's scared as he comes in close.

"No touching my arse," I says, which gets me a punch in the side and doubles me over, being near the rib Westal got a heavy fist into earlier.

"Knot's good, Quarterman." He shoves me down into a chair and levels his spear.

"And you, you have our seal?" Which they then hold up before them.

"Excellent. You'll understand my caution, seeing my two advisers dead. Well, it is our good fortune you arrived when you did." He looks over at Gressop and Westal, their blood pooling out from their backs. He can barely hide his relief; his brow softens, and he takes a deep breath.

"She won't have told you she's got a splendid bounty on

her head from Chief Othbutter. Murdered Crogan and been on the run ever since. I'll bet she was the one killed all those poor Kelssens in their theit not two days ago and is selling those children."

"We'll run her into the port and your uncle, Chief Carlessen. It's where we're headed back to," says Leyden.

Leb's in a fine mood as he realises his freedom from the gangers. "Do you need Hekkl or another of the dock guards to go with you?"

"No need. We'll get her on the droop until we reach port," says Cherry.

I can see the room better now with the mix clearing out my eye. Leyden's still got that look of a beaten dog which has served him well in many scraps, while Cherry's red hair is still thick and proud as sedge.

"The duts, well, Gressop didn't get to selling them on," says Leb. "Ydka left on a barge a few hours past though. I'd guess whatever fee was agreed is on his body somewhere. You two, find those children and take them to my uncle, he'll get some good coin for them and you'll get a cut in return."

"Where are the children? How could Ydka fucking leave them?" I stand sharply, get the point of Hekkl's spear in my chest. "Sit back down, old girl," he says.

I'm sure they find it strange my seeming so attached, and it eats at me why I'm so suddenly desperate that they aren't lost or hurt, why I'm cut so deep about it. It don't stop me being angry at the thing in me thinking I'll somehow be making a difference to them, or making up for what happened to Mosa.

Hekkl keeps to his duty while Cherry and Leyden head off, and Leb goes and fetches some of the other dock guards to drag out Gressop and Westal's bodies. There's some noise as that happens, I even hear a cheer.

161

"You do it? You kill Crogan?" asks Hekkl.

"No. Don't matter, does it? Samma Khiese's coming for all of you, and Othbutter."

"We've heard things, few barges come from up north now."

"I got no problem with you, so when I tell you you'd better get anyone you love out of here south, think on it."

He's about to say something when Cherry comes back with the duts.

"Blackeye!" shouts Dottke, who starts to run over to me with Litten and Aggie but then sees Hekkl's spear at my chest.

"Don't kill her," she says, "she's my friend."

"Where's Brek and Jorno then, Dott?"

"Brek's gone with that man to look for him. Ydka left us, and Jorno was shouting and crying and ran off after them. Brek couldn't run because of his shoulder."

"You're tied up," says Litten.

"She is," says Hekkl "She killed Chief Othbutter's brother."

"Who?" says Litten.

"She killed lots of men, I saw her," says Dottke. "They were whiteboys and they killed my ma and da so she killed them back."

"I'm hungry," says Aggie. Cherry bids Hekkl go get some of Leb's stores to feed the children. The three duts come over then, each one putting their arms around my neck, Aggie finding her way onto my knees to sit against me. I look up at Cherry, hoping somehow to tip the tears back into my eyes. Mosa would sit on my lap and I'd pick pieces of cheese off a wheel to drop into his mouth or I'd hold the jar while he dipped his fingers into our lingonberry jam and push them at my mouth to try and feed me back, catching my gums and lips with his fingernails, which Aude always promised to cut and never did.

Leyden comes back a while later. "The two boys are in

the boat; Jorno won't come in. I'll get a sheet for us and I'll stay with him rest of the night. We leave first light."

I'm untied from the chair and tied instead to one of the stone posts that hold up the roof, even given a mat so I can better sleep. I sleep like the dead and grateful for it.

The following morning Cherry comes in the boat with us, Leyden takes their horses and follows along the bank, Hekkl seeing us off. Soon enough, when she takes off the ropes binding me, the children realise the two vanners have come to help me escape and they're pleased. It gives me a chance to sit with Jorno. He won't look at us, or he shouts at us, but he doesn't say anything when I sit next to him or fuss when I chance smoothing the hair back on his head. The only way of getting him to rest is lying to him about seeing his ma again.

Cherry looks at my rib, there's a bruise there and I'm having trouble breathing so I take a pipe with her, which helps a bit. She puts some more of her mix on my knees and legs where Westal must've kicked me as I was out cold after our scrap. Honestly, I'm bruised all over and cheek's swollen again from the whack I took. Lucky there's hardly any teeth in that side of my mouth anyway, but at least my attempts to talk keep Dottke and Aggie laughing. Mercifully it stays dry, just an icy breeze as we pass through trees or steep hills. We pass some boats and barges coming from the south, only a few, and it's for appearances and what gossip they'd otherwise pass to Leb that Leyden and Cherry come this far. As it gets dark we bank the boat and Leyden gets a fire going. Once the children are sleeping around it we go to the riverbank for a smoke. I need some bacca to give me some sleep. I can hardly move for the kicking I took. Cherry put some ointment on my eye that got blackened, easing it.

"Thornsen'll be pleased to know yer not dead," says Leyden. "We all are."

"I remember you come to see me when I got back from my clan up at Keppel-Kaise, when they buried my da," says Cherry. "Thought I was in trouble when you walked into the Truin shed asking after me as we were prepping the van into the Moors."

"I sent your ma something, I think. I don't remember so much."

"You came up to Truin just to see me. I'll never forget what you did."

"Cherry, you vanners risk your lives for a tally. I know, I been one. Least a master can do is recognise that it matters. Leyden, your brother back working now?"

"Course. You had Thad ride out to Linsback. He mended his arm fierce quick. He even stopped to help with the harvest or we'd have lost much of it."

"He said your sister's kiss was payment enough. I'm glad he's well."

"Now you should get away, Master Amondsen, we can take the duts downriver. Thornsen will be delighted to know you're alive, but you can't really come back," says Leyden.

"I know, he's right. But do this for me: take these instructions to Thornsen. Tell him and Tarrigsen I'm sorry, sorry for Aude and Mosa, sorry even for Crogan and all the others. Tell him to pull everyone out of Faldon Ridge outpost if Othbutter isn't putting at least a few hundred men there or at Elder Hill; I won't have our families or any more people still in my employ dying for me. Get them back to Tapper's Way. If Othbutter don't defend the Braeg river and get those Crutter and Warrens dogs to put up some men, then Hillfast belongs to Khiese."

"Can't be, Master, he can't have that many, this Khiese."

"I been months up in the mountains over winter, left for dead by him, and all the clans in the Circle are his. He's no cave worm, Khiese; he wins hearts as well as hands and he's building an army can't be bought off him. You have to get back to Thornsen and Othbutter with this as fast as you can or many more'll die than what these poor duts have seen this last few days. Cherry, get our birds at Ablitch Fort going up to Faldon Ridge and over to deliver the message to Hillfast. Leyden, you'll come with me to the port and get yourself on a boat, you'll make sure the message gets there if the birds don't. You'll take this with you and all." I give him the bag with the shirt in. "Tell Thornsen to put it in the house. Tell him I wanted something of us to get home."

"I will, Master. But I'm concerned that you'll be spotted if you don't lie low, because if the posters and criers are out, that scar on your lips is as easy to describe as to see."

"First and last time I kissed an axe. Look, I won't leave these duts, not now. I'll take my chances. I can't do much for them after getting them to port. I got no way to feed them and I'll be arrested the moment someone figures who I am. I have to hope I can find them alms before that, then I don't give a fuck what happens to me. Tell Thornsen the company belongs to him, he's earned it a thousand times over, what he's done for me these past few years."

"Don't do this, Master, please. What could have happened since you left that . . .?" but Cherry stopped Leyden from continuing.

"I went too fucking far is what happened, Leyden. I didn't think Khiese was much more than a thug that could be sorted out. But . . . but no, it wasn't that was it; it was me thinking that I just decide something has to be how I want it and it'll happen. I had a dream and saw it becoming real and I wouldn't let it go no matter what. Now everyone's dead, and I was happy to die and all but my heart kept beating, and when it stopped the fucking Oskoro made it start again."

They was quiet for a bit, sorting this out in their heads.

"So why does your heart keep beating?" says Cherry. "Must be some reason you can't figure just yet, Master Amondsen, something it's not telling you." She smiled and put her arm around me.

"Might be. But I'm going to find somewhere quiet, if I can escape, so I can let those heartbeats just get to the end. I've done enough harm."

Chapter 6

Then

"Wake up, my love." Aude kissed my ear. He was curled in behind me. I opened my eyes. Mosa was gone.

"Where is he?"

"He's safe."

I found his hand with mine and pulled his arm about me. The cussing and coughing about us told me the camp was rising, Eirin clapping her crew up as usual for their drills.

"I should do my Forms," I said.

"Or you can lie here with me a bit longer," he said.

"Wouldn't that be nice."

"Maybe once we reach your clan we can get a few days' rest." He rolled the furs back off himself. "I'll help set the wagons, save us some time setting off."

"I'd love that. I want Thad running the Forms with me, and I don't trust anyone else to do it. I want the others to see that we're doing it. I'm not having Sanger or Yalle asking questions of me any more."

"Mosa'll want to join in when he sees you."

"I know, should wear him out a bit anyway. We've got a

long day and I doubt we'll find much in the way of trails for the wagons once we're out in the plain."

"How far to the Almet?"

"We'll get there the day after, Offering Stone is this side of it, thank Sillindar."

"Been there before?"

"Twice, mostly my brother Thruun went there with my da. Auksens was the last clan to have families go there as far as I know," I said.

"What for? Well, to make an offering, I suppose, but you know."

"Didn't make any sort of difference I could see. You'd meet travellers there, pilgrims of a sort, looking for healing or to see the Oskoro. Once a king came, before I was born, from Handar, over the Sar. Most of all you'd see drudhas because the Oskoro do things with plant you can't believe, knit it into themselves, their bodies, heads. Our clan fathers taught us from the old scrolls how the Oskoro walked with magists, even Sillindar and Halfussen, and to me it seemed like something more than worth the little effort we made, on the chance that our own pilgrimage might be met by a magist."

"You think we'll see a magist tomorrow?"

"Like fuck. But, this gift of mine, I know how dearly they seek it."

"What is it?"

I unclasped my hand from his, which predictably strayed to my bab, and I lifted from out of my shirt a thick leather necklace with a waxed pouch the size of a thumb, which had been stitched shut.

"It's in here."

"Doesn't look like a fortune."

"For what I must ask of them, no lesser gift than this would do."

"Keep your secrets then, Master Amondsen. I have what I want here."

"You do, but you can't keep it." With that I threw back the furs and he cussed at me, for it was a bitter dawn, night fleeing west.

"Get us the inventory and we'll have a few of those belets Skallern put aside for us last night; we can save the fish for later." I stood up and reached a hand out for him. Mosa come over then.

"Hey, bluebell. I'm going to do some Forms with Thad. You want to join us, build up your strength?"

"Please!"

Thad was waiting, cracking his bones and rolling his joints before smiling as I walked up to him. He kept his shape good, and he went through our first sets, his eyes shut, cutting no corners, unsparing of his muscle and bones.

I was stiff and couldn't move properly, or else was trembling through them as we went through the drill. Can't say my Forms would have impressed the others much even if they was more advanced than what Eirin's crew was doing. We was sweating and heaving by the end of them, and we laughed about how old we felt. Paid for it later in the day mind, whole body ached from the drill.

The day kept dry and it warmed up as well, perfect for seeing the plain as I'd described to Mosa. We had crested a slope of crumbling stones and grass flushing with late spring. It had been a few days since we left Seikkerson land. Everyone stopped for a smoke at the top of the slope, for it was a wonderful sight. The grasses spread out like an ocean before us, a fierce wind curling over them. Thad put a bit of luta in and found some trails might make the going a bit easier for wheels and we pushed on, Jinsy sending our scouts out ahead and each side a league or so off.

We got to late afternoon when we heard one of our own horns, to the east. I rode out with Eirin and Sanger and a couple of Jinsy's bowmen. The scout was circling four people shouting at him, one waving a knife.

"Leave us! Get away!"

This was a boy of about twenty years, girl cowering behind him. There was a younger boy there, no more than twelve or fifteen years, and he had his arm around an older woman, must have been his mother to judge by their faces. She was whimpering and he was trying to shush her, not looking at us surrounding them.

"Who are you?" I said.

"Don't matter. What's it matter when you're all dead? We're dead already and they're coming. You're going to be dead you don't turn back."

"Whiteboys."

"Course it is." He pointed to the two behind them. "They stole our horses and our food and killed her keep, his da. They were making fun of us. They could kill us when they wanted. They'll get you and all with your wagons."

"Go scout another league, I don't see anything," said Eirin to our outrider.

The boy with the knife started to walk on, pulling the girl behind him.

"What's the matter with you," I said. "We can feed you, let us help. The woman there's wounded." The mother had a shirt fashioned as a sling holding her arm to her.

"She fell off her horse. They took our horses and watched us run. There's horns tonight. Screaming horns. They don't let us sleep."

I got down off my own horse. He held the knife up. The girl with him put her hands over her face, trembling like she had the betony shakes. There was a black patch on the side of her head, must have been a scab, her ear black with what must have bled out of it.

"I'm Teyr, Teyr Amondsen. Where's your theit, your clan?" I had to stand in his way. "We're not here to hurt you. We come from Hillfast, from Othbutter himself." This didn't get an answer.

The older woman was keening now, crying proper. I could see blood and scratches on all of them, woollens torn, all consistent with running through briar, burrs, mud and buffalo dung all over their leggings and tunics.

"Eirin, put her on your horse and lead her to the van. Let the boy have the reins if he needs them. You two, come on, let's walk you to our van. You need to drink. We've got a bit of ale somewhere, and some water, cheese and bisks as well."

I was looking at the girl as I said these things, and she looked up at me for the first time. They was dazed. The boy held the knife out unsteadily in front of him. Even Mosa could have knocked it aside, so I did, and as I did the boy fell to his knees, head bowed, leaving his sister stood there staring at me with no look speaking of anything at all. It felt like it didn't matter to her what come next, except that she could sleep somewhere, for she wavered on her feet without him to hold her.

"They're about dead," said Eirin. "We can't bring them with us. We have enough trouble and looks like we'll have a posse of whiteboys dropping into camp tomorrow if this lad's right."

It was only then I noticed that the boy was scratching his arm. Same arm as the other one's ma. They needed a drudha.

I pulled him up and got my arm around him, while Sanger did the same for her. He was sour with the sweat of days, smelled of his own shit, kept looking about for the girl, who did the same for him. We walked them back to camp, the older woman wailing all the while, calling out "Rebs", which must have been her keep's name.

Our outriders come back an hour later saying there was nobody else they could see. By then we'd got their names: Dyl and Eirl was brother and sister, while Yelsie and Kuri was mother and son. Turned out the arms they'd been scratching had been branded, not a few days before from the looks of the wounds, and it was the same symbol as on the Khiese banner we saw at Crimore. We'd set up camp earlier than we'd planned, but the van was unsettled and being out on the plains give us an advantage against ambush.

"Are you from the Liskersen theit?" I asked when they'd had some water and rinds. Steyning and Thad could not get near the older woman, who wailed when they tried, though the others give in easy enough.

Dyl give a brief nod. "We have to go now," he said. He'd given his sister most of his rinds. "There's something wrong with her head, like she don't recognise me since she got hit with a club."

"You should stay with us," said Sanger, whose voice was almost as calming as kannab. He always made what he said sound like it was the only and right thing to do.

"You going back to Hillfast?" said Dyl.

Sanger looked at me.

"Sorry, Dyl. No, we're going north to the Almet."

"What for? If the whiteboys don't hunt you down those fucking treeheads will. They took Brukken's boy not three months ago. Five summers he was."

"They don't take duts, that's not right, Dyl," I said.

"How would you know, coming from Hillfast."

"Shouldn't have stopped putting out the blueheart, should

we," said Kuri. "It isn't just a rhyme. My da said, 'A tenth of blue and a tenth of grey or the Almet king sings a child away.'

"You're trying to civilise this lot, Amondsen?" said Yalle, who was stood behind Steyning while she worked on Eirl's head.

"You should know better, Yalle," I said.

"And so should you, leaving gifts for monsters in dutsy tales."

"Shush, Yalle, they might be listening," said Steyning, looking about her in mock fear.

"You won't come out of the Almet if you go in there," said Dyl. "No better than taking our chances west across the plain, so we'll be going. Maybe the whiteboys'll come for you instead." Dyl stood. As he did, Kuri did too, at which both Yelsie and Eirl got up almost like puppets.

The horns sounded then, the high shriek carrying from far off. It was dark in the east as night took over. Kuri started crying and his ma held him, shaking. Eirl put her hands to her ears and began mumbling. She kicked at Dyl to move.

"Leave at first light, the plain's treacherous at night, specially as ground's softening," I said.

"I'm not waiting for them. I hope you fare better, you and these riches about you. You're all a welcome sight but you're mad as a pack of Frenzies. Come on, Eirl."

I wanted to stop them, but Yalle and Sanger was shaking their heads at me. Thad was looking for my word – he'd stood back with Steyning, the latter still mashing some roots with a pestle in a bowl.

"Sillindar watch you," said Kuri. He put a spare cloak that had belonged to one of our dead on his ma's shoulders and they followed after.

"Head for the Crith, Faldon Ridge outpost. Tell Omar I sent you for alms."

"We're grateful," said Dyl, who took his sister's hand and kissed her cheek, a touch that she seemed to welcome as she was peacefully led away.

"Nothing right with any of them," said Yalle.

"Something to ease their nerves and we might have got them to come with us," said Thad.

"For fuck's sake, Thad," said Eirin, "we got enough to feed. I actually agree with Yalle, there's going to be refugees all over before we're done and we only got what's here."

"Teyr, they're practically Auksen," said Thad.

I was going to correct him on their clan affiliation but in doing so I'd not be giving a good reason for letting them go, for they were going to die. Eirin was right: the Circle was worse than I could have thought. It wasn't politics and treaties any more, it was Othbutter losing control over the south of Hillfast to a warlord.

"Eirin's right, Thad. Many more people hereabouts are under the heel of this Khiese. Our duty is to the greater number, to get Khiese to a Walk or otherwise stop him if we can."

"If we can stop those horns I'll be happy," said Aude, who'd joined us after seeing them leave.

"Double watch, Eirin," said Sanger, "if whiteboys are hunting."

"I'll see to it, Master Amondsen." She resented being ordered, but it was wisdom and she probably already knew what to do.

I left the group to go back to Chalky's wagon, where Mosa would sleep tonight with the girls.

"Hard to see them go, I'll bet," said Aude, who walked with me.

"I need a pipe," I said. He stood behind me and put his hands on my shoulders, working out the knots while I packed the bowl and put the jumpcrick's legbones to it to get it lit.

174

"Course it was hard. On the one hand Thad was right, but on the other we'd have been fighting them for days trying to get that boy's sister right, and she wasn't coming right, I seen that look before. That other boy's ma, she was no more than a dut. Kannab gets someone so far, but all the while I got this van to run. Eirin and Yalle was right. My first duty is to us. And to you and Mosa most of all."

"I know."

"I know you know. You was just getting me to say it, weren't you, knowing I needed to get it off my chest."

He come in and put his arms about my belly, cutching in close.

"I think you know me a bit too well," he said. "We do need you more than they did. The magists watch them."

"Or they don't," I said, finishing the well-worn saying.

"You on watch?"

"No, Aude, and I need to sleep; tomorrow'll be a hard day." I turned about and put the pipe in his mouth. He coughed a bit but left it there. He looked odd with a pipe, not being one for the bacca, but he did his impression of Tarrigsen gesturing with the bit and how he stood with his hand on his hip as he took his puffs, like the old man himself was here.

We got fuck-all sleep that night with the horns blowing, screeching and keening through the night, laughter and hollering on the wind. I got a lot of moaning off the crew as I got up with the birds, but I got the whole camp up and ready to move straight off. I wanted to make the most of the bit of trail we had and send one of Eirin's on with luta to see a path for us and the wagons.

Once we saw the trees we come to the edge of the Almet without stopping, thinking we should just push on and get

there, not least because the horns was getting [...]
they stopped suddenly just short of us arriv[...]
The forest itself was vast, mighty ash trees [...]
in the rest of Hillfast. Sounds from in it wa[...]
was asleep but dreaming of trouble.

I hadn't been here in a long time. I remembered being in
the van with my da after we'd made our offering, when I
was a girl of nine summers. We thought we'd get to Elder
Hill, trading for salt and oil, before the Frenzy, when the
wolves would go wild on the mushroom spores and amony
so they could bring down more buffalo, and anything else
living. That year the Frenzy come early, and our lives was
saved by the Oskoro.

The Offering Stone was easy to see, being at the edge of
the forest and standing as it does in the midst of countless
years of offerings strewn a league about. The van pulled up
short of this lake of gifts from all the walks of life in the
north of the world. Here was weather-worn statues, likenesses
and inscriptions lost to rain and wind, figures in the shapes
of trees and men now featureless, fallen over or else bearing
rotten fronds of banners and necklaces of wood, silver and
gold hanging in their hundreds. The skeletons of long-dead
horses was variously filled now with jars of plant, smashed
and whole, countless coins, keepsakes and carvings, rusted
armour and more than one chariot now riddled orange with
rust. The ground fairly cracked with bones. None of the great
gifts was new, for few now come to the Oskoro, or the Circle.

"Take nothing!" I shouted as Mosa and the children run
past me to explore the strange and curious things left here.

"Put something over your mouths and come away from
the trees!" come the shout from behind me, then Chalky's
keep Edma run past me waving cloths before her.

"You don't need masks here," I said.

"You sure?" said Thad. "I can taste something on the air."

Edma chased after them. I put my tongue out. A hint of butter. Ahead of us the Almet was still, seemed curiously warm now, a fullness to the air in the trees. Maybe we had woken it.

"We should camp away a bit," said Thad.

I was about to answer him, tell him that I thought breathing this air might not be a bad thing, for I was remembering the giant Oskoro that stooped to save me as a girl, when I heard the hooves of galloping horses from the plain behind us. Not yet settled, everybody was ready enough, and Eirin's crew took positions while Bela rounded up the children with Aude and Chalky, moving them behind the soldiers.

It was a crew of whiteboys, ten riders. At their head a man I recognised straight away, the one stood on the tower at the back of Thende's longhouse in Crimore. He held a hand up to slow them as they approached. As they did a few pointed at what they saw around us and rode in to our right where eight giant stones stood, five in a row with three over the top of them like doorways.

I walked out from our wagons towards them, Sanger, Yalle, Eirin and Skallern with me. We had spears and Jinsy's men making a show of their bows.

The whiteboy was as big as he looked on the battlement as he got down from his horse, still bare-chested, with black circles daubed into the white mixture over his skin, radiating out from his lean gut across his chest. Those around him chattered in their form of Abra, which I couldn't follow very well. They watched him as dogs watch a master, eyes only for him and his every move. He stood before his horse, unarmed but for drudha belts. He kept his eyes on me.

"Amondsen. Jeife sends his love. Samma sends his thanks." He spoke Common well enough.

He was in his prime, mid-twenties I'd have said. He had a few scars on him, paid up, a credible drudha in his crew then. Behind him a woman stayed on her horse, white-painted but bare-chested too, a fine strong body like I had once. She looked about us as a queen might. The others had some armour, two even in chain shirts. They had got down and was going through the field of tributes, taking the coins, bickering, casting nervous glances back at him.

He whistled sharply at them, and it seemed to still all of them, including the woman. He snapped something in their Abra and the foragers worked quickly and in silence.

"You know my name, I don't know yours," I said.

He kept his eyes on Thad as he said it. "Gruma. Gruma Khiese. Brother of Samma."

"Gruma, Jeife made it clear enough he thought Crogan would not be met as an equal by your brother. I had hoped we could Walk, for Khiese talks of the Circle prospering and I too would have that."

"Swear oaths, then. We can put that drudha and your plant to work. I'm sure he knows some small recipe I do not."

"My oath's to Othbutter," said Eirin. Impatient to assert herself, her lack of fear, she saw a chance to put him in his place, I don't doubt.

"Brave words. You're wasted on Othbutter, a fat and useless leader holding Hillfast back. Hillfast could be great again, first among the citadels as it once was, and you at the heart of it."

"My archers await your word, Master Amondsen," said Eirin. I shook my head.

Gruma took a good few moments to look at the forest and the gifts about us. He was making it about him, which spoke badly of his wit in a talk such as this.

"You're here to leave them a gift," he said. "Means you can't hurt me here, believing that offal. You think they'll come running out o' the trees when you leave a bit o' shine or some dribble in a bag. Woman, what do you hope for? A Walk here?" He laughed at his joke.

"We got different beliefs on the Oskoro. We don't have different beliefs on the Circle and its people, my people included. I would have Hillfast and all this land busy with trade and the good that comes with it. Your brother would want the same."

He kept on looking behind me, at the earth and what was strewn on it, all so I did not have the respect of his eyes.

"You see some slaves of ours in the plain, last day or so?"

"No. You seen the size of the plain?"

A couple of them had an exchange then, doubt was clear in their look.

"We'll find them and they'll die. This was an opportunity to show your allegiance to Khiese. I knew you'd fail, but Samma has honour. He said that you should all turn about to Hillfast and give word to Othbutter of his brother Crogan, and the welcome he got. He said that if he should see you, now that you have received his warning, he will be savage. He keeps his word. You know he keeps his word."

Even then, despite that I didn't really believe he'd let the whole van walk free, I wanted to believe that there was a chance to turn back. I wasn't going till I saw my brother Thruun, who the Amondsens now was sworn to. Maybe behind it was a need for them to know that, me being this close, I would not turn my back on them.

His men looting the gifts filled the silence, laughing and bickering once more over treasures they found and wanted from each other. He had to shout at them again to keep silence, but at that point the paint they covered themselves in, the marks of eyes and skulls in charcoal, looked stupid, for they was no more than nokes.

He walked towards us then, fearless, and past the wagons up to the small stone column with a plain worn stone bowl on top where I'd place my offering. It was only noticeable for standing on a natural mound, though that only knee high. He looked off in the trees before clearing his throat and spitting into the bowl. He turned about to face us, held a cupped hand to his ear, then lifted his arms up into the air, inviting retribution.

"Well, Teyr Amondsen, no arrows, no spores, no death for me." He walked up to me then, closed in. Eirin and Yalle moved towards him but I held a hand up to stay them.

"Teyr!" called Aude, who feared for me. I stood chest height to Gruma. Couldn't see his colour for he was covered in the chalky mix, but there was nothing to pinch on him, a white gorilla that could have thrown me over a longhouse with one arm. I killed a few like him, but not old as I am, not without a brew to stop me from shivering that fraction that let him know he was making me uncomfortable, close to me so I would smell him, so I would do this, look at him, feel his power.

"You have your rope, I have mine," I said. "I would still parley, there is much here in this van that could sweeten a treaty."

He leaned forward. "The only thing Othbutter has that Samma wants is Hillfast. If I see you again, I'll take this van. Kill you down to the last little boy." He walked through me, forcing me back on my heels to stop myself falling over. I give Thad a word to stop still when I saw him grit his teeth and reach for a spore egg. Gruma didn't break his stride as he mounted his horse and whistled for his crew to be ready. After the last three of them had filled a sack and some pockets with coin and some jewellery they rode away. I took a deep breath. I'm sure he thought as I did that we could have stuck the other, don't think he believed I was scared enough of the Oskoro I wouldn't try. Odds weren't good enough. Fifty–fifty never is.

"Should have stuck him," said Skallern.

"Thank you, Skallern," I said. He shrugged and stood down his crew.

"Was it the Oskoro that delayed your order? We'd have shot the whiteboys all dead with a flick of your finger," said Eirin. Aude and Mosa come up and I held them a moment.

"Yes." I wanted to say more, to fill out the lie. "Let me leave them their gift."

"Can I do it, Ma?" said Mosa.

"Of course." I looked at Aude and he winked. The van relaxed as the riders left us, continued its preparations to leave.

"Do the trees thank you when you leave something?" said Mosa as we walked towards the Stone.

"No, my love. But I'm leaving it to say thank you to them – well, the Oskoro. You know they saved my life as a girl only a bit older than you."

"You saw one?"

"I did. A giant, his head covered in leaves and flowers which grew out of it, skin grey like a whale, and he had bright green eyes. I was travelling in a van like this and there was wolves had become Frenzies and chased us. I'd fallen over and I saw these giant wolves running at me, yellow teeth as long as knives. Just as one of them was about to crush me in his jaws, this giant, the chief of the Oskoro, threw a huge spear into its side so hard it flew past me. Then he picked me up and with a big club smashed the other wolf's head flat."

"Oh Ma! Is he here, will he come out of the trees?"

"I don't think so. I wish he would."

He had cradled me in his arms, which was hard and smooth as sanded wood. He smelled of malt and leather and he hardly seemed to breathe, his mouth still as though carved, like it had forgotten what it was for both as a way of showing feeling as much as talking. My da, with my uncle Kerrig and the others running the wagons, watched the other Oskoro as they killed the pack of wolves and then stood with heads bowed like statues taken root, moving only as we approached. All appeared unique, men and women that had become so with what they did to themselves with plant. Some seemed awful to look at, small buds of mushrooms growing from their faces, other plant knitted under and over skin. Yet I was convinced of a kindness in their eyes, a joy even. This Oskoro I thought was the chief kneeled to lower me to the ground, making clicking sounds somehow and then a guttural phrase that commanded the others back to the forest without a backward glance. Two of our van made to go as well, so deep and heavy was the command in our chests.

I led Mosa to the mound and the Offering Stone. I noticed a similar clicking then, sounds that might be of insects but too full, from a much bigger source. They stopped suddenly. Nobody else reacted or seemed to notice. Though I was only half a man higher here than with the crew behind me, I somehow felt quite alone, exposed to scrutiny.

I eased out the necklace and the flat pouch of leather hanging from it, stitched and waxed closed, three fingers or so in size. I picked away the stitching with my knife and squeezed out a plant seed the size of an apple pip but bright orange, like a flame. The wind died, the trees stilled as though holding their breath. It was sudden and it made me wonder if it was the wind at all that we'd felt. Everyone in the van stilled in that moment, the only sound being Sanger's sword leaving its scabbard, smooth and calm as a pebble in the moment before a thunderclap that never came. There was some more clicks, echoing now in the leaden stillness, but try as I might, looking to every branch and trunk, looking for a whisper of movement from the ferns and brush that filled the space between, nothing moved. I give the seed to Mosa, told him to hold it up high before he dropped it into the bowl, hoping perhaps to instigate an appearance of these mighty people.

"Teyr?" said Thad. I gestured him to stand with me, not taking my eyes from the Almet. He looked into the bowl and his eyes widened, a smile playing on his lips.

"Teyr, you kept a big old secret from me. I should be offended — no, I am offended — that you didn't share this little treasure. This was your gift from the great Khasgal all those years ago?"

"From the Ososi, brethren to these Oskoro, down in Khasgal's Landing. I made a vow that I would pass it on to the Oskoro here." I smiled then as he put his arm around my shoulder.

"A kingly gift, maybe priceless," he said.

"Was it worth lots of gold coins, Ma?"

"Yes, bluebell, but it is worth more than that to the Oskoro."

He squinted and strained his eyes then, desperate to see some sort of movement.

"Do you think they see us, Thad?" I said.

"I don't know. I hope so. But we still have to meet with them if you want to impress the chiefs, or now Khiese, to a Walk. Do we wait?"

I didn't know. Nobody knows. The last Oskoro I saw was at Khasgal's Landing, giving me and Khasgal our gifts. Khasgal was given a bow, a smooth grey wood that the Ososi, for that is what the Oskoro are called there, said was carved from the leg of one of his own kind, one who was "settling" as he called it. It give slightly to the touch, as though it knew it was being held, shy, I thought at the time, as strange as it sounds. Its power was unmatched, before or since. I believe it somehow knew its wielder, the draw needed matched the archer. I was given two seeds, one now with Tarry, an insurance against the possibility this expedition might fail or I might lose this seed. I had earned them defending the lives of the Ososi with Khasgal, and we saved the daughter of the Etza-ososi from ambush. I fell before her as a would-be killer swung the axe that would have split her in two, and its kiss give me this awful scar across my mouth. These orange seeds they called Afaru-Aka, or in Common, Flower of Fates, and I could have grown my own, had I not sworn I would gift them to the Oskoro. It was an ideal I stuck to despite how rich I could have become by growing the flowers myself. I would not forget that they had once saved my life.

"I kept my promise," I said out loud and I began crying, even though I tried to hold it in for I'd put off this moment all my life since then and I shouldn't have and Mosa wouldn't understand these tears. I felt proud of myself and all, in a life that held too little to be proud of, for seeing this through. I kept so few promises but this one, this one I made to Khasgal and the Ososi, who had wanted to know what it was I thought I was born to do. The only answer I had was one I'd cradled as I left my clan and had almost forgotten as the years wore on. I was stood at this Offering Stone because there was no fucking way I was dying a failure in the eyes of the Teyr Amondsen that thought she was born to change the world.

A breeze come out of the forest then, a caress. Snatches of memories was tugged up by it, my da and me arguing, I was a girl of twenty, Ruifsen holding me against a gunwale while I retched, the others jeering at him like he was moving on me. I breathed in deeper and more come to me: I'm arguing now with a captain, my old captain, Chellit, as he sent those poor duts to the Banquet of Rest. I'm punching his chest and spitting on him, Nazz has me by the throat.

"Teyr, what's wrong?" said Thad, and I come to, upset. "I . . . Something just . . . Did you have some memories come at you suddenly?"

"I did."

"Me too. I recalled you and that captain we had, first time we crewed together, when we . . ."

"Not me, I had no part in that."

Then it hit both of us that we knew we was talking about the same thing.

I turned to look back at my van, subdued, even while some went about checking horses and unpacking the sheets we'd lie under tonight.

"There's something on the air, maybe the Almet is a dangerous place to Walk," said Thad.

"I like it here. We'll stay overnight but in the morning we go south to Auksen lands, and my own family first. We don't have time to wait for the Oskoro. They know we're here."

"What about Gruma?"

"He couldn't attack us today, he won't risk it. We run our scouts out around us as we've done till now."

Most of us slept deeply. Some of the children talked of waking, seeing things out of the corners of their eyes. Chalky and Aude skirted the camp to find nothing.

The seed was gone by morning; young Jem and two of Skallern's boys meant to be on watch was asleep like the rest of us when the camp come to, but Eirin, like me, wasn't in the mood to punish them for it. It was the best sleep we'd had since we left Hillfast.

Straight south to Amondsen lands, in the Hardy Falls. The plains give way to the hills and the Hardy peaks, the Mothers mostly in cloud, further south in the range than we needed to go, for my family edged the plains. Brackie's Trail, where Thruun broke his toe as a boy, Lebbsen Fork, where Ma and Da stopped and found two bluehearts when we had ridden out for a day by Crinkell's brook. A left there to Amondell Pass, which leads into the Amondell itself. Seemed like each stream or statue or the long-abandoned theits held a memory I could share with Mosa and Aude. With summer about here, it all come alive, and though watchful as we were, we saw few but for herders or sniffers, who give us a wide berth and the mood lifted with the good going and foraging.

Amondell itself was a fort with heavy stone walls, though most of the huts and a few longhouses was out around the slopes, for there was quarries near though most were abandoned, littered with theits and smaller, exiles finding a living in the secluded vales among the hills around our bloodlands. The Amondsen Longhouse, the fort, was built in more prosperous times, when north and south of the Circle would meet, when the trade I now sought was strong, and Amondsen stone carvers was sought all over the Circle.

As a girl I could walk the length of our fort's walls and see in the blocks of stone the story of our rope, ancestors leading buffalo in a dance, the songs that tamed them long lost, the carving of Grishtid the Tree drawing the Amondsen recipe for a poison strong enough to drop a wolf in the Frenzy, so saving many of her sons. Like the other children I loved her other carving more, celebrating her sniffing mix, the envy of all the Auksen clans. Her giant nose was shaped as though sticking out of the stone itself, and I would put flowers in the nostrils whenever I could.

All of this I hoped to show Mosa and Aude, but my heart broke as we passed Cronnel's Hill and I saw Khiese's banner over the longhouse in the distance. I felt Aude's hand on my shoulder, for he led his horse just behind mine. "I'm sorry, Teyr."

I had no way of hiding my tears, for I was not prepared for how it hurt, how peaceful everything looked, no stain of war or battle, just as though Amondell had shrugged off all our pasts like a wet cloak, same as Crimore.

The mist was thickening as we drove the wagons through the surrounding trees and crops up the main trail to the gates of the fort, attracting out of their huts and houses my family.

I took the scrollcases from Othbutter out of their sack that was now mine with Crogan gone, and I waited for Eirin and Chalky to join me in riding up to the gate.

"They all look like you, Master, well, the men do," said Chalky, for the men razored their heads, leaving only their beards, while the women kept long hair at the back of the head, and this would be twisted and tied all ways as they fancied.

I smiled at him; he tried to lighten the mood for they all knew I was upset and still reckoning with the sight of those banners, my last and stupid and prideful hope gone before I even got to see my brother.

I looked over the stones of the walls as we approached. They was green with moss and dirt, grasses growing tall in front of them. There was carvings that had spikes driven through them so they could support lean-ups and small sheds for goats, hens and the like.

The two gate guards, seeing us, got themselves puffed up a bit and come out to meet us.

"What's your business?" said one.

"Don't you recognise her, yer cock, that's Teyr, chief's sister. Moving home, are you?"

"What do you think, Pavul?" I said, the man's name coming to me just then. "Dear Halfussen, look at you, you've somehow managed to grow up a bit."

I opened my arms for an embrace. It took him a moment, which was instructive, though he give me a good hug all the same.

"How's my brother?"

"Has a keep now, Lithessen woman, older than you, Skershe she's called. Seems quiet and all, but I reckon she does a lot of talking behind her teeth."

Then I heard movement from behind the walls, the deep *clack* of the bolts to Amondell House's door being pulled and the gate we was stood outside then also being opened. I never knew them to be shut before, not before nightfall anyway.

I was keen to see if he had children. Didn't think much of a Lithessen match though. I walked past Pavul and into the grand courtyard, cobbled, big and grand enough for many more wagons than we had. A lot of justice was done here way back up the rope, and hundreds would have been hanged here as well. The Auksens wasn't always chief clan in these lands.

Chalky and Eirin followed me in. Thruun was stood with Skershe and their boy, must have been four years or so. I saw she'd taken the razor, for the Lithessens did not shave their heads, and she was in weathered woollens and tunic, hands earthy from keeping their runs, I expect. He always did need looking after. The big steel chief's chain looked heavy on him, being small in his shoulders and arms, though his tunic filled out well enough at the front. Don't know whether it was because he'd always seem a boy to me, but he looked still no more than twenty, smooth round face, a feeble-looking beard dribbling from his chin.

"Sillindar watch you, Thruun."

"My sister, the second lady of Khasgal. You still call yourself Teyr Amondsen?"

I had taken a half a step towards him, but he stood still, and I felt foolish as he spat out his bitterness.

"Yes, brother. I do."

"You visit us with plenty of steel."

"We − I − have come to the Circle with a bold proposal, but I see one bolder still flies over our house."

"Our house?" He sniffed. He held a hand out behind him in a gesture. "This is my keep, Skershe."

She did step forward for an embrace and I was grateful.

"Welcome home, Teyr." She leaned back but kept her hands on my arms to have a good look at me. I knew she found me wanting, or interesting at least for I was strong in the arms and shoulders, while my head and my face must have looked to her as it did to me, like it had been dragged through scree.

"And this is our boy, Drun." He kept looking at me, then his da, maybe fearing he might be told to kiss me. He didn't look more than a few white twigs in a bag of wool, beech-blond curls, and over his tunic he wore a belt and scabbard obviously made for him to pretend he was a soldier. He sucked his thumb and stared at us without moving, but I felt myself wanting to kneel and talk to him.

"He's a fine-looking boy."

"He's such trouble, knocking his head and scratching his arms and rips in his clothes," said Skershe.

189

Hers was problems I loved to have.

"You been busy on the runs," I said to Skershe, for nobody said a thing for a moment. The banner flying over us all put a silence on us hard to shift.

"Can never have enough guira, or carrots for this one."

"Our boy Mosa would love to help, can't get him out of our runs."

I realised at that moment I hadn't told Thruun about him.

"I'm pleased for you, Teyr," he said. "Children change everything, don't they? But your friends you need to introduce, and you should all come in so we can talk more about it all." Skershe was about to speak when a voice from behind me put a big smile on my face.

"Teyr, my girl, let me look at you."

We all turned to see Kerrig, my uncle, Ma's brother. He walked with a stick now, his bandy legs more bowed than ever, and the years had sucked a good bit of fat away. There was some wisps of white hair left that he no longer razored and a beard white as long as I'd been alive, one my ma said I'd try and pull off altogether when I was a dut on his knee.

He stood before me, looking down his bruised potato of a nose, then turned to Eirin and the others.

"She gets more beautiful each time I see her." His eyes was full up and he set me off crying, the old bastard. He pulled me to him, smelled still of the seashore, the whale oil he'd make candles from, a smell I loved all my life because of him. "I missed you, Teyr," he said, muffled by my cloak. "I spoke to old Sillindar a few times asking if he'd let you know to come home, see your ma when she was ill."

"Come on now, Uncle," said Thruun. "She wasn't here when ma died, and you've seen her since then."

He held me a bit longer, then stepped back, wiped his

eyes and looked us over. "Well, you bring a van and it's led by this fierce young beauty, is it?"

"That's Eirin, Unc, Othbutter's captain. This is Chalky Knossen, a merchant who's sharing in this expedition."

"Uncle, please, let's get them inside, they've been on the trail."

"Excuse me, Chief Amondsen," said Eirin, "could we bring the wagons into the yard here for the night?"

"You're under our watch," said Kerrig, which he had no right to say as it was Thruun's place to say that we was under their shelter. He give Thruun a look then, and it seemed like he offered the watch because Thruun might not.

"Will it put you in any difficulty with Khiese?" I said, saving a bit of face for him though fuck knows why.

"We've had word from Gruma's crew, saw you up at the Almet. We have to refuse you shelter. Might be I'll be flogged or worse for Kerrig's oath. Pavul, fetch wood and coal. Captain, take Moirs there and he'll find somewhere for your horses."

Thruun turned and went inside the longhouse without another word. Skershe picked up Drun and followed him in.

Chalky put a hand on my shoulder as he walked past me.

"Don't beat yourself up, Master," he said. "We take what we're given and leave when we can."

"He won't be flogged for it though; my uncle will."

Night settled in and rain was coming down good across Amonvale. In the longhouse there was a sweaty fog of smoke, fat and kannab that we'd shredded a block of by way of a gift to my family. There was no tower in our longhouse like there was the Seikkersons. The chief has his own firepit up some steps from the communal pit, and there was only two other rooms, one for his living and one a jail. We was more cautious now, Yalle and Bela outside with the wagons and a couple of Skallern's men, while Sanger said he'd hide out in the Amondell vale with a few of Jinsy's bowmen.

Thruun had put out mutton, eggs and cheese, with a good oily soup made with duck.

I sat at his pit with Aude, Thad, Kerrig and Eirin. We spoke haltingly of weather, harvest. Kerrig did his best.

"Had a chat with your keep, Teyr, while we brushed down the horses. Told him all about you growing up. Always getting your brother in trouble."

"True enough," said Thruun. "Ma was always running after her because she'd be out the gate and in the fields or over the pass."

"I was never one for the pots, pans and scrubbing."

"You're right there," said Aude. "I never realised just how much mischief you were when I met you."

I elbowed Kerrig and held his hand while he dipped bread in his soup before him. It was quiet then about our pit, strained. I had little of the small conversation in me that night and all day we had danced around what was the real bother while I helped Skershe and the other women with the veg and the baking. Thruun made that he was busy and could not see me. I was upset, and it built up with each mouthful of food until it boiled over.

"What happened, Brother," I said. "Why is that fucking banner over our home?"

"Our home? Saying it's ours don't make it true."

"I know, I left. There's men that's left and come back after years and still called it such. The Seikkersons give their banners up too, Khiese took Crimore by showing a line of their tribute clans' boys, threatened to cut all their throats. What did he threaten you with?"

"My own boy and all our boys. They went into our theits after dark, put the dogs and the few guards out with powders,

192

probably landed them with slings, then they're helpless, it's burn and kill everyone if they don't give up our rope. Those that give them up without a fuss, he spared, those that tried to fight him suffered. He'd finish the Amondsen rope, he said, had finished twenty such ropes since he found his crew. He had a hundred or so with him, more than we could defend against."

"Was it?" said Kerrig.

A look passed between them, and Unc's hand, which I held, tensed.

"We got fifty if we're lucky, Uncle Terrig. And he caught us quiet, had our folk out of the houses past the bailey. I couldn't see them killed."

"Neither could Thende. He's dead now," I said.

"And his people live?"

"They do, as Khieses."

"Then they live, and he died well, for their rope is not cut."

"It is fucking cut, because Jeife has no heir and Khiese will put the chief's hoop on the beard of one of his own the moment Jeife steps out of line. He has captains he will have promised spoils to."

I looked over at Aude and Thad. They could say nothing. Thruun put down his bowl slowly.

"What are you here for, Teyr? I heard Crogan himself got killed at Crimore, and you've got a crew of his best soldiers following you about the Circle along with sacks of plant and salt and weapons, the last of which we sorely need and the want of which might have helped us when Khiese came. You could've brought all this years ago and made a peace."

"I'm building a road. I was going to build a road. From Hillfast to Stockson at least, bring trade to the Circle, twenty leagues a day not five or six. Such trade, the levies, these things could enrich everyone and the Amondsen clan well placed on the edge of the plains."

A smirk come over his face then.

"Hillfast to Stockson!" He said it loud, and it silenced the house, cutting over the laughter and talk at all the tables. "You should all know that our sister, Teyr, thinks to build a road, a proper road, from Hillfast to Stockson. Five hundred leagues of road by a rider's reckoning. Over hills, plains, bogs, mountains." One or two cheered then, misreading the moment. Mosa joined them but was shushed by Edma, Chalky's keep.

"You must be a very rich woman, Teyr. Is she, Aude? Is she rich enough?"

"No, Chief, she brings Chalky to share that burden, and others the cost of the bridges and the outposts she's built near Elder Hill—"

"She builds outposts, my sister, outposts in the west, while winters take our young for want of plant and stores. Bethut, sat there, a hard-working jacker these last fifteen years, you remember Bethut, Sister? You used to help his na sniff for flag root across Cratt's Bluff and you helped him with his letters so his old da wouldn't cuff him about so much. They lost their second this last winter, a boy of three. What might a few silvers worth of your coin have bought us, I wonder."

"Thruun, please, don't."

"No, Teyr, I was mad enough you come back eight years ago and took so little interest in Amondell without our ma, and badmouthing our da while about it, but I did not speak out because he would not raise a word to you for Ma's sake. Well I'm saying it now, now you're here to bring us a road, a fucking road! A road full of beggars and disease, thieves and foreigners stealing an acre of common here and there, killing some boar or sniffing and taking from us what's ours, despoiling the bloodlands our fathers died for. It'll be of more use to bandits than our trails that have done us since before even our greddas and gretnas were babes. I expect Crimore told you the same. They saw you and Othbutter, that clan bleeding us for their silks, and rightly doubted you."

"Khiese is bleeding you out, you have to see that, Thruun, painting your boys white and sending them off to die. His tithes are harsh, his laws worse. He's a savage, a warlord," I said.

"He's Circle born and Circle bred. He asks, he does not take. For the matter of his banner we have peace here, we eat, and you share it, Sister, you and your Hillfast worthies. If you're here to ask permission to build a road, you do not have it. You are not one of this clan, you don't raise its sons or work its land, you've not healed us or fought with us."

Aude was looking into his mug, but he was shaking his head. He stood then, glared at my brother.

"I would be proud of a sister such as Teyr, were I you. You mock this ambition yet many leagues have been covered with cords and bridges, outposts that give shelter to all. From her hard-earned wealth and wisdom she builds what only great kings dare to do, more than Othbutter has ever done. This plant, these weapons you sorely need, they might arrive with you the year round if the wagons of merchants were not so likely to break or be robbed by clans who have forgotten to reckon in their common interest."

He unclenched his fists, looked at me before looking down, concerned he'd spoken out of turn. A few of my van banged their cups and I shivered with love for him. My brother was at a loss then, aware that he would be speaking ill of guests.

"We'll leave tomorrow, Chief," I said. "We have abused

your watch, I have abused your watch, and I'm sorry, sorry to all of you." I stood and Aude took his cue and joined me. Kerrig give me a wink, I think to tell me that I'd done the right thing in saying I was sorry. We took Mosa out with us and went to the hay barn, where we was put up with most of Eirin's men. Mosa was sleepy and we soon got him off, the hushed voices of the soldiers below our loft in their cups and pipes helping him settle under the furs.

"I'm sorry I spoke out, love," said Aude.

"Don't be. You don't know what it means to me, the way you've stood with me and how you stood up for me in there. I'm just sorry it's all fucked. My road won't get past Elder Hill, will it, not while Khiese lives."

"They won't be helped, bluebell. And you've kept your promise to the Oskoro, all these years later. You did your best."

And there it was, a dark flash in my mind, a thought, its lingering trail mocking my words. Had I yet done enough? It fed on itself in the blink of an eye. Kill Khiese. Kill him for everyone's sake.

"Teyr?"

"What."

"You did your best."

"I did."

He pushed a sigh through his nose before putting his hand on my shoulder, his fingers squeezing the muscle there. It both softened and saddened me, for how he coped with his own sadness sometimes was to kiss or hold me, to make something loving of it, to defy it and shed his hurt or anger with me. I put my hand on his shoulder as we lay there, and he was crying silently, his body twitching while he held his breath against it.

"Aude, my keep, what is it?"

He moved so as not to disturb Mosa, wiped his eyes and

nose as, nearby, the longhouse's doors opened for the clan and those of my van still in there to leave, their voices and some shared songs carrying across the settlement.

"I'm sorry, Teyr. I just, well . . . I know you'd come with me at daybreak, we'd roll out and back through the Sedgeway, back to Hillfast and our home I confess I miss. You might run roads and outposts all over the north and northeast, Kreigh Moors, Larchlands, but it won't be enough for you."

"It will be, my love, it will be."

"It won't, bluebell, because it's not about a road, but a road across the Circle. A road for your people. I think I knew it deep down, these years it's been in the planning. You've needed to prove something to them, to your da maybe."

I wasn't sure I believed it even as I said it. What he said threw me off balance, wasn't fair and was fair. "It's not about my da, he's dead."

"I know. Does that matter?"

"Maybe I will come home, get richer, come back with more soldiers perhaps, now I know this threat. Khiese commands a few hundred at best, it would be . . ." These was the wrong words, weighing up the threat here and now. He had the truth of me and always, always, the truth from me, whether given or taken. Our silence dribbled on while the barn filled up with the rest of us taking shelter there, trading insults and jokes, helping each other with whatever plant they needed for the wounds and other suffering that come with paying the colour.

"Speak to me, Teyr."

Love is speaking the truth because it hurts, and it is hiding it to avoid hurt, and choosing right never comes easy or often.

"We'll meet early, the whole van, decide what's next."

He withdrew his hand after squeezing my shoulder, bunched his riding cloak under his head a bit more and went still. Mosa stirred then, lying in between us. I picked some snapped ends of straw from his hair, sleep as far away from my eyes as Aoig was. I rolled out from under our furs and shivered as I stood up, the night air bitter and clear. Outside, the settle was quiet, faint talking here and there. Further off, west in the trees, a wolf called out. A figure approached. It was Thruun, swamped in our da's ermine.

"Couldn't sleep either?" he said.

"No."

"Let's go to the river then."

A man named Sagga guarded the gate, I remembered him as a bab, so a bit surprised he was on lookout, but by Thruun's account he was a quiet one, preferring the nights since the girl he was cricky on decided on another.

Left out of the gate was a few of the fields long ago cleared from the forest, two hundred yards to the river.

"We could have used the cave tunnels," I joked, which made him laugh.

"Not in these clothes."

"I'm sorry for earlier. Aude is too. It's been a long time since I needed to account for the Circle's customs, or anyone's other than my own."

"I see."

"Oi." I nudged him. "You spoke well before your people. You keep Amondell in good order. The clan seem settled."

"Perhaps that's because there are no bodies nailed to our bailey's walls, as I heard was the case in Crimore. I do what my father did. I hear their disputes, I try to remember what he told me: 'Question! Question! Question!'" The last was an impression of him, a good one.

"Oh Halfussen yes. 'And when you think you have run out of questions, repeat them all and listen for any change in their answer!'"

"It has helped, I have to say."

"You're looking more like him," I said.

"I'm fatter, you mean. Skershe cooks well, and my hands were always made for a quill, never a spade or spear."

We was grateful for a clear night, the moon near full, the land all edged in a sharp, pale white, the water of the river shining.

"Good to see you with your boy Mosa. He's been raised well."

"Thank his da for that. You have a fine keep in Skershe, she thinks the lands of you. Both Ma and Da would have loved to have seen them, Mosa and Drun. Ma, well, whatever else I might have won, I lost ever having her hold my son, though Halfussen knows I'm not looking for pity. Anyway, have you made some alliance with the Lithessens, to have married Skershe, or did you inherit our da's hips?"

"Aaah no, sadly not. The Lithessens came the spring after you last left, and Skershe with them. I could see that her da thought she'd not wed as her sister had to old Auksen's nephew, for she was near to thirty years, but she seemed to see enough in me, and I think her beautiful and much cleverer than I with our scrolls."

"You're too modest, Brother. You ran rings around us all with your letters as a boy."

The river ran with purpose, this close to the Mothers. We stood at its edge, both remembering I'm sure the years we played here.

"Have you told Drun about the girl who lives in the river?"

Thruun laughed. "Of course. I told him she'd take his innocence and weave it into her hair of glass and leave him a man in his fourteenth year. He's been looking for her ever since."

"Same as me then."

"Yes, you swore she'd touched you while you waded that one day we found the wolf's skull, remember?"

"I do." It was the yellow of cheese, picked clean to a shine, half the jaw missing, perhaps the killing blow. We balanced it on our heads and chased Beikker's son about.

"Will you go home, Teyr? I would hate for Khiese to find you, not while you've a chance to escape. I might have spoken out against you earlier and think differently to you about what you do or don't owe us, but by our blood I don't want you dead. We will survive, our rope will survive, I'm sure of it. Gruma lacks wit and Khiese lacks an heir, though word is he has tried."

"What more do you know of them? I've learned almost nothing."

"What I learned I learned from Gruma. He finds himself here often and finds in me, which my belly I'll confess proves, a man who can drain cups almost as well as him and far better than his crew. In his cups he talks a lot. He told me of their da Finn, the Elder Khiedsen, who somehow got five sons out of some poor woman he eventually beat to death because he thought she was fucking his guards. He then made keep another woman, who Gruma and Samma alone called their mother, but she wasn't able to give Finn any more children. She raised them all nevertheless through the beatings she also got: Finnson, who was his eldest, Jerrik, Olof, Samma and Gruma, his youngest. They were young boys when she, Cwighan I think her name was, started to take care of them. It was from her they learned their da had killed their ma. Samma was a runt then, Gruma growing big on his gruet as you saw at the Almet. With older brothers finding him easy to take out their own pain on, Samma realised he had to become strong or be beaten all his life. Of course, he wasn't going to best them with muscle, and Cwighan knew her letters, for Khiedsen trusted nobody else with his scrolls. So she taught Samma, and so he came to be useful to her and to his da. But this only got him beaten more by his brothers, who could see a clear threat to their own prospects for weaving glory into the Khiedsen rope. The only brother on his side was Gruma, and I think their love was bonded by their love for Cwighan and hers for them.

"As sons of Finn they were all forced to learn their Forms, even Samma, but small as he was, the tutors could ask for no more dedication. He ran, he lifted stones, broke stones, he endured. Gruma grew big as you see him, a terror in the tourneys, but Samma grew hard and cold after they found Cwighan dead. Gruma said she was always nursing some hurt, but they found blood on her bed furs and she was cut and bruised from fists. Samma was eighteen now and his ability to shoot and use a spear and sword could not be questioned. His elder brothers, threatened both by the praise he and Gruma received from their tutors but especially the praise Samma got for keeping the scrolls and learning contracts, tried to take their revenge in the Khiedsen tourney after his eighteenth. He beat them and humiliated them, took his time over it, which the clan loved but his father despised. His father, for all his praise, did not look past his eldest son as his heir, as is our way, so he expelled Samma, and Gruma followed him. They knew they fled for their lives, for their brothers were quick to lead some crews after them. They escaped and over time put together their own crew of bandits to terrorise the Khiedsens. The rest brings us here."

It give me a lot to think about. I knew now a bit more about Samma's way, his painting his whiteboys and his use of the horns. It was about fear and maddening his enemies, about making up for his size with his wit, something all us

201

women soldiers learn how to do for similar reasons when it comes to fighting.

"I never had the soldiers to go up against him, Teyr. Clans have been killed to a child for standing up to him. Skershe's own, the Lithessens, they were doing well with Auksen. You never met her cousin, who was their chief. He stood up to Khiese, killed a few of his men, twenty in all, set a trap. You don't need to know how Khiese killed them, but he burned them and dug salt into the head of their bloodlands, smashing up the stones there. She's the last of the Lithessen clan."

It was nice of him to say she was the last, given he was all for Circle traditions, and as such there really wasn't any clan any more with the last boy dead.

"What about Auksen?"

"There's been no word. Khiese won't recognise the tribute Families and principal Families as they were."

"I find it strange, Brother. If I was him I'd have won the Auksens first, knowing the tribute clans would follow."

"Think, Teyr, you keep that alliance intact and they may well bring the tribute clans against you."

He was right. I was tired. A moment's more thought and I could see it. Separate the old ties and weaken the bonds. Divide and rule.

The raw wailing of lynx began somewhere off in the hills, like two women grieving. Near us some grouse cackled as we talked, perhaps thinking us a threat to their chicks.

"You didn't answer me earlier, when I asked if you were going home tomorrow. You've got a good keep and a good boy. They're worth more than some drained marshland and a few bridges. That's what I've learned since Skershe gave me Drun. I know you curse me for those banners, but when I've got Drun in my arms, and he's alive and happy, I know I've made the right choice in my heart."

202

He turned to face me then, thoughtful. He put his hands on my arms and squeezed them, as he might a child.

"You did what you set out to do, Teyr. You poked me and Da in the eye, saw the world and come back rich, no war or poison took you, no droop, no agits. I don't know what you're doing worrying over us and the Circle." He put his arm about me then, a hesitant but welcome gesture.

"Well, here's how it is with me, by way of an example. A bit before I was thirty, Ry'ylan raiders was killing the Ososi, cousins of the Oskoro, on the borders of what would become Khasgal's Landing. I was one of Khasgal's captains and he put me in charge of a hand of skirmishers, to rout them. Khasgal had made treaties with the four tribes there on behalf of the Roan Province in return for helping fight off the Ry'ylans. Then he fell in love with Curael, the daughter of one of the tribe's chiefs, who was proud to welcome him into their tribe as her keep. And I mean 'her keep' because they had it right there: women could be chiefs and she would succeed him. By the following year he'd made an alliance between his tribe and the Ososi. After all that he must have owned a stretch of land not far short of the Circle for himself. The Ososi give him gifts of rare plant, and the trade with Roan he was stewarding netted him chests of gold. I asked him one night we was out on an ambush what he was doing sweating his balls off in a mosquie-ridden jungle cutting throats in the dark when he had all that coin. 'It's never been about the coin,' he said. It's only in the last few years I've come to realise what he meant."

"I understand what you're saying, though the tales of Khasgal founding his nation have it that while it was never about the coin, it was about you. Regardless, looks like you found something to believe in. But you won't bring the Circle together when Khiese's already done it. You'd need an army."

"Would I?"

He shook his head, exasperated with me.

"Thruun, If Auksen stands against Khiese, would you stand with Auksen or Khiese?"

He didn't want to answer me, just stared ahead into the river and the blinding shimmer of moonlight.

"Auksen."

I got the answer I wanted, though he'd made it sound like the worse of the choice.

"We should get some sleep, Teyr, you've got some leagues to cover tomorrow."

Thruun woke us all a few hours later. He put out some apple pies, a few slabs of roasted deer and some akva. It was an attempt to lift our spirits a bit, and I was grateful. Last night was peaceful and much needed, though I was fretting and snappy over watching Yalle and Sanger make their preparations. If they left we'd be hard pressed to go on, and they was making a point of doing this where I could see it.

I clapped my hands. "I want the whole van with me. We have to decide what's next."

The crew started coming together in the square before my family's longhouse. It had been a warm night by Circle reckoning, and a mist was about Amondell, thick and heavy as lard in the trees.

Yalle stepped forward then, ready to ride, armed and chewing on a stalk of vadse, which spoke of her wanting to leave straight away for it's a mild dayer we use also for stopping a sore head after a night's drink or kannab. Bela and Steyning was stood behind her, Bela close to Jem, leaning into him. Sanger had barely got his leathers on, loosely strapped. He was cleaning out his pipe.

"We got to Amondell, and Khiese's banners fly behind us over your house. We need to settle the purse as we agreed at Crimore," said Yalle.

"You'll not lift a finger to help us if our van walks the same trail as you back to Hillfast if Teyr doesn't pay you to do it?" This was Aude, who was kneeled next to me adjusting Mosa's tunic and running a comb through his hair.

"We'd not watch you be killed," said Yalle, "but that's about all. It'll cost Teyr more if she wants us to run the van back there."

Aude stopped combing and looked at her, not sure if she was serious at first, but she stared at him until he smiled.

"How much?" I asked.

"We'll make out the scrolls later. I'm sure you could afford it."

"Are you not going on to Auksen with us?" said Eirin. "I hear he has a good hundred or so."

"If they're not already sworn for Khiese," said Sanger, puffing through a fresh bowl of bacca that give off an air of cherries. His morning weed.

"I need to know," I said. And that was that, for Aude picked up Mosa and walked away, back to Chalky's wagon.

"We have a duty to Othbutter. His brother killed, we have to kill Khiese if we can, before he becomes stronger, commands more men and women," said Eirin.

Her crew was stood around her, and they was clearly set. I looked in their eyes in the moments that followed, looked for the doubt, a sense of fear, but found none. She must have spoken to her crew last night, and all of them was in.

"You have to speak to Aude," said Thad. He wasn't happy but said nothing.

"Chalky, you will go back, there's no way forward now except through Khiese. I'll make arrangement for our mercenaries to ride with you back to Faldon Ridge; you should be fine to go on to Hillfast without them."

Him and his keep, Edma, walked up to me and each embraced me. "Sillindar follow you, Master Amondsen," said Chalky. They walked off to the wagons.

I turned to Thad. "You must go with them. Leave us some brews, but I want you to keep them safe."

"And if I spoke to Aude, I believe he'd say that your being safe was his only concern. Drudhas feed soldiers, not nokes. If you're going on I'll be with you. We've seen worse."

"You were with better men and women back then." This was Sanger, who come over to stand with us. "I won't be joining you, Master, nor Jem. We have the same purse as Yalle; we'll ask only half of her fee for taking your family back home, however."

We clasped arms by way of sealing this agreement. "Aude will write up the scrolls and confirm the purse. There's a bit of coin should see you forward. Thornsen or Omar will take care of the rest when you get to Faldon."

"I'd say you should come back with us, Teyr."

"I know."

Sanger moved off towards his own horse. I looked back and saw Aude helping Chalky with one of his harnesses. Mosa was sitting on the wagon laughing at something they was joking over. Aude cast a glance at me then. The smile faded. Those few yards between us seemed impossible to step into. I held out my hand instead. He spoke to Chalky, who helped Mosa jump to the ground and follow him off to help with our packing.

I led Aude to a ladder to the wall around our longhouse. He come up behind me, and we stood looking over the wall to the camp. Women, along with the older boys and girls, was milking. Further off, the sniffers' horn sounded and I ·

saw them grouped up before the bast stalukt, as we called the master forager in our Abra. It was a younger voice than that which I woke to all through my years as a girl here. Their dogs made a din barking, and the foragers stamped their boots and took their snuff while the young man finished calling them to their work from the houses: "Kom stalukt, kom stalukt, kleip i stem, i fowrist rut."

"What's he singing?" said Aude. He leaned on the wall next to me, a little too far away for me to lean into him.

"He's singing, 'Come stalukt, come stalukt, to pinch the stem and seduce the root.' Stalukt means forager." They all clacked each other's walking sticks and spread out in pairs, moving off into the forest and along the river, whistling to the dogs. "If it wasn't for these banners it could almost be a normal day. A day I dreamed of sharing with you and Mosa for a long time, here."

"I would have liked to explore this place, have you take me along the carvings and sculptings of your walls, learn more of your rope, put it in scrolls for our library. But we're leaving today, and you're not coming with us."

I listened to myself as I told him that the threat Eirin and I would pose at the Auksens would keep Khiese's eye away from them. That Eirin needed someone who knew the Auksen lands, and I might make the difference to her crew getting out of here alive. That if I failed I really would give up and follow them back. I listened to myself say all those things and he nodded at the right times. He didn't look at me, his hair fell forward hiding his expression as he stared out at the fort as the clan went about its morning. I stopped talking.

"There was a night," he said, "nearly a year ago, during the planning of this expedition. I'd said something about lumber, how if Omar could secure the Bloody Gully you might get larch for the cords from the Kreigh clans straight onto the Crith and cut out three tolls and the usual shit Crutter's men try on. We were in the greet room and you were making a fire. Mosa came in and helped you and I thought you hadn't heard me. You gave him a puff on your pipe and he coughed and was nearly sick."

"I remember it. He wanted to know why, if it smelled like cherries, it didn't taste like them. He kept hiding that pipe from then on, and then I lost it. I'd had it since Marola."

"You were never cross with him about it and I know how much it meant to you. I loved you for that. But two months later you came home from a run to Elder Hill and pulled out from your pack a contract with Two Cock Crawtte for your barges to pass through the gully. You thanked me for the idea."

"I enjoyed thanking you."

He reached out to put his hand on mine.

"You never hinted that you'd heard me, but you'd spent months securing that contract. I felt then that nothing would stop you. And nothing will stop you."

His hand on top of mine kept me still. He took a deep breath before turning to me.

"Keep safe, bluebell. Come home. You'll know you did everything and we can make other plans. Me, Thad and Thornsen, we'll help you build an empire to rival any in the north. Then we'll make Mosa master of your fleet, maybe even of Hillfast."

I couldn't help a tear getting free. It was the thought of Mosa grown up, being taller than me. I needed him to be proud of me, and it would take time. I thought perhaps Aude was teasing me out of my course of action by not standing against it. I couldn't be sure, for really he was cleverer than me.

"Ma, Da!" Mosa was below us, at the bottom of the ladder.

"Climb up," said Aude.

"What brings you up here, young man?" I said.

I helped him up onto the wall, and he looked out for a moment, pleased to have a view across Amondell and into the trees and hill that flanked us north and west.

"The wagons are ready. Chalky told me to tell you."

Aude and I looked at each other then. He picked Mosa up and sat him in one arm, his legs around Aude's hip.

"Your ma has something else she needs to do. Something dangerous, so we can't be with her. That's why we're going back home."

Mosa reached his arms out to be held by me, and I held him up in the air before bringing him down to a hug. He'd been running about again, his neck hot and damp with sweat against my cheek.

"Are you going to drink a brew and grow big and strong to fight them?"

"I might have to."

He scratched my head with his fingers, he loved the feel of the stubble there. I blew into his neck, which made him squeal.

"Captain Eirin and her men are coming with me and Thad. You'll have Sanger and Yalle and their crew to look after you on the way home."

"Is Drun coming with us, and his da?"

"No, they'll stay here. This is their home. They'll be safe behind these walls. Will you keep your da safe for me?"

"No, Ma, he's bigger than me."

I held him for another minute, the moments seeming to quicken to our parting. I put aside the fears that slithered into my thoughts as I closed my eyes to better breathe him in. I felt better to know they was heading home.

I watched them all leave a short while later, our van rolling out west, having settled the scrolls with Yalle and Sanger. Mosa waved all the way till the trees took them. I turned back and saw Eirin lining up her crew for drilling the Forms.

I took my place in their line and become a soldier again.

Chapter 7

Now

Cherry, my vanner, left us, heading to Ablitch as I asked, to send birds and raise the alarm about Khiese up at Elder Hill, Faldon Ridge and Hillfast.

She's a good woman, seemed to have become good friends with Leyden, them promising to meet up back in Hillfast someday soon for a few ales and pipes.

Leyden's said they're looking for women who paid colour all about Port Carl. This won't be easy. Steid Carlessen is still the chief. His sister is Othbutter's keep and he exploits it richly. And Othbutter. He has a finger up the arse of every merchant and half the herders that come to market. Othbutter might well think he's getting a good slice of the take, but that's a joke.

I call to Leyden, who's leading his horse on the riverbank beside us. "We'll pull in shy of the jetties. Best to go in on the trails, fewer eyes."

Three days since we left the docks and we'd found a measure of peace. I'd taught Brek a few stretches for his shoulder and he was in better spirits. Dottke chattered almost constantly, asking questions of me and Leyden, or she was humming and singing, teaching Aggie the words to one of their churning songs that the women of their theit used to harmonise on. Even Leyden joined in. I was able to talk to Jorno a bit more in those days as well, reminding him we was getting closer to his ma. He didn't say much back. Today, after Leyden got us some cheese and eggs from a theit we passed, we dragged the boat to the shore for the final time.

"You should go on ahead, Leyden," I says. "We can't waste any time, and if there is a purse up for me, you can't be seen with us."

"We don't know the tide, might be I'll come find you if there's no boats leaving till the morrow."

"Go ahead then, tell Carlessen what's happened to the Kelssen theit and theits further north in his own lands. Then find a way around the coast."

We stand in a meadow of cotton grass, out of the trees that crowd the banks. In the distance on the side of a hill a line of people lead packhorses along the main trail as it rises, beyond which is Port Carl.

"Sillindar follow and guide you, Master Amondsen, you and these children. I hope I'll see you again one day."

I embrace him. "Give my love to Thornsen and everyone back at the sheds."

The children all embrace him in turn and he has a quiet word with Dottke, no doubt to look after us all, for she nods sternly.

We follow him up to the trail and up the slope towards the port. As we crest the hill there's a breeze unmistakably off the sea, a cold that only the sea can give the air. Before us are Carlessen's main export to the Old Kingdoms, lobelia and greymint fields, vivid blue and green, a patchwork of fabulous rugs over the soil this southern clan enjoys. The air's full with the sound of bees, the smell of tea and jams, a summer smell that lifts our spirits as we follow the trail winding down the slope towards the port. There's few guards out here, making it easy to filch some leaves and lobelia seeds for my belt. I cut a handful of mint leaves and put them in a square of linen, soaking them. Brek puts the compress to his shoulder and a smile flickers across his face as he feels the mint seep into his shoulder, cooling and softening it.

"I never knew you could use mint for this," he says.

"Knowledge is power, Brek. Knowledge can help a small power always overcome a much greater power."

Port Carl squats against the river to our left, its jetties like spiders' legs fanning out. The port is up from the coast and the sandbanks there, somewhat safe from the pirates of the Sar. It's mid-afternoon when we reach the port itself, many wagons passing us as they leave the market for the day. The children on the wagons look down at us, some wave, others are pulled into the laps of their mothers for we are filthy. As we get closer the noise of the port builds: horns are blowing on the river, whistles and shouts come from the docks as trade turns to cups and pipes. The mint in our noses gives way to the dung of pigs and deer, deep sticky furrows of it, pools of mud that suck at our boots as we hold hands and thread our way through into the streets proper. These are the fisherhouses and sheds, builders and smiths' shops.

"What's the matter?" says Dottke looking up at me. "Your hand's shaking."

How could I tell her that I could barely stand to be here, my heart's pounding? I haven't been in such a crowd since I left Hillfast. Had solitude for so long all this is overwhelming me. I can't look at anyone without feeling sick, like I'm being judged or assayed, circled, somehow guilty. I try to stone my breathing with all this chatter, these narrow runs and people pushing past us, leaning into each other to whisper. I can't bring myself to believe they're not looking for me, that there won't be whiteboys. A horn sounds then, deeper than theirs but enough that I swear and stop still. Poor Dottke hisses and I realise I'm squeezing her hand.

"Sorry, Dott. I've spent such a long time alone, up in the Mothers. The last people I met before I found you all and your theit were, well, the last was trying to kill me, and those who live in those passes also would have killed me if they'd caught me, for everything I ate I took from the mouths of their own."

They had nothing to say. Aggie leans into my leg now I'm stood still.

"Where are we going?" asks Brek.

"I told Jorno I would look for his ma – any of that man Gressop's friends might have her – and I need to find the whereabouts of almshouses. Aggie, I bet you're hungry as well?"

"I am, Blackie." It's nice to see Litten smile a bit, for Aggie was always on at me for food and it had become a joke among us.

"But we've got nowhere to stay and no coin," says Jorno.

"I'm going to look out for someone what's paid colour like me, might be they'll have a bit more sympathy for us all than fearing the colour like most nokes do. I don't exactly look like a soldier these days either, I don't look flush."

Truth to tell I looked like a lot of old mercenaries I used to wonder at when I was in my prime, thinking back then they'd made bad choices for themselves. I'd give them a bit of coin though not, at first, from choice. It was my friend Ruifsen, who I hadn't seen for a good few years now, who told me that even those who paid out was always paying the colour, and you should help them where you find them, when they can't help themselves.

We go through the market, now only a dribble of people closing up. I'm spat on from an open window above us, a whorehouse, and a prostitute's cussing me for a slaver of children. Brek's about to shout back at the man when I shush him. Dottke tugs my arm to lower it and she wipes the spit off with her sleeve.

"Ach," she says, "there's black bits in it."

"It's blood, little bluebell, that man's not well."

We find a well in an open square and queue a bit, filling our flasks. Carlessen at least has the good sense to keep the wells free next to a river. I'm looking about us for someone who's paid out and I see a man leading a big old draft pulling a cart on which are kegs of sati, the sweet, lemony smell of its juniper strong both in my nose and a wavering blue in my eye. He's a big man, must do his own tasting, but in looking at him and closing my old eye, I see a man at ease, honest, but how that comes into my mind with the altered view of him I can't say. He has a big old leather apron and a grey beard, a wolf's tooth through his ear he must have grown the hole for. His colour's faded with the years, olive now.

"Hail? Common?" I call and walk over to him.

"I never seen such a horse, Blackeye," says Litten. He'd said in the boat that he used to love riding out with his da, when we was all talking and me trying to get them to go through their upset, not hide it away and let it rot their spit and spirit as I've seen it do.

"Her name's Feather, for she was a bag of sticks as a foal, I'm told." He nodded at me as he said it, by way of saying hello, and he spoke Common at Litten, which answered me.

"If they wasn't walking free I'd have said you were a slaver, not a very successful one either."

"I'd rather kill myself. I'm Eirin," I says.

"Nirdde." He lifts Litten up onto Feather's back. The boy's delighted, and Aggie puts her arms up to follow him.

"You and all? Why little dut, you're naught but a tunic full of feathers yourself. Is that one behind you your brother?" Aggie looks at me and bows her head, running Feather's mane through her fingers.

"We need somewhere to stay, Nirdde. Their theit was raided, they're all that's left alive. They're from upriver a week or so, Kelssen Family."

"I see. I'm sorry to hear it. Explains how you all look, if you'll forgive. I got nowhere though, I sleep in the sheds myself as I've got little need of a house I'd never visit, but there's a spot against the wall the kiln's against, has a bit of overhang should it rain, and it tastes like it might soon enough."

I smile. "I knew someone said he could taste the rain coming. We're grateful for your help."

"Where'd you serve?" He starts walking and the children fall in.

"Farlsgrad, then further south." I don't want to say too much, don't want to lie to him either. "You?"

"Forontir, Argir. Lot of troubles around their borders years back as you may know. Ran some vans with Legger Black along the Lagrad borders, to Tirinmoth and up as far as Alhglish."

"Legger himself? My old Forms master taught him, a few years before me. There's stories there. Headed into the Wilds and never come out again, I heard."

"Same."

I wait at his wagon while he drops off three of the kegs

at a flophouse. There's a cheer as he enters and he's had a mug with them by the look of his beard when he returns. The rest was empty, and we follow him back to his brewery. His trade makes him a popular man, so I walk the far side of his wagon to where he's leading his horse. I need a cap from somewhere, something to hide this scar across my lips that'll give me away.

We're soon at his brewery. A big archway runs through his storehouse, which stands on the edge of the lane, beyond which is a yard leading to his two sheds, one for the malting and one the fermenting. He has some quiet words and gives instruction to a few of the men waiting to help him with the wagon and Feather. He gives Litten some hazelnuts to give her as a thank you, and he pats her head and seems right at home with her. She drops her head at his words.

"Get that boy a mouthpiece, he's a natural," says Nirdde.

"Seems to be," I said, thinking of how Mosa struggled to make a good soothing sound out of a singer's mouthpiece, our horses bolting rather than settling with him.

"I've got to get on, fair bit to do with the gruit and juniper, and a barrel of wort to be pitched before I get to my mat."

"Can you fetch me a candle? I got some bark needs oiling."

"Course. Need help with it?"

"I'd be grateful. This eye needs doing as well."

It isn't long before he's done and hands me back the melted bit of stick. There's a few comments from his men who are watching as I lift my shirt, but they're soon pulling faces as he rubs the end of the stick over my Oskoro eye. He also gives me a couple of furs for the duts, and I lead them around the side of his shed into the alley there. It's short, only two houses opposite before there's a wooden fence closing off the end. A woman opens a shutter and closes it again on seeing us. There's some swearing at a man in there who seems to cut her short with the scrape of a chair I'm guessing he's stood up from.

"It stinks here, Blackeye," says Jorno. He's right, the brewery's sickly smell is mixing with the shit around us slopped out from the houses. My wounds feel better, but like these children I'm struggling with how hungry I feel.

"We've got to make the night here, just the one. I can get you to the almshouse tomorrow." I put the furs over Aggie, Litten and Dottke.

"Can you come in there too with us?" says Dottke.

"They won't take someone like me or they'd take every beggar. I can't give you a life, can I, Dott? Look at us, sitting in the shit here with these flies and no food. You know what Leyden said, there's people after me. If you're with me when they catch me I won't know what will happen to you, and in an almshouse you'll be fed and have a mat of your own. Let me show you something Leyden and Cherry give me the night before she left us. You was all sleeping."

Out of my sack I take a scroll. "They know their letters as I do. This scroll says that the almshouse that takes you will receive some coin every month for as long as you're there. That'll persuade them to take you in."

We squat down against the wall, the brick warm at our backs from the kiln behind us.

"How can anyone drink beer when it stinks like that?" says Brek.

"I used to say that and all. But life might get harder than this, if you can believe that, and for people who hate their life or have a lot of sorrow, they might tell you beer makes it all go away for a while."

He shakes his head. "Don't see the point if all your sorrow comes back the next morning."

"Me either. Right, we're a bit out of the way of any militia down here, they'll be on the jetties and around the main lanes and sheds. I need to get us something to eat. We'll get nothing proper if we're on the lanes, we'll just get hurt by the militia moving us off. Brek, you need to look out for the others." I take my knife from its scabbard. It'd be more use for whittling than killing but was better than a fist that hadn't ever punched anything properly.

"I in't ever used a knife, Blackeye," he says.

"I know. Hope you won't have to, it's just in case someone does take a look in here and think they can try something. I won't be long."

I hold a slip of linen over my mouth as I leave the alley and walk down towards the docks, keeping a note of the turns I'm taking, the square we passed earlier with the well, a flophouse with a hanging sign showing a badly painted poppy. Then, as I turn a corner above which a torch has been lit, I see a tavern opposite, The Rubber Smiles. Under the sign hangs a large piece of black leather cut into a circle. It means the tavern welcomes those of us with colour, and that is usually because we don't like trouble 'less it's paid for.

My head brushes the top of the doorway; it's a solid little stone house, room enough for maybe thirty at most in there and near full as I enter. The serving tables are along one side and I see a few of Nirdde's kegs on them, FEATHER'S SA branded on the sides.

I swerve left away from the tables before the keep can offer a welcome or pour out a cup for me. There's two men, still wearing swords and belts must not long have come in. They've got a tray before them and there's some bones and some crispy skin, the ends of some bisks.

"Please, can I take these? I've got some children with nowhere to live."

The one of them is packing his pipe, fairly young, thinks he's a bad boy. He looks over at the keep and flicks his head at me.

"Get out, no beggin' in here. Off back to whatever whorehouse you been droopin' in," shouts the keep, who, to his shame, had paid colour himself.

"You're hanging the leather. Have some pity."

"I got plenty of pity for those with some coin, so unless you want to start sucking some cock out the back, fuck off."

"Just these and I'm gone, sir." I point to the dregs of the tray. I feel like smashing it in his face but I gather up what's there into the square of linen I'd had over my face and nip out ahead of their jeering and threats. I curse when I hear the word "scar" being said. It was a chance I had to take, but now I'm running around a few corners before any of them can share whatever might have been understood as the bounty on me.

I almost run into a young man with his head down leading a pony along. I can smell the cloudberry jam he must have in the sacks that's hanging off the pony's back, the glass jars chitting together.

"Oh, sorry, lady, I wasn't watching, I . . ." He paused, looking at my eye. My belly was turning over with the smell of the jam, I could feel my mouth wetten.

"I'm looking after some children, orphans. One jar of that for a rich man's table could feed them for a day."

"I'm sorry, my cleark, he'd . . ." He's looking about, then back to me, he lingers on my babs, then my eye, he's flushing a bit, nervous, pity tugging against duty and a noke's fear.

"You're not going to . . . to steal it, you're not a thief?"

"I'm not. You know I'm not or you'd be shouting for the militia. I've paid colour after all." He needs to be calmed. I need to use his nerves, his youth. I've got one chance at getting some jam before some militia appear and take an interest. To our right there's a rotten gate half open and beyond it a scrap of yard and a dark doorway from which I can feel and see nothing with my black eye. It'll do. I put my hand on the nose of his pony, whisper to it, take a step closer to him.

"You were looking at me just then, looking at these." He takes a longer look at my babs before looking up at me.

"I . . . Look, lady, I'm dead if I take my hands off this rein."

"Lead her to the doorway there. I've got a strong grip, I'm a very strong woman. You won't take long."

One punch was all it took, he'd wake soon enough.

I'm walking back to the brewery, sun's setting. I smell the frying and baking in the houses about, there's the smell of maple sugar, opia blocks burning from low doorways, bored-looking militia in their cups, for droopers was no trouble, feeding Carlessen's coffers. I hear Dottke calling me, but I'm not near Nirdde's. Ahead there's a crossroad in the lanes, there's a man and two older boys, bigger than Brek. They're in leather vests, wearing gloves, bearing weapons, probably gangers. The man's dragging Dottke along, and she's howling and pulling. Litten and Aggie are held by their arms by the other two, their heads bowed and whimpering. None look down the lane I'm coming from and they go past. I run to the corner, judge I'm not going to be able to get near them slow, too few people, and decide to sprint at the man holding Dottke. He hears me splashing through the mud and turns, she shrieks. The others turn. He barely has time to let go of her tunic and reach for his knife before I run into him, arm at his chest and shoving him back against the wall of a house they stopped alongside. He gasps, winded, he's big but he's

221

soft, a splash of colour you might have from a few dayers. I give him a right hook and I catch him clean. He staggers back a step and falls, stunned. One of the boys pulls out a long cleaver you might use to clear undergrowth out with. I put my hand to my sword.

"I punched your man here because I won't be killing nokes that don't know no better. These duts are with me, you'd best leave them. Don't give me a reason."

Dottke kicked the man in his face as he got onto all fours trying to rise to his feet. She must have caught his nose, blood pours from it.

"Wait!" says the other boy. "It's her, the scar on her mouth. Ryigg said to let him know if we saw her." He runs off in the direction they was headed. The boy holding Litten lets the pipe he was smoking fall from his mouth as he starts shouting for help. I draw my sword and he lunges at me to keep me off before putting the cleaver to Litten's neck.

"Don't you fucking try it!" he shouts. He's shaking. I feel sick, I see Mosa for a moment, Khiese.

"I'll kill you both if you don't let go of him now." He looks behind me, a tell, and I spin out to the side. The man's dagger catches in my tunic. He's stuck me but it's not gone in more than an inch or so into my side. I run him through and pull the sword out with a cut to open his belly. The boy screams at the same time as Litten does. I turn. The boy's dropped the cleaver and he's running. Litten holds his throat and I vomit, my head's gone light. Then he pulls his hand away and the cleaver's made only a small cut. I put my arms out for him. A whistle sounds. The lane steepens in the direction they was going, and there's two men running up it, helmets and spears, quite unfit. I wipe my tears away and take a breath, then take Aggie up into my arms. "Dott, Litten, run!" We head back up the lane to the brewery. Mercifully there's no militia as we get to the end of the lane. Jorno's there on his own, he's been crying.

"What's happened?" he says. He sees Litten's got blood on his neck and I'm splashed with it from the man's guts. I then notice Dottke is splattered too; she'd slipped on his blood as we fled.

"Where's Brek?"

"They hit him, broke his nose. He's gone looking for you, he said he wasn't going to let you down."

"Shit. You did well to stay here."

"Hey, it's Brek," says Jorno. He runs over to put his arms about him, glad to see him.

He's pinching his nose, and he's covered in blood and all.

"We have to go, the whistles mean they're looking for me, we have to get out of the port, into the hills, at least tonight." I put my arms around Brek too.

"I couldn't fight them, sorry. They took your knife and beat me. I followed so I could tell you where they went."

"You was brave, a really brave man. Help me, take up Aggie, I'll carry Dottke."

Out of the port was away from the whistles. I keep my head down and we get out of the lanes and onto the main trail as it rises away to the hill and the trees about. There's nobody following us, it seems, the whistles lost in the general noise of those around the docks getting rowdy. I put my hand to Litten's head as we walk. He looks up at me.

"Let's see your neck," I says. The blood's dried, barely a cut, but I've stopped walking and I'm looking into his eyes. My hand trembles on his head, and the children see I'm trying to stone that other grief.

"What's the matter?" he says.

The words come between shuddering breaths. "There was a boy I couldn't save. My son. I just remembered him, back

223

there, and it's upset me. But you're here, which is good. Let's eat this bit of food I got us."

I share out the bits of chicken bone and pieces of bread from the tavern as we walk and then surprise them with the cloudberry jam. I offer it to Brek first, and as I guessed he refuses and passes it to Aggie, which makes me glad. We make short work of the jar, sucking our cheeks in with the jam's sharpness and sucking our fingers with the joy of it, for it was finely made.

As we're walking along by some of the lobelia crops a woman whistles out. She has a lantern she's holding up and she's walking her land with a dog, which barks at her whistle.

"What's this then?" The dog growls as they approach, but she's inside a fence that's there to keep out deer. She's about my age, leather leggings of a farmer, shorter tunic. In the lamplight I can see a fullness to her figure that speaks of comfort and a face that's used to smiling, smooth round cheeks and dark hair tied back severely into a bun. She has a bow and quiver slung across her back and I'd bet a few coin she was sharp with it too.

"This is Blackeye," says Dottke before I can say something back. "She killed fifty men in our village but they still killed everyone except us. This is Brek, he got hit in the shoulder with an arrow, and this is Jorno, we're looking for his ma, who left him, but we'll find her so he isn't sad. And this is Litten and Aggie, they're brother and sister. I'm Dottke. What's your name?"

"Well, young lady, I'm Grenna Carlessen. This little yapper is Scruff. What brings you out on the main trail at night? You got no packs and you're not anywhere near sneaky enough to be after crops." She finishes this comment with a big smile for Dottke before she looks up at me.

"I'm Teyr Amondsen. I helped these duts whose theit was

being burned to the ground and I've got a price on my head for killing Chief Othbutter's brother, though it's not true."

Brek steps back. "What are you saying that for, Blackeye, you told her your name?"

"I did, Brek. I get a sense she takes people as I do, on what she sees, and you tell good people the truth, because otherwise you're lost." Truth to tell I surprised myself in saying this, and I'm saying it almost word for word as my ma said it to me when I was packing to leave her. I lost much of that faith over the years, but Grenna stands here calm and assured of herself, she's read us right and has chosen to talk over nocking an arrow.

"This isn't something I was expecting to hear from what I suspected were trespassers. You got nowhere to live then. Maybe I can help for tonight. I'll get my fat old keep to put some extra broth on, neckbone it is. Go back and follow the edge of the fence round. Our hut and sheds are there, just in front of those three birch."

She puts a couple of fingers in her mouth and gives an ear-splitting whistle before walking off through the run between the flowers.

How to speak of the rest of that evening? I cried, Grenna a bit too, after the duts were put to bed in furs in the cutting shed which was hung full of posies of mint to keep the moths and beetles away. Her keep wasn't as fat as all that, his name was Boneit and his broth was fine; peppery with a good film of lard on it. After we washed all our tunics and put them up around the fire we shared a pipe as I told them my story. They asked me to tell it, and for their kindness I did and I decided to leave little out of it. I watched them hold hands, make each other pipes, and I told her a recipe that would help Boneit's gammy shoulder. They told me in turn of their son going to sea, and there was little I could say to that given what I did to my ma and da. Didn't seem time or right to talk of other stories of my life for we hadn't the acquaintance that made it easy. I lived an interesting life, they said, and they meant no bad by it of course, for it was a saying that was meant as an understatement. Looking about us there seemed almost nothing in their only room that spoke of leisure: old tools waiting for a smith piled in one corner, firewood in another along with the rich, cosy smell of peat blocks. They had a stand for lying on and on the walls was a few rough shelves on which they put everything else. I asked them how they used their coin, for they must have earned a bit. Grenna said they kept some with Carlessen's own clearks and she smiled to recall Boneit going into the port one day and coming back with some fine wine their second cousin, the chief himself, sold them. I kept my mouth shut on that count, for they farmed for him of course so why was he selling wine to them? I thought too that they should have been thinking more about investing the coin they made to make more, but seeing their eyes still lingered on each other as they talked, I was reminded of what was important.

I asked them about taking one of the duts, for they spoke fondly of them. We talked about which one and we agreed we'd ask them in the morning what they thought about it. I think Boneit was quite taken with Dottke, and Litten seemed to go to Grenna easily when she asked him to help put the broth in the tin bowls. It was late when I left them to join the children in the shed. She held me and kissed me, head, cheeks and lips.

I said earlier that I cried, and it was as she held me. It was because she told me I was a good woman.

We was up early, Grenna and Boneit dressed ready for their day. We led the children to the big iron bath they let fill with rainwater from their tank and we enjoyed their screeching and splashing about as we got them cleaned up for the almshouse that Grenna told me about. She said to mention her. Then with some cheese and beets they'd boiled up we got them all together.

"I spoke to you all last night about how today I needed to put you in alms," I says. "Grenna or Boneit can't take you so I can get away. This isn't so much because they're busy here, but it's because we talked about them maybe looking after one of you. I thought it might be Aggie as she's the littlest, but I'm not sure you'd want to leave Litten, would you, bluebell?"

She's holding his hand and she looks up at us before giving us a shake of her head. Litten squeezes her hand.

"I want to look after her."

"I want to look after them too," says Brek.

"I know," I says, "and I reckon Dottke wants to look after all of you, don't you, Dott?"

"We have to stay together. You can't split us up!"

"Well, you know what I was thinking? I was thinking if Jorno was willing to stay and work on the farm here, he might earn some coin and learn to sew and get himself some fine clothes and go and find his ma with Grenna. And if Ydka is in some rich man's house, then Jorno will be clean and smart and show his ma he's become a man and make her proud of him, and more than that, they would more likely let them see each other. Grenna and Boneit know the chief himself."

I give it a moment, watch Jorno as his eyes fill up and he shuffles his feet and plays nervously with the ragged ends of his tunic. He's torn between his ma and them.

"What do you think, Jorno?" says Grenna. "Me and Boneit here would be glad to look after you."

"He'll visit us and all?" says Brek.

"Course we will," says Grenna. "I'll bring him often as our work allows." She holds out her hand. He takes a deep breath and turns to the others. They fold in on each other. Their words are the plain, clumsy things you say when you can't get at how you feel, which is almost everything when you're a dut. After their hugging he walks over and takes Grenna's hand.

"Sillindar follow you," says Boneit. I give Jorno, Grenna and Boneit all a kiss and lead the duts off out of the farm and back onto the trail. I have a mask I can put over my mouth and a cloak and hood. It looks fishy enough but might buy me enough time to get them to this almshouse, Jostein's Haven, before someone wonders if I'm the woman they're looking for who's paid colour. They thought I should take the sword I had but that would make things worse. I decide to leave it here. Killing anyone while I'm near the children will go badly for all of us.

Carlessen helps keep the almshouse, and I'm sure the skinning of fish, spinning wool and a hundred other things are done for the price of some food and a roof and nothing else. These duts are going to have a hard time of it.

The walk back into Carl is quiet, among us at least. I'm sucking on a vadse straw, which sharpens me up. We're making our way in with the merchants coming to market; wagons with great sacks of wool stacked high, trail-worn vanners leading their packhorses in laden with plant in bushels, bottles and blocks; herders and their snickering sheep and deer are crossing open ground to our right to the large stock market on the edge of the port and the rapid stuttering calls of the auctioneers.

It isn't very long before Sillindar abandons me, taking with him my saying a proper goodbye to these duts.

I'm holding Aggie and Dottke's hands, the boys behind me. The lanes are busy; I don't see the boy who yesterday had Litten by the throat, not straight away. The smell of the bacca he smoked I haven't twigged right off. He had seen us of course. We walk through busy lanes, around the hot piles of dung in the mud and cobbles, trying to keep our boots clean as we move into the main runs towards the jetties. I sense a shift, a seller of shells stops his hollering a moment, his eyes lingering on something behind me. A movement to my right, a door opening out and someone behind it. I pick up my pace, recalling Grenna's words to head for the gallows, then a lane rolling downhill to the left towards the almshouse and a big anchor they called Broketooth set outside it. We come out in the triangle that's got the gallows stage at its heart. I turn quickly, the boy with the pipe is about thirty feet behind me and he's pointing at me when he realises I'm looking at him. He drops his eyes and bumps into a couple of men who push him to the ground as he goes to turn away from me. From a lane next to the two a militiaman steps out and badly plays at not looking in our direction. Litten tugs my arm.

"What's that man doing walking up on the roof?" He points at another militiaman, similar leather vest to him that's behind us. Then the whistles blow. I keep us walking to the gallows stage knowing that the space will give me a chance to judge where they're coming in from.

I whisper to the children. "I'm going to stay here. There's militiamen around us who are going to put me in chains and take me away. You need to walk on now, down that hill till you see the anchor. Here's the scrollcase that Leyden wrote for you."

Dottke goes to hug me.

"No, bluebell, keep walking, all of you must keep on

because if we stop they might catch up and get you too. If anyone asks where you come from, how you got here, tell them . . ." I remember then the look in that noke herder's eyes as I swung about with his spear in me, the terror in his face because I should have been dead. "Tell them the Ildesmur saved you. A black-eyed War Crow. Keep my name out of it for it might go worse for you if it's known."

Brek nods at me and he takes Dottke's hand. She can't help herself, she's waving at me, so I force myself to turn away and walk back towards the militiaman. This alarms him and he puts his hand out to slow me down. Hawkers and fishers, merchants and clearks all pause as they hear him call my name. There's a flash of some sort, colour or smell I can't say with this eye, but I know someone's moved in from just behind me. The militiaman who was on the roof of a cooper's shed drops down. They're sounding their whistles. I glance quickly beyond the man behind me as he pulls a club from its belt loop.

The children are gone, nothing out of sorts with those ambling along the lane they took. I'm sure they was on their way now, and I feel released, like I'm lifted up. I did something right. Now I'm ready to go for there's no more good I can do and there's much to atone for as I untie the strap of leather over my mouth and wrap it around my fist.

Chapter 8

Then

With naught but our horses we made good time. From Amondell it's a short run east to the Auksen settlement. We didn't take the short run, the trails would be watched. We had a three rolling on luta day and night. With caution we picked our way across the stony hills that was the toes of the Mothers, their bodies to the south cold and beautiful.

I remembered Thende telling me of the chief's sister he never married, the nose-picker. Chief Olnas I may have met when a girl – he must have been a boy then – but I remembered nothing of him although expected to be reminded on our meeting.

We come to a dell beyond which I knew was the farmlands of the Auksen clan, a proper fort wedged into the curacs, which was what we called the rolling stone-strewn land that faded into the plains of the Almet. The sniffers would have already come back to the settlement as it was getting on in the day. The broken land made for copses of trees. One offered a good vantage over the settlement and we settled in for the evening watching. There was no Khiese banner flying over the Auksen longhouse, no sign of whiteboys. We scouted out to increase our perimeter and there was still no sign.

I agreed with Eirin to wait until the sniffers was out in the morning, by which time the dogs would likely pick us up, so we'd head in if there was no sign of trouble. I washed the luta out of my eyes and got to sleep for I'd likely need my wits tomorrow if I was to bring Auksen into my plan.

Thad was up at first light mixing the crew's brews and rubs. Eirin and I did each other's rubs as the sniffers and their dogs leaving the settlement woke us. Three of Skallern's men signed that there was still no whiteboys. I agreed with Eirin that she stay out of the camp and I go in with four, two spears, two bows, nothing to cause alarm. Olnas had either not yet met Khiese or he'd defied him. Either way we had to be wary of Khiese or a crew of whiteboys coming at the Auksens.

The five of us led our horses through the fields of arnica, amony and flag. North of us the hills which settled down into the great plain was hidden in a heavy mist. The sniffer dogs, being mostly brown or white chutters, was friendly, and was looking to be patted or given their snivets. Our colour, our presence even, didn't attract comment. I didn't know how to read that and it set me on edge. Sometimes people get nervous round people with colour, or pretend they don't see us.

The Auksen settlement was built on a natural rise with the longhouse at the back, where an escarpment made a natural defence behind it, the same as at Amondell. Their banner still flew, green edged with grey links, atop the giant pole carved from a single trunk of a black pine, rare enough when it was brought down from Tusker's Vale, and fully a hundred feet high. That was Old Auksen's gredda, who won over our clan to be called the high clan in these lands.

At the gate was only the one guard, and I looked about expecting to see at least a couple more, if only to keep an eye out for the poachers looking to get themselves some of the plant grown in the fields about.

"Are you mercs? I've been told by the chief to ring the bell for any mercs that come in."

"Why's that?" I asked.

"Pigeons coming from some of our Families tell us there's a warlord about."

"There is. I've come from the Amondsens, I'd like to speak with our chief, Olnas."

He rang a bell just inside the main gate and pointed the way up the slope.

As with Crimore, the settlement was quiet. It was bigger than Crimore as well, and the plentiful stone in the lands about allowed them to wall in properly their runs and plant patches; solid cottages and carved stone blocks that I had admired as a girl that marked those on the rope who had strengthened it. These stood on or formed the corners of some of these walls, or else buttressed the settlement's great walls, their ancestors standing guard, watching them with a range of expressions from disdain through to joy.

But again, the children sat in twos or threes and didn't look at us, frightened to, I thought.

"Something's not right," I said quietly to Eirin's guards with me. "Cough if you see anything at all looks like trouble."

"It's quiet, Master," said one. "Usually can't stop women going on, can you?" The woman next to him give him a nudge.

"Please pardon." But he was right.

Two more guards come out from the longhouse. I could see, from the fresher stone and thatch, that the house had been expanded, what must have been a room half as long as the main house added on to the left-hand side, which was furthest from the escarpment.

"Weapons and belts," said the one. Looked relaxed enough, spear leaning on the house behind him and sword still sheathed.

"I'm Amondsen. I'm here from Thruun, I have his seal."

"Still need them." The other held out his hand to receive them.

"Give them up," I said, and we all did. Thad had given us all a dayer. I stood a bit closer to them as I give up my sword and belts. Neither had much colour, probably only paid pennies as we used to say of those who never got on to full fightbrews with all the trouble and the staining they bring.

They pointed us inside. The flat stones was smooth as glass on the main steps and the short run to the longhouse doors. Shutters was open along walls and roof, but the heavy air and cloud left the tables inside gloomy all the same. Two men raked through the firepit, throwing ash up into the air.

"Hail!" I called as we entered. The dayer helped us see better than we would have. Olnas was at one of the long tables with a man must have been his drudha. Nobody in the Circle other than chiefs hooped their beards, and that is how I could tell these two men apart. They sat chopping and mashing cicely roots, by the smell of them.

Olnas stood up and gestured us to him.

"Is it you, Teyr Amondsen? I believe it is."

"Hail, Chief Olnas. Thank you for your welcome."

"You are family. Sit with us while we mash, tell me of your brother. You've come from there?"

"I have. I'm sorry to say I didn't recognise you, it's been many years. Am I so similar-looking to the girl who last come here?"

234

"You're not easy to forget, colour or no. I was too young to beg for a kiss back then, and too old now, sadly." His hair, its wave, was common blonde. Perhaps it was that he'd gained weight, his skin was pebbled with red blotches, like it had never been young.

"My brother sends his respects, but also requests your help, as do many clans in the Circle. There is a bandit, more a warlord. Samma Khiese."

As I said it one of my men yelled, "Whiteboys!"

I looked out through the shutter on the side wall and saw two of them appear outside it. They'd not drawn weapons and the dayer kept me even. They was fidgeting, grinning.

"I know Khiese," said Olnas. He rubbed the dirt and root fibres from his hands and wiped them on a piece of cotton-leather.

"He knew you'd come and wanted to meet you."

Olnas got up from the bench we was sat at. For a moment I thought of stabbing him, severing his rope. But he'd done that himself, as much a puppet as my brother. Killing an ally of Khiese would make the parley worse. I was wrong.

"Teyr."

From the newly built room off to the left near the back of the longhouse Khiese walked through with six of his whiteboys. For all that they looked strong and capable soldiers, taller and larger than Khiese, it was him that I could not take my eyes from.

He was my height, wore a simple brown tunic, a plain belt at his waist with only three pouches. He had a short, coppery beard, close-cut hair. His colouring was similar to that I'd seen on soldiers far to the east near the Wilds, the yellow of mustard seeds, flushes of green around the veins that seemed also to have affected his eyes, for they was a pale green instead of white.

We clasped arms. I didn't hesitate for I wanted to begin this well. His skin was like hot rough stone, hands scarred, knuckles blown and round, an experienced unarmed fighter.

"Your brother told me much about you and your adventures over the Sar. Yet you come home to the Circle spreading the good word and bribes of that imbecile Othbutter. How did you come so low? Come, sit next to me so we may talk. Olnas, take your drudha outside, tell my captain to begin looking for the rest of Teyr's crew. They'll be in the copses, no doubt a vantage point somewhere past the fields."

I looked to my men. They was unarmed, while Khiese's men had longswords. I gestured for them to sit at a nearby bench, for there was no fighting our way out of this. I sat side by side with Khiese. He was lean, a strong posture. Despite my dayer I felt nervous now. I'd walked into this simply not believing that Khiese could be here, much less lay this trap. My heart had lifted when I saw the Auksen colours over the settlement. It had softened my thinking.

"You may have heard something from Jeife Seikkerson, but it's important I outline why I've come from Hillfast. It isn't Othbutter that's proposed this, though he backed it with coin. You're right, as are all the clans of the Circle, that he hasn't come here, has chosen instead to stay around the coast. I could have done that, I was making good coin as a merchant, but I felt Hillfast needed better. I have ploughed much coin into roads and bridges leading to the Sedgeway. Now I've learned that you have risen to control many of the clans. There's no reason why we cannot work in the Circle's common interest."

He listened with half a smile on his lips. "I've heard this much from my brother. Teyr, you don't share my ambition for Hillfast, for the Circle is the first step. I won't be led by the cap by guilds of merchants. I won't ship away our larch,

236

our plant south and west for profit. You want us to rival the Old Kingdoms, to be a partner to them, to raise our standing in a game of dice they've got rigged. And they've always had it rigged because they work as one, those countries, they oppress as one. The citadels is the game I will play. These chiefs can't see past their bellies and cocks. Othbutter is first, the rest follow, and then we might be able to stand for ourselves."

There's movement outside, I hear horses whinnying and then galloping away.

"I believe Gruma passed on my warning, at the Almet?" he said.

I struggled to recall it. "We do not pose a threat."

He raised his eyebrows. "Well now, you've wounded Jeife Seikkerson and helped prisoners of mine escape. You have two drudhas of some renown and a good number of soldiers, all well appointed. I'd say you were a threat, except I have you now without any weapons or plant. But most importantly, Teyr, I asked you to leave and you didn't. My brother was clear on the price you'd pay for ignoring me. I might have asked you to join me had you not already disobeyed me, but you are too much the sort of leader that must win the minds of those you command. I win the guts of a man, for in the wild here, hearts and minds follow food and shelter. Our lives can be broken on a patch of ice on a mountain pass, a bad measure of a mix, a bad harvest. My men and women know this, it is woven in their ropes. Our lands prepare us for the hardships of war, they prepare us for death. You know this because you are one of us. Or you were."

He turned then to his men and flicked his head towards mine. They took out their longswords. My men stood, looking to me for support. Khiese was turning back to watch his men kill mine, so I brought the edge of my hand up hard into his throat. He was quick. I hit his throat but he leaned back, taking the edge off it. As I brought my other fist round he blocked it. His wrist might as well have been an iron bar, cracking mine to throw the blow off. He punched me hard in the ribs and his other hand came back, the heel of it, into my nose. My head snapped back and I was done. My men started shouting, moving back and spreading out around the whiteboys. Khiese twisted from where he was sitting and put his knee in my belly as I tried to move away, my balance gone, fiery pins crackling like fat through my head and eyes from his breaking my nose. I fell forward unable to breathe. My men, Eirin's men, screamed as the swords slid in and out of them, the whiteboys working silently. I hit the ground on my hands and knees, unable to think. I looked up enough to see my men fall to the ground themselves as the whiteboys stopped, breathing hard, wiping their blades on their tunics.

Khiese coughed, tried to speak, which gave me a flash of comfort, before putting his boot in my belly again, taking my breath further away from me. I reached out, helpless, then heard him croak, "Beat her, then round up the rest of her pathetic crew."

My ears rang. I became aware of sucking breath through my mouth, something like a heavy serrated stone sitting squarely in my face, behind my nose and eyes. I thought one of them gone, I couldn't move it, couldn't blink, my hands feel cold. They're behind me, a sharp pain in my wrists, so I'm tied. I can't feel my feet, but my legs are together, tied as well. I am being moved. The rattling of a wagon, my head bounces against it. I can't tense, can't bring my knees up to try and bring myself upright. Something smells, no tastes wrong, raw meat or blood, it's close, must be if I can taste it. My eye is shut, muffled and constricted by the blood of a bruise. I open my

238

other eye and it's full of tears. I stretch the eyelids and try to clear them of their water. Before me, twitching with the rolling wheels over the rough trail, is a head. Though most of his face has been cut away, I see it's Thad. The hair, matted with blood, is unmistakably his, his hairline, creeping back either side of his forehead. I gasp, try to cough and spasm with my body's rejection of anything so violent as movement.

For all that I couldn't speak or cry properly, I said his name over and over, whined helplessly, kept looking at him.

A voice. Khiese, from behind me, speaking softly, as though of pleasantries.

"He gave us many good recipes, even without his lips. I kept his head because I thought you'd like to say goodbye before I let our dogs have it. Sleep now, Teyr, you'll see your family soon. You'll see as well that I keep my word. It's all I'm doing, Teyr: keeping my word."

I could barely move, a roiling wave of hate and despair, a desire to offer my life for theirs, before a cloth was put over my face, the greasy musty tang of hemlock filling my throat.

The next time I woke, there was a lot of noise, children crying, Khiese swearing.

"I lost twenty at the Auksens and now you're saying twenty-three more? To two mercenaries?"

Gruma spoke, I couldn't hear what he said except for a name. Sanger kept to the purse, Sillindar bless him.

I was still bound. My throat was swollen but I could taste piss, it was sharp and sour, all about me. I'd been covered in it at some point. I rolled my tongue about my cracked lips.

"She's awake, Chief." A voice above me. Someone jumped down off the wagon then.

Fresh wood was spitting, a fire nearby. Chalky's keep, Edma, was begging for their lives.

"Give Teyr a splash, she needs to see all of this," said Khiese.

Someone mounts the wagon. I'm pulled up, pain flares up my arm, it feels wrong, hanging in an unfamiliar way while bound to my other wrist.

Someone else takes my legs, and I'm lifted down before being dragged along grass, further from the fire. Edma is closer, Chalky too.

"Ma!" It's Mosa.

"Oh Sillindar, oh no." Aude.

I open my mouth to speak but nothing comes. A wet jelly is rubbed over the eye that isn't swollen. It's carefully wiped. It's Khiese, the hard skin of his hands unmistakable on my chin as he holds it up.

I open my eye. Aoig is setting, long shadows of trees across a frost made gold by it. The hemlock has made me sick, I'm queasy being upright on my knees. I lean forward to lie down but I'm held at the neck of my tunic. A small gob of spit gets as far as my chin, I can put nothing behind it.

"Chief, she stinks. How long do I have to hold her?"

"Hold her."

"Yes, Chief."

Aude and Mosa have tears in their eyes. Aude is trying to hug Mosa into him so he doesn't have to see me. Two of Khiese's whiteboys have spears on them.

"Amondsen, what have they done to you?" said Chalky.

Chalky and his boy Calut are on their knees like me, bound. I look about and see to my right Edma and the girls, Silje and Lees, kneeling as well, though they are not bound. They don't look defiled or hurt.

"We've done what I promised we would do, Merchant Knossen. I vowed to deal with you if you did not leave the Circle when my brother told you to do so at the Almet.

240

Teyr — and you shouldn't call her Amondsen because it's not right — Teyr chose violence, and you are all that's left of her van, apart from Yalle and her crew, one of your mercenaries? They bade farewell to your van barely having left Amondell, abandoning the purse. I expect they went south and you can't blame them, so few of them and so much to protect. Sanger wasn't so lucky, nor Eirin and her crew. All now dead."

He could have been telling a story to a friend in a tavern.

"Now, Merchant Knossen, let's begin with your family. I have a proposal. I can kill you and your son Calut, and your keep and girls go free. Or I can let you and Calut live and go free, and your keep and girls stay with us. They'll be well treated enough, could even be keeps for my whiteboys, when they're old enough."

He smiled and watched Chalky and Edma closely. This was a form of pleasure for him. A stunted life under a brutal father had killed something in him early on. I'd seen it in others.

"We have to take the second choice," said Chalky. "Don't we, Edma?"

She didn't say anything for a moment, her gaze was cold. "You might have told this horse gobbler he could have your coin and your ships, even that he could have our own lives if he but spared the children."

"Come now, Edma, that's not what he said."

"Think on it. You spoke awful quick in favour of me and our girls being slaves all our lives."

"He did, didn't he?" said Khiese. "He might have offered me his shipping interests. Anything really."

"No, Khiese, you wouldn't have taken them; you gave your options. Of course I can sign over my main ten shares in ships and sheds."

Khiese looked over at Edma. She bowed her head and started crying.

"Edma, he just wants you all to suffer; he's got no interest in coin," I said.

The rest of Khiese's whiteboys stood in a circle around us, watching this play out while they chewed on bread or drank from the flasks of wine from our wagons.

"Indeed, Teyr, what does coin buy out here?" He gestured to one of his crew. "Fetch Knossen and his son a couple of flasks and a pack of bilt and bread. A knife as well, in case they come across any wolf packs." A few of them laughed as his man walked off.

"Any final words for each other?" he said.

Chalky began crying, as did Calut, who leaned into him best he could.

"Why are you doing this to us?" cried Edma. "Why be so evil?"

"Evil?" Khiese pondered this a moment. "No. I'm only doing what is necessary. Perhaps I'm cruel, but I've never seen kindness achieve anything worthwhile."

"You . . ." I began, but stopped myself. Appealing to the memory of his mother Cwighan might play badly and get my brother in trouble.

"I, what? Go on, speak."

"You could let us all go, now. We'd ensure that your message to Othbutter got through. Those two won't make it alone. I could take them. I'm sorry if we did not heed your warning clearly enough. We heed it now."

"I won't dignify that with an answer."

His man returned with a small sack. Khiese gestured for Chalky and Calut to be untied.

"This expedition continued into the Circle after I commanded it to leave. This isn't your fault, it's Teyr's. I would say I hope you make it back to Hillfast, but I couldn't care either way. Go." He threw the sack at Chalky's feet. Chalky leaned down to pick it up. His girls tried to rise and run to them both, but the flat of a spear was laid across each of their chests.

"I love you," said Chalky. He wiped his eyes as Calut took his hand.

"Take care of the girls, Ma, we'll see you again," said Calut.

"Go, Calut, before I change my mind." Khiese turned to the men guarding Edma and the girls. "You two, take these three back to our camp, find them something to eat and drink." Two whiteboys lowered their spears and walked towards Chalky and Calut, who backed off, unable to take their eyes off Edma and the girls, who was pulled to their feet and dragged away, Edma managing a single punch in the face of the man holding her arm. He dropped his spear, put both hands on her shoulders to face him and drove his head into her face. The girls screamed as they watched their mother being dragged along the ground, her guard cussing to himself, the other whiteboys hollering and laughing after him. It wasn't long before Chalky and Calut had vanished from sight into the darkness, goaded and threatened by Khiese's men.

Khiese took a deep breath and waited for his soldiers to turn their attention back. This was for their benefit.

He turned to me and took out his knife. It shone, clean of poison, a polished curved blade sharp as the edge of the moon.

"I cannot be as lenient with you, Teyr. You are a famous soldier, though years past your best. You had this great ambition to run trade through the Circle with your coin and Othbutter's soldiers. You've let nothing stand in your way,

243

ignored my warning, killed one of my chiefs, lied to my brother. You haven't given a shit about anything I've said. You've shown me no respect at all." He walked over to Aude and Mosa. He nodded to one of his guards, who kneeled down behind Mosa and held him by his shoulders.

"I've thought about this. I'll explain shortly why I think I have to do this."

He stood to the side of Mosa, grabbed his hair and pulled his head back. He drew the knife quickly and firmly across his throat.

A red slit, a spitting of blood, the thin rolling curtain of my boy's life leaving him, coursing down his neck and into his shirt as he convulsed in the hands of the man holding him up. He clicked his tongue, gagged, mouth wide for air, his wild eyes on mine, disbelief, then fluttering with shock. I heaved, vomited and jerked myself up, only to be kicked back to the ground. His blood flooded his shirt, a black smear creeping through it. Aude screamed, a high and animal cry, throwing himself to our son, pulling at his bindings in a frenzy to free his arms, to somehow save him. But Mosa's head fell forward and he was still.

I smashed my head against the ground. I called his name. Aude wailed, "My boy, my boy, come back to me". He could not stop, the words descending to a guttural lowing.

A cheer went around the Circle of whiteboys, some mimicking the choking sounds he made. I was kicked a few times, then Aude was kicked and spat on.

I watched as the blood slowed. Mosa's hair hung over his face. I waited for him to speak, to look up again. I begged him to look up, thinking, *In just a moment he'll see me.*

Through it all Khiese stood, waiting for us to wear ourselves down into a stupor. He had cleaned the blade of his knife on a rag, discarded the rag, and was looking away to the last of the light in the west, calm as a cow. Then he come over to me and sat down next to me as I lay there shivering, blowing, my heart galloping in my chest. He leaned in towards me and spoke.

"Aude will stay with us, Teyr. I'm sure my soldiers, my whiteboys, will find a use for him. This should discourage you from coming back here. You wouldn't want him to die as well, would you? In fact, I can imagine that after a few days reliving what's just happened, he wouldn't want to see you again anyway. You might also wonder, in the days to come, why I didn't kill you, as you're the only threat. Well, this is because I believe one or more of the following things will happen, and they are all preferable to just cutting your throat. You'll be cut loose shortly and sent from here. You'll most likely die of cold, and that will take time because you're stubborn. But if you don't, one of two things will then happen. You'll find your way back to Hillfast and you'll tell Othbutter that the Circle is mine. You'll beg him not to come here with whichever soldiers he has left now I've killed his best, because I'll then kill Aude. Or, and I think this is more likely, you'll be questioned, but you'll tell him nothing, you'll find some way to explain what has happened, anything so that Aude may live. And you'll live out your life there, under my rule, unless, yes, perhaps at some point between now and then you won't be able to live with yourself, and you'll draw a knife over your own throat or thigh."

He put his hand to my cheek before smoothing my head. I threw my head around till he stopped.

Then he stood, spoke to the man behind me. "Reinid, cut her bonds then strip her. Her arm's broken, she won't be able to stop you. Once you're done, see she leaves our camp, see her on her way. I'll make sure there's a flask of wine kept back from her excellent supply."

245

"Yes, Chief."

Khiese turned to the circle of men and women around us.

"My whiteboys, I once again keep my word and the rewards are plenty. We'll leave this woman to her dead son."

They all dispersed. The man holding Mosa let him fall forward to the ground as casually as he might a sack of grain and also left. I looked over at Aude, who immediately fell forward himself and wriggled himself closer to Mosa, still whispering to him, talking to him.

"Goodbye, Teyr. I won't see you again." Khiese walked over to Aude and pulled him to his feet by his bound wrists, which caused him to cry out again. He punched Aude twice in the face until he stopped writhing. I watched them leave. I called Aude's name, but he did not look at me, his head straining back to linger on Mosa, fronds of blood swinging from his mouth. I was left alone with Mosa and this Reinid.

He cut my bound hands, and my left arm swung free, the pain a sudden, savage burning. I held it to my side instinctively, it was limp, the forearm bruised and swollen with the break. Reinid cut through my tunic, cut it off my body, and then cut off my shirt. Then he cut away my leggings, the bonds about my legs and finally pulled off my boots and socks. He groaned at the smell, for I'd been in these clothes for days and besides having shit myself I had been pissed on.

All I could think about was that I needed to bury Mosa. I could die the moment it was done, but with a fierce clarity I knew that I had to return him to the tapestry, though far from his bloodlands.

"Can you get up?" said Reinid. I whimpered as my arm moved with my attempt to stand.

"I'm burying him. Give me a stone, a plate, anything I can move soil with."

"I'm sorry, you have to go."

With a heave I got to my feet and cried out, my legs shaking with the effort. Blood ran down my ankles from the cuts the binding had made. I edged myself forward but collapsed to my knees, my feet numb, the blood needling its way back into them. I inched my way on my knees to my boy.

There was many that I had caressed as they lay dead. He reminded me of them, the boys and girls that never got to their twenty because plans go wrong, commands are misheard or brews aren't up to the job. As far as that simple truth went, Khiese was right. But life isn't ever simple. Mosa let me be his ma, let me feed him and dress him, go sniffing for bluehearts and throw him in the sea because he loved the shock of it, screeching for Aude to throw me in after.

I looked back at Reinid. He was trying not to look at me. He was chalked up white, but now I got a good look at him I could see he was as old as I was, and in his manner he was fretting.

"Reinid, I beg you, let me bury him. I want nothing more, no help, no clothes, no food, just something I can dig with, then I'll be gone."

"If one of the Khieses comes back I'll be whipped."

"If this was your own boy could you leave him, unable to return to blood, to go in the tapestry?"

He looked at Mosa. I'd put my head to the floor, begging him. I was shivering now as much with the pain of my arm as the cold.

I felt something land next to me. It was a wooden cup.

"Sillindar follow you," he said, then walked away to the distant fires and songs of their main camp.

There's never been, before or since, a longer night. The songs my ma sang to me through my fevers or while soaking my hands blistered from work, I sang to him. I told him all

247

my stories as I dug with that cup and my good hand, to take with him so he could sing them to his own mother. I found a stone I could cut through his bindings with and I took off his shirt, for it smelled of him, something I could keep while I pushed over his delicate, pale body and freckled face the icy wet soil that would set him free.

Part Two

Chapter 9

Now

Hillfast.

The soldiers did some work on me during the days we tracked the coast in an old cog from Port Carl to Hillfast, but I proved a bit too much trouble when they tried to give me a beating early on the voyage. Two of them still had wrappings around their hands; I heard one was still pissing blood, and that cheered me up. Their captain remarked on my capacity for pain before putting me in a neck trap. Now they cut my breath off whenever they're bored, and take bets on how long I'll last before I pass out.

There's little left of me. Those children give me something other than myself to worry about, but now I'm facing the gallows. Fuck it.

We're on the Gellessens' wharf. They was tight with Carlessen. Looks like my bounty will have to be split a few ways. Shavings of sunlight flutter through the deck planks with shadows moving above me. Beyond them the dockers' calls and greetings, the gulls will be breeding, their yakking fills the air, though the swelling around my ear makes it sound like there's a cup over it. I'm sure my face is ruined now. I lost two more teeth, I think, but one of them was giving me grief anyway. I've got cuts over my eyes and cheeks – I think one of the guards had a ring on his finger.

The dockers are unloading bolts of cotton, boxes of plant and other cargo. Then the soldiers open the hatch and climb down the ladder to where I'm standing, fixed in the neck trap to two poles.

The one that's been pissing blood, he's in charge of the other three. I can see his jaw twitch with the need to hurt me, but there's a shimmer to him that I'm seeing it in as well. It's taken time for these two eyes of mine to find a way to work together. The headaches have all but gone, and yet I think I'd rather not have had both eyes replaced, for all the trouble it's caused me. The world isn't the same when I close my left eye. I've struggled to see out of the left eye anyway after the attentions of clubs and fists, and I have tried to fathom what it is this black eye sees, besides what everyone sees. It sees the story of things, or rather, the riddle, for I feel as though there's things I sense but cannot make sense of. My eye sees intent, sees shifts in feeling. Sillindar told us of the song of the earth, a sense of our belonging and place. The Oskoro must know this in a way my one eye can only signal.

Two men unlock the poles from the beams and hold them. Their letnant steps up to me.

"I'm going to untie you. You can walk up the ladder or be choked out and pulled up it by your trap, if you want to try kicking me again. That clear?"

"I'll be quiet." I hadn't spoken in days. It was a croak, lispy with my broken lips and bruises.

"Good. You look a mess."

"Sip of water?"

"Didn't think the dead was thirsty," he says.

My arms and legs are untied and I'm brought out into the light. I manage to breathe a bit of the sea through my nose, the sour tang welcome on my tongue. The trap's too tight for me to look about, and I want to look up over the dock, the port, to the Crackmore path that winds its way up the hillside to our house.

There's a gathering on the narrow run of the quay, Othbutter's militia waiting at the bottom of the gangplank. A number have stopped their work in the sheds facing the front.

"Gallows!" and "Hang the ugly whore!" are among the shouts, but as I'm led down the plank the spitting starts, a few stones are thrown, one of which gets me good in the back of the head and causes a cheer as I buckle for a moment. Word passes quickly along the quay that Crogan's killer is being led along. I keep my eyes down, seeing cobbles I walked for years after I come home from Marola, inspecting cargo and running my tallies. I feel a trickle of blood running down my neck. I suppose it doesn't matter.

"Teyr!"

The first anyone's said my name. I look up. Tarrigsen, aghast. He's on the steps of the guildhall with some other merchants, who look away, though Iddie Trups and Kieltsen know full fucking well who I am and how I stood for them in years past against tithes and strikes they brought on themselves with their meanness. Tarrigsen doesn't say any more, and I can't turn my head, pushed onwards I'm guessing to Othbutter's chamber of justice or the Hill, the jailhouse dug into the cliffs that rose from this end of the bay.

I hear, in among the Common and Abra, many other languages: Juan, Farl, even Vilmorian.

"The tourneys been already?" I shout to the letnant in front of us.

"A few weeks ago, a success it was and all, people from all shores come for it, except for one Farlsgrad lord I heard lost his recipe book on a side bet. A recipe book! I'll bet my balls Farlsgrad'll be coming after whoever won it. But don't worry, if the Hill's fuller than usual we'll rig up a hammock in the cess there."

"Kiss my cinch."

I'm shoved forward by the soldier wielding the pole behind me, and this forces me to cough.

"We're here. Let's see if the chief's flag is there." By which he means the yellow flag that showed hearings was under way at the chamber.

The chamber is set at the heart of the markets. Here all manner of catch fills my nose and makes my belly ache, but the smell of roasting nuts most of all, a smell that would have Mosa tugging my dress and pulling me over to get him some.

The letnant is talking to one of the militia at the door to the chamber, the soldiers around me taking turns to light up some pipes and fish for the attentions of women or girls unfortunate enough to get near them.

Soon enough he's back, telling us no flag, but word was being sent to Othbutter that I was here.

I'm taken to the lower level in the jail, known as the Coffins. One of the floor grates is opened, not much more than a coffin-sized space, carved out of the stone. I'm stripped from the waist down, which gives a few in the coffins nearby a chance to ask me to join them. I'm forced down into a coffin by pressure from the poles on the neck trap. My backside is pushed against a trough carved to take down into the caves whatever I expel, an innovation that made this one of the better prison duties a guard could be put on.

The grate is pushed down over me, heavy, trapping me still as it does the others. After an hour of this weight there's a savage sharp aching across my body, beyond which I can barely hear the noise of others telling me how they'd like to use me. They are only distracting themselves from the pain they also are undergoing. I let it fill me. It drowns out Mosa.

It makes little difference, I shortly learn, where they put your backside in relation to a channel for whatever you shit, because later that night a couple of the guards come down to the Coffins. They relieve a night's ale over us, aiming at the faces of those sleeping especially. I guess it's the newer prisoners that make the most noise about it, for they're told to get used to it by others.

One of the guards kneels on my grate and starts pulling himself off over my face while the woman that's with him is cheering him on. The woman laughs hard at this, tells me I shouldn't feel honoured, he does it to all of them in here. I feel him finish himself on me. I tell him that I feel sorry for his keep if he's that quick with her. He hits me once on my head with the pole end of his spear before she cusses at him to stop. Turns out they're eating food and wine they was bribed to give me, and getting food into the Hill, down here in particular, requires some sort of clout. Tarrigsen, it must be. I feel like taunting them, but they've been soaking in cups, and guards fit for this sort of duty make all sorts of bad decisions when they're soaked.

As they leave the others calm down, some muttering, some singing muke-thickened verses of old songs, and there was two kept arguing about the mistakes the other made that got them here. Tarrigsen didn't look well when I saw him earlier. Thinner. There's a rot gets in your pipes and eats you up from inside and I fear it's in him. Might be he's thinking of some way to get me off the gallows. He runs much of the dock, though these two wouldn't have eaten what he'd sent down if they thought there was a mosquie's chance I wasn't going to hang.

The hours pass, shifts change, measuring the night's coming and going. I snatch sleep between the men's agits. One asks me if I really did kill Crogan. I tell him I deserve this, and nothing more.

The door's bolt is drawn back with a heavy crack and it swings open.

"She's there. Tell her Kristluk's going to save up a big shit just for her when he's in later."

"Tell Kristluk that if this happens, I will end his rope, for they will no longer be able to work in Hillfast."

"You're a cleark, go fuck yourself."

Thornsen, a voice varnished to a soft shine, my immaculate high cleark. My eyes fill up because he will see me like this. I had not wanted to see him for all that I loved him. That was another and better Teyr Amondsen.

He holds a torch out towards me and squats down to get closer to me. I can barely move my head, my neck seems frozen in iron. He's typically well groomed, a clean short beard, his cap, tunic and leggings navy and grey, also clean and well sewn, for he apprenticed as a tailor for years before his letters earned him work as a cleark.

He too has tears in his eyes and he comes forward onto his kneecaps and puts his hand to my cheek. "I'm so sorry."

I had cried enough these last few seasons since I left Mosa's body and went south to the Mothers, but his sorrow cut me open again. I had taken our friends away and killed them.

"Please go, Thornsen, I can't bear this."

"Othbutter won't return from his hunt until evening. I will petition for your release then."

"No. No, don't. I can't bear to be alive. My interests, my ships, it's yours, yours and Tarry's."

"But Cherry found you, she told me what you said had happened. You didn't kill Crogan, Seikkerson did."

"Fucking shut it!" barks the man in the coffin to my right, and he says it again and again.

"We can't talk, Thornsen, there's too much to say. The Kelssen children that was with us, with me, Cherry and Leyden, look out for them and prepare for war, for Samma Khiese's coming. Now go."

He's about to protest when the cunt next to me who's shouting starts a chain of others off that brings the guard.

"You'll have to leave, your silver in't going to cover this lot gettin' the agits, and all the extra work swilling them out when they get angry listening to you."

"I'll see you tomorrow, Master." He stands up, both knees clicking, something he used to moan about often, and the torchlight fades with his footsteps. With him goes the foul smell of the dipped torch and the fine smell of orange oil that he's used in his beard since we first met.

"We'll all see you tomorrow, and watch that old neck of yours snap," shouts one of the guards back at me.

"It'll be worth it not to have to listen to your shit any more."

I can't help but cry out as they unlock the grate pressed on me the next day. I cannot straighten myself, though they pull me up by my arms and slap me about, as though that will move the cramp and deadness from my limbs. I'm thrown to the ground and a robe is put over me to spare those in the justice the sight of my body, I'm sure. I shake and shiver with the effort of trying to move even slightly. A few kicks are meant to encourage me, but it takes hours for a body to set itself after being in the coffins. There's many I've seen deformed by them when their punishment sent them back there too often.

It's hard to say how I'm feeling otherwise. The end of a life, the hands of the dying I've held down the years, it all goes this way: a shallow mixture of the fondest memories drowned out by the unbearable vivacity of the world around you, a gluey wax of sense, the cold on my bare arms, the scratch of wool hardening my nipples, the thickness of smells: sweat, oil, wounds.

Eventually I am pulled to my feet. The guards put a shoulder under either arm and drag me out. Torches provide miserly pools of light on the worn, slick steps of this dungeon. The light of morning, when the iron-braced door is dragged open, hits me with the grace of a cooper's mallet. I'm given many names by the guards clustered in the irons room, changing shifts over pipes and bowls of nettle tea. I'm a "bald cratch", a "spim-drunk drooper". "Dead cunt walking" is the truest of them. I hope they can get me in the noose before the day's out.

There's little fuss at the sight of a prisoner as I'm dragged more briskly out of the Hill and through the market to the chamber. I haven't been given boots, the earth and dung are cold enough to numb my toes as they scrape the ground. It's a blue sky; snow-white clouds thick as butter shape Aoig's light. The black eye softens the edges of the stalls and buildings around me, the notes they sing in concord with the melodies of laughter and prices hollered.

I wonder at the beauty that must fill the days of the Oskoro who have been changed by the Flower of Fates, those who receive the seed. I wonder too if they can pass on how they've changed to their children as the rest of us do our noses, eyes and hair. It stops me thinking about the judgement that's coming as I'm led into the chamber. It takes a moment to realise that the yellow flag isn't flying. The chamber doors are opened by militiamen, and beyond the beams of sunlight draw hard sharp squares on the dark flagstones of the main floor. I'm dropped to my knees by the guards before they turn and leave. I feel like a child, but I have no choice and I cuss as I lean forward to find a way to hold myself free of the spasms of pain I'm suffering in my spine. Then, for a moment, I could believe I'd woken up from some awful dream, for Othbutter sits in the simple wooden chair, Tobber to his side, a table for a jug and a cup at Othbutter's other hand. His hair might be greyer, he might be fatter, his belly filling his lap. His tunic is a rough woollen one, the one he's always preferred for passing judgement on ending a life, pretending he's a servant to the law of the land while before the poor.

But it's not a dream. Aude isn't standing behind me. I'm no longer full of the future I had for us.

Then I sense another here with us, in the shadows behind the beams of light, but I'm standing in one, shielding them from sight.

"Teyr, of the Jonassen clan," begins Tobber, giving me Aude's name since I'd become his keep.

"I'm an Amondsen, Tobber, you streak of shit, and you did me the honour of calling me Amondsen the last time I was stood here. But back then you had an agreement on my wine shipments that you kept off your scrolls, I believe."

I hear a laugh choke itself off. It sounds familiar. Othbutter raises his eyebrows.

"Othbutter, I didn't kill your brother, the Seikkersons did. If you won't believe me put me in the noose and get this fucking thing over with. I'm done."

I get a dig in my ribs for that, but I keep my eyes on him.

"Amondsen. The Seikkersons are loyal to us. Jeife

259

Seikkerson brought my brother's body back to his bloodlands to be buried before winter just gone. His tithe was true, generous indeed. He told me you left Crogan to the whims of this warlord Khiese."

"He's smoking Khiese and he's played you. Khiese now knows your strength, or lack of it, and the lie of land from Elder Hill through here. I expect you're recruiting for war?"

At that Othbutter looks off to his left, to the person standing in the darkened corner. "You are the only reason I'm not having her flayed where she sits." He turns back to me. He wants to say more, but what I said about Jeife must have made him think.

"What makes you speak of war, Amondsen? What can you tell us of this Khiese?"

"What is there to say? He has the Circle united against you. He's harder than you, cleverer. He'll end your rope before taking the rest of the citadel."

"You seem keen to die, Amondsen. You've met Khiese, assessed his numbers, how they're armed, the way they work? Will you not show your loyalty to the staff? To me? Your knowledge could spare you the noose."

"I'd rather the noose than a few months in a cell before Khiese takes over this port and finds me. You don't have the soldiers or the loyalty in enough clans for the army you'll need."

Othbutter stares at me for a moment, thinks better of replying and reaches for his jug to fill his cup.

I remember Khiese's words, his threat to kill Aude, but Aude would be dead now, all this time later. I can't bear to think of him alive if I'm honest. The sun is warm on my head. I wish I could be left alone. I catch Tobber's eye. He looks to his feet, hands clasped behind his back, clearly pleased.

"You should smile a bit more, Tobber, give your keep a shock when you go home later. You was right though, wasn't you? I failed. And I lost Aude and Mosa, Thad, Eirin. I'd like to know if Chalky made it back with his son?"

"No sign of him, his keep or his children at his sheds or the guildhall. I've taken on his interests as he had no brother," says Othbutter.

Poor bastards. Even if Khiese had truly let them go, they just wouldn't have survived the journey back on their own – no snowcraft. They might have shared the truth about Crogan had they made it.

It occurs to me as I look about me that there can't be more than four or five people in the room: Othbutter, Tobber, whoever it was that laughed and the guards behind me.

"Brilde, Hamskke, leave us," says Othbutter.

I hear them turn and walk out, the heavy black larch doors closing.

"No witness to rolls? Are you going to kill me here?"

"No. We should talk about a way out of this for you, Blackeye. Isn't that what I heard you've been called down in Carlessen lands?"

This voice comes from the corner. It takes me as long to place it as the speaker takes to step into the light.

"Nazz?"

Where do I begin with this fucker? I knew him all my life from the day I arrived in Hillfast on a van as a girl looking to change the world, through to the day in Marola he set me and Thad up to die. He'd shared both our beds. I'd loved him as a keep, then as a brother, and we wandered half the world with Ruifsen and Threeboots. He had long-knots then, hair the colour of pine, but age has salted it all over as it has mine. He moves like he still does his Forms, but he's a ganger now, and it doesn't pay to look weak. Even his colour looks like it's had a shot recently. I realise as I take him in that his skin, often so bad in the field from a reaction of some kind to guira, was less blotchy, fewer white flakes and crusts of skin mottling him.

"I'm sorry about Aude and your boy. Sorry about Thad too – I loved him. Where you been since before winter?"

"What do you want?" I want to spit on him, scream at him for how false he is in saying all this, but I'm on my knees, leaning forward on an arm, and that wobbling with the effort of keeping me in a position free of pain. It's all I can do to keep my breathing even.

In the years since I've been back at Hillfast I knew he was about of course, saw him from time to time, but he lived in the nights and I the days. He wouldn't meet my eye when we did pass in the lanes or on the quays, but I shared too many pipes with him before Marola to hold such proper hate in my heart that I'd go after him.

"I'm here to find out if you want to get some revenge on Khiese," he says.

"Why have we lost my guards?"

I know the answer, I see it in Othbutter's eyes. I see a flush as well, a shiver of colour of sorts, close to anger from what I'd learned of the way this black eye sees. Khiese may have spies in Hillfast.

"The fewer that know of this the better," says Nazz.

"How much land has Khiese taken? He's reached Elder Hill and he's got whiteboys a few days from Port Carl. Is that about it?"

They share a glance. Their faces, eyes searching for what to say, speak of much that is left out, much they're not sharing, but I cannot fathom what.

"I'm putting a crew together," says Nazz. "Khiese threatens us all."

"I supposedly killed your brother, Chief. Am I a threat to you or not?"

"Not where you're going, to the noose or elsewhere,' says Othbutter. "I'd have you in the fucking noose, you old cratch, and I'd drag you there myself, but our mutual friend sees a use for you, maybe even recover your honour."

"You're right, Teyr. You were always right," says Nazz before I can reply. "Mercs and soldiers from the north will take time to assemble. They're being mustered, but a needle in the heart's as good as a hammer to the head. We can be the needle, and you know all about the heart it needs to find."

Kill Khiese.

I see him again, dirty yellow colour and copper hair. I hear his flat, calm certainty, his purpose rooted deep and cold as Sillindar's Eye is fixed above us.

"We had near fifty, including the chief's best, my own best, Sanger and Yalle, and Sanger and his man Jem did for near forty of them on their own trying to save the lives of my family. It did us no good, all the clans are for him. You're against all of them, to the last."

"Sanger was fierce, I'll grant you, but you took a van in there, Teyr — families. We're going in there and we're killing everyone between us and Khiese, just a handful of us, able to ride fast, hide easily. We'll do it better with you." He come closer to me, to get a better look. I read all too clearly in the lines of his face and set of his eyes how troubled he was by all the damage I carried.

"What happened to you? Your eye?"

"Infection I picked up."

He knew that was cow shit but said no more.

"Teyr," says Othbutter, "you seem ready to die, old girl. I can give you that, out on the gallows. Tobber'd tie the knot himself, wouldn't you, Tobber? Or you can find death yourself, if what you say about Khiese is true. The second way of dying puts a sword in your hand and gives you the chance to avenge your family. Kill Khiese, then you come back and droop yourself out on the purse you'd have earned, gold of course, fully thirty Hope pure and a stretch of Khiedsen land too for they will be punished for the sins of their son. I can't hide that I can see the threat Khiese poses me, which is why it makes sense for me to be generous, even to you, if it'll turn your head towards our common enemy."

I roll my arms at the shoulders, the pain makes me hiss. I look between Othbutter and Nazz. Something's not being said. Nazz is making coin by the barrel. There aren't many sheds or merchants clean of him. It seems like suicide if the point of it is turning some coin. But here he is, with that sure look in his eye, that "One more brandy; what's the worst can happen?" like we're soaking it up way past wise in a tavern after beating some poor debtor about for Fat Steppy.

Khiese.

I don't much give a shit, now I think about it, what it is going on between these two. My belly's aching for something to eat, like it knows I'm no longer going to the gallows. More than that, the healing the Oskoro have done, the plant inside me that keeps me alive, tingles sharply, making clear its own need perhaps.

I think about putting a sword in Khiese, right up to the hilt. It brings a tear to my eye.

"I'll join your crew, Nazz. I just hope you remember everything I taught you after all these years frightening poor debtors with what's left of your colour. Chief, Tobber, I'm going to find some boots and then some wine. I'll need some coin though."

"Chief!" began Tobber. Othbutter raises his hand and cuts him off.

"Nazz, she's your responsibility now. As are the others. We'll meet once more before you leave." Othbutter gets out of his chair with a grunt of effort and leads Tobber out to his office at the back of the hall, whispering to him all the way along.

"Yes, Chief," says Nazz after him. He comes up to me and puts his hand on my shoulder as I kneel. I am both too sore and too shocked to react and push him off so I let it happen, feeling his awkwardness.

"I'll have Talley, my drudha, look at those wounds," he says, "and give you something for what the Coffins have done to your bones."

"Not today. I just want to find something to wear, something warmer than this, get myself a bath and razor my head. You can give me some coin for that and then find me a fieldbelt and a good sword if you want to be useful. For the belt I'll need luta leaves, whatever dayer you've got, preferably a galerin mushroom base. What's the base for the fightbrew you have? Walnut and butterbur twist?"

"Something like that. There's a spread of fireweed, bark, shiel, lark in the scabbards, arnica presses, betony mix for paying colour. Othbutter will have guards following you, you know that."

I don't answer, I just want to be let outside. I hold my hand up for him to pull me to my feet. He takes my weight as I heave myself up and holds me steady as I whimper at the pain in my knees and hips. I shush any words he's about to speak and he waits silently while my body remembers its duty.

"You should come to the Mash Fist tonight," he says. "Threeboots will be there, she'll be cheered to see you after all these years."

"Let me have some coin, Nazz. I want to go." I think of

Threeboots a moment, one of my old crew, but then I can't be bothered, I can't work up any anger, let alone regret. If she ever listened to me on a purse it was only because she loved Nazz. Betraying me and Thad down in Marola wouldn't have caused her a wink of lost sleep.

"You made the right choice coming with me, and you're field-ready, Teyr, deep colour, all cut stone corners as we used to say. I'm trying to persuade Ruifsen to come, Threeboots is with us, she's on my purse anyway, and one of my cutters told me he saw Salia on the quay, which is a sign Sillindar watches over us – well, if we want to believe that shit and if she'll take the purse. She apparently came in on a ship two days ago. There's a few of your friends from the Coffins who know their way about arms and'll be happy to avoid the noose. Then there's my own people, and I'd stand my coin on them against anything in the Circle."

I say nothing. He shrugs, takes two silver pieces from his belt, Hope stamped, a lot of coin for most who live hereabouts.

"I know where to find you, Nazz. How long before we leave?"

"How long do you need, Teyr? To recover from your stint in the Coffins and pay back in I mean, proper colour. You'll need a few flasks and a week or so, I'd say. Stop in at shed twelve for your belt, sword and flasks tomorrow. Would you go to see Ruifsen? He's at the farm, has been a long time, as you probably know, but I'm sure if you asked him to come he would; there's nothing he wouldn't do for you, and he hasn't changed."

"Meaning there's nothing he would do for you. There's a time you'd both do anything for me, Nazz, until Marola, and he had the droop for an excuse when you all rode away and left me and Thad with forty-odd mercenaries paid for a crossroads on us." "Crossroads" meant they had to kill us or die trying. Serious purse.

I let go of his hand. I'm steady so I turn and leave him standing there and shuffle up to the doors to the just, and I open them to the day, the sea, the life of the port, salt and sweet, ignorant of what might be coming. Fucking Othbutter.

With no yellow flag flying, nobody's slowing as they pass in the hope of seeing hangings or floggings at the stand.

I look up to the hills. I can't help myself. I'm looking to where our house is, looking to get away from these crowds, find some sky with a flask of wine and a thick piece of ham.

I head along Ridsen, left off the justice and I walk around wagons that have got themselves in a mess, one with a broken wheel. Alik's is open, one of the places Steppy used to run. The air's greasy with heavy, bad bacca and rot in the mortar and wood, but that's always been its air and it hasn't fallen in yet. One of the silvers gets me their "finest Juan imported" brandy, a muslin-wrapped hunk of salted bacon and a half-wheel of cheese. I give a handful of pennies to go around those that serve and cook.

If I'm being followed I don't see them. I wonder if Nazz has had a word.

I turn right off Ridsen onto Wadey and right again onto Packham, the east quay's merchant quarter. Then I'm through the shadows of Folken alley to the tall gate, up through the farmers' huts and the hill beyond them. The stony path is warm on my soles as I climb the hill. It quickly turns muddy and the nettles at the top catch and nip me all over. "Paths need walking," Aude had said. "Our boots make them strong." And I'm watching his boots a few steps ahead, his odd gait that I felt belonged to me, his fine legs. Finally I crest the hill above the harbour at Hillfast, and before me, a hundred or so feet off, is our house. I see a bright new fence post and planks, fresh and proud amid their weathered and weary neighbours, speaking of a recent repair. Thornsen. I remember now he'd come up here on his day off to give his children somewhere to run among the old apple trees, but it seems he's also keeping the place in some order.

The path from the gate is swept, the gate opens silently, recently oiled.

"You haven't oiled the main door though," I say out loud, for it cracks open with a rasp. The rooms are empty, silent but for the feathery scratching of a mouse somewhere nearby as I move to the windows and unlatch the shutters. We had goat-horn plates put into a frame before the shutters, so that we could have some sunlight in my little office and our main room without the cold. These were the first such windows many had seen, though they were everywhere in Marola, a legacy of the wealthy Harudanians during their occupation of that land.

The plates bleach the sun to the colour of butter. Only two chairs remain in the room, and like the desk they're thick with fronds of dust. Each bare nail in the walls is a marker, a needle of remembrance for the embroidery or carving that once hung there but now lies in a chest in our bedroom. I follow the nails that mark the walls through the hall into the kitchen and scullery beyond, though with the shutters fast only my black eye can see. I see instead Mosa and a kitchen girl I can't now recall the name of watching Aude skinning a rabbit; the soft crack as the feet are severed, his swift cutting, the easy pull and twist of the fur leaving the glistening, vulnerable-looking body, the length of it always a surprise. I close my eyes to wish this memory away, but the smell of its blood is making me light-headed. Mosa is speaking, saying something I can't quite catch, the girl's head is tilted as though listening to Aude, who may have been instructing her.

I have to get away and walk back along the hall. I'm at the door to our bedroom. Two candles, one at Mosa's bedside, one at ours. I'd wake earlier than them, always, the price of the colour, the pain seeping through whatever salves and kannab give me sleep. Every morning, turning back at the doorway, candle in hand, checking to be sure I haven't disturbed them. Aude's hand would move over the cooling fur where I'd lain, Mosa only a tuft of hair visible in a ball of wool on his own mat.

"Then I'd crack out my bones before I made the fire," I say, "cussing and fucking freezing until it got going." The echoes of my voice slip and slide through the house, as though the house itself doesn't want to hold or bear me speaking to it. It makes me shiver.

"Why am I here?"

"You don't know?"

I spin, startled, I go for my sword instinctively, my hand brushing the wool of my tunic.

"Thornsen! Fucking Sillindar, you move quiet."

"And you're still quick. That sword would be through me if you'd worn it, then I'd be sorry. I guessed it might be you but couldn't be sure."

He's standing at the front door I left open.

"I spoke to ward off the ghosts. They don't want me here."

"I've brought up some kindling, candles, some oil and a flask of uisge. Would you sit with me, Master?" He takes a cloth from a pocket in his cloak for my tears the moment before they fall. My crying takes over and he hugs me close and waits.

"Come on now. Let's get a fire going here, see if the house'll remember you then."

With some wood I hadn't noticed was piled in the corner of the room, he gets a fire going in the hearth while I'm

269

sitting there, breaking off mouthfuls of cheese and swigging them down with brandy. He pulls up the other chair next to me, and we watch the flames lick the bark of the bigger cuts, building its appetite.

"You bring Epny and the children here?"

"Yes, Master."

"Fuck it, Thornsen. Teyr please, just Teyr. I'll not be Master again."

"Of course. We came for the apples after you'd all left last year and I thought they'd need some cropping anyway to get a good yield this year. Epny baked you some in pastry if you recall, with that bit of sugar you gave us from the *Thirsty Crow*'s cargo. Anyway, I wanted to keep the house in some order for you, for your return. We had some good feasts here over the years, all your crew's children and . . . you showed us all such kindness." I take his hand and hold it while I nip at the brandy, warming up my throat, filling my chest with oranges and browns. Epny was beautiful, a bawdy bark of a laugh, happiest in the vortex of their four children, the sister I never had.

I tell him what happened to us. I don't tell him about the Mothers and the things I did there to live, only what come after, with the Kelssens and today with Othbutter.

"I'll have Leyden visit that almshouse when he's back at Carl, see how our coin's being spent caring for those duts," says Thornsen, before tipping a measure of uisge into the cap of the flask. It catches in his throat and he coughs. I never saw the appeal, but then he's never tried to swallow the awful mulch and curd of a fightbrew, closest thing to a throatful of nettles there is.

"Is his shirt here?"

"It is, Teyr. It's in the bedroom. I found a lovely satchel to keep it in. Do you want to see it?"

I always see it.

"No. I'm just glad it's home. I hope he will have been able to follow it."

The fire's warmth is welcome, the flames echoing in the chimney. My feet are warming up.

"I want you to have my concern, Thornsen. You've run it, you've helped me and guided me all the way since I hired you. You and Epny have sacrificed so much to see it go well. I don't intend to come back here, even if I was carrying Khiese's head."

"You said that to me yesterday. I'm not interested."

"Who will run it otherwise? There's too many good people relying on you now."

"We can't talk about this now, Teyr. Too much may still happen. There's much good still to do."

"The only good I can see is killing Samma Khiese, and who will that bring back from the dead?"

He gives me a sympathetic look, lays his arguments down and huffs his way through another mouthful of uisge.

"You're going back to the Circle."

"He said he would kill Aude if I did," I says.

"Do you believe him?"

"I don't know. Aude must be dead. It's been so long, and we both know he's got no wild in him."

"Can you live not knowing? Does he think you'll go back after him?"

"Khiese? He probably thinks I'm beaten. Always in his speaking he was sure of himself. Not sure, certain. What have you heard about matters east?"

His face darkens. He struggles to meet my eyes as he looks for what to say.

"It isn't good, Teyr. The Crutters have been to see Othbutter, according to his guards, and his guards talk when a bit of plant is wanted of course."

"Of course."

"Crutter's lost three Families now and then half his remaining men trying to claim them back from Khiese. Othbutter's lost the Crutters and given they won't side with Khiese the merchants are expecting a coup. Crutters and some Kreigh clans they're tight with might well be marching in with more soldiers than Othbutter can muster, though he's had the call out for a few months now for any and all mercenaries to come. The worst is, I'm sorry to say, Elder Hill and Faldon Ridge have fallen to Khiese."

"Omar?"

"No word. I sent three scouts separately, none have come back. Families taken care of."

I have nothing to say for a bit, remembering how Omar's jokes was dry as sand and he'd always be getting our apprentices to ask the smith for a left-handed hammer or to see the carpenters and coopers for wax nails.

"Best castellan I ever saw, they all loved him at the Ridge, loved him wherever he went."

"We took the last chests of coin only a few weeks before it went quiet. His report spoke of some trouble in the Circle — bandits — and he'd requested coats of chain and arms, ingots as well."

I know what I'll find when we get to Faldon Ridge. I see no point in sharing it with Thornsen.

"Othbutter's fucked," I says.

"Quite."

I sip the brandy, feel him watching me.

"You should come to the house tonight, Teyr. We'll put a bath on for you, Epny'll take care of you." He struggles to speak. "You . . ."

"Look the wrong side of sixty? I know." I feel like a sack of gravel. I'd be worse, fingers and toes only saved from

272

frostbite by whoever the Oskoro have that pass for drud-harchs. My hands are lumpy, the colour blackened in places by bruises, cuts and whatever they put on my fingers. I haven't had salts or rubs for a long time and I got used to everything being sore and hurting.

"I was going to say you'll let us fit you out properly for this purse. If you have some time you should get back on the brews and the rubs, it'll help you with your Forms so you can go and execute this bastard and bring Aude home."

I think briefly about refusing to go with him, drink myself under and sing to the darkness filling the house beyond this room. That would be too easy, too soft. I think I'll put up with their love for a while, straighten myself out for what's to come.

Chapter 10

I'm standing over a bench in the Mash Fist, where I'd spent the previous few days sleeping to avoid seeing any of my old company. I'm fixing my belt, packing a bedskin, bilt and other bits for the walk to Ruifsen's farm. Good as their word, Thornsen and Nazz had fitted me out proper with what I'd need for a return to the Circle.

"Teyr?"

Her accent hasn't changed; she always made my name sound more exotic than it is, like some breathy and beautiful sigh.

Salia.

She hasn't changed since she was in my crew; at six foot tall she draws all the eyes in the room to her. Perhaps the beauty in her face which tapers like an almond is a little more set, hard work and age thinning out the softness of youth. Her green eyes are lit up by the deep brown and blue-shaded skin of the colour she's paid. She still has her black hair, though it's tied back in a thick tail. She was the difference on more skirmishes than I can count, a killer as cold as they come. What I recall of her dry and unforgiving humour, her beautiful body as we shared skins on nights out in the field, was long worn out with her betrayal back in Marola.

She walks over from the doorway, and I put my arms out for an embrace, a chance to get a sense of how ready she is, because I feel like we'll be talking about Nazz's purse very shortly. I'm suspicious of why she's here at this time, even if Nazz isn't. She feels hard and strong, square cut as Nazz would have said. I hold her hands as we pull back and they feel agreeably rough and callused.

"You still move like a dancer and your hands still feel like they hold a sword," I says.

"I can choose my work these days, though it's all for Farlsgrad's king and it pays well. Word's crossed the Sar regarding Othbutter's troubles in the Circle. I thought I'd see for myself. I saw you yesterday, coming in here with a freshly waxed pack and that new scabbard you're wearing. A new sword as well?"

"I'm off to see Ruifsen. He still lives about, his brother's farm. Thought I'd walk it."

She gives me a feeble smile, no interest in Ruifsen but too polite to say otherwise.

"Are you taking that handsome lad that's pretending he's not watching this place from across the lane?"

"I am. A long story."

"Like that beautiful eye of yours. What caused it? Is it some new recipe?"

"Salia, it's good to see you alive and looking so well, but let's not pretend you give a shit about me and I'll pretend you didn't leave me to die in Marola. Why don't you find Nazz, whose purse I've just taken, and join the crew he's putting together? I suspect it's why you're here."

She nods slowly, taking that one on the chin. It surprises me that she isn't protesting ignorance of Nazz's crew and

275

that perturbs me all the more. She was a frighteningly good merc back in our prime, and her leathers, her colour, the strong smell of her plant speak well of her coin and status now. I'd wager she's been sent by someone close to the king to report on the state of Hillfast.

"Seems like you've had a hard few years, Teyr. It would explain you paying in again. Give Ruifsen Sillindar's blessing from me, would you?"

"Of course I will. May Sillindar follow you."

I had no desire to suggest we meet up on my return, for all that I guessed she might have felt at least a bit awkward about seeing me again after what happened. So I walk past her and out of the Mash Fist onto the lane. I gesture to the man Salia had pointed out, the guard that was to watch me.

"I hope you've got your walking feet on, lad. Get yourself a pack, we're leaving for the North Four farms. Did they only send you?"

He sulks and whistles to another further along the lane, signs to him what we're doing.

"I have to have your sword, Teyr," he says. "I don't want to be run through the moment I fall asleep out there."

"Get a fucking hold of yourself, boy. I'm wearing this sword and I have no desire to run and save my life, let alone kill you to do it. I'm just looking for a few chalk-faced traitors I can die with. Bring your friend along, he'll give you someone to talk to."

I fret about Salia appearing like she has, but if she joins Nazz's crew I reckon there's time enough to work out her position. With the two guards and their bows at the ready keeping some way out of my hearing I take them onto the Sixty, which refers to the number of trails that connect the farms in the quarters which are all worked by Othbutter's own family.

Pair hadn't set camp in their lives, so needed some telling about what to fetch and how to do a watch. Seems like they never did night work either, not even a recipe for night seeing, and both fell asleep, needed waking as the weger birds started their scritching at the turn of Aoig.

Few bother us as we pass through with Othbutter's seal. The big galerin mushroom sheds cluster like villages amid the runs of celery, shiel and henbane. Seems little awareness out here that there's trouble east. Thornsen knew many of the clearks on the lots here and visited often, securing us prices that others couldn't get in return for ensuring the people here had a few kickbacks and someone in Hillfast they could trust on their visits to the markets there.

The point of me visiting Ruifsen was to persuade him not to come with us though, despite Nazz and whatever he and Othbutter was both plotting and paying in coin. I know it hasn't gone so well with Ru in the years since we come back to Hillfast. He put his coin into his brother's farms but his brother's become a soak and a dicer and lost one of them. Now Ru works them, I guess to protect his investment, managing the two left and trying to bring his niece and nephews on so they don't lose everything, and I'd have him do that for he deserves his happiness.

Like a lot of things I wish was different, I wish I had time to have seen him more in the years I was building up my own interests and got taken up with Aude and Mosa. It's always easy to put off seeing those you love if they're a way away. Perhaps you think they'll always be there, so there's no rush. But it isn't true.

Ru looked after me all my life, from when I first left Hillfast for the fighting on the Farlsgrad border. He had served for Hillfast for a few years by then against Northspur in the Larchlands, so he was quieter than the rest of us new recruits, who didn't know better what killing does to you.

When I first left Amondell and my family all those years ago I joined a van that was passing through to Hillfast and for passage I signed a contract they call the Beggar's Blood, for I had no other way of getting out of the Circle without coin, and it's blood, back and bone that's taken as you're put to work. When the old Othbutter come to Fat Steppy to raise some soldiers so he could win favour with the Farlsgrad king, Steppy put me, Nazz and a few others on the ship over the Sar.

I wanted to be out of the citadel. Getting a crew to look past my babs, legs and youth was a daily war and I had to break some faces and bones on occasion. There was three of us girls on Steppy's Blood, and the fuckers we had for masters to train us always said the girls worked hardest. Don't think that meant we got an easier ride for our work; Grilde, our one master, was brutal but straight as a line. Riebsen, however, was crazy, a vicious cunt I'd seen cripple a couple of boys that stood in the way of me or one of the other girls he'd try and give night shifts to when we all knew what he was after.

All in all I was told I'd pay down my contract a bit quicker and I'd be away from all that shit for a few months at least. Thing is, I'd got close to Nazz in the years we'd come through together with Steppy. He was a handsome boy then, reckless and immortal with self-belief, loyal to a fault, for a while, and all of that bound a crew to him fierce. I was full of juice for him, his soft lips and deep-set eyes; he made me laugh like a gull and got us into all kinds of trouble in taverns or break-ins, and, well, we couldn't keep our hands off each other. Seemed all the better at the time that my paying colour stopped my bleeds. By the time we got on the ship going west to Farlsgrad I'd stopped going with him for I'd heard he was free with his cock and he was taking different jobs to be away from me.

Of course, being Nazz, surrounded by a lot of men and women he didn't know, he was acting up, as it was his way of figuring out who was who, by their own reaction to him. Ruifsen, on the first day of the voyage, had come over as I was sicking up over the gunwale and asked if he could have my wrists. I turned about, chin still dripping, and held them out because it was that or throw myself overboard and be done with it.

He put his thumbs down hard on each wrist and faced me. He was a giant then and a giant now, a good foot taller and wider than me, his whole family, he said, seemed to have a bit of tree sap in their veins. The sickness fell away.

"I got some ginger in my pack, always pack a bit for a rough crossing. I'm Ruifsen."

Nazz was nearby, had shouted over that there was others sick, not just pretty women. Ru give me a rag to wipe my mouth and otherwise ignored Nazz, which pleased me no end. Nazz had a few about him he was entertaining, but I too ignored him because I knew that wound him up the most.

The trails are signposted. There's no fence as such when we get to Ru's farmland, at least part of it. He and his brother gambled on growing food rather than the plant that goes in mixes. I knew from my last visit that the twenty acres before us was wild-looking; slender spruce and birch grew amid the rich soil that his family had spent years cultivating to fill with cloudberries. Before us we could see eight or so pickers in the nearest few acres, surrounded by the small furnace-orange fruits on their beds of papery singed-looking leaves. It's beautiful land, left to itself, and their cloudberries are famous hereabouts because they can breathe the soil a bit more than other farms.

Further on we come to their great fields of barley and beyond those the fields of cattle.

My guards lose a little blood to the mosquies and flies that live off the cows as we tramp through their fields, one thing at least my colour saves me the trouble of. They're fussing and complaining about them when we pass through a gate and I spot Ru talking to a few of his hands. They're in their cups, a cool late afternoon and work's done. His brother's keep, his sister-ken, is with him, a basket of bread in her hands.

Something's said, a nod towards us, and he turns about. His huge beard splits open with his smile. He slaps his thighs. His sister-ken I just about recognise, though she looks like she's had a hard day on the land and her hair is tied under a scarf. She smiles and waves, obviously recognising me.

Ru runs over, delight all over him, and I shriek as he lifts me up off my feet and into his arms, crushing me and spinning me about and kissing my cheek as he does.

My eyes fill with tears, my black eye not so much of course, and I hug him back. He's sour and wet with hard work and when he drops me down again we get a good look at each other. He's got older, browner mostly, grey flushing through his beard and stache. His hair's soaked to his head and he's losing it at the crown a little. There's a stillness in him that my eye somehow picks up, he seems rooted to the earth; the song, a hum, barely breaks between him and the ground.

He won't say it, but my face is a concern to him. We both know it's broken up.

"You get more beautiful, Teyr."

"Fuck off, Ru. It's lovely to see you."

"Who are these boys?"

"My guards. I'm under a death sentence. And I'm hungry."

"Right then. Well, you'd best join us at the house – we were just seeing off the hands for today. What do I call you two boys then?"

My guards aren't in a great mood from the mosquies.

"I'm Bridmas, this is Niks," says the one. "We'd be grateful for something to stop the itching of those bloody mosquies."

Ru's sister-ken come over then, Bridie.

"I can see you two poor things itching. You didn't have a nettle cream about you?"

They shake their heads.

"Teyr, it's good to see you again after all these years." Like Ru, she's staring at the black eye, the scars and broken nose, but is too polite to say anything about it.

"And you, Bridie, how's Jol?" I was meaning her keep Jol Ruifsen. I never used Ru's first name, Niel, he was always just Ruifsen to me.

"He's away at Hillfast, he says. Won't see him for a few days and he'll want cleaning up and straightening out when he does come back. Always glad of Niel, in't I?"

Ru shrugs and smiles at her.

"I can't wait to see those duts of yours, though I expect they'll be my height now, will they?" I says to her.

"They'll love to see you, I'm sure. We're grateful for the oil you still bring up here. I never got to tell you that before now."

"That'll be Thornsen to thank."

"How do you mean?" she says.

"Well, I've been away a while."

*   *   *

281

"I knew it," says Ru as we're in our pipes on the porch to his brother's house. He has a hut of his own nearer the cows, just the one room he sleeps and washes himself in. It's late in the night, and the two *guards*, in fairness, got stuck into helping with making cheese and then making a few rye loaves, or kuksas as we say in Abra. Far as I know they're sleeping in one of the barns, the mead Bridie makes could take down a buffalo, but they thought they knew better.

"I know you got that funny eye, but I knew something was wrong from the look in them generally. I never seen you so sad, Amo."

"You seem happy though, Ru, and that's cheered me up. Sorry I been away so long."

"You were getting rich and must have been busy. Your van that comes through and drops the oil off would give us news of you and your trading over the Sar. Then they were telling us you'd met a man and then that you had set up your posts over the Ridge and down near Ablitch."

We'd been over it all the last few hours.

"How's the two farms now? I look about and see it all in good order, from tools to wagons to fences."

"Bridie's managing it all now she's got her letters. Jol didn't want her to have them, didn't want me near his scrolls either, but when the first farm got signed away on a bet she give him a right going-over and then I hears him hitting her and I put him out on his back, after which I said I'd be taking on the scrolls and tallies, and sure enough it was a right fucking mess. He got right for a while, because she wouldn't have him in her furs until he did. Didn't last. But I taught her letters so she could teach the duts. She's running the scrolls and I'm keeping my eye on the hands and training Ilda and the two boys."

They might have been his own children the way he loves them, and they are fond of him, Ilda the most.

"Nazz sent Threeboots up to see me a few weeks past. I'm thinking your being here has something in common with that."

"How is she?"

"Still paid up, working for Nazz, probably running one of his crews. She's got a bit of grey at her roots, dyes her hair a bit now, I think, and the plant's took hold as well, like she's shrivelled a bit. You know how it goes, one moment she's full tilt talking about the thieving she's been doing and the next she's gone quiet or stops in the middle of what she's saying and changes to some other subject."

"How are you now, still off the betony?" A lot of us mercenaries have had trouble with betony, some it gets hold of and it's a fight to get away from it. Ru was under for a long time in Marola.

"Aye. I got you to thank for that still, not been tempted by it since."

I squeeze his hand, pleased, besides which I'd not seen the shakes on him all day.

"What did she say, Threeboots?"

"Nazz has a purse, a big one, going after this Khiese. Didn't say it was a crossroads job, but she said it would clear the debts we got from Jol's dice."

"How much?"

"Teyr, I don't want to go into it now – first night we seen each other in years. You're going though, eh? Going back for Khiese?"

I nod. "Bit surprised Nazz is going though," I says.

"He is?"

"He is. He's leading it."

"Don't make any sense that. Nazz has his fingers in almost

283

everything going on among the sheds except, it seems, yours. He got deckhands, vanners, cutters, runs dice pens, droop joints and taverns, whores. Can't see what reason he's got to go except to protect all that, but still don't mean you'd go yourself."

"What I was thinking, Othbutter's got something to do with making him go. I was up for the noose for them thinking I had killed Crogan Othbutter, and it was a pardon if I went and did this. Nazz and the chief have something cooking and I don't have an idea as to what it is. Then, as I'm leaving a couple of days ago, to come here, I see Salia in the Mash Fist, first time she's been in Hillfast in years, has to be. She didn't seem surprised Nazz had a purse for this job either. Don't smell right, Ru."

"Salia? Haven't seen her since she took a boat over the Sar from Sukenstad in Jua. Well, I'll be by your side at least. We'll figure it, Amo."

"No! No, you mustn't, Ru. I come here to tell you to stay. You can't go out there, the Circle, because nobody's coming back, I know that much. I can't help thinking it's something Othbutter and Nazz must know, but regardless of what it means, you have to keep Bridie and the children safe. They're your world now and all your coin you put in these farms — I won't have you lose it all. My coming here was about me, well, saying goodbye, I guess. I missed you, Ru, but I come to make sure you didn't do anything stupid for that spimrag Nazz. I can settle your debts if need be." He puts his arm out and takes up my hand in his, brings it to his lips to kiss it. He's quiet for a bit, looking about him at the fields darkening, but he's breathing a bit harder, trying to stop some tears, I think.

"You tell me this Khiese is come to rule all Hillfast. Caring for this farm and my interests is at one with caring for you."

"No, Ru, please."

"Amo. How many times you saved my life? Nazz forgot it for his greed down in Marola, as the others did, but all those years you cared for us, did our worrying, got us our due. I wish you'd asked me to go with you last year. Don't know if I could have made the difference but you're stupider than my brother if you think I won't be there for you now."

"The farm, Ru, all this. It's something you should be keeping hold of. I saw you earlier, laughing and eating with the hands and all settled. I would've turned back if I knew I was going to put ideas in your head. I didn't keep us straight all those years so you'd be paying back in again, taking colour again. It was so you'd pay out ahead of all those broke-up mercs we see on the docks stammering and begging, lost on the betony, which we was close to."

"You telling me I can't pay you back for that love you showed me?"

"For fuck's sake, Ru." I tipped my head back, stars was out and a nip was on the breeze. "You've got to be paid up, on your Forms fierce. I worry about you on the brews again. Might be that Farlsgrad send a force if they see their interests in the citadels harmed, so your farms would be safe, I reckon. But Ru, you stand a chance to get away if Khiese does come. You got no chance in the Circle." Can't believe I didn't ask Othbutter about Farlsgrad.

"If you're so sure of dying, why are you going in there? What do you want to be dying now for? It don't bring Mosa back and it don't help Aude if he in't dead already. You know that, don't you?"

"I do. Course I do." What I'm so sure of seems slippery when I'm trying to force it into words for they don't come easy. "I've got a reckoning with myself to make. I thought I deserved what I had, I thought I should have got what

I wanted just because I wanted it. And I wanted it all. I wanted to never be made keep to some Auksen runt and be pushing out duts for him. Then I wanted to be Khasgal's queen and rule an empire. When I couldn't have him I took you all to Jua and the biggest purses we ever had, though fuck knows it wasn't enough. Then I come home and within a few years I'm trying to prove I can run a road where no one else dared and I'm thinking nothing can stop me because I'm Teyr Amondsen. Now I'm old and I got nothing worth having, only coin, and that gone with this death sentence.

"This is about me settling all that best I can. Just carrying on making coin like it matters a fuck isn't going to fill that black hole in my head. Drowning in brandy won't bring Mosa back to life. Maybe running Khiese through won't fill the hole either, but I can't think of anything else might work in place of getting revenge on him."

He's quiet for a bit, then he smiles and lets out a good big breath of smoke.

"What's that smile for, Ru?"

"Only ever seems women have to apologise for a bit of ambition, don't it? We all believed in you, din't we? Me, Nazz, Thad, Tarrigsen, then Aude. We all been with you and for you."

He takes my hand again.

"If I'm paying back in I want you to second me. Run the Forms with me in the morning, show me how far away I am, because I been doing them regular for years but without a second you get bad habits."

"What about Bridie? You're just going to leave her to your cock of a brother?"

"She'll manage." He says it a bit quieter. I know why.

"You love her, Ru. I can see it, she can see it, I'm sure,

she's sharp as a needle. I followed your eyes all day and they was much on her. And I think she's fond of you and all, for I followed her eyes as well."

He narrows his lips, gives the smallest of nods, like he thought better of trying to put up some sort of denial.

"We can stop another day. I can have a word with Thornsen to have a cleark come by now and again if you are coming with me. My two guards haven't looked so happy since I led them off the quays, I'm sure they'll stay a little longer."

"Aye. Perhaps we can take a day."

We leave two days later.

Bridie and the children give all the assurances that everything is in order and that both he and I need to look after each other. They all give me Sillindar's blessings and Ilda sings us them as we all used to sing them. The boys give Ru a beard hoop they'd been making for his birthday; it is black larch, his favourite wood, carved in which was the Ruifsen emblem of the striking falcon, his family being renowned breeders about Hillfast. Him and Bridie have a good long hug but the children are too young to read anything into it. Bridie's eyes are full when she asks me to try and bring him back safe, though she makes sure none of the others are about when we say our own farewell. I can't say anything then she won't want to hear, for she knows well enough what being a soldier means, what paying colour means. Might as well juggle axes blindfolded as take a fightbrew.

Good as his word, it looks like he has kept up his Forms and it give me some comfort for what was to come.

We wave farewell to Bridie until a slope in the fields takes the sight of her and we push on till Aoig's on the wane before rigging a shelter for us to lie under. Ruifsen has been doing this for years and is fierce quick about it. Just as well because the rains come to stay all the way back into Hillfast.

Salia had left word in the Mash Fist I was to head for the market sheds east half a mile from the walls, the Thesselday after the half-moon. Nazz would have the crew ready to go that morning, which was the following day, given my stay at Ru's, but we decided to make a night of it there with the carters, soaks and others anyway. Me and Ru sang, even danced together the jigs we remembered from our army days. I won a few arm wrestles, was reminded of why I was barred from most other taverns on the quays, mostly fighting and getting juicy with men whose keeps found out and come after me. But all that was long ago. Last night me and Ru just washed everything away with a rare old barrel of soraki, a strong juniper ale few there could afford.

I felt free.

Today's a busy one on the docks, at least seven ships on the water, four cogs and three whalers already in and gulls and dockers alike are maddened by blood and blubber, crew-masters hoarse, waving their whips at the teams over and in the carcasses. One man's being carried away dead and two more are howling with breaks as we hop and step around the hundreds giving it their backs and bones amid the black pools, fat and barrels.

We take Skipson Lane, move off the front and into a warren of flophouses, droopjoints and workshops of those that service the quays. We're heading for the meeting point when an old man calls out from behind us.

"Master Amondsen!" He has the bearing of a life's service in his straight back and measured, almost ritualised gestures, hands behind him, eternally waiting on the next instruction.

"Luddson, it's lovely to see you." I put my arms around

him despite him being professionally unable to return the gesture, but I feel his smile widen as I kiss his cold cheek.

"Always a delight to see you, my child. Master Tarrigsen was much moved by your condition last week. You'll be Ruifsen. I've been told a giant might be accompanying the young master."

"Do you want us to come to Tarry's?"

"Ah, no. He has sent me. My disapproval of his excessive working fails to excite him to any alternative pleasures, but he's unwell. I fear that his interests take too much."

"We should go – there might be something I or Thornsen can . . ." But Luddson raises a hand.

"He's not well, Master." The words are said with a subtle, practised weight, forbidding further dissent. He pulls from a pouch on his belt a small waxed leather wallet.

"The Oskoro have spoken with you once, I see." He gestures towards my eye. "I hope they will do so again, Master."

"As do I. They can no longer watch from the shade of the Almet if they wish to survive."

Having handed the wallet to me, Luddson stands straight once more.

"Master Tarrigsen wishes you well and hopes that you'll share with him the last of Thad's leaf on your return. He has another gift, but it must wait."

"Tell him I love him, Luddson. Tell him also that Thornsen will take over my interest and will cut him in, so that they can maintain our people's livelihoods. May Sillindar follow you all."

He bows and walks off with a grave and measured stride, leaving me upset for the news he's brought. I know in my heart I won't see Tarrigsen again and I'm angry that the last we saw of each other was that moment on the quayside as I was led off to the Hill.

"Come on, Teyr, let's go see this crew we're joining. And if that's what I think it is in that pouch, I feel a good bit better about our chances."

I try to smile. "You shouldn't."

"Took your fuckin' time you black-eyed streak. Is that dried-out bag o' twigs what we waited for, Nazz?"

This is Drogg. Like me, he's been offered this purse over the gallows. Come from somewhere on the east side of Mount Hope. He's almost Ru's size, like someone piled up some big rocks, pebbles for cheeks and a chin, smooth and round.

"This is Teyr Amondsen, Drogg. I'm sure she'll answer to Blackeye as well. And this is Niel Ruifsen, who I knew she'd bring. Good to see you again, Ru. You look ready."

"Looks like you paid back in less than I have, Nazz. You ready for this or shall we let Amondsen run it?"

"Fuck you, Ru." Nazz might have laughed this off years ago, but there's an edge, a stress on him I think comes from not having had to draw a sack of misfits together tight and strong for a long time. You get nothing but your will done as a feared ganger.

They're all mounted, the whole crew that's waiting for us, with our horses and a couple of spares outside the stables of what must be one of Nazz's farms.

"Master Amondsen!"

It's Cherry. She dismounts and runs over, throwing her arms around me. My face is full of her wild red fuzz of hair, thick as a pillow of soft grass.

"Thornsen came by," says Nazz. "Brought a couple of extras to look out for you, make us easier to see out in the hinterland. I hope they're fucking good enough for this."

"Helsen's volunteered," says Cherry, "you know, that

sniffer we use over on the foothills of Crutter. His keep passed on. He wants to do something worth his while, he said. Thornsen didn't make us come here, Master, he just asked for those willing to help on a crossroads job to go alongside you and make a difference. You been there for me, there for those duts and all down in Carl. We're there for you."

"Fucking Sillindar! Stick a few fingers in her cinch while you're there and finish her quick, Blackeye, we got ground to cover," says a big haggard-looking woman I learn is Agura. She was in the Coffins for poisoning her sister and sister's family, hoping to get their plant concern west of Elder Hill. Used to be a legend among the vanners up in the Moors, renowned double-hander, but later in camp I'm going to give her a going-over.

"Who else we got here besides those I know?" I says.

"Good to see you again, Teyr," says Threeboots. She speaks slowly, pipe in her mouth probably got some threaded bacca in there calming her. There's half a grin through the smoke, black leathers as she always wore, though Nazz's people were all in them, new belts and all. She's kept her shape like Salia has, though she's nearly a foot shorter, an acrobat as a girl growing up in Khasgal and still no fat on her. Her colouring had darkened like mine, hers browner, almost bruised-looking in patches.

"You met Salia, of course," says Nazz. "She's got a drudhan with her, Yame, the girl there with the olive colour from over Western Farlsgrad. My own people are here: Talley, who's our drudha, Heddirn Thordsen from the Larchlands with the shield there, Caryd, who won me the singleton grand prize at the tourney and finally along with Drogg there's Gravy, both taking the purse over the noose."

Yame looks restless, might be a vadse addiction. Thick

long ropes of brown matted hair, the front of it tied back and up like laces on a shirt. Gravy's got a pickaxe of a nose, jacker's build, he's with Drogg and it's clear they've known each other a while. Caryd's from Mount Hope if I go by the name, but also the green eyes, and black hair worn short. I can see her hands tremble from fifteen feet off, she's somewhere on betony's road, but heading in or out I can't tell for all she's young. It's her eyes, the eyes of a far older woman. Heddirn's trying to look bored because he's young, but mostly he's just glancing at Salia's backside, his horse being behind hers. Like Talley he's been inked, something Nazz likes from his people. Talley's shaved her head bald, and she's got tears inked all over her head and face, all drawn to fall down to her neck. Heddirn's just got the Thordsens' kissing trees crest over his face.

Fourteen of us all told. There's enough here with a bit about them we might last a few weeks, hopefully enough to get to Khiese. I'm sorry for Cherry and sniffer Helsen of course, but like Ru they've chosen this and I don't want to let them down whatever else happens to us.

"We calling you Captain, Nazz? It isn't right calling you by your name, not if we're operating as a crew," I says.

"Hasn't seen you in years and she's giving you orders again," says Threeboots.

"Seems to be," he says. "But she's right. It's Captain now. Crossroads purse. We're after Samma Khiese, his brother's a bonus but he's fuck all, so once Samma's done we'll mop away whatever's in our way and Othbutter can come and sort out the Circle. We ride for Faldon Ridge. Teyr's got an outpost there and it's a good base for Othbutter to hold and retake Elder Hill, close the Sedgeway. It'll be full of white-boys, full of killing."

292

"Should've become soldiers, shouldn't we? Getting paid to kill 'stead of all that sneaking an' stealing," says Drogg to Gravy, making it obvious Gravy is running him.

I see Salia shake her head and lead her horse about to head out east. Nazz takes the cue and we ride out for the Circle.

Faldon Ridge

Agura hasn't spoken to me since I hit her a couple of times on our first night out. Her fault for keeping going on Cherry and Helsen for their following me. Big as she is she's slow and has a bit of fat on her. There was some cheering, Drogg and Heddirn among them, thinking I'd really have her, but long gone are the army days where who ran what tents was decided on the first day of each campaign. We used to call it the Ladder; dayers, gloves, blades, oaths. Me, Nazz and Ruifsen was tight, Ruifsen's size settling us on the Ladders with little fuss so's we'd get our pick of tents and be first at the drudha and tally benches for plant and pay.

We wait in the rain, in trees near my outpost, Faldon Ridge. I had to say something about the Oskoro eye, so I thought I'd tell them all how I come about it. It shut a few of them up, and I might have said that I could see a bit more about each of them than I really can, if only to get some peace and quiet. Now the night hides less than it used to. A great sorrow for me as the first to make a sortie. The fine red gates of Faldon Ridge have been burned, but they're still there, the walls have bodies all mangled and black nailed to them. Large and small. Cherry left me for Ablitch as I'd asked when we was down in Carlessen land with the Kelssen duts, and it was there she learned that the Ridge had been taken, no birds flying north or south, no people coming or going either. Khiese had let one of my people go, to spread the word of his success, and he was likely pushing to Ablitch when she was heading out of there to Hillfast.

Then I see Omar is nailed on the gate itself. With tears I remember him and the joy of his company, but anger's taking hold of me, not grief, and I relish it. A few guards are standing in pairs, holding sheets over their heads, probably to stop that stupid fucking chalk from running. They're not up for this job, not tonight, so tonight's when we go in, I reckon.

Nazz melts out of the trees behind me, and Threeboots I sense a flicker of to my left. I turn just as she looks at me, and I think she's a bit surprised not to have flanked me.

"Report," Nazz whispers.

"Two up there, two on the gate. There's two the far side, the rest hidden behind the walls out of this rain."

I'd found a patch of earth earlier on to draw out the layout of the outpost with a knife so the crew knew the layout thorough.

"Good," he says. We move back to the crew. There's no fire, just a silent group that haven't been getting on very well.

"We're going in," says Nazz. "In line both of you." Meaning me and Threeboots. Been a long time since I had a captain giving me orders and I'm happy about it. I told him what I knew, now he has to show he can make the right calls and start pulling us together.

"Caryd, Teyr, Salia and Yame, you're all good with bows, you'll work on the guards nearside wall and the gates. Threeboots is going over the wall with Gravy and me at the back. Hedd and the rest of you are going in the gate once Threeboots has it opened . . ."

"Wait, when—" begins Drogg. Nazz steps forward and slaps him across the face. Drogg brings his arm back to flatten Nazz when Heddirn thrusts his sword between the pair.

"It's not fucking difficult, Drogg. You do what the captain says." This is Heddirn. Nazz gets in Drogg's face then, or close as he can get given Drogg's height, but it's clear who's on top and Drogg just nods.

"Right, Talley, get the brew round. We'll give Drogg his first," he says.

The drudha slips off the pack she's got over her shoulders and from it pulls a leather bag. The brew inside gives off the smell of rotting grass and don't look much different. My eye can see the vapours coming off it and I feel the nerves, my throat drying. I shake a bit. None of us enjoys taking it, let me be clear on that. Nobody takes a brew for pleasure, no matter how strong it makes you feel, how it changes you. Helsen will stick to a strong dayer, he's never done a brew, and without work it'll kill you.

The thirteen of us that's had fightbrews all go quiet as we do whatever we've been taught by our different masters to stone the brew, preparing our minds for it. Talley comes to each of us in turn. There's a mouthful of a prepper that I can smell has at least juniper oil, something we used to have down in the Roan Province, and garlic. She's learned recipes off Nazz's old drudha at least, before he went and paid the Drudha's Share, throwing himself off a cliff, according to Thad.

Then she pushes the mulch in our mouths, and it's chew and swallow as fast as fuck because you can't throw it up no matter how much you want to. Nazz helps her, putting the strap over our mouths so we have to swallow back anything we reject.

My throat burns with something like raw ginger, fire ants, hot seawater, then the strap comes away, taking its faint scent of mint, and she's on to Ruifsen next in line.

No going back.

The moments go by slow. Slower. My belly fills and my heart quickens.

I'm waiting for the wave, the one that rises far over a ship to take it to the dark depths with a violent, shattering inevitability.

Some recite rhymes as the brew takes hold. I have a single note I hum. It must not break, it is a slender steel rod, smooth. I hum its flawlessness as the wave rushes up, the spasms start in my belly and the heat bleeds out of it, gouts of heat, thick bubbling liquid meat and bone, and I force it all through the steel rod, the single line that must be flawless, smooth, that must grow and control all my new strength and sense, flawlessly, featureless and calm. My eyes see too much, my black eye feels like it's come alive, it joins earth and sky together for me, leaves and rain, clears them, brightens them for my inspection, every inch, through the mist, into the knots of bark, the rumbling of the soil and the stone beneath our feet, rustling of the worms, twitch of spiders hiding under leaves, mushrooms stretching their veins, exhaling their spores . . .

"Move!" It's Nazz, teeth chattering, hopping as though on coals, grinning and licking his teeth, sword shaking in his hand. How stupid he looks, like he's playing in some drama the role of a fool. I take my bow in hand and I'm running. The smell of the dead comes heavy, the frying bacon beyond the walls of the outpost, the sweat and the hops on the bodies and breath of the guards. Salia stands next to me as we take our positions to shoot, her skin changing, bright enough I almost tell her to quieten, that they'll hear her colour. She's ignoring me. She's so beautiful, arm extending out, arrow on her finger, drawing back the string to within a whisker of her full pink lips. They mesmerise me. I'm in love with her, I want to pull her to the ground, but there are men and women we must kill together, those that took everything from me. I draw, we loose together, arrows leaping like wolves off the bows, shimmering, bending with their release, a moment to the guards' soft necks, their death already a truth before our fingers have rolled off the strings. This is the song my eye sees, the sight of Sillindar himself.

Salia runs forward. I run forward. The guards are dead at the gate, a shout comes from inside the outpost. A shadow up on the wall – there, gone. Threeboots it was, a brief orange glow I knew was hers as she scaled the wall in a moment. She's lifting the gate bar with someone else, Nazz maybe. I get to kill now, close. I splash through the mud of the trail and follow Heddirn and Drogg through into the main run. There's nobody on more than a dayer in here. Most are whiteboys, some aren't. It makes no difference in this cold, soft rain. A sword's raised, a stance attempted, but my bind rips it from his hand and I've got my sword through him, my hand on his shoulder to get it further into the hilt. I realise my bow is across my back, no recollection of drawing my sword. This delights me and I can't help but laugh. Someone blows one of their high reedy horns, a cry for blood. I breathe like a buffalo now, my leathers tightened by how I've grown, what I've become. A door opens, the almshouse, now a billet for these boys and girls. Ruifsen leaps past me, his spear driving into the man that was readying his own, and he pushes him back, making room for me to run in behind him. The light of candles is the light of Aoig, brutally exposing the five or six who are jumping up, naked from their sex or slumber. They scream for we are bright

298

and blackened with mud and rain. We screech like War Crows. I see flesh and helplessness, chalk faces and necks, pink bellies and chests and legs. I feel like a butcher starting her day. One tries to run, to duck to my right near the wall by the door. I drop my sword to better grab his hair, holding him squealing, twenty if he's a day. My left fist, the stubs of nails stitched into the glove's knuckles, tears open his cheek, smashes his eye to a mess and I keep punching just to see how far I can go.

"Stone it, Amo!"

Ruifsen's right. He's speared each of them once, then again, each in turn as they hold hands over the holes he's making, retching or whining feebly. He seems calm, a bit sad, like being on a brew is putting on an old and favourite coat that don't quite fit, and that was how it always was when he was risen. I only feel sad because I have to let this boy drop when I haven't finished breaking his head up, and I take up my sword, hope there's someone else I can kill.

I'm outside. I can't think. Talley's overdone the brew, I want to squat and shit it out, but I can hear screaming and I want to be about it. It didn't used to be like this, did it? Yame, Heddirn and Caryd step out of the longhouse, Cherry following. She's singing a song, bits of flesh and bone in her hair, on her cheek. Caryd's hands are shaking as she tries to fill a betony pipe in the doorway, green eyes filled with hunger for it.

Then I clear, I resolve, a drooper cresting the hill of her return to the brew's bab, peeling the scabs off to better infect herself. Helsen is lifting and smashing a heavy mallet into a couple of bodies, putting his heart and back into it. He got wounded and he's telling them about it. To the side of the longhouse, at the smithy, I see Gravy holding down a man before him, over a horse trough, knife at his throat, other hand pulling down his leggings.

"They're not all dead, Gravy, we still got work to do. What the fuck are you doing?" I shout.

He flashes me a look, his eyes are empty, wild. The brew's got hold of him when it should be the other way around.

Agura comes up behind me, says, "Leave him. Least they deserve and he probably hasn't had it in a long time."

"That's right, Ag. I'm takin' this one, goin' to give him something big to die on."

"No fucking way." Course it shouldn't matter to me after what these whiteboys have done, the good people nailed to the walls, but we're not them. Take the life, pay it back clean, win over the beaten, whatever side they're on. I run over, and being honest, I don't like Gravy. Rain's heavier now, a frenzy in it, a hate. I'm behind him and get a good swing at his side, his ribs, as he starts jabbing at the man, who's keening and cowed with fear.

Gravy don't feel the blow at first, kicks the man's legs a bit further apart. So I kick the back of his knee and he falls to the side, jumps back up, knife held out, leggings at his feet. The other man hobbles away, unable to move much either with his own pants at his feet, and he begins pulling them up. Nazz steps up to the whiteboy as he's dragging his leggings up to his waist and flattens him just as Agura splashes up behind me, a moment too quick for me to react, her own fist smashing into the back of my head, sending me to my knees. Gravy steps to me then, and his arm goes back, ready to stab me. I spin out of the way to the side of him, my balance gone. She hit me good.

"Put your cock away, Gravy, we're done," says Nazz. "Agura, step back or I'll cut you to fucking pieces."

My hand twitches, the blade in it is too dry, thirsty. "In't there more to kill, Nazz?"

"No, Teyr, we're done. They're all dead bar this one Gravy

was fancying. You need to stone it out now, go cold. And it isn't Nazz, it's Captain."

I smell Ruifsen then, the underlying stink of peat in summer seemed always to be his smell when he was wet and worn out from a battle. He comes over from the almshouse, head to foot black and slick with blood. The smell of them all, alive, new dead, old dead, comes at me like a thousand voices demanding attention. I put a hand to my nose, start crying. Ru kneels next to me, puts a hand on my shoulder and begins the hum, the note I use for stoning. There's no other sound now than the rain, the breathing of us all about the outpost, the sickening smell of the dead that have been opened. It don't last a moment.

"I'll fuckin' kill her. I'll kill you, Amondsen, you pox-ridden cratch!"

"What's up, Gravy?" says Drogg.

"No fucking, apparently."

"No rape, no," I says.

"Amondsen, leave it," says Nazz. He looks up, looking to the cold rain for his words.

"No rape, not this crew. I learned once you have to win the hearts and thoughts of those you leave behind, or they'll just be an enemy behind you."

Gravy snorts at that.

"Don't fucking push me, Gravy. No rape." I look up at Nazz and he's struggling, as much, I expect, to stone what the brew's taking as he is laying down his orders. This isn't how a successful raid ends. And it gnaws at me that something's not right with him.

"Happy to agree to that," says Cherry, calling over from where she is looking after Caryd.

"Me too." That's Ruifsen.

"And me," says Talley, who was up on the outpost's wall

near us, her bow still in her hand. The inked tears on her head shine with the rain and the torchlight. She should be prepping us for paying colour, but her speaking seals Nazz's authority, as it should. Drogg is about to say something but Gravy knows better and puts a hand up to silence him. You might think many things of the captain you've been given to lead you, and you might feel that a few bad calls give you the right to mutiny, or slack or make his life hell. But if your drudha speaks, you listen. Your drudha's your life, raises you up, brings you down, heals you, mixes your copper coin recipes, even improves them if they're well disposed towards you.

Ru's humming has stopped. He's putting an ointment on the back of my head where Agura's glove broke the skin.

"You," says Nazz, calling over the man Gravy was about to mount. He stands up, stumbles forward, head bowed. Nazz motions for Heddirn to step forward from the longhouse to the man's side.

"You don't need much imagination to know how many ways we can make things bad for you, so let's do this respect-fully. Can we do that?"

He nods. Heddirn puts a hand on his shoulder, which he tries to shrink away from, shoulders all turned in with fear. He's a young man, lumps of the white chalk gluing fragments of his beard and hair together where he hasn't washed them properly. His cheekbones draw strong lines, small nose, fairly obvious why Gravy had juice for him.

"Where you from?"

"I'm Eeghersen, east of Elder Hill."

"Eeghersens have sworn for Khiese, then."

He nods again.

"Elder Hill?"

"Belongs to the Crutters."

That got a murmur, and my heart sinks a bit. Might as well be a war now. I see Nazz look up at Talley. Threeboots has joined her, slippy enough that none of us noticed, but that was always her way. Word of this seems to give them a shared pause, like it means something else. I look then for Salia and she's standing under the bit of thatch overhanging the doorway to the stables. She's also watching Nazz and Talley.

"Where's Khiese?" he says to the whiteboy.

"I don't know. I really don't. You don't have to—"

"Don't I?" Nazz growls.

"We were to hold this until more of us – well, his men – got here. He don't tell us where he'll be; it makes sure we're ready in case he comes."

Nazz looks at him, eyebrows raised, for here we are, him the only one alive. He glances at Heddirn. It takes a moment, his arm hooking around the young man's throat, a jerk, his neck cracks and he falls to the ground. Nazz turns to face us all then.

"We're going south in the morning, to Ablitch Fort. We need to know it's still loyal to the chief. We move into the Circle through the Gassies. Sedgeway'll be rife with wagging chins, and seems like the Crutters might've cut a deal with Khiese, the way they were going on at Othbutter. I seen some big pots of this chalk paste they're using in the longhouse there. I think it'll help us."

It was miserable news for all it was the right call. The mosquies and the bogs'd be hell, but first we had to pay the colour. The next day or so we spent among the dead while we retched and shat, cried and smoked mixes that give us feathers and stopped us from breaking our bones with the shakes.

303

Ablitch

There's theits around Ablitch that have dug out dykes to drain parts of the marshes to plant barley, flax and wheat. Going into Ablitch was easy in that regard for these are the older clans that live about, more trails making the going easier, and a few of these trails was where my own company had started to drain the land around before it all went wrong.

Takes three silver pieces to get one of the marsh Families to give us rubs to help with the bites and leeches, for we have much further to go east and none of us knows the ways. No amount of coin is going to get anyone to join us however; every good hand is priceless making good the harvest while the plant and crops was growing freely and the birds, deer and salmon in such good supply. Who'd go into the Circle now anyway?

Ablitch Fort is where things start getting worse, though it's not Khiese's yet. There's about fifty of Othbutter's men there, some of which come with me on the first trip. They ask how things went and I tell them, and they have been wary of the news north and the whiteboys, though Ablitch won't be easy to overrun till the Gassies marshes freeze in winter. The men are repairing the walls with the trees about.

We stop for a day and a few of us help Helsen sniff about for the plant for our belts. He sniffed plant for me prior to all this of course so I knew he was good and the drudhas Talley and Yame are glad of him. Those at Ablitch that had come with me on the first run through the Circle light candles for our dead. Some remember Mosa fondly for he was always about the van asking questions and wasn't shy. Nazz makes a good impression while we're there, is good telling them to hold Ablitch and protect their own families. At one point he says that a big crew didn't do us no favours first time through and it won't now. His comment has Cherry mouthing off, feeling he's insulting me and Eirin; and I'm not able to calm her much. Feel like we need to kill some whiteboys to give us a sense of our shared purpose.

We're a walking banquet in the marshes. The rubs we bought were shit, might as well be adding seasoning to our necks, eyelids, hands and anything else exposed while we walk and sleep. Horses are all jumpy with it and all. Those of us with proper colour don't have it as bad, but it seems the mosquies are willing to drink almost anything. I laughed at Gravy yesterday for his lip and an eye was puffy with bites, told him it looked like the mosquies had the better of him in a bar fight. Took Heddirn and Ruifsen to get him off me and he split my lip in exchange for me flattening his ballbag. I think we all felt a bit better after that, letting go some of the bitterness we was feeling.

Now the afternoon's getting on and we have rain, no cover either out here barring the odd few copses, just the bogs, lakes and grasses, treacherous going for all it feeds us and gives Talley some fresh plant for her recipes. Helsen proves himself again today as he has done since we got into the Gassies, finding butterbur and blue flag, and fresh lobelia most of all, for it is strong at easing the price of the colour.

"You seem to have an eye for a good path, Teyr, so how come we're here?" says Salia. Salia's drudha, Yame, laughs at this, standing with us at the edge of a lake I'd led us to. The reeds and grasses I thought was a path disguised a treacherous run of big pools, deeper than they first looked, and then this lake.

"We'll set here for tonight," calls Nazz. "Hedd, once we've set camp, take Gravy and Helsen with you, back to that copse, get us some wood. Keep to the markers, the Gassies is always hungry."

I spend a moment looking for something to come back at Salia's shitty comment with but I'm tired.

"Why don't you try a spot of fishing instead of behaving like a puckered cinch?" I says. This gets a snigger from Heddirn, sensing something's off.

She smiles then, reminding me of better times. "I meant nothing by it, Teyr. Bad enough with Gravy, Drogg and that awful Agura. The purse will bind us, hand and heart."

"Hand and heart," I say, looking to draw a line under it so I can get on my pipe and get some sleep.

"Didn't seem to matter down in Marola, the purse," says Ruifsen.

"Back off, Ru," says Nazz. "This is old, it won't help us now."

"Besides," says Threeboots, "you in't exactly blameless, as I recall."

"Wait, wait," says Caryd. "I want to get my pipe for this, enjoy it properly'

"What happened, Master? Can we trust them?" says Cherry.

This has gone bad rather quick. Fucking Ru. I love him, but I can see now, the look that's on him, he's still carrying the guilt he felt when first we saw each other back here in Hillfast after Marola, when he was cutting himself with the betony and had to be tied up so his brother could do his nails to stop him ripping his skin off. None of us was innocent in Marola, but I thought we'd never shit on each other till it happened.

"We got greedy, if you lot want a story," I says. "Might as well get it out there so we can put it away again. We landed in Jua, me, Ru, Nazz, Threeboots and Salia here. There was a drudha with us too, Thad." I take a moment, remembering us at the Almet, his delight at seeing the seed. His arm around me.

"We picked up with a company of Juan spears going south into Marola. This was the end of the Orange Empire, the Harudans, who had occupied Marola and all those other lands about. The Marolans wanted to resettle their lands, which had Harudan families on them for generations. Started out as a bloodbath. Our job was to see the Marolans and Harudans agree a peaceful repatriation. Soon enough we got the Harudans moved off the lands without much bother, taking whatever wealth they could pack on a wagon, leaving soil, crops, groves and the rest unsullied. We did some killing at the start, while all this was getting settled, but soon we found ourselves earning plenty of coin for little more than overseeing that the Harudans did just that, leave peacefully taking nothing more than they was due. In turn we'd ensure the Marolans didn't get bloodthirsty about it.

"Soon become obvious that coin could be made on top of the purse to ensure that the scrolls was forwarded and processed more quickly, or that a bit more might be taken away than was formally agreed and scrolls adjusted with the rubbing of some treated guira. It all got even easier when we was moved down to the border between Harudan and

Marola, where the disputes and the opportunities to profit from them multiplied as land was parcelled up and split. I was given more and more of the responsibility for the central borders, more clearks, more soldiers, and so Nazz here said he could pick up half of it. He used to be a good captain, he was my captain for a while so I know. I just didn't think this lot would fuck me over. I thought I could trust them to keep things easy and quiet, not get greedy." There's a heavy moment then, those not in that old crew thinking it would kick off, but Threeboots and Salia are making their pipes, Ru has his head bowed and Nazz is just staring straight at me, cold as ice.

"Word gets to me of some Marolans and Harudans who wasn't so badly disposed to each other finding Nazz and his clearks are skimming them both. I have to assume he's a useful ganger these days because then he learned how completely fucked-up stupid that is. So I'm put on the spot, aren't I? I have to investigate him. Well I told him, didn't I. I said, 'Nazz, what the fuck is going on. Cool it down while I make amends.' And I made out it was scroll errors and got rid of some clearks, even cut a couple of hands off, sold them out to protect this one here. 'You're right, Master,' he says. 'We'll settle it down.' And they didn't."

"You're forgetting, Teyr, you'd been stashing the gold that Khasgal showered on you all over the Sar, your castellan tithes, while we had only silver to count," says Nazz.

"Fuck me, you whining bastard," says Gravy. "'Only silver to count'. Hear that, Drogg? He's all miserable at the silver coins they got themselves piles of. You got no fucking clue what suffering is sat on your dock fleecing honest workers of their coin at the tip of a dagger from one of these bootlickers."

He's forgot himself. Threeboots stands, as do Heddirn and Caryd – her betony shakes gone, with some of her good sense. Caryd takes her bow from the ground, arrow from the quiver next to it, and I don't even get the chance to do more than breathe in to shout before her arrow's through Gravy's face. He tries to get up, his eyes looking down a moment at the shaft in his cheekbone. Then he's gone, a moment later. Heddirn's sword is up at Drogg, who's also risen but looks shocked at what's just happened. I look back at Caryd, and she's already aimed another arrow at me.

"You should, Caryd – put an arrow in me. It'll stop me dreaming. Stop me waking."

"Shut up, Amondsen. Nazz is our captain. You've forgotten how a crew works? I'm not wondering any longer why you fucked it last time out, and now your self-pity and bitterness is getting people killed."

I look down at Gravy and I'm sorry for him. I got no answer for her, despite her twisted reasoning. I told my story and got bitter about it in the telling. Silence, barring the life around us chipping, croaking and calling. Ru's on his feet, then everyone is. I stand and step forward, a movement she matches.

"Teyr," says Nazz, "don't. She'll do it. She's cold." And she is. Betony takes a lot of what makes someone sympathetic. Caryd seems empty, for all that she's shining with that sureness of being young and rightful.

"She's right, Captain, I shouldn't have talked about you that way. I'm going to take a spade from the packie, going to bury Gravy just over there, it's high enough he won't be led in water. Tomorrow I hope I'll find us a way out of here. I've had some luck so far. Helsen, Ru, can you help me with the body?"

Digging's good for working out anger. I need to save it for Khiese. Nazz goes over to Drogg, who had obviously known Gravy some years. He's shouting and stabbing his finger at Caryd, and Nazz talks him down.

It quietens after a while, Drogg working through his brandy and some pipes and singing softly to himself off away from camp.

I've led us for three days through the Gassies, or rather an Oskoro has. I haven't said anything about that fact. We spent a few days out of Ablitch waist deep, roped and fighting the mud and reeds and roots tripping us, pulling at us. My black eye caught sight of a bright stone then, almost giving off its own light. I was about to point at it, for it shone like Aoig and appeared all of a sudden it seemed. Nobody else noticed it; indeed, Threeboots and Salia passed over it as we walked. I took it up, and closing my black eye it looked like a normal stone. Switching eyes, it shone near painfully. I've seen others since that first one, and they've led us true until today. I have no idea why the Oskoro are here and helping us. Can they sense another seed on me? I find it hard to believe. Maybe they think there's still a debt to pay or I've earned their trust. Now, morning after Gravy was killed, I offer them thanks, sing softly over our burned fish and the scrawny ducks we caught, my back and body aching from the digging last night:

> On sill and run, in bowls of tin,
> You leave your gifts, our tree-blood kin.
> With wool and iron, cheese and brin
> The oath is honoured, tree-blood kin.

The drudha Yame catches on to it. She's from the mountains of Western Farlsgrad. Seems they like to drink and sing there, which isn't a surprise, land being all quarries of slate and mines, which makes brothers of everyone that goes underground together. She can't get Salia to sing, nobody ever could. Heddirn and Threeboots are happy enough watching

Salia do her Forms while the rest of us share some songs. Obvious to me now how fierce she's been at it all these years, better than any instructor I've seen do them. I would join her, hoping she'd give me some instruction, but I'm cut up with a black mood so I'm packing bowls with Drogg, Gravy's belt at our feet. I spend some time sitting with Drogg, saying I'm sorry. He's soaked up on some brandy but he's had a mix to settle him. I hope what's happened don't have a lasting effect.

I look over and see Ruifsen's quiet. Preparing us the rubs for our bones and joints. He's got good at waxing my eye. I squeeze Drogg's shoulder and he nods as I leave him to go and sit with Ru.

"What's up, Ru?"

"Girl needs taking down. She's loyal, but she's got some growing up to do."

"Caryd? She's right, as far as what's needed here and now. We both have to keep a hood on it while we're out here. Khiese is all that matters, but seeing you all brings Marola back and I couldn't help it."

He settles with that. I draw on the bacca and let the smoke roll up my face. We'll be out of the Gassies tomorrow, I reckon. Crimore's next. I hope to meet Jeife Seikkerson once more.

Crimore

"You need to sleep, Amondsen," says Drogg. He's just climbed the tree I'm perched in. The sun's setting, but it'll only make my black eye and this luta on the other eye work better.

"You can tell Nazz the walls aren't guarded today either. Must think the camp is protection enough. Can you smell the boar and deer?"

"No, I can't." Might be that it's the eye confusing my sight and smell, even sound, again. The eye sees the river running past the fort shining like silver and echoing like a thousand bells through the trees. The chatter of the men and women below in the camp are plucked strings. The soil is hissing, crackling where there are footsteps; the fires wheeze like old lungs. It feels like a glimpse into the world of the magists. Some call them gods, and how else might gods perceive things if not fully in the way I have only the merest hint of?

"Crimore's feasting. We go in tonight. Talley should get the brews prepped." I look at him, see the dismay. Faldon Ridge was his first brew in years. It was also the strongest by some way. Talley was taught well. "She's a good drudha. We should make this, Drogg, if you're as good with those javelins as that hammer. Should stop a few horses if the need shows."

"I know we'll make it. I am good with them, or Nazz wouldn't have picked me, would he?"

"Well, no."

He worked mines for years. Gives him a power that suits a hammer. I just wish he'd use an axe with some poison, but he obeys orders and doesn't appear to think too much more than that.

"Did you see Khiese?" he says.

"Not today. He's still there, in the fort."

While we hadn't known where he would be, it was a shock to scout Crimore ahead of going in and ending the Seikkerson line as Othbutter had commanded Nazz to do, only to find two hundred whiteboys camped outside the fort, their tents spread about either side of the main gates. We watched them for two days but it was yesterday I saw Khiese, walking down from the longhouse into the camp, Jeife with him. I can only think he's massing a force for a push down to Carlessen lands. Port Carl's too important if you have designs on taking Hillfast from the Circle side of it: crops, trade, a gate to Mount Hope and the Sar.

I follow Drogg back down the tree, careful and quiet, taking a slower, different route, covering more ground to ensure there was no scouts about. We wind our way up the hill, past the clearing we buried Crogan in to the thick woods beyond. I feel peaceful. Last week or so we been moving careful, separated into smaller groups, moving at night with luta, with rain to help us. We used some of the chalk from Faldon and got no trouble from those we did see in small theits that was Seikkerson-sworn Families.

At camp our factions are keeping themselves to themselves: Salia and Yame on their own, Agura together with Drogg, then Helsen, Cherry and Ru, then Nazz and the crew that was already on his scrolls, Threeboots, Heddirn and Caryd.

All of them are preparing belts, getting their leathers on. Talley's at the fire laying out the bowls, flasks, bottles and bags that she'll build the fightbrew from.

Nazz stands to greet me as I walk into the midst of them.

"Tonight is good. There's cloud, it's dry."

"You'll go over the plan again?" I says.

"What do you think, Teyr?"

I shrug.

"Amondsen, can you mix this paste up?" says Talley.

"Aye. Helsen, want to help, seeing as you're not needing leathers?"

"Of course, Master."

We mix up the chalk that we'll use to get to the camp. Helsen will be over the river, slinging the spore eggs in among the tents once he sees us go to work. He's never taken a fightbrew, only dayers. He's become a friend of Cherry's of course, for they have at least in common the life that used to be working for me. I talked a good bit with him these last few days we was camped out and hiding. We both lost a keep, and we missed them. I was happy to let him talk about his, the years they'd had, the sorrow when she'd lost two before birth and could not face trying for a third. They had many years and he'd hoped to find a recipe to help a woman during her gravid term. But nobody has, and then she died one winter of wet-lung – come on quick and he had nothing could do much for it. He might have been called a cooker by Talley, no formal training in drudhanry, but his sketches on the scrolls he kept, his recipes, well, she wasn't too proud to offer a lord's ransom for his snuff recipe and always turned an ear on the rare occasions he spoke, seeing or smelling some flower, mushroom or weed and speculating on what use it might be. She won't be too happy if she ever learns he's left his book with Thornsen should something

314

ever happen to us out here. It was his way of thanking me, he said, for how I was the only purse who hired him out of all the merchants in Hillfast who went to see his wife put in the land, to the tapestry. The choices have become easier, nobler and emptier now, he said.

Soon enough Nazz calls us together. Skin rubs are done, we're chalked up, faces and hands, a single line under the right eye, left clean so we might recognise each other when it got messy.

"We talked this through yesterday, this morning, and I'm going through it again. There's three points we attack the camp. Once it starts, Helsen will be over the river putting spores about the tents before joining us when we're in among it, so masks up. Talley will check your eyes are pasted right or you're going to lose them.

"Me, Heddirn, Agura and Ruifsen go in one group, Drogg, Caryd and Threeboots another. Salia, Cherry and Teyr are leaving first. Count to a hundred before we set off, gives them time to get Teyr into a position to take a shot at the lookout at the top of the longhouse tower. She thinks she can make the shot with that black eye of hers, and the last few rabbits we ate are evidence of that. She'll lead Cherry and Salia over the wall after Khiese and Jeife. We have to hope they find him and kill him before he takes a brew.

"We're riding the packies in, me and Ruifsen – might look strange us all coming in on foot – but Threeboots, your crew will be nearest the horse pens, so Caryd's going to shoot the horses while you both protect her. All of you, get the guards first, who'll probably want you to identify yourselves anyway. The horses scritching will wake the valley so give us all time to get into the tents and start work. Helsen, once you've emptied your quiver and sling you join us, you saw the spot you have to shoot from yesterday. If you come under fire it's a short run from the bushes there to full cover. Head back to the horses if that's the case and ready them, because it'll have gone wrong.

"It in't likely we'll kill them all, and we won't take Crimore now like we thought we could, before we knew Khiese was here. But we can really hurt Khiese, and he won't have as few men about him as this again, so we have to take the chance even if it means leaving him alive and retreating. There'll be a fair number in the fort, which means we won't get over the walls as well, so Teyr, Salia and Cherry, once we've killed whoever we can I'll blow the horn to sound that we're leaving. You're with us or you're on your own."

"Captain," says Yame. "Going in the fort, they're not going to come out, are they? Not if Khiese's in there and as sharp as you're saying he is. I don't get it."

"It's the purse, Yame," says Salia. "I'm the best sword here; Cherry will be a good enough archer to cover us. Khiese might well be an excellent sword, so we won't take any chances if we can reach him toe to toe."

"So why is Amondsen and not me going in with Salia? I'm a better sword than she is."

I can't help but smile, for I have said it to those showing some grey myself over the years.

"I'm the only one alive here that's been in there, girl," I says. "With Salia I hope we'll be good enough for him and his drudha."

"Are you done, Yame?" says Nazz.

"Yes, Captain."

"Good. Talley, shall we begin?"

Laughter and some song echo up the slopes and in the branches about us. We've got a soft luta mix, the world all sharp and pale green, the flames of the fires dancing black.

The lookout at the top of the tower swigs from a flask and stares down at the camp. We're to his left, near the back of the bailey in the trees. I step out and take my time, though in truth there is no doubt as I draw back. Breathe out. The arrow knows the arc, the air reveals it to me.

He falls. The tower is stone; there's no sound. We're running out across the open ground to the wall. I look left towards the river, see the others ambling out of the trees. I burn, burn for Khiese, to rip him open with my hands, pull him apart. The brew's so strong I'm grinding the few teeth I have left. The wall is easy to climb. We each of us dig spikes into it, find knots in the wood and fly to the top, peer over. The wall's empty. I hear the horses start up, a few shouts go around the camp. We're over the wall, Cherry stays on it, waiting for her first targets, me and Salia dropping from the wall to the side of the longhouse. Dogs growl and start barking, blackstrips. I don't have to say anything, Cherry's heard them, seen them out of their kennels, has a pepperbag on an arrow and shoots it into the ground ahead of them as their hackles go up and they make a move. It sends them into a frenzy. She's quick to follow up, killing two. Salia runs forward and spears the others. Cherry moves along the wall so she can see the doors of the longhouse.

They swing open, a mistake on Khiese's part, perhaps thinking the threat is outside the walls.

He has a sword, no leathers, walking out, three letnants with him, chalked up, armed and likely on dayers if they was guarding him.

He turns as Salia runs in, settles into a stance, his letnants level their spears. Cherry puts an arrow in one of their throats. She should have aimed it at Khiese, maybe thinks I need to be the one that kills him.

"You!" he spits.

317

I'm struck again by how scholarly he appears, his colouring aside. Then he moves, and the decades of discipline and sacrifice and pain reveal themselves. To my black eye he seems more clearly carved from the world, a keynote in its song, brighter, harder than everything around him.

As I close on him I can't speak, my blood is roaring, boiling, the brew pulls my strings, shakes me to pieces almost as I smack one of the spears out of my way and two strokes – stab, hack – and put the slow man down.

Salia's on the other spear, who's moved in front of Khiese, blocking both her and Cherry. He has to watch us both, calls out for support against Cherry, who has started putting arrows down the slope into doorways as they open, shouting and hissed commands sparking like coals in my ears.

I leap at him, he cannot be faster than me. But I'm predictable, frenzied. He cannot stop me but he uses it, my power; he is bright and clear, passive, quite aware of our disparity. An arrow flies between us, a moment of wood and feather splitting the world in two, and Khiese has struck me, just under the ribs. I step back because this is all wrong.

"Teyr!" Cherry's shouting. Salia steps in front of me, moving like hot oil, pushing Khiese back away from me.

"No!" I run forward, another arrow, the whip of it rolling up my neck to my scalp as it whips past me. "I had him!"

"Archers, I can't see them. Teyr!" shouts Cherry.

Salia drives Khiese back further, he makes a step to run, but I see what he's doing even as he tries it. I throw a knife as he twists and strikes out at Salia as she becomes aware of the archers shooting at us. It stops him, grazing his arm, not quite connecting but throwing him off. Salia thrusts at him, tip catching him just, but he drops and rolls. An arrow scuds the ground, missing her leg by inches. He backs away. She also edges backwards from him. The archers are easier to see now. Cherry once again tries to pick them off but they have doorways for cover. Salia's hand is on my shoulder, strong as eagle claws.

"Shoot them!" Khiese shouts. He is reluctant to step forward, and he sees Salia is too good to risk us both.

"Salia, no! We've got him!" She's pulling me back. Cherry must be out of arrows now, the way Khiese stands unflinching, his chest heaving and his face flushed, surprise and anger in him, that he's been proved wrong, that he has underestimated me, that his truth, his spells of command and control, are defied and fractured. I'm a knot of gristle in his meat, spoiling it all.

"You will die, Amondsen. There is no way out of the Circle that I will not find you and bring you to Aude. I keep my promises as I keep him."

I'm lost for a moment, for I had not believed Aude alive still and I now know him to be, but is he speaking true? There is a shade to his speaking, his claim, that makes me doubt him. I dare not hope what this might mean.

"Cherry's out of arrows, we'll die, Teyr," hisses Salia in my ear. "He's trying to draw us into his bowmen. Stone what you're feeling. It was only ever a whisper of a chance we could get him; now we have to go." She's a head taller than me, fierce strong with it, doesn't wait for her good reason to soak into my hate, crushes my leathers in her hand and with a grunt she lifts me to Cherry, who hauls me up the wall. I catch Khiese's eye as we leap over the wall, arrows following us, him bellowing at his men to man the gate where the noise of Nazz and the rest fighting carries from.

"The trees," says Salia. She and Cherry sprint away, but I'm still shaking with anger that we didn't get him, my blood's burning in me for killing, so I turn and run alongside the wall towards the camp, to Nazz and Ruifsen, for the fort

319

will not open and whiteboys will not come, knowing Khiese's called for the gate to be guarded. Those outside the fort are on their own.

I see two whiteboys, one with a bow, the other handing him arrows, absorbed in the fighting among the tents before them, cussing as they try to get a line on one of my crew. Their backs are to me. My sword slides from its sheath slick with poison, wet and hungry. Khiese is gone, but I can still hurt him, take his power from him, one body at a time. The bowman turns at the last moment, I leap at him, sword through the side of his head. It's a woman that's next to him, brew running down her face, not risen, slick with sweat, overcome, no chance to stone it. Her hand is on the hilt of her sword as I drive my blade into her, cracking through her ribs, fast and deep, stabbing. I can't help but salivate at her shock and that brief moment of sadness as death blooms and snuffs her still.

There are bodies all over the ground, tents ablaze, smoke, flames and screaming like rippling silks in the wind. Ahead of me, nearer the gates, Drogg, Nazz, Heddirn are harrying and falling upon Khiese's soldiers, those alive now brewed up but disorganised, leaderless. As I pass a tent, two men burst out of it, one's got a pike, the other a seax, had been waiting for their rise and saw their chance to get one of us. I twist and parry the pike but trip and fall back. A cry then. Helsen it is comes in, moving quick, but they're risen. As the pikeman turns I roll back and to my feet, the seax caught in a moment's indecision, which is an age on a good brew. Helsen forces the seax back, it hasn't got anything like the reach, but the pike goes at him. Helsen slips as he adjusts to the thrust, foot giving way briefly on slick grass, just a fraction, enough that his shield moves up as he instinctively tries to keep balance. The pike stabs deep into his thigh. I'm running at the pike, a moment too late, but he's not got the head of the pike out of Helsen's leg before I've run him through, and I step in to hold him, moving him between me and the seax, who's charged me. My sword's got reach. Helsen's crying out, bleeding out despite our brew. A shout behind us, Talley it is that's seen us at it. The seax knows he's beaten, has to try, a misery on him. He parries me, but the intent was to roll the parry into another strike, and I get the sword in his guts, don't wait, follow with another thrust through his ribs. He spits blood and falls.

I'm about to move on to the gate, Talley passing me to get to Helsen, when I catch a movement to my left, a slithering shadow from the back of the same tent away into the grasses. I turn and run at the figure. He hears me, turns, sword and knife in hand, in stance.

Jeife.

Some light from the tents burning nearby makes me out clear enough. He stares, wide-eyed.

"Teyr! How? Khiese said . . . He said . . ."

"He said he had killed me. But I have not died. This red drum in my breast beats and beats without mercy, there is no end to its beating though I am killed twice. Khiese is not the man you think he is."

"There was no choice, not for our people. There is still no choice. You'll die." He stands up straight. He knows his chances, his options, have vanished. "Enough of you for an unready camp, but did you mean to also take the fort from Khiese with this number?"

"What does it matter to you? Your rope is severed, a new high clan will be sworn."

"Wait, Teyr! You don't need to—" He lunges at me, thrusts his sword, moving forward, filling the space and hoping to force me back. But I move and bend quickly and unnaturally on this brew, I am almost able to pick my spot as I win the bind, throw his balance off, a neat thrust to his belly. He sighs softly, as though he's just tasted a fine wine. I didn't get much in him, he's wearing chain over leather. Recovers his stance, waits, seeing some advantage as Khiese did in using my brew against me. But he's no Khiese. My strength, balance and movement, my eye's knowledge of him, it feels like a story I've read before. He might as well tell me what he's going to do, his intent filling the air around him, as though it's leading his body. Another exchange, another puncture, his side, another wound like the mouth of a purse. He's breathing hard, trying to maintain his form, trembling as the poison starts in.

"Drop your sword and knife, Jeife. There's no honour for you in this."

He does as he's told, looks very old then, his easy confidence dried out in him, emaciating him.

Tears fill his eyes and he spits out at me, "You mean to revenge Mosa's death and kill Khiese because there's nothing left of you, is there? You lost it all for your greed. Now you stand there with that unnatural eye, like one of the Ildesmur returned, like a War Crow, 'risen for revenge, bringer of woe'. But it was just a story to scare duts." He winces, falls to his knees as he weakens. "I've no more fine words for you now, War Crow. At least I'm on my bloodlands. Get it done. I'll join my brother in his rest, who himself did too little in life."

His head comes off clean, his body falls forward. I pick his head up, blood pouring from it. At the gate I hear shouting. Nazz and the others are standing out of bowshot. They're blowing on the horns that the whiteboys use to terrorise the nokes, letting out their noisies, the lust spent on a field full of dead. Whiteboys line the walls around the main gate to the outer bailey. They're waiting, still and silent, ten, twenty of them lining up, but the gates stay closed. The smoke from corpses that have fallen into fires is thickened by and stinks of them. A breeze then moves a thick plume and reveals Khiese standing over the gate as it reveals me to him, my movement catching his eye. Bows rise for I am within range. He raises a hand to still his guards, says something to them in his Khiedsen lingo.

Nazz's crew, my crew, quieten as I move closer to the main gate. They're wondering if I'll be shot until Khiese's hand goes up.

I stand twenty feet from the gate, the smell of guts, of fat burning, is in my nose, coats my face, thrills me on this brew.

"The Seikkerson line is ended, as Othbutter commanded." I hold up Jeife's head. "Ildesmur he called me, War Crow, come back to doom the living that took their children." I throw Jeife's head high over the wall. "They will see his head for themselves, this Family."

Khiese doesn't watch it as it flies over him and into the settle. "You'll die by my hand, Teyr. Not some arrow, nor the winter. I do good work with my hands, work few others are capable of."

"I'm here, Khiese. Let your men see their great leader fight a woman in single combat."

A roar from behind me, Nazz and the others. His men look to him. He gives me a weak and polite smile, the smile a teacher gives a junior who's said something stupid.

"I am not on a fightbrew, and I have no need to step into your arena. I'm not so weak I would dance to your goading words."

He turns. There must be whiteboys behind the gate, the Seikkerson Family there too of course, wondering at their fate. He looks to them to focus their attention, then turns back to face me and the crew behind me. "I decide how this ends. You are all in the Circle and the Circle is mine. You cannot outrun me for I know its face, every bitter line."

"You don't have its heart, Khiese, you sad fuck. Fear shackles these people to you, it don't bind them."

"Your fine words are wasted on me, Amondsen. I'm the runt of Khiedsen's litter, remember? You should leave." He turns and walks along the wall, a handful of guards with him, descending inside the walls without a glance back.

I walk back to the crew. They've gone over to Talley, who's bent over Helsen. He's got a stick in his teeth and he's blowing hard as she tries to pack broadleaf into the vicious wound on his leg, a deep hole and cut. The pike must have been twisted to open it up further. Strips of wool are soaking, slipping in his fingers as he tries to hold them against it, and she's cussing.

He sees me, spits out the stick.

"Poison's in, Master. I . . ." He snaps rigid, howls.

"We need to make ground, Teyr," whispers Nazz, leaning close to me. "We walked into camp and one of them was saying Gruma's in Amondell. Where's Salia and Cherry?"

"They're out, heading back to camp." I kneel next to Helsen. "We just need to bind it, Helsen. I've got some betony'll keep you still."

He clutches my arm, shaking his head, he's wheezing. We have some protection from Circle poisons like henbane, but not against a good amount, not if it gets right in.

"It hurts, oh magists, it hurts! Finish me, Master. Don't make me slowing you down the reason we didn't get to kill him." He cries out. "You have to move quick, as Nazz says."

Every moment going by was putting us back in Khiese's pocket, now the surprise was gone. I'm not proud to be

324

thinking that, but I've been here before with good men who don't deserve this shit.

Helsen takes from his neck a leather necklace with a small piece of iron shaped as a droplet. He drops it before he can put it in my hand. He's got the spasms starting.

"It brought me luck to this point, might be it brings you some. It was a privilege, Master." He nods, barely a gesture, but the command is in his eyes, my black eye sees it, him settling with the earth, like they're one in this moment.

I do it sudden, drive the sword into his chest, into the heart before he can feel any fear. Nazz steps back, Ruifsen makes a sound, shocked. I can barely hope for such a quick death. Helsen was brave, a rare vanner that knew the weight of the purse.

"Teyr . . ." says Nazz.

"As you said, and as he knew, we have to go now."

I run, away from Helsen who's died for me in this field, skipping over the bodies lying about and onto plain grass. I was always a good runner, a good way to ease the pain as the time comes to pay the colour, as the muscles shrink and the bones get sore. I hear the others and on the breeze, Khiese, shouting.

Up through the pines, luta and brew revealing the earth, the knotted roots, the pine needles a slick carpet; all can twist and break a runner's feet, a horse's hoof. Salia and Cherry are there, horses ready.

"Helsen didn't make it. We ride west for the Shield and Amondell. Gruma's there," says Nazz. There's nothing said to that. We're going to have to pay the colour so every hour matters while we have the advantage of horses. There's a moment that's curious as we mount. Salia makes a fuss over Caryd, checking she's all right. I can't see why. Nazz nudges his horse forward to where Salia is standing, helping Caryd onto her horse, trying to get between them. Caryd's trying to shrug off Salia's attentions.

"Salia, we have to go," he says. I look over at Ru, who shrugs, but it's clear he's seen this and wonders too what it's about.

The Shield

The Shield is one of two stretches of woods between Crimore and Amondell and marks the boundary of the Seikkerson and Amondsen bloodlands. We rode a steady trot, hard on the horses for the hours we was riding, stopping at a small river late the following day when the pain got too much for even our bacca and mixes to cope with. Talley was forced to look out for us, forage and see to the horses, while we paid and while Yame was busy with the cuts and bruises we had. Nothing we could have done if whiteboys had come at us right then. I killed a lot of men and women that was found paying the colour after their brews and in their pain and suffering hardly knew they was being killed.

Following few days, with the chalk on our faces, I'm sorry to say we took kuksas, cheese, even some rough uisge from the two theits we come across. Khiese, coming across them, might think to ask them if we had the manners they wouldn't expect of his own whiteboys, so we give them no sense of our identities on that count.

We figured Khiese would have to send men out to the theits around Crimore, get their horses so's they could follow us. There'd be too few for a proper force to come at us.

We found a clearing where a couple of old larch had fallen, ferns having the run. Talley risked a fire after Caryd and Salia brought down an elk earlier in the evening; their shrill whistling calls the beginning of their rutting season. Ruifsen it was who made the cuts of top round and loins. He'd hunted much more than most of us, and proved his worth to us with his read of the land, its treasures and traps. With large measures of a heavy wine that Nazz passed about, our first cheer for what we had done to Khiese since we left Crimore, Nazz's crew set up first watch.

You might say it was our mistake, mine, that I didn't give more thought to the things I saw with Nazz that didn't add up.

I opened my eyes, and the sun was already high in the sky.

In the hinterland if you're opening your eyes to strong daylight you're lucky to be alive, there's always too much to do in land that rarely gives you what you need without a struggle, without work, and you need whatever daylight you can get for that.

The woods are full of life about us. Elks have moved on, but we hear enough birds, quick sharp rustling of what might be stoats or hares. I try to sit up but my belly turns over and I'm sick on the grass, getting onto my knees to better get it up, two soft twigs for legs.

The horses have gone. I look about and see Nazz at least gone, then Talley, Caryd, Threeboots and Heddirn, it goes without saying.

"Cunt chose a good wine for that sleeper," says Drogg, trying to stand but like a drunk he can't accept he's unable to.

"Wake up!" I shout. "And sit down, Drogg, give it a bit. Get an emetic out of your belt, or something to give you the shits."

The shout brought them awake. They all stir, roll about and realise they've been poisoned too.

"Least he didn't kill us," I says, though it upsets me bad, what he's done. I can't believe it though it might seem obvious he was capable given our past.

"We have to shit this out or bring it up, I don't mind which. Nazz has fucked off and left us in the way of Khiese but I got no idea why. We have to go hard for Amondell because I know the land better than Khiese. It'll give us a chance to regroup a bit more safely, figure out the next step. It's also where Nazz said he was going, and any chance to find him again I'd be happy to take."

"I know why he's gone," says Salia after she'd put her fingers down her throat and thrown up. She's led back, propped up on her elbows. "Yame noticed it first, was watching Talley put the fightbrews out for Crimore and saw how she set aside Nazz and his crew's. She wondered why they were in two lots, why they all had theirs together first, then we had ours. So I embraced Caryd, as we left Crimore, and she smelled different, different to us – her breath, her skin. It wasn't the same fightbrew. And I know because I tried it once before, six months ago. The reason I was in Hillfast, the reason I'm here, with Yame, is that we work for King Crusica." Crusica is the king of Eastern Farlsgrad, the great power around the northern Sar and Sardanna Strait.

"Nazz's girl Caryd was quite easy to bet against in the singletons at the Hillfast tourneys a few months back. She doesn't give the appearance of a good fighter, does she? One of King Crusica's nobles thought his champion was so much better than her he put down state secrets on a side bet, a fightbrew recipe called Gaddy's Mash." The side bets was always where the real action was at any tourney, and Hillfast's was making a name for itself in that regard. I recalled then

329

what the guard said to me when I was dragged off the boat in Hillfast. Salia was the one Farlsgrad had sent to find who had got hold of the recipes.

"We was on Crumper's Rot when I was taking a purse in their army," I says. "I take it that's Gaddy who's made it, a second to Drudharch Crumper back then."

"He's drudharch now. His mash resists horse chestnut and datura preps better than the Rot, and gives a clearer song." By this she meant that the song of the earth, the sense of what is and will happen, must somehow be sharper.

"They fought well, quick to us even on Talley's prep, and Threeboots was a piper, quite the storm of steel, and moved as fast as I've ever seen her move. It was nothing like at Faldon Ridge. I knew Nazz had the recipe when I found out he owned Caryd, but I couldn't be sure what Nazz would do with it, whether Othbutter had some part to play, and I had to know – well, the king has to know – because of what it could mean for Hillfast and Farlsgrad. Then Nazz takes this purse to come out here to kill Khiese, so Othbutter's involved in some way."

"That could mean war, if you're right," says Ru, mixing something up in a cup for his belly.

"Farlsgrad and Hillfast haven't ever been at war, but with Othbutter looking likely to be dropped as the high clan chief by the council of clans, this Khiese's threat has almost done him. I had to find out why Nazz was making a trip he's rather too rich to need to risk. It makes me wonder whether Othbutter has a cut of Nazz's little empire in return for going easy on his gang."

"We left Khiese behind. Makes no sense going deeper into the Circle, even after his brother. Where's he going, if he's got this recipe? He must have the cyca?" says Agura, by which she meant the key for understanding the recipe, for all recipes are written in a drudha's code so they can't be stolen and understood easily.

"He'd be mad to bring the recipe itself out here, never mind the cyca, given it's the Circle," says Yame. "What he does have are flasks of the brew. A drudha with enough of the mix in question stands a chance of working out what the recipe is from working out what's in it. Might be that there's a drudha in Forontir or Argir good enough to do it."

"What do you think, Teyr?" says Salia.

She's guessed at it, wants confirmation, I suppose.

"It makes good sense. We've come east. If he has the recipe and it isn't about some appeasement of Khiese then he's looking to get to Stockson, Forontir at least, maybe Argir. Going against Khiese in Crimore would confirm it, for Othbutter rightly don't see appeasement or a pact with Khiese working, and it would ruin his and Nazz's arrangement on the docks besides. The gift of a brew like that might bring an army back through the Circle and solve Othbutter's problems at a cut. Makes sense if you've seen them meeting a lot in the last few weeks. It would give Nazz some hold over him as well, strengthen his position on the docks. Clever game he hoped to play, only like me he was thinking that Khiese can't be as bad as all that. Seems clear, on that reading, why he's gone now, don't it."

It was plausible to the others given their quiet.

"Best we don't lie here then," says Cherry, who seems a bit better than us, strong enough she can get up and move about. "I can help with the rubs and mixes so we can move on. Not wiping your arses, my gredda needed enough of that at the end of his life. I'm done with shitty leggings."

She's got a sure touch, better than Ru's when it comes to waxing my eye, given how his former drooping's left him with the tremors. She finds it easy, the small things you say that settles people, while she's helping Agura and Drogg, who would normally never have let her go near them to help with their belts and leathers. They do their best to move themselves about for her, despite the weakness in their bodies. They're old enough, I can tell, to have a sense of this being life or death now. They can see nobody's mocking them for needing help; nobody out here in the wild can be proud and alone at the same time. Makes me smile, seeing Agura thank her, but she's been on vans most of her life, she knows the rituals, unlike Drogg.

The horns start the following night, robbing us of all but snatches of sleep, hour after relentless hour they wailed. Our trail's been picked up. We're doing our best to run, some struggling more than others, but death follows us. We keep to scrubland, spread out so's tracks are harder to see and we're pissing and shitting in any water we find, on dung too if we can find it, to hamper their sniffers. We're headed for the Shield, straight line to Amondell. Our only chance on foot. Land gets hillier, harder at least to spot us, easier to counter ambush, though we're not prepared for it, being tired from running and we'd be against mounted soldiers as well.

Drogg's the first to lose it over the horns one night, the thin wailing as bad as a bab scritching for milk. Takes me and Agura to keep him calm and not give away our position as he suffers. By dawn, after a mouthful of bilt and a few swigs of water, we're moving off again. I find the land easier as we go, recalling the trails, the bluffs, ruins of hilltop outposts. With our chalk faces we hopefully will pass without suspicion from those stationed in them, small figures that must be on seeing mixes, but seeing nothing they need to send guards out to us for. I keep us in whatever streams and rivers I can find, to slow those that follow us. They're not stupid, they will have been told that Amondell is our likely path. I hope Nazz has created tracks that will entice them away from us, but I don't know where he'll have been headed, away south of Amondell if he had any sense.

Horns are louder the following night when they start up. Closer. I cuss, for my efforts to throw them off or slow them have been in vain. We don't speak as we prep for watches and take our rubs and mixes. I think even a word would set us all on each other.

Yame has an idea we could put guira in our ears. We have to sacrifice our pouches of crowell's root, it being the least likely plant we'd need in the coming days. Pressing out the roots, we manage to get enough guira for half of us to plug up our ears. It makes a little difference, but the relentless howling of the horns blows and echoes with the wind. Hard to place how far off they are, how they keep their minds through it all. Then I remember the Kelssen theit, and how their mixes made them frenzied, not quite people at all.

We make no camp, huddle close together two on a watch. We're up as soon as the gurgling and chittering of snipes begin, another day of burning muscle, our woollens stinking, salt-covered leathers and the skin of our feet rubbing away, blood in our boots, trying to repair the mess before we snatch a few hours. It's bonded us if nothing else, even saw tears in Drogg's eyes last evening as Salia helped his boots off and pasted his blisters and bloody skin. He told us a tale or two of how his life went when I got out a small flask of brandy to lift our spirits, one I always pack and keep for cold and hopeless nights. Easy enough to fall to villainy if you get your bad breaks in luck, whether you're born to a bad da or ma, or crops rot, you lose your wife or fall in love with one who herself is in love with another, your friend as it

333

happens, and you don't hate him for it either. All this happened to him, and Gravy it was stole the heart of the woman Drogg himself adored, Adeik, who was the third in their banditry of vans, including one of mine. He was saying sorry now. But he's worn out with lack of sleep, as nice as it might be to think he could change who he was now he's an arrow away from dying and us depending on each other.

Next night, the horns are louder, there seem to be more of them. Makes no sense why they're not pushing on to catch us when our path now must be so obvious to any among them boys that knows Amondsen lands – Rikele Way, Eirkeden's Theit, Amondell. Yame it is barks us awake, her and Agura's watch that night. She's screaming, and I want to cuss at her as she does it, then I see she's loosed an arrow, points to a knot of trees across a clearing. The horns are further off still, but I'm sad to see that one of them's got Agura. Arrow in her chest. She's fading. Salia kneels next to her, gripping her hand, but there's nothing to be done.

"I fell asleep a moment, I did!" Salia says. "I would have seen these fuckers." Ruifsen it is that grabs her as she makes to go off from the camp. She doesn't resist him as he puts his arms about her and leads her back. Drogg goes to the edge of the camp and he's bellowing at them, hands high, urging them at us. I kneel with Agura, Yame next to me. She looks about us, takes Ru's hand and beats the ground because she cannot form words for lack of air. Then she's gone. I can't think then, I want to shout at Drogg to shut it and I want to bury Agura but we can't. Cherry at least is thinking. She puts her hand on my shoulder. "Come on, we have to prep." She goes round each of us. It should be me but I'm still coming awake, I can hardly stand. Cherry does Ru's luta first, him and Yame on lookout while the rest of us put luta in and pack up in silence.

"They're picking us off, Teyr, one by one," says Salia then. "Because they can. We can't even keep a proper watch."

The others are looking at me for instruction or command, but I've got none.

"We have to keep for Amondell," I says. "There's hills about, passes that can be easily defended against many. Chances too to counter them, lose them, trick them with the chalk."

"I've got thirty arrows, Teyr, and that's the most anyone here's got. We should attack. Why go on like this?" says Salia.

"Out here we're dying either way, like this or running at them," says Ru. "I'm sorry for Agura, I am, but while they aren't coming at us, we use it to get to land that gives us more of a chance. Teyr's right."

"We need rest, water," I says. "There's shepherd hides and huts up in the passes we can find some food in."

"We're not going straight for Gruma then?" says Drogg. Yame laughs, earns a clip round the head from Salia.

"Maybe we would have, Drogg," I says, "if we'd not been betrayed by Nazz and the others. And it's them's as guilty as those cunts out in the trees for all this. But we go near the fort anyway on our way into the highlands, we might have a chance of scouting it before pushing past and up the slopes to the Middry Hills, towards the Mothers."

There's nothing more said. Agura's belt and food are stripped. A long day's running ahead.

Following afternoon the rains come in heavy as we get through the woods and copses of the Shield. The wind's howling, a storm. Sheets of water come at us like spray off the sea as we cross the hills and valleys of my bloodlands. My eyes hurt, my right eye most of all. No fire we can heat up the wax stick for it. I have only a vague sense of where we're going, I'm in and out of my head, exhausted, mind curled up behind my eyes. But still I see a glimpse, feel somehow the hooves of horses far to our left. I'm about to say we should be careful, with the mist so heavy, the wind and rain so loud, when horses crest a hill behind us that we'd not long descended and others appear from our left. The lie of the land sharpens to me as I take a proper look at it, first in hours, I'm sorry to say. We'd run into a dell, my fault, for it reduced our ability to anticipate attack. The running's lost me in my muscles, in the need to keep my feet moving. Tiredness, lack of sleep, had robbed me of the proper caution I should be taking, like it took Yame last night.

I hiss at Ru to take Drogg and run for the nearest tree, get in its roots. There's patches of spruce about, thickening at the sides of the dell. Where we are there's younger trees growing amid older ones that have been chopped for lumber, and we're grateful for them for they offer good cover from arrows. Salia's already moving with Yame, splitting away from Ru to make things harder for the whiteboys. Cherry gets it pretty quickly, and runs for a fallen tree to crouch against. Hard to know what seeing mix the whiteboys are on. My life depends on whether I take a fightbrew or a dayer now. Then a few arrows come in, the horns starting up around us, savagely loud, almost splintering the air. I keep low and find my way to another tree while I try to keep sight of Ru and Salia, the only two I can trust to make the right calls here. I sign to Ru, using field Farlsgrad, for that's what Salia would also know. They reckon dayers are what's needed, the whiteboys indulging themselves in putting some fear into us. If they were on their fightbrews they'd be running in under the illusion they're immortal.

I slip luta into my eyes and punch the earth a bit while it gets in them, for it's that or pick them out with a knife if it would ease the pain of it. The black eye comes good for all it hurts. A roiling whiteness flickers and sparks at the edges of its sight, the noise of the horns it must be, but I see clear enough where they are, the air they disturb. Fifteen horses at least, groups of five, two groups back the way we come, one to the left. They're on foot now. Three, four of them are moving away from their horses, Cherry closest. I whistle and gesture for her to get luta in her eyes and watch for that movement. One flank covered as long as they don't run at us now.

Over to our right, no horses there, no horns, and it feels like that's exactly where they don't want us looking. I gesture over at Ru to watch there, for the air don't seem right, and then two thrushes fly out. Ru sees them, waves at me in thanks. He hasn't even got a chance to pull Drogg out of sight of that flank, he being focused on the horsemen that followed behind us and their blowing, when a volley of arrows comes in, seven, sharp and clear to me. Drogg's hit by one of them, and Ru's pulling at him is all that saves him from a second finding its target. It's hit him in his side, above his hip.

Salia sees what's happened. She whispers to Yame and runs for Drogg, who's led on the grass. Yame shoots at the first of the whiteboys on the right to see Salia breaking cover, misses by a whisker, but a fine reflex shot in this wind and rain and it'll keep them behind their trees a moment. The boys at the back of the dell think they're far enough off and us too occupied that they don't need to stay behind their trees. Maybe they think it's a taunt that'll distract us. Seeing nothing of those advancing to my left, I get a line on one of them blowing his horn, a bit prouder than the rest, a bit too much belief in their control of what's going on. He's worth an arrow, the sighting of him once again a thrilling

337

certainty, raindrops running down his puffed-out cheeks, spare hand on his hip as though he's casually calling muster. I can't draw the string quite as far without a brew in me, but the arrow lands square in his chest. He falls back a couple of steps and drops dead. The others run for cover, the horns falter there and it brings a smile to my face. I look over at Drogg, and it's cheered him too to see it.

Cherry spots the ones on the right moving away now, maybe thinking better on the odds they've got, the quality of our shooting. I'm grateful for not even needing a dayer, for Salia signs too that they're moving back on the left, the horns stopping. She carries on then treating Drogg.

Fucking whiteboys.

I sign for us all to move to where Drogg, Salia and Ru are, seeing nothing now by way of movement.

"I got the arrow out of him, sucked out what I could, but the poison's in there. Touch and go, he shouldn't be moved today, we have to let the bark and the mix do its work in there."

"We can't sit here," says Ruifsen.

"We can't leave him," says Cherry. "We're not losing another one today."

"You have to," says Drogg. "You made the right call, Amondsen, to keep going. This land is better odds – well, would have been."

"I'm sorry, Drogg, I am. I was leading us. I didn't . . . Cherry's right, sure we can get you moving somehow."

"Don't, Amondsen, they're on us, there's only going to be more and I can't walk. It's bad luck is all it is." He reaches up to hold my hand. "Helsen knew, didn't he? He saw out the purse proper, and I have to do the same or even his death's in vain, isn't it, if you're caught carrying me. No, I won't let him dying or even Agura's dying be pointless for me slowing you. Cherry, you look after Amondsen and this crew like you've been doing. Can you give me some of those spore eggs? Might be I can still do some good and take a few down if I hide in these roots and they come past this way."

I glance at Salia, who looks up to me as he says it. Her eyelids flicker agreement. I kneel next to her at Drogg's side. He's sweating badly, grimacing a bit as the poison bites in.

Cherry looks away. Her heart's too big for all this.

"It was better coming out here than hanging at the gallows, Amondsen. I hope you kill this Khiese and have a drink to all of us that's died." He smiles then. "Be good to see Gravy again. I know he don't blame you for what happened, Amondsen. I don't either."

I lean forward to kiss him. His cheeks are wet, for no one readies for dying without some feeling.

"I'm grateful to you, Drogg. Sillindar keep you."

"Try getting to your knees when you hear them, if they're coming straight through," says Salia. "The longer you rest still, the more chance the plant'll give you the means to get up, if only so you can throw those eggs a bit further."

Me and Cherry give him most of our spore eggs, five in all. Might do for a few of them, but at least he can break one himself to save him being tortured. She leans to kiss him too, whispers something to him which makes him smile. Then we go, passing through the spruce and into a thicker copse as lightning and an awful great crack of thunder send the air that I see, the song's weave, into a violent rattled spasm.

339

Amondell

The horns have echoed on through the woods around Amondell, before us and behind us. We've used the last of the caffin, fought off a charge on Dedssen's Fields and got into some thick trees, coal-dust gloom, the steep rising crescent of the start of the Middry Hills, the Amondell longhouse and my family a short walk away. We haven't spoken since we left Drogg; there's just me, Salia, Yame, Cherry and Ruifsen slapping each other about to stay awake, picking each other up if we've stumbled. But before I can think about where around here I could hide us for some rest, to stop and turn on them in trees I know like the back of my hand, there's shouting ahead and four whiteboys are running up the slope, oblivious to us as we freeze still. An arrow comes back past them. Sword work echoes from the far side of the rise that looks over my home.

"Who the fuck's fighting?" hisses Salia.

"Caryd," whispers Cherry. "I saw her up the hill just then, running as fast as a wolf."

I'm glad. "I don't know what they're doing here but I'm glad we found those fuckers. Ru, I'm going to take you and Cherry up the hill after those whiteboys once you've had some brew."

We help each other to keep it down, hold our heads, hands over our mouths as we suffer through our change. Seems like we're so tired we stoned the brew hardly trying to, like it just stands us up and opens our eyes proper. I gesture them all to follow and creep a few trees further up the slope. "Cherry, see the two ash, they should have circs on them, Auksen marks carved into their bark. Look up in the branches. There'll be a few that have their branches aligned, ten of them in all running a line that overlooks the fort. You'll get a good view around you from up there. Set up and shoot anything around you — you'll find ledges have been nailed in to give you room to move about. I have to assume Gruma's in the fort with my brother. Don't let them spot you; sign me when you can see me, tell me what's going on in there. Go. Rest of you with me."

A childhood playing hunt the wolf; sightlines, vantages. I sign, Salia interpreting, creeping our way to the ridge overlooking our fort, moving in and out of great thick ropes and fingers of roots. We wait. Grunts, whistles, sounds used by the whiteboys to position each other and instruct. A rustle through ferns ahead of us, two more whiteboys running low uphill. Threeboots, hidden the far side of a trunk not forty feet from us, spins from behind it, prefers sword and knife. I'm taken back by seeing her, can hardly believe it. Nazz and the others are really here. The first of the two whiteboys also surprised by her manages a parry before her run carries her into him, her knife into his sword arm, drawn along it, out, into his chest. The other chatters and howls, his fight-brew leaving little sense in him. The Khiedsen drudhas never cared much for how the colour was paid, only that it give them an edge in battle. They had no edge against the brew Threeboots would be on, and Salia knows it. The other whiteboy goes at Threeboots, her back to us. Salia leaps out

341

and runs at her, not a moment's hesitation in seizing an advantage, even against a woman she ran with and shared pipes with all those years. The whiteboy might have lasted a moment longer had he not spotted Salia coming at them. It's all Threeboots needs to go at him, force a bad riposte, and she runs him through. Hears the footsteps behind her, turns and, seeing the chalk before seeing it's Salia, defends well as Salia presses the attack. It dawns on her then, who it is she's fighting. As she tries to counter and press Salia back, her eyes widen.

"No!" She manages, swords ringing, a step back as they circle. "Don't do this, Salia, please. Whiteboys are everywhere. Gruma is in the fort, he thinks we're all here fighting as one. Where's Teyr?"

"Fuck you, Threeboots, fuck your betrayal of us. Drogg, Agura, both dead."

She thrusts, rolls the bind, but Threeboots is back out of her way. She's fast. Salia is far the better sword, but Threeboots licks her lips and comes back at her, sword and knife. Threeboots gets a score with the knife, slicing the back of Salia's glove, the back of her arm, but the leather takes the worst of it, the blood thickening quickly because of her brew as it runs out.

Ruifsen spots a couple of whiteboys, and Yame nods at him, getting arrows ready. There's screaming coming from the fort. I try to keep sight of the world about us, the brew now lighting me up. I ready myself to jump to Salia's defence for I'm no longer sure she'll end it. Salia and Threeboots move in and out. Salia initiates; each time Threeboots is quicker, escapes where her lesser skill might have got her killed. Then she attacks, two blows parried, the third gets into Salia's shoulder, but she rolls back and is spared a heavier blow. As she comes back at Threeboots, the smaller woman's power tells, and in two swift strikes Salia's knocked back, her sword swept out of her hand. Threeboots stands a moment before Salia, savouring it. As I burst forward, as she brings her sword back to thrust, an arrow punches into her chest, its angle high. It's Cherry, above and behind us. Threeboots drops her sword, hand to the arrow shaft. She looks about her, sees me as I approach. In these moments it hurts me to see them fight, how all those years we shared pipes and cups had come to this bitter steel.

"Teyr," says Three, looking down at the shaft and the dribble of blood seeping from it, looking back at me, "we had no choice. It was a recipe might have saved Hillfast." She shivers. My black eye can see her song diminishing, blending with the world.

"We know. Salia's purse is to recover it. For Farlsgrad. But if it was for saving Hillfast, why fuck us over back there? Don't matter though, does it. You're dead now, old girl."

She's bewildered by this, shudders, falls to her knees. "Nazz, he . . ." Her eyes widen, death quickening in her. "Tell him that what he gave me I had no right to expect. He saved me. Tell him." She falls to her side, dead a moment later. Shouts go up nearby, whiteboys move on Ruifsen and Yame. No more time to look upon this girl, the troubles she had and the troubles she give me as we made our fortunes over the world. I draw my sword and Salia wastes no time either in getting hers and coating it again with the paste in her scabbard.

Ruifsen and Yame do a good enough job with the white-boys and cut them down. I look up in the trees for sign of Cherry but she's moved, hopefully to get a better view down onto my fort.

"They might have moved further uphill. I need to get in the fort — there's a way, cave around the far side, a narrow tunnel into our longhouse. The only sure route bar scaling a cliff is down and right around the fort. Salia, I need you with me. I got nothing for the white spiders in the tunnel, so we'll have to hope we don't get our faces in a web."

She raises an eyebrow.

"What about us?" says Yame, looking at Salia, nervous about being left with a far less capable sword for a partner.

"Kill whiteboys. Use the chalk, act like one of them till you're close enough," says Salia.

"She's right, the confusion Nazz and his crew have caused will be enough to make them think twice," says Ru.

"Salia, can you find Cherry and get her read of what's going on in the fort, then follow me." I point out the route around the fort to the river at the far side where we'd meet before I take her to the cave.

Far off, a deeper horn sounds. More like a war horn. It's only then I remember where I'd heard it before, for it brings a tear to my eye before I even recognise it. It sounded in Khiese's camp, that night, in triumph as I dug the hole for Mosa.

We say nothing more, we have to get in the fort and at least try and kill Gruma, hurt Khiese as much as we can before he comes and ends it.

I move swiftly downhill, no more whiteboys ascending towards Nazz's crew, no guards on the walls of the fort, though the shouting and crying is increasing. A horn then, blowing its screech, silencing them a moment.

Gruma calls out, "Khiese comes! You should run, Teyr Amondsen. You do not want to be killed alongside your brother and his child. Let them pay the price for your return, as Mosa did, as Aude will."

The children in the fort can't help themselves, they cry out again. I don't break my stride. I pick my way through

344

the thickets of trees on the far side of the plant runs that fan out from the main gate. As I near the river, a clash of swords. There's bodies of whiteboys lying about, as good as a trail. I duck behind a tree, hiding myself from that direction, and I see to my right Heddirn's body. Blood still rolls out of his wounds, the steam of his body on the brew still giving off a wisp. Around him are eight or nine whiteboys dead. I lean out and see Nazz, two whiteboys on him. He's holding his side, his glove black with blood. Looks like there's four or five more dead around him. His sword wavers as they move in, a trick. He parries with surprising speed and power, runs one of them through, brings his sword up just as the other one, with an axe, swings side on at him. His sword takes most of the force out of it but the axe still hits him, the blade unable to bite, stopped by his own steel. I sprint towards him as the whiteboy goes to swing the axe again, Nazz on one knee, dropped and gasping from the power of the first blow, but I'm too late, the axe lodges in his collarbone and he cries out in fury more than pain, that it ends like this. The whiteboy turns, eyes widening as he sees my sword slide into him. Held by his ribs, I use the sword and my free hand to pull him down, then finish him.

"You'll finish me as well then?" Nazz says as I stand over him. He's breathing hard with the brew. There's a fear in his eyes that he thinks I might mistake for anger or hate.

"You look done as it is and I'm not sorry, Nazz. Marola was evil after what I did for you, but leaving us to die out here? You was never going for Khiese, were you? We worked it out. Salia come over from Farlsgrad to track who it was won the bet for the recipe, and your girl Caryd was the subject of the wager. She smelled it on you all back at Crimore – Gaddy's Mash. You're on their army's new fightbrew. But Othbutter finds out you won the recipe, don't he, and he's

345

got his claws in you, which is why you been a success so long. So before Khiese comes for him he's looking to make some sort of pact then, with who, Citadel Forontir? Argir? An army to come in and take the Circle back for him?"

"Clever girl, Salia. Caryd didn't look much going through the tourney, but that's her way. This lord of Farlsgrad had his champion, a good one, and the betting was against her. I made a lot of coin, but the recipe was going to set me up purple and gold. Until Othbutter found out. Othbutter threatened to have me shipped to Farlsgrad — it'd ruin him if they thought he was involved — but then this cunt Khiese starts up and Othbutter knows he's fucked and got nothing more to lose. He can't sell it to Khiese because he's a zealot, a man of ideas, not coin. He won't be bought because he's after the staff. Othbutter can't turn to Farlsgrad of course, while the Crutters and Kreigh, even Carl, they all got an idea to be chief clan so he can't go to them. We both know he's fucking useless. So yes, I was going to Forontir, Argir, whoever would put up soldiers to help him, if we gave them this fightbrew. There was nobody better to get us through the Circle than you, but then we hit Khiese in Crimore and it was clear he was mad to get at you. I can't pretend I'm proud of what I did leaving you back there, but everything I worked for is on the line and you weren't getting in my way. Khiese finds you, he forgets about me and my crew."

"Why did I expect anything more of you? But why you, Nazz? You could've sent a crew, not come yourself."

"I told you, this brew sets me up for life. I wasn't trusting anyone else to bring it through and couldn't trust many anyway if word got out I had it. Gangers' friends are only a good purse from being enemies. So he sends me out here hoping he can make some proper alliance if we can get through. You being caught and back at Hillfast sealed it. We knew you wouldn't come back out here, not for a purse, not looking at what you are now."

I want to cave his head in, but it won't help me. "I'll have the recipe for this fightbrew and the bags of it on your belt. Tell me you don't want me to get revenge on Khiese. Revenge for my son."

"Won't bring him back, will it. You made your choices, I made my choices. We got people killed we wish we hadn't, all our lives. Only difference between us is you think you can pay out, but you can never pay out because the colour takes everything you have, one way or another. I didn't hide from it."

"No, the only difference between us was that there was a point where the killing started to hurt me. You never got that far. You got cold about it. I got nothing more to say to you, Nazz."

"You haven't. She hasn't, has she, Talley?"

Fucker. The tip of Talley's sword touches my neck. "Sword, Amondsen."

Nazz can't smile, like he would have. He's blowing, trying to control the pain even through the brew. I hold my hand out, drop my sword. I loved that face once, his eyes that could speak almost better than he could, though he never learned how to use them. I throw myself forward onto him, for Talley's high on their brew and will be too fast for me to turn and attack her. I unsheathe my knife as I drop; my knee hits his chest, and I cut away a bag of their fightbrew from his shoulder belt before rolling off him and away from her. He grunts in agony. She steps forward to engage me, caught out a moment, but I'm crouched and stepping away in a stance. Bloody stupid really, with only a knife. I'm betting she doesn't have the heart to finish someone so recently sharing her cause.

"Another time then, Teyr," she says. "Have you seen Threeboots?"

"I have." She's not showing an intent to take me on; her mind's on her own master's wounds, a challenge to heal him, keep him alive.

He'll know what I meant by my words, and her last words I'll keep for he didn't deserve the comfort her final words might have brought him. I run on through the trees, feeling like they'll somehow, he'll somehow, get away from this. Like he always does.

Salia is at the river signing to Cherry up in the trees on the far side of the camp on the hill. She's already seen me running towards her.

"What's happening?" I says.

"Gruma's got the whole family out in the main run, outside the longhouse. Ten whiteboys in there, thirty or more killed out here. Nazz's crew did some good work at least on Gaddy's Mash."

"We have to get in there. The tunnel, we drop into it. Won't be pleasant – bats, other things, the spiders that live on them all. I know the route through. Stay close, I'm immune to their venom."

We run low along the side of the river, out of sight of the walls, facing the sheer side of the hill that the fort is built against. Over the noise of the stream there's shouting, screaming. Something awful is happening inside the fort. Salia isn't saying if Cherry has signed what it is.

I find the footholds and handholds. She follows my lead, up twenty feet or so to a lip, edge along the lip, the face of the rock flattens, the size of a bed perhaps. There's a hole there, our family's secret exit out of the fort. I look down inside it, my black eye revealing the heat off the mound of bat dung, the crawling insects and beetles over it are loud

348

enough, as is the scritching of bats, a sharp green flicker to the eye. I drop, land shin-deep in their shit, near the bottom of the mound. Salia drops rather more stealthy behind me, a sharp breath as she tries to control the urge to gag and vomit. I find the leftmost of the four holes dug to lead any unwanted people away to their deaths and whisper for her to crawl after me, her luta allowing her some sense in the blackness beyond the cone of light from the entrance. Hoods up, masks on and heads down, we move through the tunnel, thankful the bats wasn't aggravated by us.

Water runs over our hands, holes in the rock around us, a larger cave then, the ledge cut across it slick with dung. I feel the subtle pressure of a web, smooth as a Roan headdress, as my hands and head push through it. It gives me pause. A big web anchored here and no doubt the cavern's roof a few feet above us. We're being watched. I doubt Salia feels it as I do, but still she senses the web.

"How big?" she whispers.

"The only ones I saw was about the size of your hand. Da said he saw one bigger, size of a dog, but I think he was trying to scare me. What would it eat down here?"

"Keep moving, Teyr."

Something skitters in front of me, eyes glowing. I flick my hands out as they move forward, but it drops away out of sight before I can get it. Then we're back in a hole for a few feet more crawling and out into a space where we can stand again. This at least seems clear of webs. I'm dizzy with the thick hot air from the dung; there isn't long before I'm going to pay the colour.

"What's this?" she says, feeling the wooden boards before us.

"They lift off in a specific order. I have to hope that it's only the store cupboard that's still in front of them."

349

Taking each down from where they were slotted, I listen against the panel behind them. Nothing nearby.

The panel creaks as I move it aside. The cupboard is in the longhouse larder. Before us are piled furs — musty, feeding moths. I feel for the catch and open the door into the larder. The door is shut at the end of a narrow room that is piled with shelves on either side, smells of oil, cheese, barrels of barley and beer, though all are overpowered by the stench of us, what we've crawled through. The longhouse beyond is also quiet, all the noise outside now. I risk opening the door a touch. Salia is unshouldering her bow, unbuckling the cap on her quiver. She covers me as I step into our longhouse, lets me take her sword, a simple weapon of exquisite steel, almost as beautiful as she is.

The doors at the far end of the hall are open. The firepits are lit, smoke making it hard to see the gathering beyond, but the wailing is clear enough. I get a lump in my throat, for the cries are hoarse and beyond despair.

"Your rope is ending, Amondsen! How many more must I kill before you have the belly to face me?"

Gruma, calling out still. I sign what I can see to Salia behind my back with my spare hand as I walk through the hall and out onto the steps that lead down to the main run; four spears left of the doors, three spears right, bows right forty paces, left thirty and sixty, eight more spears, Gruma with two letnants, two guards and the children. Two dead, one with Gruma, knife at his throat.

"I'm here, Gruma Khiese." I have to call it over the crying, a woman I don't recall kneeling over her boy lost in her grief. I feel weak for a moment, me and Aude the same before Mosa. Now Gruma stands, chain armour, my nephew Drun against him and a wicked knife at his throat. Thruun and

Skershe are also on their knees, as though he's prepared the same scene for me. I grit my teeth.

"I knew you were here, for Samma sent us ravens to warn us of a crow. Your crew are giving us good sport up in the trees about us."

"Your whiteboys are all dead, Gruma. Let Drun go. These people have sworn to your banner; you need kill no more children."

"I need not have killed any, old crow, had you and your crew obeyed sooner. Not your uncle Kerrig, who put up something of a fight early on. He stood facing us on his own, all these good people leaving him to die, not one standing with him. Not even you, Thruun, though your keep scritched and scritched at you. Not had time to hang what's left of that old cunt on the fort's gates, but we will."

"My brother's a noke, Gruma – what could he have done, what good would it do?" I look over at Skershe, hoping she'll not speak against me for this. Her eyes speak plenty. Thruun's eyes are only on Drun and the knife. I swallow, for I cannot let Gruma see my tears for Kerrig.

"You killed my son and you thought you'd killed me, but here I am, back like the Ildesmur from the dead to avenge him. You'll die first, Gruma Khiese, then your little brother."

He's quiet for a moment, before a smile and then a hearty laugh break out, a cue for some of his soldiers. The guards holding Thruun and Skershe are the two chittering idiots from the Almet who stole the offerings. The woman that was with him then stands as one of the closest spears. Her eyes are moving from him to me. She doesn't see I am still signing positions to Salia, for I have not stepped forward enough for anybody to see the fingers of my free hand working against the small of my back. Once I'm done I bring my hand round to hold the sword in both. I breathe deeply and focus on

351

Gruma. Prick isn't going to knife Drun, but I need to make sure of it.

"Your crew will tell Samma that I offered a duel, a chance for you to subdue me yourself, being younger and stronger than me, but you turned it down. You talk of my rope, Amondsen rope, being cut for good. Yet these are all sworn to Khiese now; it's your own rope you are killing. No honour in that, as you know. I saw cowardice in you at the Almet, Gruma, a shortened step when you stood at the offering bowl and spat. You're no master, Gruma. Your woman there, your crew, all grovel to your runt of a brother, the littlest of Finn's boys but the cleverest. Tell me, can Gruma subdue this old crow, from whom his brother has taken everything but he has taken nothing?"

It is silent now in the fort. His jawline tenses, relaxes, tenses.

In these moments he is reminding himself of his size and strength, his youth and speed, for I have reminded him of them. A flush is coming over him, fuelled by his brew, which they either cannot or choose not to stone, and it's persuading him that whatever skill I have, I cannot hope to match his bind, resist his parrying or his blows. He glows now with the sense of his own power, breathes in, that great chest stretching his mail shirt, arms the equal in girth to Drun's legs. He's almost shivering with his brew's bloodlust, as I'd hoped, though hope's a strong word for I cannot see the outcome of this until I get a sense of his training, his tells.

He draws his sword to a cheer from his crew. I see the woman who shared his horse back at the Almet lick her lips, smile at me. From his belt he takes a rag and wipes his blade clean. Whistles and more cheering, for he is giving me the advantage in a sense, though he cannot afford for his poison to kill Samma's prize, for Samma has promised I would die at his own hand.

The knife comes away from Drun's throat and Gruma lets him go. He runs to Skershe, whose hands are bound and cannot hold him so she kisses him desperately, savagely.

"Come at me then, one sad Khiedsen spimrag about to get cut up by an old Southie cratch with one eye."

Hard to believe the goading works so well as he steps forward to test me. The tops of our blades are close enough to kiss, both middle standing form. He moves in, swings low. We bind, but I read his line, his weight; I drop the blade to parry, step in and kick his knee, snapping it back flat before pushing his blade off. He steps on the leg gingerly, shakes it. One of his men laughs but cuts it off quickly. I rush him, a thrust, test his footwork. His parry is strong but I keep moving in. He hasn't anticipated I'd be willing to get close enough for him to use his strength. He's lost initiative. Before he can grapple or hold me, I kick the side of his other knee, step back ready for a counter.

"Come on, kin killer, this is easy."

There seems to be a well of heat in him – my eye reads it well – like he brightens, cut out from the air about us.

Two blows, predictable, but he's using his strength, asserting himself. A moment later he almost kills me. I'm a fraction late in recovering from a cleverly concealed blow, and he's thrust, sword passing between my leather and the skin of my side, a long cut. It holds there a moment, my armour and body's movement stopping him from withdrawing the thrust for another. I twist, cry out as the sword bites into my side, get a hand on his wrist to hold him and push my sword into his thigh. I step back as he freezes, stiffens. There's a thin, vicious line of pain and warmth as I step away from his blade. I'm not bleeding much, feel the leather beginning to stick to the blood as it thickens and clots with the brew in it.

I smile to see him sweating and cursing as he hobbles. I choose to wait for his own brew to work, stop the bleeding.

"Did you know," I shout out, "that Gruma and Khiese killed their own brothers? Know also that their father Finn killed their mother, then their second mother. Nobody cuts rope like a Khiedsen. You stopped cussing now, Gruma? Your crew are quiet, you might ask them to cheer you on a bit."

"They are silent because Samma Khiese comes. They want you to hear his horns sound on the wind. These people are just waiting for you to die; they're loyal to those who give them justice in hard times. Not merchants whose loyalty is only to their coffers. We rule the Circle, the Sedgeway, the rest of Hillfast will fall to us. Nobody here is standing with you. You're on your own."

"She isn't. I'll stand with her." It's Skershe. She gets to her feet. "She's my sister-ken. She isn't here for coin, she's here to stand for her blood."

"Skershe no. Gruma! I beg you!" shouts Thruun, fearful of what they'll do.

Gruma nods to the idiot standing over her. "Cut her open slow."

The whiteboy's eyes widen with delight and he reaches for his knife, dropping his spear so he can get hold of her head with his other hand. I'm about to move on them, force Gruma to focus on me, stop it from happening maybe, when Thruun stands and jumps at the whiteboy holding Skershe. Hands bound he can do nothing but put him off balance. Drun jumps back, screams. The whiteboy that was standing over Thruun wastes no time, puts his spear in my brother's back as he falls. Me and Gruma lock eyes. Act. I run at him. He sees Salia over my shoulder, shooting from the longhouse,

354

and he stumbles back. An arrow whips past my ear. Another takes the guard standing over Skershe, two more follow, each finding a whiteboy. Then Cherry, up in the trees, takes her cue from Salia, and shoots down on the bowmen in the fort as they raise their own bows to reply. My people run for their houses, ignoring the whiteboys now confused by the arrows coming in from behind them, up on the ridge.

"Kill them all! Burn this fort!" screams Gruma. He raises his sword and runs at me. I'm forced back towards the longhouse as he swings at me. I read his movement, though he's hampered by the wound in his thigh, lost some balance. I see the moment to move in and attack, forcing him onto his weak leg. We bind close to the hilts but he can't meet it properly, his leg giving way with the poison. I roll it easily and slice through his neck. Blood spits out as he staggers back. His hand's at his throat looking at me, eyes wild. He thrusts at me. I pat his sword away and watch him fall. Might have been different if he'd had poison on his blade. The others near us, his woman included, come at me screaming, for their fate is sealed either way. Salia shoots her mid-stride, arrow knocking her askew. I put up a guard and move to the spears next to Thruun, lying on the ground with the two idiots that are dead there. I take one of the spears up, leave Salia's sword on the ground.

I know my brew is waning, the pain is beginning. I go after the spearmen who are attacking those running from them, men and women being run through and cut open as the whiteboys screech, frenzied, panicking. They too have not been taught well, some not at all. One freezes as I approach, no brew in him, pushes his spear out to fend me off, but I win the centre, thrust into his face. Another smacks at my spear as I come at him. I skip the shaft off his and thrust to his face and throat, far quicker than him. I hear leathers creak behind me, thrust my spear backwards but it's parried.

"It's me," says Salia, flicking the thrust aside. "I'll take the rest. You're hurt, see to your brother."

She sprints off, signing to Ru and the others in the trees.

He's on his side, a woman with him, next to Skershe, who's pressing cloth to the hole in his back. Drun stands quietly, unsure what this means, fearful of being in the way.

I fall on my knees before Thruun.

"Skershe, take this cotton, soak it in this." We learn our belts so we don't have to think, to open pockets and pouches, ties and buckles blind. I soak some bark in alka and jam it into the hole the spear's made. He swears.

"Who told you to be brave, little brother, eh?" Skershe hands me the cotton. I squeeze gum from a pouch onto it and press it into the bark and the wound there, keep my hand on it though he's hissing and crying with how it hurts.

"I'm sorry, Teyr."

"No, no, don't say it. You kept these people alive."

"I tried to tell Kerrig. I should have stood with him, Gruma was right." He gasps then.

"Skershe. Drun!" His voice rises, he's dying and he knows it. I take Drun's hand and draw him down to his knees.

"Hold your da's hand, Drun, give him your strength."

Skershe leans over him, kisses him. "I'm proud of you, my keep. You are Amondsen."

I hiss with the pain of the colour demanding its price. I'm coming down off the brew. My head begins pounding, the backlash of my body as it sheds what has taken it over. I weep, for I cannot be still, cannot say anything to my brother. I can think of little more than a drudha, a mouthful of something to take me out of it.

"Teyr," says Thruun. He's looking between Drun and

356

Skershe, looking up at me, but death takes whatever it was he wanted to say.

I ease myself to the ground, muscles twitching, sharp and burning. A sliver of betony perhaps, just a little for this pain, to ease the paying, calm me down. I fumble for it, my hands shaking badly, as Salia walks up, panting, soaked in sweat and blood.

"The others are coming, Teyr. Let me get to your side."

I can't see Drun or Skershe. I submit to Salia as she rolls me to get at the buckles of my leathers.

"She all right?" says Ru.

"She's fine, a cut just needs treating, no poison."

"Horns are closing. Do we make a stand?" says Cherry somewhere behind me, drawing deep ragged breaths.

"The Almet. The seed," I says. Salia has to repeat it for them.

"We're all paying the colour," says Yame. "We can't do shit here."

"How far's the Almet?" says Cherry.

"Two days' hard ride."

The betony glows in me, makes me smile, sleepy. "Send them after Nazz." I point about me but know it won't make sense to them and I chuckle.

"She's taken some betony, bit more than she should have," says Salia, cussing.

"You take their horses and ride then. You might be safe in the Almet, safer than here." This is Skershe's voice, rough like shale from her crying.

"Nazz. Talley. They're about." No, no point in speaking, I just need to sleep.

Salia shushes me.

"She's got a seed, Flower of the Fates," says Ru. "Might be the Oskoro in the Almet will help us in exchange for it.

She told me they've saved her life, helped her in exchange for the last one she gave them."

"The Oskoro, Ru?" says Cherry. "That's a story, they're just crazy bandits."

"Monsters more like, child eaters," says Salia.

"It's all bullshit. This seed, they'll help us for it, if we can get to the Offering Stone. We can't get Khiese now, like we are. The Oskoro might do it for us, or help us at least," says Ru.

"These people will be killed – Khiese won't leave anyone alive," says Cherry, not helping.

"We'll hide in the caves. You're the only chance for the Circle now," says Skershe, who looks down at me then. "Take her, find the Oskoro."

I realise, as the wave of honey, the golden-brown river, runs across my skin, through my bones, that I have Nazz's fightbrew. I pull Salia's hand to my satchel. She does the rest as I fall away into troubled dreams.

The Almet

"She's waking up."

Thruun, take my hand. No, it won't wash you away, you've seen Da swimming in spring, even when it's strong like this. Might be the girl in the river is waiting for you today. Nearly fourteen summers you are, she'll take your childish fear for a single kiss and you'll be a man. Da will be proud.

"Teyr?"

"He said she was there, in the river," I says.

"Fuck. Ru, give her some vadse, we're going too slow."

I frown. "Did we tell Da she come for him?"

"I think she recognised your voice, Caryd," says Ru. "I'm sure she won't kill you when she comes to."

"Funny old man, in't you," says Caryd.

"You know how the betony goes, Caryd," he says. She don't say anything. "She's dreaming about her brother, I think."

"Wake her, we have to move." Salia.

"Why can't I see?"

"It's dark, Teyr," says Cherry.

Horns of the whiteboys. The horses are skittering. I can hear them, unhappy, nervous.

"Only advantage we got is that they can't push their horses like we can, or it's a long hard way to wherever they might go once they've killed us."

"That's the spirit, Caryd," says Yame.

"Chew these, Teyr," says Ru.

I blink, try to move quickly, to sit up, but I'm hurting all over. The colour. Every muscle's been fried, every bone dried out and sore, it seems. Soon enough I'm awake and looking about, checking my belt bags without thinking, inventory of what's there.

"You have a bag of Gaddy's Mash, the fightbrew," says Salia.

I nod. "Couldn't get the recipe. I think Nazz and Talley got out."

We're in the plains. A strong wind up here whipping our furs. It's been snowing, but little's settled.

"Yesterday was bad," says Ru. "Had to tie you to that horse to get you over the river and through the woods about Amondell. We saw them last light yesterday, clearing the trees behind us. I think Khiese thinks he's putting a fear in us, just following, not aiming to give chase."

"Might be his horses have had little or no rest getting to Amondell, he can't push them," says Caryd.

"I don't believe that," says Salia.

"Caryd?" I feel a flash of rage but it melts to confusion. "How are you with us and not Nazz then?" I says.

"There. I told you she'd recognise it was you."

I put my hand out for Ru to help me up. He pulls me up onto dead legs, holds my arm while I shake them out.

"Take this," says Salia. She puts a vadse stick in my mouth and some bilt in my other hand along with a few caffin beans.

"It was wrong, stupid and all out here," says Caryd, "splitting off and trying to run for it across the Circle east. He

360

had no idea where to go, and when we came across a theit we couldn't speak their lingo either and they sent us up to Amondell, we got on the wrong trail. Your lands are fucking impossible to work out — cliffs, bluffs, curacs, as bad as Hope. Foothills is always a problem 'less you know them. Saw Ruifsen and Yame coming at me as I was going at some whiteboys. They showed me mercy."

I hobble forward. Need to get myself moving about, and it'll shake off the colour that much quicker. I walk up to her, put my hand on her shoulder. "You might have lived if you'd stayed with Nazz, but I'm glad you're here now."

"How much of that Mash she got in there?" says Yame. She's sitting at the moment, going through her belt checks and freshening her scabbards with poison.

"Those bags can do four," says Salia. "We'll have an edge, those of us gets a dose, but not on seventy horse."

"What?"

"That's the count, Teyr, he's got a good number with him."

"More reason to find this Offering Stone and even up the numbers," says Ru.

I don't say anything to this. Maybe I'd like to think it's true.

We ride hard for hours. These horses aren't going on, even if we live. We get to the Almet. After that we don't have a plan.

The horns don't let up of course, and they're gaining over the wind. Khiese must have thought it was time to run us down.

We come across a stream and stop for a few minutes, give the horses a drink. Caryd and Salia are better with them than me, talking to them. Salia has a mouthpiece, a strange instrument carved with channels she puts in her mouth and breaths into. Makes a sort of whistle, a call, somehow gets her horse to settle. With the aggravation we're getting from the other horses it's clear only those two stand a chance of fighting on horseback if it comes to us going at Khiese in the open.

We run out of the caffin beans we got from Caryd's belt after Amondell, use them and some luta to keep on. Nobody's speaking, we're just looking for the treeline in this ocean of grass swelling and falling like green waves. The tall grasses are as hard for Khiese's horse as ours at least.

The sun's high when Cherry spots it, a faint purple smudge, could be low cloud, strengthening and defining itself as we ride. We all holler at each other and look to finish the horses. Salia comes across to me as we gallop.

"Need a rise, a hill of some sort, something that'll unsight us from their bowmen but give us elevation should we need it over the grasses." She looks behind. "We're not getting into the trees, Teyr, we won't make it."

I look behind me. Two, eight, twenty horse crest a swell in the land, more, scritching and shouting and blowing. They might well be killing themselves for his cause. He demands no less.

"They're getting close!" shouts Cherry. It's clear now that their horses are fresher, better fed and watered.

"No more than a few miles now!" I shout at the others, the trees becoming distinct in the afternoon. I'm whispering to the trees now, hoping we've been seen, but how will they know that I am here for them, to give them the most prized of gifts. Would they wait until I'm dead and take it then?

Ruifsen's horse rears up then, nearly throwing him. It's done, eyes wild, shaking. It's the oldest of them, but the other horses stop as well, like they've drawn their own line. I look desperately on at the trees but I can't leave Ru, not now.

"Teyr, here's a hill of sorts we can use," says Salia, accepting that we now need to make our stand.

I stand up in the stirrups, take the seed pouch and slit it with my knife. I hold the seed up, high as I can.

"An offering!" I yell. The others, themselves flinty and worn, join in, shouting and bellowing. Caryd gives a fierce whistle then, like a knife in the ears, which skitters her horse and she has to jump from her.

"Teyr, we need to prep, they'll be on us," says Rù.

"All of you, off horses, get behind the ridge of this slope," I says.

I jump down into the long grass. As I do there's a movement, a rustle, thirty or so feet to my left.

"Someone's there," says Cherry. She points, but we see nothing. Then bird calls. Close. We freeze, for there are no nests here. Salia's drawn her sword. I hold my hand out, asking her to keep still. I feel a hot rush of joy, hope even, for the Oskoro are near, might have seen us all coming at them such is their sight if their eyes are better than mine.

"I have another seed, a Flower of Fates, that you might birth another drudha." I hold it up again. "Help us!"

Silence.

"Where the fuck are they?" says Caryd.

She gets a cuff from Salia. They're all looking at me like I know what's going to happen.

I lower my arm, walk a few steps onto the rise and look over the plain to the woods. Grasses move against the wind, like eddies in a current. All I see with the black eye are vapours of a sort, shapes of smoke. It is as though I'm seeing only movement, not that which is moving. When it stops, there seems to be nothing there. There are numbers of Oskoro about us, I just cannot tell how many, or few.

Hooves in the distance. I turn to Salia.

"It's me he needs to see. If I show him we've stopped here, they might stop themselves, and we'll have a bit of time to prep." I walk up the rise to its crest, the length of a few horses, enough for us all to stand there if we chose.

I look back at where we've come from. I see Khiese, it must be him, as the whiteboys slow to a canter, a mile or so off, fanning out, wider and wider as more of them are revealed from the line they was running to help the horses behind follow those that flattened the grasses. I turn my back on him, look down at my crew, a captain again.

"Good, they've stopped. Let the horses go, all but Salia and Caryd's. Four shots of the Mash, shared as follows: one for me, he'll come for me. One each for Salia and Cherry, lastly for Ruifsen. Caryd, your bowmanship will be sufficient on Talley's other brew, Yame, you prefer a bow and your powders in a fight as well, so you'll take Talley's brew. Give the horses a good measure of their own brew. It'll kill them once the fighting's done, but we need all they have.

"Talley went through their belts, those we killed back at Faldon Ridge. Our fightbrew's good for cuts and the poisons, but prep the alum and waterdock skin rub. Damn that fucking noise!"

They was lifting their horns to blast, seventy horns filling the sky.

"Caryd, tell me about the Mash, how hard does it hit, how fast and how long?"

"Captain. Better in all ways than the other. Rise is cleaner, fierce fast. Might get another hour out of it and all."

"Won't need an hour to—"

"Silence, Yame. I don't know what the Oskoro will or won't do. It's just us. We take the brew the moment they ride, can't chance taking it and they just wait there for whatever fucking reason Khiese's got in his head. If the

Oskoro start something, anything that sets Khiese off, we also drop the brew and we go. Salia ride left, Caryd right, bring them back towards Cherry and Yame, in range of our bows if you can. Caryd, bow only, then lead them back in range of us if you can. We hold here, me and Ru. He's going to come for me."

I step back down the slope, beckon them all to join me. We clasp arms and look on each other. There's tears of course, for we have suffered together since Crimore and we don't want each other dying, but there's odds on us the dead wouldn't take.

"I'm after Nazz once this is done," says Salia with a wink.

Caryd clasps arms with me. She didn't need to stay.

"Think I might have signed up for your guild, Captain, had we got a bit longer. You give me something I hadn't ever understood wanting till now."

"You ready, Cherry?" I says.

"Captain." Her hair's foaming out of the rim of the helmet she's got on, brings a smile to my face, but she's dealing with her nerves and can't say much more than that.

Yame just clasps arms before returning to her horse to retrieve the rest of what she needs for her belts. They're all too young to be looking at the end of it all. It's never easy, though you somehow manage to tuck it down until the brew comes on and burns the fear away.

"Amo."

Ru's hand pretty much circles my forearm, and mine don't make it about his. I look up at him, steady and warm like a tree in the sun.

"I still wish you hadn't come, Ru. Would give me some peace knowing you were out on the farm with Bridie and the children, not dying here with me."

"Don't be stupid, girl. I couldn't be anywhere else and

365

live with myself. Don't think this Khiese knows what he's up against. Just keep the brew stoned; you burned a bit back at Faldon."

"Stay close, Ru. Khiese will work whatever he can so's he can get to me and make a show of it. Both of us I hope is too much for him."

We hardly got to work pairing to smear the skin rub and fix the leathers when Caryd whistles.

"Brews!"

The Mash has been salted to help with how bad it is. It's threaded into guira, which I haven't seen before, and that helps a bit with the swallowing. While it's getting in us we pair and switch for the luta. I hear the hooves, the rumble building as I unshoulder my bow and step up the rise a bit to push my arrows in the ground. We only got five or so each, the rest going with Caryd and Salia.

My eye's been waxed, feels hot in the socket, like a coal put there to warm my head. I see the vapours then, clearer outlines of the Oskoro, who must be bare-skinned, for their natural colour is as the grasses about us, though it's mixed with bark and moss, even stone. There's more of them than I could have hoped, but I can't tell if it's enough. The rise keeps building as I begin humming to stone it. It's a cleaner brew for sure.

Whistles start up all around us, closer than Khiese's crew, a strange sound. From the ridge I'm on I see two groups of horses coming at us, Khiese staying back a bit, but also moving in. They're fanning out further left and right, cautious about what might be behind this rise, taking no chances. The whistling gets louder between us and the whiteboys, and then I see arms rise out of the long grasses, spinning what look like lengths of bone, holes in them, and the whistling becomes its own kind of screaming, a calling to the earth and sky, louder and louder as they are spun faster, a blur. Khiese's horses rear up, though ours can be settled at this distance. Salia and Caryd wait on my command to ride out. Khiese's whiteboys dismount as their steeds throw them or buck and turn. The horns that they've been blowing fall quiet under this strange and haunting cry, which seems to grow with the wind, tones that blend and fade, confusing the ear, like the air is being wound about my head, making me dizzy.

It stops so suddenly the land seems to hold its breath. We all feel that beat of stillness, though many of the white-boys' horses have gone, running free, the letnants shouting for order, settling lines. I sign for Caryd and Salia to ride out, expose their bowmen, give us a read of their range. Me and Ru stay on the ridge, I have to tempt Khiese in, and I'm better with a bow than a sword. Yame and Cherry move forward, low into the grasses.

There's a cry then, far off, bows are raised, arrows loosed. Khiese's group brings its remaining horses under control and they move down the middle while his flanking groups shoot. They're communicating in whistles, blasts on horns, and the group coming at our left start running at Salia, shooting as they come. Four horse remain on that flank after the Oskoro's whistling bones, and they ride after her as she turns away, screeching and laughing at them, readying her bow to shoot. Those on the right now inch forward, using the swirling grasses. Caryd returns arrows to those bows she sees raised at her, whiteboys standing out of the grass, aiming, missing her and being dropped in turn. Soon there's screaming as she gets our first kills, the poison finishing the wounded. She is remarkable. Then others start screaming on our forward left flank with the poisons from our arrows. Salia is leading their horse towards us, goading them on. Figures then seem to form from the air, the grass shifting into the shapes of Oskoro, who wield slings, hurling what I think are stones into the grasses near where the whiteboys must be advancing. They choke and retch, and I can see the dust of each sling-shot puff a moment before it clears away. The whiteboys stand straighter to get in the breeze above the grasses, clawing at their throats, on the edge of our range. Yame lets loose an arrow, but I see there's no need, these whiteboys are choking to death. Khiese shouts, points at these Oskoro that have begun their own assault, and the rest on that flank run or ride straight for them though they are suffering with what I have to think is spores.

"Shoot, now!" I shout. Cherry and Yame stand and pick their targets as they close on us. The powders from the Oskoro work quick, many of Khiese's crew dropping before a count of ten. This is fierce drudhanry. Shortly the Oskoro there, eight in all, stand and hurl more of their powders at the incoming whiteboys, but they're masked, they'll be holding their breath, and then they are on them. These Oskoro are not fighters or soldiers. Why would they be? But they are out here killing Khiese's men, and I'm grateful.

Salia's now riding at the four horsemen on that flank as they close in on the Oskoro there, spear at her side, a supreme rider. Cherry and Yame are putting arrows where the white-boys advance beyond the Oskoro, who must have killed near fifteen. The Oskoro on the right, where Caryd rides, I count five or six, retreat as they sling their stones, forcing the whiteboys to slow, Caryd harassing them, killing a man with every other arrow it seems. Still Khiese's main group moves forward, most on horse, and six break from the group to ride down the Oskoro who have now stood up between us. They manage to throw some of their stones and take the horsemen out, but volleys of arrows, twenty at a time, catch

them as they run back towards us. I see then as I ready my
own bow for a shot that the volleys have changed direction,
are higher.

"Get down, down!" We drop back on our side of the
ridge, a cry nearby, Yame it must be, hit with one or more.
She's calling out to Cherry. I run to the edge of the slope,
look over and she's looking back at me, thigh and belly hit.
There's screaming all over now as the powders work around
the field. The Oskoro are getting cut down, whiteboys hacking
at their bodies and throwing arms and heads in the air towards
us as they advance, wild and lost on their brews, but many
more whiteboys are dropping dead, the powder stones spread
far and wide and too refined for their masks, the mixes too
potent perhaps. Still there's too many coming for us, scritching
and screaming and mad for blood. Now the arrows have
stopped, Khiese realising they have to get closer to us to get
away from the spores.

Cherry's closer to Yame than me, looks back at me and
signs her position, her wounds, then runs over to fix her
up.

"No!" It's Ru, who's looking over at Caryd, her horse hit
by arrows. She leaps from it, drawing her staff from its loop
on the saddle as she does. Nazz was right about her: she's
assured and, familiar with the brew, she engages eight or
nine of them that side. I nudge Ru to run out, to put some
arrows among them, help her out. I cover him from the crest
of the slope, use all but one of my own arrows as he moves
out low into the grasses. I don't miss.

We're not enough of course. Then one of the letnants,
next to Khiese, breaks and gallops to our left, towards Salia,
whose shield has taken seven or eight arrows though she's
killed the horsemen there. Salia begins riding back to the
slope, not knowing Yame's dying. A handful of Oskoro remain

in the middle, nearer to us. They must be out of their slingshots for they're whirling the bones again to scare back the horses that advance, breaking Khiese's line up. Khiese raises a hand quickly and his crew dismount, running at these last Oskoro on foot. I can see him better now, his drudha to his right.

I shout out to Salia, who sees the letnant riding towards her. She wheels about and rides for her, spear ready. The letnant's posture is strong, steady. Salia's spear misses, she twists and bends back, the letnant's spear glancing off her shield. Salia can't stay on with the force of the hit, jumps up and back, letting the horse run on, dropping into the grass, ready.

"Cherry, Salia!" I yell, for she's out of my range. Cherry stands, sees the letnant wheeling about to charge Salia. Cherry's quick with her bow, nocks the arrow, aims, looses, sends it ahead of the charging horse, but it's close, the horse's head turns, leads it off line. Salia, on a better brew, tracks the line and plunges her spear into the horse's flank, sending the letnant off into the grass. I'm confident Salia can kill her, but Cherry and I see three other whiteboys emerge from the grasses, so Cherry runs for Salia. I realise a moment later it's because she's out of arrows. I run down to Yame. Cherry's done her belly, not a great job, but she hasn't had a chance to start on the leg. I go in my belt, look for the bark and the leaf mash ready for binding the leg, but she stops me, hand on mine as I go for the arrow. She squeezes my hand, gestures with her thumb back behind where she lies, where Khiese is. She's gasping with the pain of it, there's blood all over her leathers and in the grass about her, the arrow in the thigh has done her, caught her in the main vein. She was dead the moment it hit. I lean forward and kiss her, then stand as she falls still.

Caryd's over on the right flank, fifty or so yards off. She

has the balance of a master, but with so many on her there's inevitably a moment's mistake and I see her run through. There's dead all around her, it's just a matter of time for her. I can only see the top of Ru's helm from the grasses now, but he's no longer shooting, out of arrows.

Then it's over. All at once. Cherry's killed a few as she made her way to where Salia is, but she's taken a sword or something, and now she's working at a wound in her side. Salia and the letnant are circling. I see her shield drop, her arm hanging there but still strapped in. An arrow must have punched through it. One-handed, poison in her, she can't keep the letnant off her, and she takes two jabs to the chest from her spear. But Salia is calm as stone, she's the kind who can talk you through the dressing of a wound as you stitch her up, and had. Salia drops her spear as the letnant pauses to watch her die, whips a knife from a sheath on her back and with an instructor's precision throws it hard into the letnant's face. She falls before Salia, who has time enough to turn to me, looking into my eyes as she reaches for the pouches to staunch a fatal wound, her training taking over her hands as she nods me a goodbye. She drops to the ground. Khiese and his drudha walk towards Cherry. She looks up, then back at me, and I start running towards her. I feel tremors in the earth, the stone beneath, waves running through it. Thunder?

"Fight me, Khiese!" I shout, looking to save Cherry. Salia never took back her sword; she took another, and I have it now. I won't reach Cherry though, we both know it, so she readies herself, her own sword held out, hand on her side, holding some bark in place, unable to gum it in. Khiese has a two-hander, his drudha retrieves a bag, powders. Taking no chances. He opens the strings as Khiese closes on Cherry. Just as he flings the powders he jerks, an arrow through his temple. I can smell Ru behind me, who must have taken my last arrow that I had left on the slope, but the line he had meant the drudha must have blocked sight of Khiese. Now Khiese has let Cherry, in her fear, thrust at him. He steps to the side and in, a savage slash across her belly opens her guts, then a thrust into her throat, driving it in as he turns to see his drudha fall, to see where me and Ru are.

The roar grows, the song of the earth crackling and booming, like a mountain being dragged by Sillindar himself. Something's wrong with the world, and I've been too close to this fight to notice it building.

"Teyr, buffalo! Fucking buffalo! Far as the eye can see and coming right at us!"

Khiese sheathes his sword to refresh its poison, drawing it again.

Three of us left, it seems. There's some crying out, some dying where Caryd was. I look over and don't see her. She's gone down as well.

Ru comes to stand next to me. "It's death to stay here; we have to get to the trees!"

"All those horns, Teyr," says Khiese, closing the distance between us, thirty yards, twenty. "The horns of those tree animals, those Oskoro, they've called the buffalo on us all."

"Yet they only killed your clan."

"Some allies, if they have brought a stampede on you."

"Suppose we'll not find out, though I expect your own horns had as much to do with it. You find your brother? My gift?"

He doesn't flinch, might have been talking of the weather. "Yes. She thought she was brave, Thruun's keep. You know, she stood before the gates of Amondell alone as we rode in, Gruma's head in her hands. She told me you'd be heading here, that you would avenge Thruun, Mosa."

"You killed her, killed Drun?"

"No. She expected it of course. But your Family did not wrong me, did not kill my brother. You did. I kill in order to assert order in these lands, to bring the clans to heel, no more. I make a spectacle of it because it promotes order. If I killed all of those Amondsens who would farm that land and give tithe for my soldiers . . .? I found them cowering in the tunnel hidden at the back of your longhouse. The children were scared of the dark in there, and they also feared for their lives. But they did not wrong me, as the Seikkersons did not wrong me, nor the Auksens. They all live because they obeyed."

I have no clever words for this. I'm happy that Drun and Skershe live.

Ru's hand goes to my shoulder, squeezes it. "Don't think we're going to make the trees, Amo." He looks over at Khiese: "Least you won't either, you cunt." Khiese looks west, the cloud of dust rising with the buffalo. He's thinking, like he knows there might be a way out of this. "Shall we get on with it, then?" he says. "None here would be satisfied with just waiting it out, would we?"

Ru and I split. Khiese goes straight for Ru, as I thought he would, confident he'll kill us both. Ru's form is good, a clash of swords and I move in, forcing Khiese back to engage me as Ru steps to his side again. He attacks Khiese again, a fast and savage bind, Ru slightly stiff. Khiese softens, rolls the bind and stabs Ru in the guts, just under his right ribs. I close on him, Khiese brings his sword up, stepping away from Ru. Ru is working his belt, closing up the wound while I cover him.

"I fancy you see well with that strange eye. You do not prefer the other in your posture." Khiese thrusts, doesn't know how much this eye sees, the script of his lips, his shape, doesn't know either the supremacy of this brew over that which filled me in Crimore. I smash his sword away, quick steps forward, watching him move, his positioning. He's moving back towards Ru.

"Get back, Ru, he's mine."

"It's no tourney, Teyr, we give him no advantage." He has to shout to be heard over the thunder of the charging buffalo, tremors through our legs. He forces Khiese back, pushing him, looking hard for an opening. Khiese blocks twice, comes back at him as I move in. Their swords come together, Khiese's wrist rolls his blade off Ru and he leaps in, sword thrust down deep into Ru's shoulder before swinging back at me to meet my own blade. He steps away from Ru again, who's bent over, drops his sword to better get at his belt, still thinking, using the time I've given him.

Khiese glances at the buffalo then, I read his face, the brows knitting a moment as he realises perhaps that he won't escape the vast and wide wall of the herd as it bears down on us. He takes a deep breath, sets himself and gives me his full attention. In another life he would have been a feared but successful king.

"I will fulfil my promise, Teyr, though it may be my last."

He tries to bring me on, tease an overreach, but I can feel the pressure of the air itself on my skin, feel the fractional breath of its movement as the steel of his blade comes sharp at me. I see it with the eye as much as I see the anticipation written in his own, a glance down, an intention to slap my blade forming in his muscle, to twist his shoulder and thrust at my leg. I step back, pivot, meet his blade as he thrusts, leaning, putting his body into it. His blade goes past, just enough. If I was on a lesser brew he would have had a chance to correct himself, raise the edge of his sword, but I'm already driving my blade under his arms, through his ribs, the jolt

374

stilling him, each inch of steel passing into his body bringing me closer to him. The tip punches through the leather on his back, lifts the chainmail up an inch before I draw the sword back, swing and take his right leg off at the knee.

He looks at me, his eyes wide with shock, for I have moved as thought itself moves. He is becoming aware of his death as I bring my face close to his. He drops his sword, instinctively reaches for my shoulder to hold himself up without his leg, trembling and gritting his teeth with hate.

"Mosa's with his ma and his da. I put him in the ground myself so he could find them. And I will join them, Khiese, for these are my bloodlands. Their gate will be closed to you."

He falls dead at my feet.

I turn to see Ru on his knees. "War Crow," he shouts with a grin on his face. I look behind him at the buffalo, a roiling black wall of them in their tens of thousands beyond sight to left and right. I'm about to drop to my knees to hold him, but he holds up a hand.

"Take a gob of our old brew and take Khiese's with it. Drink them and run. There might be rocks, some channel you can escape in. You die here for sure, but you might not die on the brews."

"It won't—"

"Shut the fuck up, Teyr. Go." He thrusts his bag of brew at me.

"It's done, Ru. Let me lie here."

"Fuck you, Amo, no, you get home, you go to my farm and tell Bridie I love her. I came here for you, now you pay it back. Run!"

I look up again then back at him and begin shovelling the brew into my mouth. He smiles, leans back on his hands as though he's relaxing by some river.

375

I cut Khiese's pouch from his belt, and I run, throwing off my own belts, Salia's sword.

"Live, Teyr Amondsen! Live while the red drum beats!"

For a moment I think it might be another voice, closer than Ru as I sprint, but who else is here?

The pounding crashing hooves close, I scream and scream as the brews scorch and light me up; my heart shudders, grows, my veins thicken to ropes and I pick up speed. Still they close till my bones rattle, a run of shallower grass, I go faster still, and at the corners of my eyes the wall of buffalo edges into view. I'm spattered with saliva then as I close my eyes to die, the heat of breath coming in hard fast snorts washing over my back, hitting my neck stronger and stronger. For a moment, a nudge, a head on my back. I open my eyes as their hooves come down at my sides, see ahead a hard sharp slope rising, an outcrop of rock, thirty feet across, six high. A final step, deeper, springing up as the buffalo part for it, I hit the ridge of the outcrop with my shins and I hit the top of the rock hard, head, arms and chest. And I'm rolling down the far side. The world darkens, stones loosen as the herd moves past in its unnumbered thousands. I hold my head, try to move, but blood pours from my nose, from my black eye. I hold out my hand, convinced Sillindar will take it.

I realise I'm laughing because all of life has been shown to me.

But I am done.

Her service begins.

There's a stillness only snow makes with the air, brings a hush. It falls on the trees above me.

A face appears. I cannot see its colour for it is dusk, but the skin of his head is shaped and sewn into ridges over the ears, though where the bare skull should be something grows, a spongy moss, pale slender roots thick around the nape and throat and running down through a huge chest and bare shoulders. A heat comes off him, dry like a baking stone. His hand slides under my head, almost the size of it, lifting it gently, bending my neck for him to hold a cup to my lips. Things live in it, wriggle in my throat, taste of yeast.

His words are for others moving around me. He shapes an exhalation, a deep whistling. A mouthpiece or has the plant in him found voice? Another stands over me briefly, a thin red shirt, dark hair, beautiful, like he comes from the south, and no colouring from plant on him I can see. Children sing in a strange language away in the trees. The beautiful one lays my head back down on the earth. There's something like the trickle of sand tickling me as he raises his fist over my head. Whatever he smears over my face, closing my eyes with his fingers, soaks into me, bringing visions of places I cannot understand before I am swallowed by darkness.

As I slip away he leans to my ear, wraps string about one of my hands.

"Ljam." Abra lingo.

Gift.

Part 3

Aude

Aude lives.

With each step a pain, those words are the salve for it
and all else I endure in covering these wintry leagues east
towards Eastmarch and the border between Citadels Hillfast
and Forontir.

The Oskoro have no need of horses, so I walk, but I cannot
walk properly now, will never walk properly. A smooth shaft
of wood serves as a staff, and I do my best to keep my weight
off my left leg, for it is misshapen, a bow in it, something
the fightbrews did to the bones. I expect, I hope, I will grow
used to it, once the rest of me twists and sets itself to the
new shape of my movement.

I've seen no one since the Almet. I sleep at night clutching
Aude's amber necklace, the gift from the Oskoro, the proof
he had somehow fled Khiese.

The furs have been made to fit me, for winter comes to
the Circle and it rouses the ghosts of these lands, howling
over the rocks, clawing like a bear. The Eastmarch is unfamiliar to me, but the Oskoro who watched over me walked
me to the edge of their forest and pointed this way.

I have a fieldbelt, one of theirs. It's unadorned but strong, skilfully made. They did their best to tell me what plant lay within the pouches, bags and pockets, little of it familiar, all of it pungent and strong.

The plains give way to emptier, meaner lands beyond the Circle, whitened with frost and ice as winter hardens itself to stone and earth, feathering silver the leaf and bark.

A standing stone, some seven feet high on a mound to give clear sight of it, has carved on it the Drunessen clan sigil, a single flame on a shield. At each theit I say his name, imitate his walk, easier in a way with my own bad leg. I take their welcome where it's offered, find one or two who know some scraps of Common or Abra. They're courteous enough when they see I've paid colour and bear still a sword – Salia's. I thought I had lost it.

They tell me of whiteboys and the dreadful horns, though no foothold was established here, not with Khiese's focus on Hillfast far to the west.

It's as I scramble up a ridge to get a look at a wide valley I was told of that I see a distant figure whistling to a dog, a big one. I find myself trembling, dizzy, and it worsens as the figure straightens from some poking about in heather – the roll of his hip. If he puts his arms up in the air to stretch then rolls his shoulders it's him.

"Aude!" I would shout for him again but I'm crying and I can't stop myself. He turns. He must see me, see someone at any rate using their staff to help them balance as they slide down with the scree they loosen with their boots.

I fling back my hood, can't see for tears, and I have to stop at the bottom of the slope and wipe my face, hoping I haven't lost sight of him, that he hasn't somehow ignored me or vanished like a wish.

The dog bounds towards me and I find some bilt from a side pocket in my pack. The dog is unsure of me. Chutters are the best breed in the citadels for sniffing work, which is what Aude must be out doing. I flick the bilt at the dog and wait, for I'm not sure if she's been trained to protect him; most are. She jumps at the bilt however, no killer, comes over instead, tail wagging, licks my outstretched hand and then starts barking, for she's found plant about me, and an awful lot of it.

I watch him as I wait, my heart pounding. He's using his sniffer's catch to walk, a steady dull chink as it hits the stone, for the bottoms of citadels catches are iron for breaking ice. He walks as I remember, an imbalance in his gait, his back straight as a polearm. He's hooded still, and as he gets closer he seems more hesitant, more sure it's me, I think.

Slowly he pulls back the hood of his cloak, takes the mouthpiece out that he instructs the chutter with, gives a yip for her to return to his side. Tears fill his eyes till they shine.

We are still before each other, then he puts his arms out, dropping the catch. His hair has gone; what bits are left are matted like Caryd's was, but only a few thin threads. He's so thin, those sharp high cheeks drawn, the skin scarred on one side of his face. You'd think I might rush as best my leg allows, but I want to look at him, this man I love and thought dead. I wonder briefly if the Oskoro are watching, that there is more to this, something to stop me from putting my arms around him.

He smiles. He has a proper beard now but this too is unkempt, patchy with whatever ails his skin. He has teeth missing, and he sees that I'm looking at his smile, his mouth, and he covers it with a hand, leaving one arm out to me still.

All too suddenly I'm holding him, my head against his chest, so little meat and warmth there as I weep into his tunic and squeeze him to me. The beard feels strange on my head, but his smell is the same, warm soil and wool. He brings a hand to the back of my head, as he used to do when he saw me worry, scratches the bristles there in slow circles. As he does so he traces the scar from my black eye, the bark that runs across my temple and the side of my head there.

I cannot think of a thing to say as we stand there. His heart thumps in his chest. He's had to push his fingers underneath my pack to hold me properly.

"Khiese?" he whispers.

"It's over, my love. He's dead."

He breathes deeply then. I think he starts to cry but he tenses up and stills it. I squeeze him a bit more, hoping he'll let go of his hurt, let it out, but he coughs and clears his throat.

"I'm looking for shiel and labror, last of the season," he says. "I'm not much use at sniffing, but Flicker there, she gets enough for us both, and I'm hoping the family I'm stopping with will have a use for me through the winter at least. Will you walk with me?"

He leans back from our embrace and the scars are clearer now, the fine nose sharply broken, hooked. His eyes are miserable, they flit about. He can't look at me. His beard is wet with tears, and he sniffs back the flem that comes with crying. His hand goes back to his mouth, seeing me watch him, then to his face where the worst of the scarring is. He steps away, puts his mouthpiece in and calls and whistles Flicker into the bushes about us.

I wait for him to say something, as his eyes follow the dog and he goes still. But he doesn't.

"They give me this, the Oskoro, pointed me this way to Drunessen lands so I could find you." I lift his amber necklace off and walk up to him. I want him to look at me.

"Tell me . . ."

"Not now, bluebell." He looks at the necklace, the amber

dangling from my hand. I drop it into his as he holds it up to feel the stone. The leather of the loop is almost like paper.

"We should find a new loop for it."

"No. She gave me this when she had Mosa in her belly. Had been her ma's." He kisses it and tucks it in a pocket quickly. "I . . . I can't remember how her ma came about it. But I used to know. A lot of precious things I used to know that I don't any more."

He rolls the mouthpiece back into place, whistles and waits again.

Flicker comes running back, a bunch of amony held gently in her jaws.

"Good girl, good girl." He drops to his knee and gives her a snivet, cradles her chin and scratches under her ears.

"Come," he says, holding out his hand for me to walk with him.

We say as little as we did that first time we rode out of Hillfast, having left Mosa with Tarry. And as happens with keeps been together a long time, he asks after Tarry just as I'm thinking it.

"Sorry to say he's sick, my love. I saw his man Luddson. He bid me farewell on my coming back here." It's too hard for me to say any more, and so I understand his own reluctance, the sorrows that stand between us.

He squeezes my hand and we walk on, back towards a theit, where he must be a guest. It's at the top of a long hard rise out of the valley at the far end, a path winding up that he helps me with for it's broken in many places and prone to giving way. As the path curves around the side of the slope and beyond, in a high vale open to the sky, I see twenty or so houses, pens for reindeer and dogs, though they must be out and away. Flicker runs ahead of us to one of the larger houses, all of them here having thick and heavy stone walls, roofs bound and thatched, kept well, as they must be. A bell rings moments after we crest the slope, for no good comes of strangers out here. We approach the edge of the deer pens, two men digging out foundations for new posts, hard work in hard ground. They heft their pick and spade when they see my sword, but then they see me better, see my colour, and they go back to resting on them.

"Aude!" says one. "What did she find?"

"Good bit of amony, labror and all, though not so much of the latter, I'm sorry to say."

"And what did you find?" says the other.

Aude looks at me. His eyes fill up again, but he tightens his lips and looks at his feet, still holding my hand.

"This is Teyr Amondsen. She's come looking for me and has found me."

It's evening and I'm in the kitchen of the family he's staying with. They've had to borrow a stool for me from the shed that Aude sleeps in, at the end of their kitchen garden. Jelmer and his keep Vuina sit at either end of the table as is custom for the hosts. He smokes a long clay, I'd bet a jacker in his youth for the size of him. Vuina makes a fuss of me under his approving gaze. With us around their table are their two children, girls, who I learn are Lina and Nietsa, nine and seven years and curious to look at side by side for Lina is paler by far with straight hair, white as snow; Nietsa's hair is a very dirty yellow, and a bit more blood about her. However it seems my eye and my colouring are the entertainment for tonight, for Vuina has to hiss at them to stop staring.

"Did you steal it from a fish?" says Lina.

"Must have been a big one. What did you do with your real eye?" says Nietsa.

"Nu! Nu!" says Vuina, remembers then her bit of Common. "You don't ask these things." She holds her hands out, her sign of apology. I had no idea how the Drunessens felt about the Oskoro, I could not risk causing any hurt to Aude by mentioning where the eye really come from.

"Are you blind in that eye, Teyr?"

This is Vuina's sister Ruisma, more or less the same age. She wasn't given the lips or lashes must have got the boys of this theit out of breath for Vuina when they was girls, but she's strong-looking, hard hands and to my eye a stillness about her, a bit of me in her, I'd like to think, not soured in any way by what their ma or da must have wanted for her, I'm sure, as she passed through her tens and into her twenties and now beyond that without a keep. She helps Vuina serve up the deer broth and pitties. Through the curling vapours of his smoking, Jelmer orders the two girls to fetch his jug of beer and some cups.

"I am blind in this eye, yes," I says. "Nearly shot dead with an arrow, can you see?" I lean forward to the girls. Lina reaches over the table, hoping to touch the scar and bark there, but her ma yelps with a further exasperated apology.

"I'm fine to let them, Vuina-lap." This is an Abra custom, adding "host" to names when you are a guest.

The girls reach across the table over the bowls and board of bread and they take turns to touch my face, the scars and bark there. Satisfied with that, they fetch the beer.

"Can't say much for this beer," says Jelmer. "Sure with your colouring you been paid coin enough to drink the finest in your prime. We brew this out here with what we can. Bloody kill myself if I couldn't, eh."

"Jelmer, don't say that." Vuina smiles, glances quickly at Ruisma, then Aude and me.

Aude is quiet through all this. He glances about him nervously again. Much of the time he's got his hand to his mouth or runs it over his head. His other hand he keeps below the table, holding a thigh that bounces with nerves.

I put my hand on his and it stops him still a moment. Soon enough his leg starts bobbing again.

"So how did he find his way to such good and kind people?" I says, knowing that he's not about to talk of it.

"He was walking through the valley," says Ruisma. "No care for any danger or anything else about him, so one of the hands came and told Jelmer there was a stranger about the theit." She looks at him. "You were in a sorry state. This must have been near two months ago. Had a few dribbles of water in a flask and you'd been eating grass. The girls wouldn't have us move you on."

"You have to be kind," says Lina; "you die without kindness out here." Must have been a saying, such words coming from a girl her age.

"You asked to work for your food if you could fix up the shed and stay a bit," says Ruisma. He nods only slightly. "Seen better with a hammer and chisel though." All the family laughs at this. Even Aude flashes a brief smile. Ruisma's fond of him.

"Then we finds out he has his letters, don't we eh?" says Jelmer. "That give us some good straight dealings with Drunessen's collectors, not to mention the few others we seen from the Families about. And he's kind enough he's going to teach the girls. We're grateful, Aude, grateful you came here to us from whatever you had escaped."

"He'll teach those girls well. They'll have their letters come spring, I reckon." Though I said this because it was right to say, I knew it could mean he'd stay here at least that long and the thought of it hurt.

388

"Where might you be from then, Teyr? Who do the Amondsens swear fealty too?" says Jelmer.

"Oh Da, you should know," says Lina, "it's Auksens."

"She's right, Jelmer-lap, I'm Auksen clan, a southie." Meaning south of the Circle.

"I thought your way of speaking was familiar," says Ruisma. "Haven't been over that way in ten years."

"Clans got out of the habit of meeting and keeping a common interest."

"That's true, Teyr. I keep saying to Da and the others that we should look to see what can be traded west and north."

"You've not said anything as I've heard," says Jelmer.

"Oh, of course she has," says Vuina.

"Where will you go from here then, Teyr?" says Jelmer. Aude looks up from his lap then.

I think about Omar, dead and strung up on the gates of Faldon Ridge. I see Mosa, kneeling.

"Hillfast, I think." I look at Aude, but his leg starts bobbing again and he looks once more into his lap, touching his head again like there was something there or something missing.

Nobody speaks for a bit so Vuina gets the girls talking about their jobs the following day. Not used to silence I daresay in such a noisy warm house as this. I struggle to make table talk, can't ask questions that usually get people to open up and win them over. I'm tired, more than I thought with only half a day's walking, but I've been on edge these last few hours I was welcomed and introduced. I know we've got a talk coming, know that he's just trying to get things done for the family while he gets used to me being here.

Soon enough though, night getting on, they're all yawning and making their excuses, the duts doing what they usually do and protesting they aren't tired but go and get all grumpy about being told they are instead. Ruisma and Vuina go and settle them in the next room. Jelmer puts the jug on the table as he stands up.

"I'd be happy for you to finish this between you. I get the sense you have a bit to catch up on. Aude, we don't need you sniffing in the morning, but your help looking over the scrolls before the old man's collector comes would be welcome." He quickly knocks out his pipe on his plate, winks and leaves us. Vuina and Ruisma make their own excuses, and soon we're alone in their main room.

"I can't do this here, Teyr. Can we go out?"

"Of course."

The night's dry, bitter too of course; so we put our furs on. There's a porch to the house, for it's raised up to help against snowdrifts. He lights us a lantern and bids me sit next to him on a bench that overlooks the empty pens. We fill our cups from the jug and put them on the ground a moment.

"We both thought each other was dead then," I says. "But you're here. Beyond any hope I had for us, here you are."

He's not looking at me, just staring ahead as I speak. His hand goes to his mouth, his face, again and again.

"How do you feel? What happened?" I says, for all I want is him talking, to hear him and watch him speak.

"They hurt me, Teyr. I can't tell you the things they did, but they broke me because I'm not strong like you. I couldn't take it like you can."

His voice is softer than it was, partly the effect of him losing so many teeth, the change in his nose and how he breathes perhaps.

"You got away though, you escaped."

"Only because I was going to kill myself. I meant to. I and a few others were being walked along a path beside a steep drop to a ravine. I thought that would do me, make really sure of it."

That bit makes me cry. I lean into him, and I'm grateful he doesn't move away. He keeps on with his telling though.

"I threw myself off the edge of the path, fell hard onto the scree, rolled and broke to pieces it felt like, stones flaying my hands and face as I fell. I hit the bottom and found I still breathed. I thought then it was stones, big ones, following me down. I looked up, hoping for something to land on me, but it was a whiteboy. Not sure if he was sent down or he was risen on some plant and thought he was being brave, but he lands near enough on top of me and he's hurt as well. They must have thought I hoped to escape, and the whiteboys would do anything Khiese asked, even something like that, but he had paid colour and he was trying to get up. My hand – I'm trying to get up as well – closes around a stone, a big one. I wanted to die so you'd think I'd let him finish the job. But I wasn't going to let one of them do it. I had to do it. They had no right. I rolled over and hit him with it, hit his eye. He grabbed my arm – much stronger than me – but it gave me the leverage to get my other arm around his throat. His other arm's no good, it's landed behind his back, must have broken. He can't stop me choking him to death." There's tears in his eyes now, his trembling worse, and he's looking at his hand like it's still got the rock in it. "It's a hard thing to do, isn't it? Kill a man."

"It is, bluebell. Only madmen say different."

He takes my hands in his, runs his thumbs over my knuckles. He's damaged, brittle, like the marrow's been scooped out.

"They shot a few arrows down the ravine at me, but I was obscured by rocks above me, and the falling scree had kicked up some dust. I'd hurt my ankle. I was dressed warm enough to survive the night lying there, but in a few days of hobbling along I was in a sorry state, starving. I must have passed out in the plains. I woke up with the Oskoro. The Almet."

"They've given us both life and here we are. Maybe Sillindar was watching."

He snaps at me then, angry. "Course he wasn't, or he'd have got in the way of Khiese's knife, wouldn't he?"

I curse myself for it was a stupid thing to say, looking for some words to settle him when he never did have time for notions that magists come and go from the stars when we need them.

He leans down and picks up our cups of beer. We sip in silence for a bit, but I finally break, for treading around on eggs isn't how I used to be and I'm not good at it. I'm not helping put him at ease. I'm cross with myself as well for that bit of me wishing he'd have been happier to see me, for I cannot take my eyes from him yet he can barely put them on me.

"I miss him every day," I says. "I got no right to, have I? Everything's gone but what I got in that pack in the kitchen there, and you sitting here with me on this bench. I want to go home, and I want you to come home with me, stand under the falls with me, sit by the fire in our socks."

His thoughts pass clearly through his eyes, as they always had. The truth is written in them, the answer's quivering on his lips, the one I don't want.

"Might be this is my home, for now anyway. This might be as close as it gets."

"Why? How is it your home?" It comes out stronger than I'd wanted.

"You want me back in Hillfast? His bed's in our room, the wooden ships, the pictures of me and you he carved on the seat of his chair and under the table in the kitchen, they're there, the tree he watched us from, the big branch that stretches out over the plant run by the pantry. He won't ever be sitting on it again, and I'll always look up at it and wish he was."

"I know. I want to make it better and I can't because I was always bad with finding the right thing to say. Might be we can make a start somewhere else, look after each other. I got no more desire to run a road through the Circle." Aude's eyes flash at this, but I go on, like the fool I am. "It was something I wanted so long as you and Mosa was there, something'd make you both proud of me and we'd build it up together. Now I found you again I just want whatever means I can be with you, whether that's home as I thought or not."

He drains his cup and pours another. It hurts to watch how his nerves make the pouring of it harder. He finishes that in a long gulp as well. He drops the cup and shakes his head.

"You're giving up on the road? I'm sorry for that. He died for that road."

"No, Aude . . ."

"Yes. I walk off with you now, find some the'll have us if not this one, or go back to that house and all those things that remind us of him. We'll sit in our chairs in a room and make a fire and get in our cups and pipes, have Thornsen and Epny and their four children around for pie and sweetmeats, the finest Juan wine."

"Don't, Aude, please."

"We'll be doing all those things we were doing before we left on that van, only we won't have my boy with us. So what was the point of it all?"

"Our boy, wasn't he? Our boy?"

He pauses. Nods slowly. "Sorry, yes, our boy. Teyr, if he's died then it should be for something."

This last thought seems to strike him deep and it seeps into me like dye into wool.

"If he was here, Teyr, what do you think he'd tell his ma to do? What would he want?"

I stayed for three days with Jelmer, Vuina and their family. I didn't presume to join Aude in the nights, so slept in a chair in their main room. I wasn't much use on the runs, give a bit of advice where I could, but they got these lands under their nails and noses as the saying goes.

Jelmer's is the Retsien Family, sworn to the Drunessen clan. He was chief of the theit and was fair with his Family right through to the hands they hired and the mouths they fed, mine and Aude's too. It was good to see.

Aude and I talked when we could, but I had to leave him be in the days, when his conscience wouldn't permit him to idle. He wouldn't tell me what Khiese did to him; was difficult to ask given I too was reluctant to talk of my own suffering, but I told him something of what happened after Mosa died. He was happy to hear of the children of the Kelssen theit surviving, but it upset us badly as I talked of them, and it was the following night I told him the rest of it and what happened to Thruun.

That night too I told the family I was heading back west. He didn't say anything but left the table shortly after.

On the last morning he walked with me after I said my farewells. Ruisma and Vuina both vowed to look after him. He walked with me through the valley a way, and the air was still, snow falling lightly, nothing that would settle, we reckoned, but it brought a peace to the land.

He kissed me when we come to the standing stone. It was brief and tender and it lifted me.

"Give me some time, bluebell," he said.

Letters

467OE

For Aude

I'm writing to you from Autumn's Gate. It might well be high summer but there's a fucking cold wind raising white-caps on the sea below me and it's blowing right through my woollens. I'm in Farlsgrad of course, and wish you were here with me. The port is built on land that rises steeply, something like Citadel Argir, and the king has put me in a grand house overlooking the docks, where I sit scribbling this.

Took me a while to get back over the Circle, but that was fine with me. I did get a horse from the Auksens. Auksen was fair horrified to see me, even when I told him I killed Khiese, maybe because of that. There were no whiteboys about. He said they'd followed Khiese out of there and hadn't come back, but those few that did to collect tithes had word of trouble and it was me that was the trouble. He said they called me War Crow, but he didn't know it was me they were talking of. It left me cold seeing that longhouse where Khiese got us and killed the crew that was with me. I told him I just needed a horse and I'd be on my way. Time enough to reckon with Auksen, and I had no crew with me and I'm unable to fight now as you saw.

I went south to Amondell. Khiese was as his word and had not killed them. Skershe and the rest of them rushed out and cheered me and broke open kegs of what they'd had brewing to celebrate the Amondsens seeing off a warlord. The children called me Blackeye there, much as Dottke did. I went to see our bloodlands and stood over my brother's grave. Couldn't help thinking then, him in the ground and me standing there in the state I'm in, how it might have all been different, a wish for a different future dreamed about in the sorrow of the present, though Khiese would still have come. I remembered when we were duts, Uncle Kerrig had Thruun on his shoulders, a spoiled boy and a happy boy shining with laughter on a hot summer day, and I held hands with my ma, who sang a harmony with him, for she and her brother would sing beautifully together at gatherings. I had doubted Thruun and shouldn't have, and so I told him anyway for he was in the land hereabouts with all our fathers and mothers.

Then I went up to the Oskoro in the Almet. They came out to meet me. I told them how grateful I was for their help against Khiese. One among them was moved so must have lost someone close in that fight. Easy to tell their drudhas, they tower over the others, and she bade me shut my own eye so I'd look on her only with the black eye. I saw then how we might speak without words. They took me into their theit, though the few lofty buildings of wood and stone I saw there were crafted to look as though they had grown naturally from the land itself, though I never saw such work as could make stone seem like weavings, with the delicacy of spun sugar. I wanted to draw it all that I might share it with you, but my eye for a picture is worse than these words and they are sadly too poor to relay the wonder of it all.

I gave them Nazz's fightbrew, what was left of it, and asked if they could tell me what was in it. There were a few among them that put bits of the mulch on their tongue, one just rolled it in his fingers and smelled it, and they came to the same conclusions and wrote down a brew and how to prepare it. They made me a flask of it, but it smelled a bit different and they smiled, suggesting they had somehow improved it. The recipe is safe and I'll say no more in this letter.

You're probably asking why it is I didn't go straight back to Hillfast. I was going to, and going to tell Othbutter what I thought of him for the shit he pulled with Nazz. I went past Faldon Ridge and saw that the Crutters had a flag flying there and it was being used as a barracks for their men. Protecting the Sedgeway, they said.

The roads we'd made were holding up however, bridges as well, and it was easier going to Tapper's Way.

Back at Tapper's, Fitblood was there and doing his best to feed many had come from the Circle looking for help. I was moved to see him and see he was well and we had a drink for Omar and remembered him. He hadn't heard anything about Edma and the girls taken from Chalky. Nobody had, for the whiteboys had gone to ground or fled.

He told me that Thornsen was still running things and couldn't wait to get word that I was on my way. But he told me also that Nazz had already come back through with his drudha and they said to him I was likely dead.

I realised that if Nazz knew I was still alive he knew that I would most likely expose him or try and go after him. He'd want me dead, and that meant Thornsen or others working for me might be in danger for Nazz runs a serious ganger operation and now he's back with a better brew he'd be dangerous.

I knew then I'd have to go south quietly and get on a boat over here to Farlsgrad. I was in their army for many years and Salia and Yame had given their life for a Farlsgrad purse. Seemed to me I could solve a lot of problems at once coming here and telling the king what happened and where he could get the recipe and cyca. I left a message with Fitblood to send to Othbutter. I told Othbutter what I'd be doing, told him that I'd left him out of it. This would save his life. In return I expected to be recognised for that. Or he could run for it, see how far he got.

The king received me upon my landing here and I told him what had happened in the Circle. I told him the recipe for Gaddy's Mash as the Oskoro told it to me to confirm my story and he was satisfied with Salia and Yame's pursuit. Thornsen had been developing our interest well alongside Tarrigsen's, and the king saw fit to ensure that we had reduced tithes for berthing and the loading gangs as well as a contract drawn up for farlswood at a reduced cost to us, which will net me a very healthy profit across the Sar in years to come. Assuming I live that long.

The only bad news during my stay here, and I embark tomorrow for Hillfast on a Farlsgrad war galley, is that Tarrigsen is quite ill, bedridden now.

I am desperate to see him. If I do I will give him a kiss from you and send your love. I fear even now it's too late.

He was a father to us both in a way. I won't pretend, with all that's happened, you would feel even a smidge grateful for him having brought us together. But he helped me to have a life, for a time, that was happier than I had any right to. The same I say for you, my love.

Your Teyr

467OE

For Teyr

It was a great pleasure to receive your letter, though a crew of five well-armed men must have cost you a lot of coin for this purpose alone. I worried about you, crossing the Circle on your own like that, even though you know well from your life how to travel without being seen. You have good friends at the Almet, I believe, and perhaps they watch over you even now.

It is easier for me to write how it is I'm feeling than to say it, and still it isn't easy. I cannot imagine the hardships you've endured since we were captured by Khiese. It moves me to think of you walking out of that forest with my amber necklace and coming looking for me. Nothing ever could stop you when you had a mind for it.

I'm sorry I didn't make it easy for you. I'm sorry that I bit out at you over something as stupid as the necklace's leather. I have a temper now where once I did not. Sleep comes and goes. Vuina puts something in my beer or my tea, I think, last thing at night. I have scared the children more than once with the dreams I have. You cannot escape them, can you. I say this yet I am forgetful among other things and I need to be alone a lot. I'm changed in many ways and not for the better. I'd be alone all the time, leave here I think if it wasn't for their kindness and that I couldn't survive a day not knowing which belets I could and couldn't eat, which seeds. But they've given me solitude with the chutter, and I wish to work hard and earn what goes in my mouth each day.

I'm healing. I'm glad as well that you might be, that my speaking of any sort of debt to Mosa (though I hated myself for weeks afterwards) was in fact something that would bring you back into life from that place where you sought only death. I had only hoped in saying it that he would inspire you now as he did when we were together. I know that you inspire me.

Aude

468OE

For Aude

I hope this letter finds you with better spring weather than we have here. We could drown in rain, but it seems the bridges Omar and Fitblood built are holding up to the floods at least.

You shouldn't worry about the expense of getting letters to you. I have no better use for soldiers than that they can keep me in your mind and let me continue to talk to you.

There was quite a scene on the quays of Hillfast when six Farlsgrad war galleys anchored offshore and one sailed in to my main berth full of soldiers – and me of course. Othbutter's roused and the bells tolled about the docks. Everyone's come out for a look. I walk down the gangplank with Tusahl, King Crusica's chief diplomat. She speaks for the king in all matters and betters me in wit and thought in every way. Her seal and scrolls she hands to that pathetic high cleark Tobber without so much as a word and strides past him for Othbutter's chambers, announcing to all that are there she is here for his help in a serious matter. This calms the crowd somewhat, and the soldiers stay on board the galley of course.

The moment wasn't lost on me that I last landed here on the Gellessens' wharf in a neck trap and was spat on, and now I meet Thornsen in rather more finery than I'm used to. Oh Aude, you should have seen them all at our sheds. We were all crying for I'd missed them so badly and I could tell as well how upset they were about what happened to Mosa. I could see also they thought I'd changed, and it upset them to look on me, I knew, though of course they wouldn't

402

say it out loud. They all asked after you and sent you their love, glad that you're alive and have survived. They all still called me Master, though I told them Thornsen was the one deserved the title. He's proved to be as good and canny a merchant as anyone. It was such a delight to see him and his family again.

I followed Tusahl to Othbutter's chamber, where she had laid out the terms under which her king would continue trading with Othbutter and the merchants of Hillfast.

The terms were that Nazz would be given up and his operation transferred to me. Likewise I was to be given rein over rooting out corruption on the docks with the other merchants' help. I expect you're thinking this might have been met with some resistance, and you'd be right. Fuck them anyway, it'll be good to see them have to work for their profit. More than that is that I hate gangers, always have, doing honest people out of coin by putting a sword to their neck, or the threat of it. Whether it's droopers or those who want a fuck, or want to sell a fuck, you got gangers making them all miserable while they make themselves rich. I have plans for changes in that regard that'll really get Hillfast's rich gritching.

So the soldiers that had come from Farlsgrad fetched Nazz out of his office that was in a droopjoint and tavern he owned. I waited in the street with Tusahl. His gangers didn't have much grit about them in the face of a crew of soldiers shining with colour and ready for war. A crowd gathers of course, shutters open up all about us, including from his tavern, and whore, sailor and drooper alike cheered as he was brought out in chains, Talley and all.

He hid his surprise well at seeing me.

Tusahl read out for his benefit what it was he had, in her word, stolen, and what the punishment would be. He came up to me then, bit of a strut as he tried to play the crowd as he always does.

"You tell them Othbutter was behind it all, did you? I don't see him here in chains."

"Might be Ru and Three and Caryd, Salia too would have lived had you not betrayed the purse, abandoned the plan to kill Khiese. Now all this is mine, you cunt. Mine." He was about to say something to that when his chains got pulled and he choked. Talley I had no words for.

Soon as I could, after seeing him put on board that galley, I went to see Tarrigsen.

He's not well. The best plant keeps him comfortable, but he can't walk about much, no puff in him. As long as he's still he seems himself and like everyone else he sends you his love and Sillindar's blessings, which he knows you'll hate and he said it with a wink.

Shortly after, I went to see Cherry's family, Helsen's too, and I gave them a sum to help with the future and to say how brave they were and what good they did.

Then I went up to Bridie's farm. She comes out of the house, seeing me hobbling up, and she falls to her knees. She's crying for I come alone without Ru. Jol steps out then, looks down at her. Then she gets up and pushes past him and goes in the house, and he comes down the road to me.

I ask to be let into the house to tell Bridie and Ilda and the boys, for they deserve to know it and hear it from me who can give an account of how brave their uncle was. Jol tries to say I shouldn't bring such news in there, that he can take care of them. I put my hand on my sword hilt, tell him he needs to find somewhere else to be, and he moved sharp. I expect I'm a monster to worms like him.

I was able to tell Bridie that Ru loved her and I was able to tell them all what he meant to me. I had with me a bag of coins, his purse paid in full and a lot more besides. Jol came in later with a couple of his Hillfast friends, trying to make things awkward, but I saw him off. He wasn't going to fleece this farm or do anything wrong by them, and she held my hand and we sang a bit after Jol and his friends left, drank and laughed till we were sick, and it was a good night, best I'd had since last I saw you.

Also, I saw vanner Leyden appear at the sheds the other week, who was broken when he heard about Cherry for they spent months on the roads together. I told him he should go down with a roll making a promise of payments to the almshouse the Kelssen orphans were in. I'm surprised, though I shouldn't be, with how much I think about them. He said Thornsen had taken care of it, as I'd asked him to do when I was last in Hillfast, a prisoner in the Coffins. I'd forgotten that I asked him, though I was a mess then. One more reason to add to the thousands that make me love the man.

Two more things worth telling you anyway in terms of how I aim to advance the road. Crutters were occupying Faldon Ridge, as I told you. Othbutter gave authorisation and some soldiers to help me get them out of there, so I went with them to do that. I think I made some more enemies of course. I'm sure those men will send that back to Old Crutter. Faldon Ridge is again mine and I have work to do to make sure it can run as well as Omar ran it, for there are few in the world better than he was at the role of castellan.

On our way back we got ambushed. They were desperate enough and on a brew so I lost four men in all before we could rise enough to fight them off. I am sorry to say that while I had the Oskoro fightbrew and wore a fieldbelt I found I couldn't bring myself to swallow the brew. I haven't spoken of what happened to me when I escaped the buffalo.

405

I had two fightbrews in me and I was dying, like they were turning me to mush on the inside, and that is what must have caused my bones to bend as they did. As I lay there I lost all sense and tumbled through a darkness, that awful feeling when you jump from somewhere high. The countless thousands of the frenzied herd stamped out all thought and memory. Then I heard others, Oskoro, speak to me, speak together as one. My armour was being taken off, my woollens. Desperate to end the spinning emptiness, I sent my fingers down into the earth and found its hot veins and its cold fields of bones, worms and seeds that wait for another world to come. I fled into the earth, barely tethered to the skin and bones of me. I called out to Mosa, to comfort him so far from his bloodlands. He couldn't hear me, nothing could with the crashing of hooves above us. Silence followed that, though there was no ability to reckon time. Knives of warm bone were put on me, then hands moved inside me, leaving their gifts to work and grow, draw me back.

As with so much in life, these words are frail against the experience. But it was this experience that froze me and stopped me from fighting, the fear I might fall into that place again and never come back. I expect you'll say I should be thankful if it means never again choosing to do something stupid with only one good leg.

Turns out those that attacked us were from Families sworn to the Crutters, men who had profited for a time stealing or extorting from the few travellers or refugees who had come out of the Circle. They were burned, not buried. I will take extra guards in the future so do not worry.

Write soon, my love. I have to leave it here despite everything to tell, for I have tallies and scrolls as tall as you to work through, and no you to work them through with!

Your Teyr

406

468OE

For Teyr

A year since last I saw you, bluebell, or near enough. It's hard to believe.

I am glad you felt able to speak of your suffering at the reckoning with Khiese. You've a strong heart to endure the war of those brews with your body. Few could have withstood it. You cannot and must not blame yourself for not drinking a brew in defence of those whose purse was to defend you. Your wars are with your quills now, my girl, not your sword, and your quills are quite sharp enough, going by your account of your plan to play Othbutter and Nazz and strengthen your hand with Farlsgrad at once.

It must have been a relief to see Nazz taken away. I look forward to your plans for his interests. I know you'll do right by the people that deserve it. You always have. Sometimes the right things happen to the right people.

The girls Lina and Nietsen I've taught letters to, and you should see Vuina and Jelmer, such proud parents. Their aunt Ruisma's asked if I'd teach her as well so that is under way. She thinks that she might become a teacher to others and put the Drunessen clan in good standing in these parts. Of course, when Beddy Drunessen, the chief, heard about me and what I'd done, he asked if I'd visit there to help with his clearks and his interests, so I have gone along, hoping that I could speak well for Jelmer's Family and improve their standing as thanks for their making me part of their lives.

It appears that, talking to Drunessen, he's lost a Family to the Amersens to the south. Seems he's not given justice

407

well enough in their interests these last few years for their liking. It took me, being an outsider, to tell him that was my reading of it, and he was grateful for it.

He also has trouble to the north. Whiteboys have been seen.

You might wonder why I am telling you this, for these are small matters when put against your current concerns. There are still challenges on this road you wish to build. You have killed Khiese but the Circle is still a dangerous place. It is this work with the chief, this guidance that he's begun to look to me for that has stopped me from taking one of the two vans that have come through here for Hillfast, one of them yours, as you surely know. I might be of use to you, bringing some harmony to the clans out here so that you have fewer problems when your crews do manage to drive trails out this way.

I must warn you that if you return here you are likely to be given a hero's welcome, for word has travelled regarding your killing Khiese and his brother.

I would also reassure you that I am much more settled, more myself these days than I was last summer. I find time enough for solitude and have taken to wandering further and further from the theit. I have enclosed my observations of the land hereabouts, which may also help you with your planning of the road, and I have included the accounts of those who have seen bandits to help also in advising your vans if they come this far east in the near future.

Please send news of the children in Port Carl if you hear any. Although I was much moved to see you talk so happily of them and their characters, they have made an impression on me and I would see them make something of themselves.

Aude

468OE

For Aude

It was lovely to receive your letter. It was also worrying to hear that you've taken to travelling far from the theit in what are still dangerous lands. I know you are finding the wilderness to be good for your happiness. All I want is for you to be happy. Still, you see anyone outside the theit, run or ride back. Don't trust anyone you don't recognise.

Last I wrote to you it was spring, and now autumn is here and the Crutters run the citadel. The council met as they always do in high summer, and this time there was widespread agitation that the Othbutters be removed. Almost the whole north and northeast clans came out for the Crutters. A lot of merchants about me in the gallery looked on with pleasure and knew well that it could harm my interests, for they had their claws in the voting for sure. A lot of clans could expect reward for their loyalty, and the Crutters surprised me in that regard, for it must have taken some modest level of organisation on their part, though they don't lack ambition. Not many families came out in favour of the Carlessens, but it's their fault and I'll speak to them on it when I get a chance. They might be the only clan capable of making Hillfast a bigger interest in the Sar and I mean to see that interest find its way to all the clans.

Not one of the merchants except for Tarry's interests speak to me since I took over Nazz's own interests. I put the whores in charge of their own houses and supplied their security at a fixed rate agreed in scrolls. I am the "queen of whores", "the cocksucker general" and worse. Merchants meanwhile have had to pay me for the use of the same guards that Nazz supplied them, but the guards now have more money to take home.

I write this from my outpost in Faldon Ridge. My hope is that I can see you soon, perhaps before midwinter. I miss you. I would have left sooner but for the matters to attend to at Hillfast but also because, given you asked after them, I have been down to Port Carl.

Sorry to say the Kelssen children were in an awful state when I saw them. The almshouse was badly run, the children worked to the nub by an evil old fucker, and that was another thing I'd then ask the Carlessens to change, for they made good coin off the efforts of these duts, who were mostly rope making. Aggie, Litten and Dottke's hands were in a state from the hatchelling, and they had Brek spinning. Least they weren't tanning. All their heads were shaved for the lice of course, but they were thick with them in their clothes and stinking besides. They all shouted and came running at me when I was brought through to the barracks they were kept in with about fifty other children and some young men and women who had the minds of children. Brek was bruised and his eye closed over from fighting, and I learned about how he got into all kinds of trouble, whipped as well, for doing what he could to stop some of the older ones from picking on them. Dottke asked if I'd go and kill the four or five been causing them their grief, and they were shaking in their boots when I walked over and they thought I'd do it. Dottke had been telling them that Blackeye was coming for them the whole time, and it got her a few beatings, so now they saw it was true I think they feared the worst, me being there with my soldiers and all for I go about with a lot more of a crew after being attacked here.

I was never going to leave them there of course, and I

brought them here to Faldon. Aggie asked me if she could call me Ma and the others started saying it too. Course I cried at that.

We took the trails up through Ablitch and we got through a few jars of cloudberry jam, and they told me about their lives and I told them a bit about mine. I told them a lot about you and they all wanted to come with me to meet you, but the Circle is still the Circle and I couldn't bear it. The girls aren't sure what they'll do now. Brek though, he was after learning his letters. He wanted to pay me back, he said. When Dottke heard that there were those about Faldon calling me War Crow, however, she said I had too many names and none was very nice! Call me Teyr then, I said, but she said Ma will do.

We head out tomorrow, north from the Sedgeway to the Khiedsen land that was promised by Othbutter and has been upheld by the Crutters and the clan that has replaced the Khiedsens, the Jamessens. I then hope to come south through the Almet to see Skershe and Drun before heading east to you.

I know I have talked much of my plans for my interests in this letter. I tell you because you would see this road and all of these interests serve that purpose. If you think I have not thought of much else you would be wrong. I said I missed you and I do. It makes me sad on the one hand to think you might have come to Hillfast if not for the Drunessens and their chief, but on the other you are happy there and you do much for us and Mosa's road. I look forward to riding out with you if winter allows it. The foretellers seem to agree on a mild winter for once. Who are we to dispute them?

Your Teyr

469OE

For Teyr

Midwinter has passed and you have not arrived. The fore-tellers are wrong once more, it seems, for it has been hard on us all here. The iron, oil and coin you sent with your last letter were most welcome to us all, and the clan sends its thanks to you.

I had hoped we might see you while at the Auksens and at your home in Amondell for we visited Skershe and your nephew Drun. Drunessen asked if I would go along as he was keen to repair relations with Chief Auksen. Ruisma came with us as well, for you have much inspired her, and she is determined to do what she can to help unite the clans for a Walk.

When I spoke to Chief Auksen he said he had banished from their bloodlands six men who had hunted the Oskoro on the plains not a month ago. Seems the Oskoro had come a bit further south than they might usually, I expect in part due to your efforts, and were blamed for a number of missing deer. Other families, fearful for their own herds, went hunting them, and the chief found in one of his theits the head of one of the Oskoro.

It's easy for him as it is for us to understand that they might not be a threat, but this is winter in these lands. A few of the men banished spoke of Khiese's plan to burn the Almet, which you might not have been aware of. They spoke of it as a good, for they think the Oskoro to be animals.

I suggested we go to the Almet, and your sister-ken Skershe wished also to come. Chief Auksen was shamed into going for he did not seem happy to suggest accompanying us.

412

The buffalo had gone through by then. We camped under the eaves of the Almet, boldly perhaps, though not far from the Offering Stone. The morning after the first night we awoke surrounded by ten of them, though they bore no weapons. One of them, one of the least changed, spoke Abra lingo, snatches of Common even. He, or she, for it was not clear to me which, said that the Oskoro wished to send a delegation of their number out to the theits and clans around the Circle. They hoped that with our help they might meet the clans and prove they have no use for people's children or babies or even their animals, for they do not eat meat, or much of anything as far as I can tell.

I was much moved by your writing of the children of the Kelssen theit calling you their ma. It's certainly better than Blackeye, isn't it? I want you to know that it gives me great comfort, your managing to save them from Khiese's whiteboys, save them and give them a good and secure future. They've lost more than you and I have lost, if we're honest with ourselves. I think they understand their debt to you, or will as the years go by.

Finally, Auksen wanted you to know he had no truck with the Crutters in the vote for the high clan, but could not bring himself to support the Carlessens, who as everyone knows don't pay their dues.

Best wishes,
Aude

470OE

For Aude

I'm so sorry my love for how late this is in arriving. I got your letter a month or so after you sent it. I think you'd left it with that fucker Auksen, and one of my scouts eventually got it back to me here in Hillfast.

I might have been near Amondell when you were there, from the sounds of it, but while I was up visiting the lands taken from the Khiedsens that are now mine I got news that Tarry had died.

I don't expect anyone else has been out your way to tell you. I wish I was there to be able to tell you in person, wish some great eagle could have carried me there, for I know he was a da to you and saw you through all your joy and sorrow with Mosa's ma and then bringing him up. But when I heard the news I had to come straight back, for his life's work needed his heirs, one of them anyway, to be here to manage the scrolls and affairs, for he had more than peas in every pie you could think of, he had most of the rest of the filling and all! I say "his heirs" because he has made you and me the main benefactors of his interests. Aude, you wouldn't believe it. His interests are worth, to us both, many thousands of gold coins. We own five ships each, were we to split it so. I know that you are not one much moved for riches, I don't think we could have been each other's keep if you were. But if there was a time to come back to Hillfast it would be now, bluebell, to understand better your fortune and what good could be done with it. For the present you know that Thornsen and me will keep it all going. The scrolls that come with this letter inventory your main tens, your ships and their crews as well as the farms, herds and houses along with the tenants of them. They list all of it, for I am not about to carve up what we're given without I talk to you first about what you'd like to see done, and I'm not thinking about it like that anyway. I'm not separating me and you and I'm just saying it as it is, I'm sorry if that is forward or wrong. Me with my own interests ongoing, it's more important that you decide what should happen to all this and feel happy with the outcome, which Thornsen and me can then arrange.

The other thing that's kept me busy and, it feels, run all my days into one, is that the crews and vans that will continue our work on the road over the Circle are already on the Sedgeway moving east. I have found enough soldiers and workers, organised the supply and had the crews give us the lie of the land. They've helped me to work out what route we should sign and what roads to build. My aim is also to build an outpost like Faldon's but at the Almet, to the south-west of it. I believe that it will encourage north and south to visit and trade, something you have told me you are trying to encourage anyway with Drunessen.

I'm going to be in a van heading for the Circle tomorrow. Theik tells me there's trouble with the whiteboy gangs that now wander about, and others might be coming to fill with their own greed the hole Khiese left. The clans think it will help a good deal if the War Crow herself brings them to heel. Gertsen, our drudha, has made up the Oskoro fightbrew for these crews, and their first taste of it has got them excited. This fightbrew may well be better than anything in the north. They will need reminding that there's always some way to die, however.

I won't speak of how fucking stupid the Crutters are, how

in the pockets of merchants and how prone to bribes. This also has kept me, Thornsen and our crews busy, rooting out those we found to be fucking us over across all our interests.

All of these things that have needed my attention have meant I've been getting my food and drink and sleep at the sheds. Easier to put up a mat there than take the trail back and fore to our house every night. I decided therefore to give Thornsen and Epny our house. They've always loved it up there, his boys and girls too. They protested for a while, but they're moved in and we have had some lovely evenings there. The house seems to like them, like it's breathing again and got some colour in it, like it had with us. We went up there after we buried Tarrigsen to finish his tapestry, sharing stories of him. Most had gone home and I was alone in our main room when Tarry's man Luddson come in just before he was leaving, said there was one more thing he was asked by Tarry to give us. Seems that Mosa had saved all the coins we gave him over the years we went sniffing for bluehearts. He kept them all under the window in our bedroom, made a hole under the floorblocks to hide them. Then, the day before we set off for the Circle, you remember Tarry was at the house? Mosa gave him the coin and some instructions. He was to engage a fine woodworker to make us all walking staffs – him, you and me – with farlswood catches, fine steel bobs and carved into them the flowers we most treasure. They were to be ready for when we returned and then the three of us might go walking again, out beyond the farms, Krellen Woods. I use mine all the time, and you should have yours with this letter. It's the most beautiful thing I ever saw. I would like to know what you think we should do with Mosa's.

It might be some time before I get to you but as always I think of you and miss you badly.

Your Teyr

470OE

For Teyr

I have the staff at my side as I write this. I too take it everywhere, for he would want it used and my word it is fine, the blade keen, bob weighted just so. Your nephew Drun should have Mosa's. They would be of a close enough age that they would have been good friends in another life. Drun should learn to sniff and to use one of these, all boys should. Mosa was a natural though, wasn't he, a fine nose for the work.

I've thought a lot about Tarry of course. I enclose a letter for Luddson, one as well for his clearks, for we were good friends when I worked there. I think of him every day. I am sure you will take care of them, but my share of Tarry's fortune must go towards ensuring their considerable comfort from hereon.

Jelmer has had his family help me build a small house on their theit, and I have taken the white cut, bloodied their shield, and a new rope was woven for the longhouse, my white thread added, sworn to defend their rope for life. My weapon is my quill of course, but I'm told it's sharp enough in clan matters. It means I would like to live out my days here, for all that I might travel about.

This is home for me now, Teyr. I am part of a family.

Drunessen and Jelmer agreed to give me a bit of my own land I could run some hands on and help grow the theit, but I asked that I remain a teacher and sniffer for I have become happy with that life and its rhythms. Anyway, could you see me managing a crew of hands? I never had the way of talking to them when they needed a kick in the crack that you had. You only had to narrow your eyes at one of your crew and he or she would scurry off.

The house has only two rooms but a fireplace in each. Such extravagance! The main room is a good size so I can keep a desk in it, and the bedroom doubles for supplies of ink and scrolls. Getting this house built has taken most of the summer, and now autumn is here and I've been helping with the harvests, the air turning cold frighteningly quickly. Winter will come early this year. Keep yourself safe if you travel out in it, crew or no.

Aude

471OE

For Aude

I looked today for your last letter. It was a year ago and as you know it's been a hard year in the saddle overseeing the trails, bridges and blockwork, as well as all the dealings with the Families to put stables along the road.

It was lovely to see you this summer just gone. You have changed, I'd say a bit weather-beaten though you might not like to hear it. The wind and the sun have baked you a good colour, I think. You're right my own colouring has faded. It's a welcome sight to me, though it leaves me looking strange now, the bark in my skin stands out darker, as does the plant in me, which is growing from where it was put in, while the scars all over me make me look like a dolly's been stitched from straw and badly at that.

I'm glad you were honest with me about us. We rode out a few times, didn't we, and as the hours went by on those rides I felt it was coming, your telling me that we wouldn't be together again, that we'd no longer be each other's keeps. I did my best to hide how much it hurt, and I'm sorry if my visit was difficult or that I made it more difficult when you'd finally spoken of your feelings. It hurt so much because I found in you what I thought was my keep. You used to make so much effort to make sure I was happy, like I was the most important thing, well, Mosa and me. You never got cross with me, or if you did I deserved it and fuck knows I wasn't easy to be with. Out there on Jelmer's land you held yourself back, and it was the first time I realised it wasn't grief but something else. You said

419

it felt like a bit of you hadn't come back though most of the rest had, some bit of the feeling that made you love me was gone but it wasn't my fault. I don't fully understand it but I have accepted it.

You should know, for I couldn't say it at the time, that if there's someone that becomes dear to you, you should not hold yourself back. I have to get on, but it would hurt me more if you didn't go on yourself and find someone to love.

When I left you said that you hoped we might have a friendship to treasure, that we shouldn't forget the love we had. That's easier for you to say and embrace than me, but you're right of course. Don't ever stop writing to me. I will always write, there's always so much to say besides the dry progress of our shipping and plant interests. You and Thornsen, and those Kelssen duts, are the dearest things to me.

We pushed on from your theit and arrived at Stockson safely, to talk with them of the road that I aim to bring through to them.

Stockson's as I was told it was, as we both knew it to be – a big, stinking spread of emporia around the barracks and customs for Hillfast and Forontir's border. Much bigger than I thought, a lot of gangers. Saw rivals' tats all over the taverns, sheds and offices there. Soon as we saw the place I knew we had to set up an outpost, so we've begun the work of finding families that'll let me buy some land from them. Course, the chiefs I've spoken to, merchants, tavern keeps, vanners, all of them think the road's as stupid as they all did back in Hillfast. One or two gangers tried it on, but the black eye gives me two things, a better and better read of people, but also it gives them pause, for the word's got out here that I'm the one they're calling War Crow and I'm the one did for Khiese.

Thornsen will come out here soon, I hope. Things seem to go more smoothly when he's about, but that's normal as the north hasn't ever taken a woman seriously.

Your Teyr

472OE

For Teyr

I hope this letter finds you well after that dreadful winter. The Drunessens lost more of their old and young than they had in many winters. I had hoped we might see each other again with you being that bit closer over in Stockson, but I can understand why you haven't managed it. You are working yourself too hard. When you were here you were distracted constantly by the scrolls and your managing the plans in the kind of detail that you cannot maintain with such large and diverse interests as you have, on top of which I am selfishly leaving you to manage mine as well. I hope you and Thornsen have plans to bring on to a high standard your set of senior clearks? You should give my interests to one of them. If it doesn't make all the profit it could it's not as much of a concern to me as your health.

I've worried more particularly about you since we talked about us. You spoke well of it in your letter. There's some piece of the puzzle that's frozen and gone, as I said. You're the same beautiful, kind and strong woman you always were, and you need telling as much now as you ever did, it seems! But the heart and blood that goes with me thinking that you were my keep, that there was an us, it's gone.

Between the lines of your letter I saw that you suspected that I might have found somebody else to love. You probably also suspected, for the time we spent together, that it was Ruisma. She's become my keep here and now shares my house. A letter isn't the place to talk of it or explain it. You've met her. She's been a great comfort and a good friend, and I'll say no more for words are small.

I should tell you that Vuina's not been well. She caught a cold while out in the winter, it got her in the chest, and while the worst of it has gone it's left her short of breath and with coughing and muke. We've all helped Jelmer with the nursing, but we're afraid that the busy woman pulling up her family and keeping Jelmer in his comforts might not come back. She gets out of breath if she moves around too much. Lina, who's fourteen summers now, does a lot to help Jelmer while I'm not there, for I'm travelling a great deal now on Drunessen's behalf.

There's little more to tell for it is only the struggles with winter and Vuina's poor health that has filled our time. I wanted only to write to be straight and true with you as you deserve and to also communicate my hope that we can remain good friends now our lives have taken their new shapes.

Aude

473OE

For Aude

Stockson's neutrality on the border of these citadels is a curse and a favour. The troubles we've had are gone far beyond anything I'd have anticipated. One half-built outpost has been burned. Stone, wood, nails, rope, everything you can think of has been stolen in various amounts over the months, two crew killed in the taverns at Stockson, six more wounded, nine found pilfering for themselves or worse at the order of a couple of the gangers. All of which is the curse.

The favour comes from it having its own jurisdiction. We learned after a while which interests were behind trying to arrest my own from developing, and when we had I took a crew of mercenaries in and we butchered our way through to them and finished them in a good public messy way that's meant we've had a bit of peace since. Stockson needed to see how far fucking with me gets them.

So the outpost is being built on Fullersen land, a small clan with no sworn Families of their own. Of course they didn't trust me for a moment so I had to sweeten their appetites with some favourable terms, but they'll see they bet right soon enough.

I don't know if word has reached you that the Crutters have been removed as chief clan of Hillfast. The shortest reign of a chief clan in all the history of these lands, it seems. It doesn't take much raising of tithes to turn the people against you, even those that put you there, especially if they see that you have started in on southern ways with wines and silks and the like. Justice was done rarely and poorly, so around Hillfast it's got more dangerous as the chancers realised they could get away with a great deal more misery-making — extortion, robbery, all of it. The Crutters thought they could use soldiers to deal with the dissident voices on the council and among the merchants. Three merchants were killed, one of my sheds was burned while almost full of cargo bound for export, and seven died, for we had farlswood in there and as you know it burns thick and hotter than Aoig. Got even worse then when what must have been one of the merchants sent an assassin after Weiden Crutter and killed him, but he got killed himself trying to escape. Fucking chaos. We protected our interests. I drew back some soldiers from Faldon, and they got some order restored about our sheds and ships. Thornsen it was visited the families of all ours who died and we helped them.

We'd planned for the Crutters being useless, and Thornsen has been working with the Carlessens to better present their interests in Hillfast and actually be seen to pay their fucking tithes properly. Ah, but I'm raving about politics. You'd think I had nothing to occupy me.

There's some news of my children. Yes, I'm calling them my children in part because they call me Ma and in part because that love is returned, though I cannot call myself a ma when I am away all the time and not seeing to them directly.

Brek has his letters, apprenticed to Theik at Faldon Ridge, and is taking his duties very seriously. I think he will make a good cleark, and it's decided he'll stay at the outpost there. Litten, Aggie and Dottke have gone back to Tapper's Way. There's an old stablemaster, Glyn, who's putting them up in his quarters next to the stables there, and Aggie is smitten with the horses it seems so she tries to help where she can.

Glyn is a Carl and had dealings with the Kelssens many years back so he has some sympathy for them. Dottke is telling everyone that she wants to be like Blackeye when she grows up. I hope not, though I fear for the world and everyone in it if she does. Litten's been put to work with the smith there, but he's being trouble. I think he's upset that they've parted from Brek, but Brek's studies are best pursued in the busier outpost.

I hope you're not wondering what I might have said about you and Ruisma because you know well enough that for all I'm hurt, I don't want anything but whatever gives you comfort and joy if you can now find it. She's a lucky woman.

If I can find time I would come and visit. I think it isn't likely. You and Ruisma I believe have been travelling about and improving relations with the Auksens, Amersens and Drunessens. It might be that a Walk in the Almet becomes possible.

Teyr

473OE

For Teyr

Winter is here, and while we were away in the summer, we did not go too far for the sake of Vuina and the girls. I'm sorry we didn't get to see you.

We did get to see Skershe and your nephew. They are both well and Skershe is raising Drun to become head of the family, though he's only twelve summers as yet. Drun has much to learn, but Skershe is clever and runs the Family at this time. I understand from meeting some of the Family chiefs that a council will remove the Auksens from being the high clan and the Amondsens will be raised up. Olnas is old and his boys have earned little respect.

In respect of your road, though you'll have heard it from your own vans I'm sure, Skershe rode out with me for a few days to show me the outpost at Almet and the road coming through. It is a remarkable thing to see. I am not ashamed to say that it made me weep to see it all. So many working at the stone, the organisation of it leaves me dumb. You do not speak of such things in detail in our letters for you might think it boring, as you've said. It is the greatest and most inspiring thing I've ever witnessed, and there is a grudging acknowledgement of that fact even in the most sceptical among the work crews I shared cups with when Skershe and I stayed in their camp near the woods. More remarkable still, delightful in fact, the Oskoro venture to leave the woods to share their own strange brews with the workers, even what they cook. There are hearts and minds there, in the earthiest of folk, that are having their fear and prejudice turned by

427

the presence and familiarity of these strange people, some of whom are losing their resemblance to us all the same. Their kindness, and I don't know if humility is the right word, is up with the best of us.

Mark these words, Teyr Amondsen. This may be your greatest achievement of all.

Aude

476OE

For Aude

It's done.

There's a man, Farah, rode out from Hillfast four weeks ago, alone. We put horses all along the way in the stables we built, the outposts. He ran the horses hard and the stables swapped them out. I wanted to see how quick it could be done. He is in his cups in the outpost here at Stockson and there is a celebration about me as I write this.

Why do I feel so sad then, now the road is built and my dream's come true? I can barely look at them, these beautiful people, those who have toiled for this road, those who have died for this road. It's cost us all too much, hasn't it? I have lost crews, and the soldiers with them as they cleared and drained lands, built roads and bridges and put up the posts to mark it all out. Stables have been burned and looted, those in them killed. We have had our revenge on those that attacked us. The attacks have stopped this last year although I have had to fund a small army to do it, both soldiers and letnants, for, as Thornsen has said, the hard work could be said to start now, no matter the coin and cut of tithes we give those who man our posts. We may yet lose much to the corrupt and those whose lives are threatened with it.

You told me all those years ago that I should do this for Mosa. It's not something I've done, it's something we've done. You have done much to ensure peace in the Circle, Aude.

When I saw you last year we were close to the finish, you recall. Only the impending winter had put a stop to the building being done near the Amersen borders. All we seemed

429

to talk about was the children, wasn't it? The girls have grown, haven't they? Nietsa's a worry to her da the way she's carrying on, and it didn't appease him much to hear me say that I was like her as a girl. Vuina's death hit them hard of course.

I'd like you to thank Ruisma. It cannot have been easy for her to see me, for you both perhaps, but I'm glad of it. It helped me a lot to see you together, helped me to see you happy about each other, despite your efforts to spare me!

You said that you both might not try for a child. But you should. She seemed less sure of that than you – perhaps she wants one before it becomes too late for her. You cannot think of being too old to become a da again. I hope you think about it again.

Since I met you and returned along our road it seems that Theik is lining Brek up to become a letnant for him. I'm told he's getting a reasonable beard now at twenty summers. Theik is pushing him, but I knew he would. Those other clearks who might have thought their family names give them something more than Brek have underestimated him. He is a quick mind and devoted to this company, indeed he has proposed a name for it beyond the Amondsen Guild; he has proposed it be called the Good Company. He sees and believes in the good we have been trying to do, the good you and I spoke of, the good I dreamed of since I paid out as a mercenary. There are years yet before anybody believes that we might become this company as he calls it, but it is a good word, it speaks of solidarity. It's inspiring. Brek might be a little too earnest in this regard, for a twenty-year-old man. He shuns the cups and is shunned in turn by those who enjoy them or believe merit is only one part of a preference they ought have of Theik's time. But capability and graft is all. We toil that we may deserve our dreams. And we have toiled.

I wish the same could be said of young Litten in Tapper's Way. Fitblood despaired of him, and now he is lost to us. He was caught arranging with various merchants and others additional scrolls and small chests that could be fitted outside of our own records and the profits split between vanners and himself. He was confined to his quarters in the outpost and denied drink for he has taken to cups hard and had made a nuisance of himself and has caused his sister and Dottke much hurt. Then it got bad enough with Glyn and Fitblood after a run of his broken promises that they put him on a van going up the Moors. They hoped that a good captain and a bit of hard living would straighten him out of the comforts. Might be, looking back, he needed to stay with Theik and Brek, but I don't know, Theik wouldn't have had the time for him. So the van sends a rider back saying that he left their camp one night on the Moors and never came back. They spent a day trying to track after him but there was no sign.

The girls knew before me of course, me being all the way out here. It upset them terrible. Aggie had been trying to help him but he seemed even to turn on her and she's become the gentlest of spirits, everyone around the outpost loves her. She's tall now, beautiful too. Glyn says she is a wonder with the horses and she has even had a go at making horseshoes in the smithy, though Dottke it seems is the better one with the hammer. He's a good smith, Skarrer, for we need quality work, and he won't have wasters about the smithy. Can't talk highly enough of those two however. But since Litten's gone, Dottke's written to me and asked about going back to their old theit, the Kelssen bloodlands. She said she'd been thinking about what had become of their home, for she remembers it a little, Aggie not at all. She's been getting her letters with Fitblood and helping him manage things, which has been a blessing for him for he is struggling to get about the outpost as he once did, he said. I gave approval for a van to be put together for this expedition and Leyden would join them, which she's delighted by and he's pleased of course. I would have written back to tell her to be careful. I worry about her making this trip, but then it's Dottke. She won't be stopped, will she!

Thornsen has been making plans for what would become our largest outpost, one that would house the fifteen clearks now working for him and fortified as well so we might store a great deal more of our cargo and coin there safely. The Kreigh Moors clans welcome this for some of their families are in difficult and remote land and they speak warmly, I'm told, of being able to have somewhere nearer to trade. Thornsen's own Family is from the Moors and he will move Epny and their children there when the outpost is built.

Well, I've just read through all this, and so much of the world about us is changing and we have been significant in that.

The vanners that use the road we built across the Circle call it Mosa's Road.

It is.

Teyr

481OE

For Aude

Nothing prepares you for the Old Kingdoms.

I write from Credezka, the great port of Mount Hope. It is a magnificent sight, all marble and white stone in the heights, worn iron and stone buildings crowding the wharfs and quays away down the hill from the rooms I've taken here. If you have written to me it's possible, with the travelling I've done, that your letters keep missing me. But if you haven't, I hope you'll indulge me the odd letter to you for I think of you often. Please give my love to Ruisma. I hope you are keeping well and keeping those girls in order. Perhaps there's one of your own you might tell me about!

The reason I'm here is clear of course. It's the Old Kingdoms. These networks of trade cannot be undone easily and they are bound together by centuries. They have, as Thornsen puts it, tenure. He is here with me for I am heartbroken to tell you, having to write this even after all this time, that his wife Epny died suddenly not six months into their own stewardship of our great outpost, which the crews and clearks all now call Outpost Epny to honour her – and him of course.

His children are grown up now – they all are, aren't they – and while one of his girls trains to be a drudha no less, another has made a letnant there her keep and they are due to have a dut soon, I understand. Thornsen will go back for that, much as he insists otherwise.

With regard to that subject of tenure, there is a poisonous and annoying history to everything here that you are made to feel you are intruding upon. I've been called a flatback.

433

I had no idea what that was, but it means I've become rich suddenly, not inherited it from someone else, not "old money". So I'm here to prove myself from the beginning, to make our case with Thornsen, to sit and wait in the halls of lords and the even more grand halls of the merchants despite being richer than all of them, made to pay with my time and coin for every inch I gain, mocked too for that inch behind their fans and lace handcloths they have the habit of here. They all appear to wear silks and so I have tried to do so, not least because woollens are too warm here, and they make their decisions as much based on how you appear to them as they do the merit of your proposals. It's fucked, and my appearance does little to help me as you can imagine.

But I struggle here for many reasons. As my interests have grown, corruption has crept in where my eyes have been the least. Our reputation is hurt, the name the Good Company is mocked roundly in certain towns and theits about Hillfast and Forontir especially. I seem to pay far more than other merchants for the diligence of those that run my company yet receive only a little more in return, it seems.

Brek had been thinking over these years the same things of course, for he sees the backhanders and bribes and filching for himself at Faldon, I'm sure, and hunts it down there and elsewhere.

He has sent me letters with ideas for this company. He thinks we need a sort of emblem, not just one that identifies that boxes and barrels are ours, but one that performs as do clan colours, something to rally around, something that helps give those that work for our coin common purpose, something perhaps to stand as a symbol to others. He thinks the colour red should do it, the red of farlswood. All the outposts and stables have, as the main gates to their enclosures, huge doors made of farlswood and iron, as I have been rigorous in specifying. All remark upon them who see them, and he has reminded me of this quite obvious fact. How then, he argues, might it be used if we had cloaks and flags and banners that themselves were of the same red, that a van to look on be decked in red where it can be, red for the covers on the wagons? Thornsen widened his eyes as he read this letter, for red as you know is not an easy dye to make, though I reminded him what he told me I was worth. He did think that it might be a potent symbol for this reason, the red. A bright rich colour that all of our men and women could rally to, might fight harder for, would also be happy to wear, for it isn't a colour you see much outside those with coin to spare.

At a time when the flaunting of wealth was accepted around me only because it had come from the toils of fore-fathers and the accident of nature in respect of their fertile lands and mountains, I had more desire then to flaunt what I was building. Thornsen to this day I don't think believes it a wise thing, that it might cause more problems than it solves, but I am willing to give Brek his lead and see if his judgement is correct because Sillindar knows I second- and third-guess my own when trying to order some food these days.

For now then I am here, and I am listening with interest to the reports from the Roan Province of unrest there in the court. Part of me is sorry to hear it for I have good memories of the place. Thornsen sails there in two days. I don't feel well enough to make the journey. These last few weeks I have had strange dreams and they have woken me. Sometimes my black eye will see movement that I cannot track with the other, though I notice my old eye is weakening. The plant that the Oskoro put in me grows. I hadn't thought much about it over the years, but it makes sense that it has. Some days I feel it move, others a leaf-like smell I give off gets remarked on and I have to bathe before any important meet that I have.

Nonetheless the black eye sees through most bluffs and bluster that I'm faced with in negotiations. It gives me a great sense of things not feeling quite right when someone speaks, the way they speak. To these wealthy people I'm a distinct curiosity, or I was. Now I'm just a flatback that won't go away and commands too much of a fleet and bargains too well to ignore.

As for the children, Dottke, with Brek's help, has arranged for an outpost to be set up on her bloodlands. Can you believe she's now twenty-two summers! All those duts are grown up now, and I mean Litten too for I feel that he still lives somewhere. She has moved to the Almet outpost as her interest and travel to her homeland has grown. She will settle there, if she hasn't already while I've been away, but Brek wishes to stay at Faldon. I hope Aggie might join Dottke down in their old theit. At the least, Dottke will set the place right, and it's a strong spot on which we might manage trade along those rivers south to Port Carl. Write soon, for I would love to hear from you.

Teyr

482OE

For Teyr

I have not long received your last letter, from Credezka. It has the look of having travelled halfway around the world, which isn't far from true, is it, and I can almost smell the salt and spices on the parch.

We've been kept busy by life here, as you have there and everywhere you go. We did try for a child but we were not able to have one. You guessed rightly that it would hurt Ruisma more than she had first let on in our talk of us trying. Now it seems we are drawn more and more to caring for Lina and Nuitsa, for Jelmer is ill and I do not have much hope for him getting past it.

It may be with all your travels you do not know that Drun has become chief of the Amondsen Family properly now, as he's old enough and ready. He does Skershe great credit and she has done a fine job there. He has Skershe's and your ability to inspire those around you. His position is bolstered by the road. He has agreed as well to a Walk, where the Auksen boy hasn't, and I think this has helped him to be taken seriously by the likes of the Eeghersens, Amersens and Jamessens. A meet is planned with the Oskoro to discuss the way such an undertaking might be planned.

I'm sorry to say that such a Walk is more important now than ever. A band of Oskoro were killed by men from a family of the Triggsens. Ruisma and I went there with Chief Jamessen himself to see the Triggsen chief, and it soon came out that they had blamed this band for blighting their crops in what was a hard year and for the death of a boy, though

437

he'd been playing near a river that had swollen with the rains of the last spring. I've therefore done some travelling myself, to bring these families to meet the Oskoro. You would be glad to see how many Oskoro now come to the Almet outpost, meriting little more than a glance from those travelling through. They are careful with their recipes, which is a shame for the rest of us, but they have saved lives and eased the pain and other ailments of almost anyone that leaves an offering at the stone. You should see now the gifts there, and none plunder any more. The old ways have returned.

Teyr, I understand why yours have been so few, and hope you understand why my own letters are so rare in return, but I love to receive them still. You may think the talk of your Good Company is just ships and profits and contracts, but you mustn't forget that our ability to talk as we do, however rare, is entirely due to the dream you had all those years ago. Part of me wishes, when I read your letters, that you'd slow down more, for you have an itinerary would kill even young men stone dead. I expect you travel in more comfort these days, but still I expect you creak worse than I do, and I do creak. Ruisma had one of the soldiers that came by a few months ago show us some of your basic Forms, for it is her belief that the exertion will help us keep some strength into our old age, should we get there. It's not this that I worry about as much as that I am forgetting things. I have hunted the house down many times now in search of Mosa's Catch, and it is somewhere obvious but unremembered. The same goes for so many things, but this, of them all, breaks my heart.

Though the years may go by before next we write, we continue to work here to secure the peace that you hoped the road would bring. The road, oh Teyr, you should see it.

As you had thought, the justices and others travel along it and save weeks. The rulings of our laws are spread, and fewer soldiers can cover more ground to meet and deal with those who wander into these lands through hunger or to hurt us.

Maybe you will come back along Mosa's Road again, soon. We will have a feast in your honour.

Aude

486OE

For Aude

More than three years have passed. The days go by like blinks of an eye and there's so little time for reflection, and I'm sorry for that.

With no thanks to Thornsen I sit once more at the end of a birthday celebration and a night's feasting and drinking, though I've little stomach for either with all this plant in me. He wanted me to celebrate that I was sixty-two summers. "Winters," I told him. "Summers is said for a happy remembrance," though be assured I said this to him in private. Who wants a miserable old woman at her own party!

It was a surprise to see Theik here at Credezka, for that is where I still am. He has left Faldon finally at Thornsen's request and will stay here to command my berths on the wharf and my sheds, for he is incorruptible. Brek has been a marvel, and he is taking over as castellan of Post House Epny. I should explain that he has been a fountain of initiatives since he oversaw our company adopt the red. Wherever my vans and crews go now they are called the Reds, it seems. He has also, without my knowledge, worked with Thornsen to establish at Epny an academy that must be the finest in the citadels, for the training of soldiers, drudhas, smiths and others that the company always needs. It is his hope that if a man or woman chooses to be a Red, to join the company, they will receive training, food and shelter, and his hope is that this promotes loyalty, and where it does not, it at least eliminates antipathy to us. He has also been working with the clearks to name our outposts post houses. Omar has a post house named after him, though Faldon keeps its name, and Ruifsen does. I expect our old friend Fitblood will have Tapper's named after him, however, for he is now sick and being cared for.

Soon I will follow Thornsen to the Roan Province, for he has summoned me, or more precisely his letter accompanied one from the queen of Khasgal's Landing. Khasgal died some seven years back. She has survived him and continues to rule there. She is much loved, revered even, but she has discovered what has become of the woman who competed for her king's heart and wishes to meet me. I don't expect it's to have me strangled or strung up by the ropes in my belly, and I only have fond memories of her despite our loving the same man. I wish I could come home. I know I can, of course, but Thornsen is right that making this last play, if it lands right, will settle the Good Company into the heart of the Sar and the Old Kingdoms. Its future will be assured so long as people believe in what it stands for. Greed builds empires on sand, love builds them on stone, he tells me.

I hope the Walk you mentioned in your last letter – for I carry your letters wherever I go – I hope that it happened, for that would be a great, great comfort to me, more than I could have asked for. I heard as well from the scrolls I get from my high clearks that Drun is now Chief Amondsen, that they are the high clan. As you said, I hear that he takes Skershe everywhere with him, and it makes me proud. I'd have thought that such a man would be snapped up by any number of good women, but I hear nothing on that front. It doesn't matter anyway. We could all as easily be dead now, long in our tapestry. I try to be grateful for every day, I try not to forget how I got here.

I hope that he will write to me one day; I would love to

receive some scrolls from him. I have received them from my children. The first was actually from Jorno three years back. It was a delight to see his, well, modest hand. He has been on the farm with Grenna and Boneit all these years. They passed into their tapestry, and he ran the farm when they couldn't but he had nothing to stay for because it was Carlessen land. He went to the Kelssen theit to see about settling there with Dottke and Aggie, but he was unhappy and got to arguing with them about all manner of things, and then they discovered he had an addiction to betony.

Despite all Dottke, Aggie and even Brek tried to do for him over these last couple of years, he fell to the droop proper and he left them and hasn't been seen since. Brek was broken-hearted, Dottke too. Still, it seems that only Brek and Aggie have come right in her eyes. Aggie, now twenty-three summers, I think, has an army of boys at her beck and call, though she prefers horses to every one of them. Both her and Dottke have taken over the staging post we sought food at when we ran from the whiteboys who destroyed their theit. They oversee the building of a post house there. Meantime they have hands working the fields where their families fought the whiteboys, and have raised stones for the dead, for Mell, Orgrif and the others.

It's come to this, hasn't it? These few letters we send are full of the illness, deaths and sorrows of those we love as life makes its cuts on us. Can't say I'm looking forward to crossing the Sar, I never did well on the water. Once our work in Roan is done I'll be heading home, I think. I hope Thornsen is doing well over there without me. He is frail these days, though a little fatter than me. We have got quite comfortable, I think, though I am shrinking. This letter has taken some time to write, for my fingers are swollen, my wrists, ankles, elbows all sore and stiff beyond any salve I have to ease them, and there are lumps on my knuckles. I eat so little now and the plant inside me and this eye pull me away from my old and normal sense of things to places that, I cannot write it well enough to describe, are unseen but still about us and within us. There is much to this world we don't notice, and knowledge, real knowledge, is there if we can pay attention to it. I have written much on this elsewhere, for I hope it is of use to our drudhas. Reasons enough to head home and see if the Oskoro will see me, if they have anything that can help me with my pain and my questions.

I hope you have managed to keep in better shape, old man!

Teyr

489OE

For Teyr

As you might be able to tell by my hand, it's Ruisma that is writing to you. We might apologise too for it being so long. So much needs doing in the long days of summer to prepare for winter and then in the short days of winter because they are short!

Aude got caught in a storm on an expedition south last winter. They were coming back through the Mothers when it hit and they were lost for a while. He should have been back sooner because the trail they planned to take turns bad in winter and winter came early there. Of the six that left, two didn't come back, but great Sillindar was with him and he returned to me. He has lost some fingers and some toes, and it's brought him low I think these last months. The cold seems to be in him, and I fear for him. He won't eat, he's thin as a handful of straw and cannot use his hands much at all and he is angry at everything. I do what I can for him but it's like he's given up. I am writing to you to ask you to come and see us, hoping that you might pass by the Oskoro for some plant that might help him. It would be such a lift to him if you could come.

We have had two Walks now, you will be pleased to hear, before this expedition of his went badly. I went with him for the first of them, and all the families turned up, I think. Many of us were moved to see it, all the clan chiefs and family chiefs together in a place and with the Oskoro as well. They led us inside their forest, and I cannot say whether I approve of all they do with their people, but they were kind

444

and let us walk about the place, only asking us to be careful here and there, for certain plants were precious to them and were easy to walk on for their abundance. There was much talk of the problems Khiese caused, and a few sought strife, raising troubles with other families from years ago, but thankfully few had the will to cause further bad relations. There was talk of you and your road. You should not be surprised by that. Drun, your nephew, spoke highly of you and how much easier you have made their lives, for now they can both trade and give help to each other in hard times, and this has been unheard of as you know, for it is why you built the road, is it not?

Aude asked that I keep you apprised of the children here. I don't know if he wrote in his last letter that Jelmer died, but he did. We celebrated what he has added to our tapestry, though his rope continues on only through his brother up at the Drunessen longhouse, who has two boys.

Lina lost her first baby. She has a keep from the Triggsen clan and has gone there to live, but her second thrives apparently. Nietsa has Aude's house that we built him, for she has a keep now, a Drunessen, who has taken her and her boy on. He's a terror, except with Aude of course, and they love each other. I wish I could have given him a boy but it was all too late. Nietsa's boy wipes the years off his brow. Children are like that. Another worry for me is that now, since his injuries, Aude does not want to see him.

I hope this letter finds you well, and that the winter, if you are in Hillfast, hasn't bitten off too much. We would both very much love to see you.

Sillindar follow you,

Ruisma

490OE

For Ruisma and Aude

I have received your last letter. I'm sorry to hear Aude is in poor health.

It seems things go badly for us all. I would give anything to command a carriage to take me along our road to see you but I cannot. This old crow can no longer fly, nor walk. My leg is getting worse and all these lumps on my bones cause me such pain. This as you can see is not in my own hand. I landed back in Hillfast just after midwinter. I could wait no longer with how broken up I am. I say "I" for I have only managed to bring back the body of my best friend, my standing stone, Thornsen. There are lives beyond count owe him a debt all over these lands, and I could weight down the scales with all my life's troubles on the one side and he would tip it swiftly to the other with his love and support. He fell ill in the Roan Province, and I stayed with him there, nursing him as best I could. To speak truly, I pushed away this company for a while to take care of him, but there was no healing him. He died in his sleep, and I envy him that.

We have buried him in his bloodlands, the true founder of the Good Company. I wish I had been able to do the same for Ruifsen and Thad, who had both stayed true to me in my life.

I had time there to see Thornsen's children, and they carry all the joy and troubles of life with them as they grow families of their own. They will want for nothing.

I thought then I might have the heart to redouble my efforts to cover his, but I have nothing left. It's time to let those we have trained and nurtured show what they are made of, and Brek is now the head of the company. You and Aude will be pleased to know that a charming young woman has managed to pierce his shell of duty and got him to love something other than this company. She has given him a girl as well. I gave him whatever wisdom Thornsen had given me on the challenges of duty and family, and I hope he has listened where I did not. He inspires me, that boy, and all I've said to him of the good work that this company truly exists for, that it bring nations together to learn and profit from each other that we might discourage war, he has taken to his heart.

I have had a letter as well from Aggie, who has had a boy and she has called him Mosa. She told me Litten had returned briefly to their theit as well. He had not died on the Moors as we feared. Near thirty years now, a grown man, he had found work on the boats for most of this time, a deckhand, turning the work of his muscle into drink by her account. He left them again, despite all they offered to do for him in their theit down there. He would not stay, said he needed to be away, but she thinks he just could not bear to be loved for he did not in some way love himself. She is heartbroken, as am I. I would love to see those girls again, south of the Mothers, but I won't now. They have a good life, I've given them that, I hope.

I could fill this letter again with the dead, couldn't I, for I recall I have not yet told you that Theik and Fitblood are gone as well. It seems this Good Company needs a tapestry of its own, so many have given it the love they would give their own blood. But how else can you live? What poverty, what waste in the life that does not give all of its love?

The Oskoro have sent someone who says he will take me to the Almet to complete my service. It is he that has written

447

this letter. I just told him he reminded me of a statue I had seen in the Roan Province, of Sillindar. I have seen him before, I'm sure of it.

He's laughing as he writes this, but my black eye blazes to look upon him.

He tells me I am out of time. I think he may be right.

So this is my farewell to you. Love that boy, Aude. And love each other while you can.

Teyr Amondsen

Epilogue

Dear Cal,

I am detained by Administrator Stroff on urgent matters, but will be with you in the morning! I trust, however, you are enjoying the accommodation and in particular the wine cellar while you wait. There is much I would speak to you of, much that must be said in person.

You'll have been given this satchel by a most trusted friend of mine, Agent Widdow, who will stay at the Old Hall Inn with you until I arrive. He won't be alone, for the letters you find here enclosed are of immense value to the Post. Very few people know they exist. You'll keep it that way.

I share them with you because not only have you kept to our oaths and delivered your van at great risk to your lives, but in our conversation last week you greatly impressed me with your passion for our aims and our work. My hope is that in reading these letters they ground such enthusiasm further, for there are great challenges ahead, I fear, and I would have your help in overcoming them.

You will know of course that Brekeuel, or "Brek" as these letters call him, was the first Red as I am the sixth. You will also have learned that he had many mentors, among them Teyr Amondsen. Yet these letters between her and the man once her husband, Aude, show that this utterly remarkable woman was in fact the true founder of the Post and had most likely saved Brek's life as a boy, becoming a mother to him. It was her "Good Company" that became the Post, and it was from her that Brek set down the Post's ideals, everything we stand for and everything that the Reds, such as I, swear by when we swear our oaths upon the Bloody Shirt.

I look forward to speculating with you on the nature of the strange and powerful "Oskoro", referenced herein, and their mysterious fate.

Yours,

Yblas

Post House Amondsen

Autumn's Gate

27 Crutma, 574OE

Acknowledgements

A big thank you to Steve Warren, Adam Bouskill, Neil Garret, Dave Fillmore, Shaun Green and Dan Bonett for reading and feeding back your thoughts on the first draft. Your support and encouragement mean the world to me.

Now *Snakewood*'s been out there for a couple of years, there are many that have shared reviews, thoughts and my updates. I'm grateful to all of you for taking the time to give my work a go, it's deeply humbling. In particular, I'd like to thank Steve Warren, Femke Giesolf, James Latimer, Ed McDonald and "Adriëlle" Ooms-Voges for doing so much to raise awareness for my work.

Thank you also to Pete Withers-Jones for his ongoing patience and support managing my web presence and all the technical shenanigans that go on with that. You ease my mind, sir!

As with *Snakewood*, I am deeply indebted to Jenni Hill and Will Hinton, my editors at Orbit. Once again you've seared away the chaff and helped me to make this book the best it could be. Thank you as well to Joanna Kramer for the face-saving 'how did I miss that!' copy-edits and the rest of the Orbit team for getting *The Winter Road* ready to rock. Any rubbish that remains is entirely my own.

Jamie, my agent, continues to taunt aggro so I can dps. Thank you, mate.

Of course, no words get written without the infinite patience, love and support of my wife Rhian. Thank you most of all x

extras

orbit

www.orbitbooks.net

about the author

Adrian Selby studied creative writing at university before eventually settling into a career making video games. When he's not wishing someone would invent a sleep compressor, he squeezes in reading and gaming around his family and writing. He lives on the south coast of England. His debut novel, *Snakewood*, is an epic and inventive fantasy about a company of mercenaries and the assassin trying to destroy them. You can find Adrian on Twitter, tweeting as @adrianlselby and on his website at adrianselby.com.

Find out more about Adrian Selby and other Orbit authors by registering for the free monthly newsletter at www.orbitbooks.net.

if you enjoyed
THE WINTER ROAD

look out for

SENLIN ASCENDS

Book One of the Books of Babel

by

Josiah Bancroft

Mild-mannered headmaster, Thomas Senlin, prefers his adventures to be safely contained within the pages of a book. So when he loses his new bride shortly after embarking on the honeymoon of their dreams, he is ill-prepared for the trouble that follows.

To find her, Senlin must enter the Tower of Babel — a world of geniuses and tyrants, of menace and wonder, of unusual animals and mysterious machines. And if he hopes to ever see his wife again, he will have to do more than just survive . . . this quiet man of letters must become a man of action.

Chapter One

The Tower of Babel is most famous for the silk fineries and marvelous airships it produces, but visitors will discover other intangible exports. Whimsy, adventure, and romance are the Tower's real trade.

— *Everyman's Guide to the Tower of Babel, I.V*

It was a four-day journey by train from the coast to the desert where the Tower of Babel rose like a tusk from the jaw of the earth. First, they had crossed pastureland, spotted with fattening cattle and charmless hamlets, and then their train had climbed through a range of snow-veined mountains where condors roosted in nests large as haystacks. Already, they were farther from home than they had ever been. They descended through shale foothills, which he said reminded him of a field of shattered blackboards, through cypress trees, which she said looked like open parasols, and finally they came upon the arid basin. The ground was the color of rusted chains, and the dust of it clung to everything. The desert was far from deserted. Their train shared a direction with a host of caravans, each a slithering line of wheels, hooves, and feet. Over the course of the morning, the bands of traffic thickened until they converged into a great mass so dense that their train was forced to slow to a crawl. Their cabin seemed to wade through the boisterous tide of stage-coaches and ox-drawn wagons, through the tourists, pilgrims, migrants, and merchants from every state in the vast nation of Ur.

Thomas Senlin and Marya, his new bride, peered at the human menagerie through the open window of their sunny sleeper car. Her china-white hand lay weightlessly atop his long fingers. A little troop of red-breasted soldiers slouched by on palominos, parting a family in checkered headscarves on camelback. The trumpet of elephants sounded over the clack of the train, and here and there in the hot winds high above them, airships lazed, drifting inexorably toward the Tower of Babel. The balloons that held the ships aloft were as colourful as maypoles.

Since turning toward the Tower, they had been unable to see the grand spire from their cabin window. But this did not discourage Senlin's description of it. "There is a lot of debate over how many levels there are. Some scholars say there are fifty-two, others say as many as sixty. It's impossible to judge from the ground," Senlin said, continuing the litany of facts he'd brought to his young wife's attention over the course of their journey. "A number of men, mostly aeronauts and mystics, say that they have seen the top of it. Of course, none of them have any evidence to back up their boasts. Some of those explorers even claim that the Tower is still being raised, if you can believe that." These trivial facts comforted him, as all facts did. Thomas Senlin was a reserved and naturally timid man who took confidence in schedules and regimens and written accounts.

Marya nodded dutifully but was obviously distracted by the parade of humanity outside. Her wide, green eyes darted excitedly from one exotic diversion to the next: What Senlin merely observed, she absorbed. Senlin knew that, unlike him, Marya found spectacles and crowds exhilarating, though she saw little of either back home. The pageant outside her window was nothing like Isaugh, a salt-scoured fishing village, now many hundreds of miles behind them. Isaugh was the only real home she'd known, apart from the young women's musical conservatory she'd attended for four years. Isaugh had two pubs, a Whist Club, and a city hall that doubled as a ballroom when occasion called for it. But it was hardly a metropolis.

Marya jumped in her seat when a camel's head swung unexpectedly near. Senlin tried to calm her by example but couldn't stop himself from yelping when the camel snorted, spraying them with warm spit. Frustrated by this lapse in decorum, Senlin cleared his throat and shooed the camel out with his handkerchief.

The tea set that had come with their breakfast rattled now, spoons shivering in their empty cups, as the engineer applied the brakes and the train all but stopped. Thomas Senlin had saved and planned for this journey his entire career. He wanted to see the wonders he'd read so much about, and though it would be a trial for his nerves, he hoped his poise and intellect would carry the day. Climbing the Tower of Babel, even if only a little way, was his greatest ambition, and he was quite excited. Not that anyone would know it to look at him: He affected a cool detachment as a rule, concealing the inner flights of his emotions. It was how he conducted himself in the classroom. He didn't know how else to behave anymore.

Outside, an airship passed low enough to the ground that its tethering lines began to snap against heads in the crowd. Senlin wondered why it had dropped so low, or if it had only recently launched. Marya let out a laughing cry and covered her mouth with her hand. He gaped as the ship's captain gestured wildly at the crew to fire the furnace and pull in the tethers, which was quickly done amid a general panic, but not before a young man from the crowd had caught hold of one of the loose cords. The adventuresome lad was quickly lifted above the throng, his feet just clearing the box of a carriage before he was swung up and out of view.

The scene seemed almost comical from the ground, but Senlin's stomach churned when he thought of how the youth must feel flying on the strength of his grip high over the sprawling mob. Indeed, the entire brief scene had been so bizarre that he decided to simply put it out of his mind. The *Guide* had called the Market a raucous place. It seemed, perhaps, an understatement.

He'd never expected to make the journey as a honeymooner. More to the point, he never imagined he'd find a woman who'd have him. Marya was his junior by a dozen years, but being in his midthirties himself, Senlin did not think their recent marriage very remarkable. It had raised a few eyebrows in Isaugh, though. Perched on rock bluffs by the Niro Ocean, the townsfolk of Isaugh were suspicious of anything that fell outside the regular rhythms of tides and fishing seasons. But as the headmaster, and the only teacher, of Isaugh's school, Senlin was generally indifferent to gossip. He'd certainly heard enough of it. To his thinking, gossip was the theater of the uneducated, and he hadn't gotten married to enliven anyone's breakfast-table conversation.

He'd married for entirely practical reasons.

Marya was a good match. She was good tempered and well read; thoughtful, though not brooding; and mannered without being aloof. She tolerated his long hours of study and his general quiet, which others often mistook for stoicism. He imagined she had married him because he was kind, even tempered, and securely employed. He made fifteen shekels a week, for an annual salary of thirteen minas; it wasn't a fortune by any means, but it was sufficient for a comfortable life. She certainly hadn't married him for his looks. While his features were separately handsome enough, taken altogether they seemed a little stretched and misplaced. His nickname among his pupils was "the Sturgeon" because he was thin and long and bony.

Of course, Marya had a few unusual habits of her own. She read books while she walked to town—and had many torn skirts and skinned knees to show for it. She was fearless of heights and would sometimes get on the roof just to watch the sails of inbound ships rise over the horizon. She played the piano beautifully but also brutally. She'd sing like a mad mermaid while banging out ballads and reels, leaving detuned pianos in her wake. And even still, her oddness inspired admiration in most. The townsfolk thought she was charming, and her playing was often requested at the local public houses. Not even the bitter gray of Isaugh's winters could temper her vivacity. Everyone was a little baffled by her marriage to the Sturgeon.

Today, Marya wore her traveling clothes: a knee-length khaki skirt and plain white blouse with a somewhat eccentric pith helmet covering her rolling auburn hair. She had dyed the helmet red, which Senlin didn't particularly like, but she'd sold him on the fashion by saying it would make her easier to spot in a crowd. Senlin wore a gray suit of thin corduroy, which he felt was too casual, even for traveling, but which she had said was fashionable and a little frolicsome, and wasn't that the whole point of a honeymoon, after all?

A dexterous child in a rough goatskin vest climbed along the side of the train with rings of bread hooped on one arm. Senlin bought a ring from the boy, and he and Marya sat sharing the warm, yeasty crust as the train crept toward Babel Central Station, where so many tracks ended.

Their honeymoon had been delayed by the natural course of the school year. He could've opted for a more convenient and frugal destination, a seaside hotel or country cottage in which they might've secluded themselves for a weekend, but the Tower of Babel was so much more than a vacation spot. A whole world stood balanced on a bedrock foundation. As a young man, he'd read about the Tower's cultural contributions to theater and art, its advances in the sciences, and its profound technologies. Even electricity, still an unheard-of commodity in all but the largest cities of Ur, was rumored to flow freely in the Tower's higher levels. It was the lighthouse of civilization. The old saying went, "The earth doesn't shake the Tower; the Tower shakes the earth."

The train came to a final stop, though they saw no station outside their window. The conductor came by and told them that they'd have to disembark; the tracks were too clogged for the train to continue. No one seemed to think it unusual. After days of sitting and swaying on the rails, the prospect of a walk appealed to them both. Senlin gathered their two pieces of luggage: a stitched leather satchel for his effects, and for hers, a modest steamer trunk with large casters on one end and a push handle on the other. He insisted on managing them both.

Before they left their car and while she tugged at the tops of her brown leather boots and smoothed her skirt, Senlin recited the three vital pieces of advice he'd gleaned from his copy of *Everyman's Guide to the Tower of Babel*. Firstly, keep your money close. (Before they'd departed, he'd had their local tailor sew secret pockets inside the waists of his pants and the hem of her skirt.) Secondly, don't give in to beggars. (It only emboldens them.) And finally, keep your companions always in view. Senlin asked Marya to recite these points as they bustled down the gold-carpeted hall connecting train cars. She obliged, though with some humor.

"Rule four: Don't kiss the camels."

"That is not rule four."

"Tell that to the camels!" she said, her gait bouncing.

And still neither of them was prepared for the scene that met them as they descended the train's steps. The crowd was like a jelly that congealed all around them. At first they could hardly move. A bald man with an enormous hemp sack humped on his shoulder and an iron collar about his neck knocked Senlin into a red-eyed woman; she repulsed him with an alcoholic laugh and then shrank back into the swamp of bodies. A cage of agitated canaries was passed over their heads, shedding foul-smelling feathers on their shoulders. The hips of a dozen black-robed women, pilgrims of some esoteric faith, rolled against them like enormous ball bearings. Unwashed children loaded with trays of scented tissue flowers, toy pinwheels, and candied fruit wriggled about them, each child leashed to another by a length of rope. Other than the path of the train tracks, there were no clear roads, no cobblestones, no curbs, only the rust-red hardpan of the earth beneath them.

It was all so overwhelming, and for a moment Senlin stiffened like a corpse. The bark of vendors, the snap of tarps, the jangle of harnesses, and the dither of ten thousand alien voices set a baseline of noise that could only be yelled over. Marya took hold of her husband's belt just at his spine, startling him from his daze and goading him onward. He knew they couldn't very well just stand there. He gathered a breath and took the first step.

They were drawn into a labyrinth of merchant tents, vendor carts, and rickety tables. The alleys between stands were as tangled as a child's scribble. Temporary bamboo rafters protruded everywhere over them, bowing under jute rugs, strings of onions, punched tin lanterns, and braided leather belts. Brightly striped shade sails blotted out much of the sky, though even in the shade, the sun's presence was never in doubt. The dry air was as hot as fresh ashes.

Senlin plodded on, hoping to find a road or signpost. Neither appeared. He allowed the throng to offer a path rather than forge one himself. When a gap opened, he leapt into it. After progressing perhaps a hundred paces in this manner, he had no idea which direction the tracks lay. He regretted wandering away from the tracks. They could've followed them to the Babel Central Station. It was unsettling how quickly he'd become disoriented.

Still, he was careful to occasionally turn and construct a smile for Marya. The beam of her smile never wavered. There was no reason to worry her with the minor setback.

Ahead, a bare-chested boy fanned the hanging carcasses of lambs and rabbits to keep a cloud of flies from settling. The flies and sweet stench wafting from the butcher's stall drove the crowd back, creating a little space for them to pause a moment, though the stench was nauseating. Placing Marya's trunk between them, Senlin dried his neck with his handkerchief.

"It certainly is busy," Senlin said, trying not to seem as flustered as he felt, though Marya hardly noticed; she was staring over his head, a bemused expression lighting her pretty face.

"It's wonderful," she said.

A gap in the awnings above them exposed the sky, and there, like a pillar holding up the heavens, stood the Tower of Babel.

The face of the Tower was patched with white, gray, rust, tan, and black, betraying the many types of stone and brick used in its construction. The irregular coloration reminded Senlin of a calico cat. The Tower's silhouette was architecturally bland, evoking a dented and ribbed cannon barrel, but it was ornamented with grand friezes, each band taller than a house. A dense cloudbank obscured the Tower's pinnacle. The *Everyman's Guide* noted that the upper echelons were permanently befogged, though whether the ancient structure produced the clouds or attracted them remained a popular point of speculation. However it was, the peak was never visible from the ground. The *Everyman's* description of the Tower of Babel hadn't really prepared Senlin for the enormity of the structure. It made the ziggurats of South Ur and the citadels of the Western Plains seem like models, the sort of thing children built out of sugar cubes. The Tower had taken a thousand years to erect. More, according to some historians. Overwhelmed with wonder and the intense teeming of the Market, Senlin shivered. Marya squeezed his hand reassuringly, and his back straightened. He was a headmaster, after all, a leader of a modest community. Yes, there was a crowd to push through, but once they reached the Tower, the throng would thin. They would be able to stretch a little and would, almost certainly, find themselves among more pleasant company. In a few hours, they would be drinking a glass of port in a reasonable but hospitable lodging on the third level of the Tower—the Baths, locals called it—just as they had planned. They would calmly survey this same human swarm, but from a more comfortable distance.

Now, at least, they had a bearing, a direction to push toward.

Senlin was also discovering a more efficient means of advancing through the crowds. If he stopped, he found, it was difficult to start again, but progress could be made if one was a little more firm and determined. After a few minutes of following, Marya felt comfortable enough to release his belt, which made walking much easier for them both.

Soon, they found themselves in one of the many clothing bazaars within the Market. Laced dresses, embroidered pinafores, and cuffed shirts hung on a forest of hooks and lines. A suit could be had in any color, from peacock blue to jonquil yellow; women's intimate apparel dangled from bamboo ladders like the skins of exotic snakes. Square-folded handkerchiefs covered the nearest table in a heap like a snowdrift.

"Let me buy you a dress. The evenings here are warmer than we're used to." He had to speak close to her ear.

"I'd like a little frock," she said, removing her pith helmet and revealing her somewhat deflated bronzy hair. "Something scandalous."

He gave her a thoughtful frown to disguise his own surprise. He knew that this was the kind of flirtation that even decent couples probably indulged in on their honeymoon. Still, he was unprepared and couldn't reflect her playful tone. "Scandalous?"

"Nothing your pupils will need to know about. Just a little something to disgrace our clothesline back home," she said, running her finger down his arm as if she were striking a match.

He felt uneasy. Ahead of them, acres of stalls cascaded with women's undergarments. There wasn't a man in sight.

Fifteen years spent living as a bachelor hadn't prepared him for the addition of Marya's undergarments to the landscape of his bedroom. Finding her delicates draped on the bedposts and doorknobs of his old sanctuary had come as something of a shock. But this mass of nightgowns, camisoles, corsets, stockings, and brassieres being combed through by thousands of unfamiliar women seemed exponentially more humiliating. "I think I'll stay by the luggage."

"What about your rules?"

"Well, if you'll keep that red bowl on your head, I'll be able to spot you just fine from here."

"If you wander off, we'll meet again at the top of the Tower," she said with exaggerated dramatic emphasis.

"We will not. I'll meet you right here beside this cart of socks."

"Such a romantic!" she said, passing around two heavy-set women who wore the blue-and-white apron dresses popular many years earlier. Senlin noticed with amusement that they were connected at the waist by a thick jute rope.

He asked them if they were from the east, and they responded with the name of a fishing village that was not far from Isaugh. They exchanged the usual nostalgia common to coastal folk: sunrises, starfish, and the pleasant muttering of the surf at night, and then he asked, "You've come on holiday?"

They responded with slight maternal smiles that made him feel belittled. "We're far past our holidays," one said.

"Do you go everywhere lashed together?" A note of mockery crept into his voice now.

"Yes, of course," replied the older of the two. "Ever since we lost our little sister."

"I'm sorry. Did she pass away recently?" Senlin asked, recovering his sincere tone.

"I certainly hope not. But it has been three years. Maybe she has."

"Or maybe she found some way to get back home?" the younger sister said.

"She wouldn't abandon us," the older replied in a tone

that suggested this was a well-trod argument between them.

"It is intrepid of you to come alone," the younger spinster said to him.

"Oh, thank you, but I'm not alone." Tiring of the conversation, Senlin moved to grip the handle of the trunk only to find it had moved.

Confused, he turned in circles, searching first the ground and then the crowd of blank, unperturbed faces snaking about him. Marya's trunk was gone. "I've lost my luggage," he said.

"Get yourself a good rope," the eldest said, and reached up to pat his pale cheek.